Montana Rising

Wordplay

LeeAnn Bonds

Published by LeeAnn Bonds, 2017.

MONTANA RISING

First edition. December 12, 2017.

Written by LeeAnn Bonds.

For Zack

love you like crazy

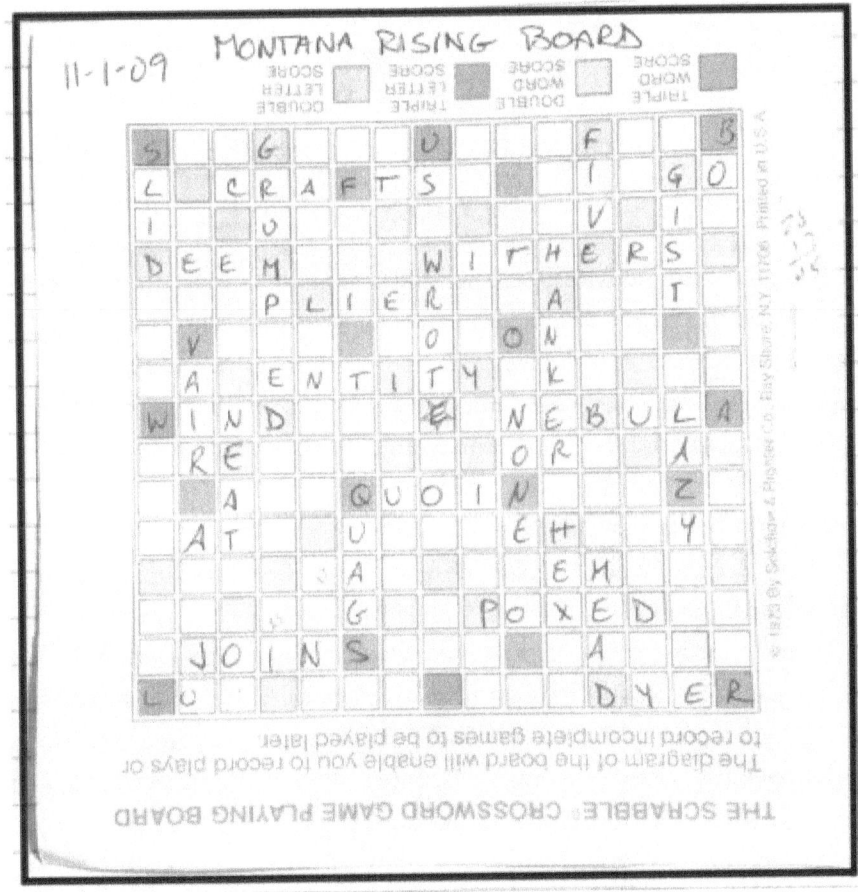

THIS IS THE GAME THAT gave birth to the book.

Back in 2009 I wasn't yet taking pictures of anything and everything with my iPhone. I think I still had a flip phone at that point. But I also had a neato-keen Scrabble score pad with a board diagram on the back of each sheet. Sadly, these now appear to be out of print. (And yes, I know I had the diagram upside down as I was recording the words. Dang it!)

Each of the words played in this game appears somewhere in the "Scrabble Story" thread of **Montana Rising, Wordplay**.

Scrabble

The phone rang as Monti scanned the tiles again, hoping against hope for something brilliant to jump out at her. Who was calling at 10pm? She stood to go answer it. Maybe inspiration would strike when she returned.

"Hello, Risings," she said. "Hi, Noelle, everything okay?" She listened awhile. "Sure, sweetie. No, it's perfectly fine, the bed's already made in there and we're just finishing a game. Any idea how long she needs to stay? No, just wondering if she has any plans at all. Okay. See you in a bit. Love you too." Monti put the phone down. "Noelle's bringing home a stray." A grunt sounded from the kitchen.

Monti returned to the terrible tray. Brilliant inspiration was not forthcoming, and it looked like her best play was H on the triple word score, giving her eighteen for 'hat'. Not horribly bad for this late in the game. She ran her tongue over a sensitive molar as she scooped the last tile from the bag. Another A to join the three already on her rack. Rats.

"All right, Kit, it's your turn."

"It's about time, Monti," her husband said as he wandered back from the kitchen, cup of coffee in one hand. "I made coffee and emptied the dishwasher. I was just reading the assembly instructions for Noelle's new espresso machine." He shooed the cat off his chair and lowered his lanky body onto the seat, bracing his free hand against the table for balance. He glanced over the board until he found her addition. "Hat. Wow."

"Oh, hush. It's eighteen points and now I'm only seven points behind you. I took the last tile." She scooted the A's around on her rack. ANT. NEAT. AAAANTE. "I think I'll go up and open the door and let the guest room warm up a bit."

Kit nodded but didn't look up from his rack. He had one hand on the Official Scrabble Player's Dictionary, 4th Edition, and riffled the pages with his thumb. Monti recognized the signs of strategic thinking. She started up the stairs. She would lose this game, not that she cared. The playing was everything, the winning or losing inconsequential. To her, that is. Kit kept track.

Montana Eloise Rising, named for her birthplace and her great-grandmother, walked straight-backed up the dark oak stairs trailing one hand along the polished banister. She wondered about the girl her granddaughter was bringing home. What had driven her out of her home and into Noelle's confidence? How there could be so many young women with their hearts smashed to pieces at eighteen, Monti didn't understand. Would this be the fourth one to take refuge with them this year?

She opened the door and turned on the light. The room waited to welcome their young guest. Dark wood trim framed the white walls and diamond-pane windows. The oak double bed with its eyelet-trimmed sheets, green print coverlet and extra pillows, the Craftsman lamp and big wicker chair made a cozy retreat where the girl could sort herself out, alone or with whatever help she would accept. Monti got some towels out of the bureau drawer and laid them on the foot of the bed. She poofed the pillows, straightened the framed print of maiden musicians on the wall above the bed and turned off the light.

Like all previous visitors, this girl would be welcomed, loved on, listened to and pampered a bit. That usually went a long way toward starting whatever healing was needed.

"Your turn, lover," Kit called up the stairs. "I have two tiles left, and now you're sixteen points behind."

Jenny

Noelle tried to keep her whole attention on the impenetrable traffic. Friday night and a home game and everyone going somewhere. Jenny sniffled in the passenger seat of the little red Geo, but at least she was calmer than she had been an hour ago.

"We'll be there in a few minutes," Noelle said. "Then we can start figuring out a plan, okay?"

Jenny nodded and unfolded another tissue from the pocket pack on her lap. She wiped at her eyes and blew her nose again. She tilted down the visor to inspect her mascara and dabbed at the streaks. "I'm okay now," she said. "I think I've cried as much as I can possibly cry in one day. Your grandparents won't mind if I crash there?"

"No way. They'll love it. Grandma adores company anytime and all the time, and Grandpa loves to give tours of his roses and his fish."

"His fish?" Jenny looked wary.

"Yeah," Noelle said, giggling. "He keeps these giant aquariums full of bizarre fish. Saltwater. Some of them are pretty, but some are just weird. Here we are." She pulled the car to the curb and the porch light came on. "Come on, you'll see. Don't trip on Gulliver. He's the welcoming committee, and he wraps himself around your legs, the silly thing."

Noelle slung her satchel onto her shoulder and led the way up the front walk. The last roses exuded their perfume on either side of the door and dropped petals in the damp evening breeze. Jenny followed her friend into the warmth and glow of the Risings' bungalow.

Grandma held the bag while Grandpa tipped the board, letting all the tiles slide into the purple pouch Noelle had found at the Women's Shelter Thrift Shoppe. It was perfect for Scrabble tiles. The newer sets came with bags but her grandparents' set had to be fifty years old, and still going strong. Except for the box, Noelle noticed. That needed more tape. Her grandma pulled the bag's drawstring tight as Noelle closed the front door.

"Who won?" Noelle asked.

"Well, that's a fine greeting, young lady," Monti said.

"Grandpa, then," Noelle said.

"Right. Come on in, girls. Gulliver, get out of the way." The grey tabby ignored her and did his best to get trampled before the two girls put their bags down. Jenny stood, shoulders hunched, hands shoved into her coat pockets, on the rug inside the front door. Monti went to her.

"Grandma, this is Jenny Conklin. Jenny, Montana Rising, and my grandpa, Kit Rising."

"Nice to meet you," Jenny said.

"You call me Monti, sweetheart," Monti said. She eased Jenny's coat off her shoulders and hung it on the oversized coat rack. "Come in here by the fire. You're shivering." Monti led her down the two steps into the living room to a leather and oak settle by the fireplace. Noelle followed and sat down beside her friend. "You two warm up while I get you something to drink. Kit made a pot of coffee, or would you like tea? Cocoa?"

"Coffee's good for me, how about you, Jenny?"

"Coffee's great, thanks," Jenny said.

Kit negotiated the stairs and sat opposite the girls in his favorite chair, a leather recliner. Noelle frowned at the care he took lowering himself into it. They all gazed into the fire for a couple of minutes, getting comfortable.

"Are you a student at the college, Jenny?" Kit said.

"Yes, sir. Freshman year, like Noelle. I'm in her AP math class."

"Ah. Another smart young lady, hmm?"

Jenny snorted. "Pretty stupid, actually," she said.

Monti brought in a tray laden with coffee and fixings and a plate of shortbread cookies. "Who's stupid?" she asked.

"You're not stupid, Jenny," Noelle said. "You did a foolish thing. We all do foolish things now and then."

Jenny's eyes teared up. "This isn't like forgetting to study for an exam, Nellie. This is...this is what you say other things are like when they're really stupid."

"I'm not following," Kit said. "Could we start from the beginning, maybe?" He took a cookie off the plate. Monti handed Jenny a box of tissues and put a cup of coffee in front of each girl. She sat in the mission-style rocker between Kit's chair and the settle and nibbled on a cookie.

Noelle put her arms around Jenny and leaned her blonde head against Jenny's dark curls. "You want to talk? Or do you want me to explain the situation?" Noelle said. The girl trembled violently for a moment, then shook her head and nudged Noelle with her shoulder.

Noelle hugged her, then let go. "Okay. Here's the short version, G and G. Jenny lives in a house off campus with five other people, and one of the boys made like he was madly in love with her and she fell for it. Now she's pregnant and he doesn't want anything to do with her. He's getting nasty about it, in fact. That's why I thought it might be good for her to stay here for a little while and let him cool down. And maybe we can help her figure out what to do."

Jenny said, "I know what I have to do. I don't have a lot of choices."

"Sure you do, love," said Monti. "You have several choices. We'll help you explore the possibilities, think things through and make a plan."

"But there's no reason to try and hash it all out tonight," Kit said. "It's late and you look exhausted. Noelle, what about running your friend a hot bath? That seems to be the universally preferred therapy for distraught women. I bet Grandma will even let you rummage through her cupboard of bath salts."

"Certainly I will," Monti agreed. Jenny's shoulders relaxed visibly. "Noelle can show you where everything is upstairs. We'll all get a good night's sleep and start on this problem tomorrow."

Noelle got up and pulled Jenny to her feet. "Capital plan, I think." She looked to Jenny, who nodded her agreement. "Thanks, G and G, I knew you'd be grand." Monti rolled her eyes. The pun was ancient, dating back to a story her grandmother had read to her when she first arrived in which "grand" was a favored adjective. Monti offered the plate of cookies around again. Noelle and Jenny took a couple more cookies each and went upstairs, arm in arm.

KIT AND MONTI CLOSED up the house for the night. He banked the fire and locked the doors. She rinsed the cups and gave Gulliver fresh water. They met in the hall. Monti put her arms around Kit's waist and leaned her head on his chest. He switched off the light and they stood together in the dark.

"This is going to be a tough one," Kit said.

"I know it. It's not rape, but still." She looked up at him, not seeing his face but knowing the look of strength and love on it. "I'll call Sandy tomorrow."

"And I'll see if Ray and Dorothy have room, just in case." He bent down and kissed her forehead. "Let's go to bed."

Some Assembly Required

Monti held the lilac cashmere pullover in front of her and judged the effect in the mirror. Fabulous. She put it on and added small, but not too small, silver hoop earrings.

Lilac was her new favorite color. She'd never worn any shade of purple in her younger years, but since her hair had gone completely princess (that's Snow White, not Cinderella, as Noelle said) she looked terrific in lilac, though she wouldn't have known it if Noelle hadn't made her try it. And cashmere for ten dollars...what would she do without that girl?

Noelle was an avid treasure hunter. Since Monti's daughter, Marla, had left Noelle with them and reeled away into a grief-sparked, drug-fueled depression, grandmother and granddaughter had spent countless hours haunting the local second-hand stores, searching for beautiful bargains. Noelle had a real eye for ensembles, even back when she was eleven. Now when they found a great combination Monti put on the outfit, posed, and Noelle took a photo with her cell phone. She printed them and Monti tacked them up in her closet. She now had seven years' worth to choose from. Looking fabulous hadn't been so easy since she was twenty.

She pulled on her jeans and slipped into her favorite Birkie clogs. Another look in the mirror to tweak her bangs and she was ready. Kit was still sleeping, poor man. His back had seized up fiercely during the night, and after a session alternating heating pad and ice pack didn't ease it he'd had to resort to a heavy-duty painkiller. That would make him groggy today which he hated. She kissed him on the cheek. Then she grabbed her journal and her Bible and went down the hall to the kitchen.

The girls padded downstairs a while later, no doubt drawn by the irresistible aroma of fresh coffee. Monti, ensconced in the window seat with Gulliver curled up on her feet, smiled up at them. They couldn't have been awake more than five minutes. Jenny wore Noelle's ballerina PJ's and Noelle wore her ninja PJ's. She had an extensive pajama collection. Heavy eyelids on both girls indicated they'd talked late into the night. Good. Noelle had insights beyond her eighteen years and Jenny needed all the wise counsel she could get.

"Morning, young ladies," Monti said. "Help yourself to the coffee. Cream is in the fridge. No morning sickness, Jenny?"

"No ma'am. I haven't had any at all."

"Well, that's a blessing, anyway. Noelle, your grandfather nearly got his hands on the espresso machine last night. The danger increases with each passing day. I think the words "some assembly required" glow like a neon light at him whenever he walks by it."

Noelle smiled, "I'll try to get to that today, Grandma. I can't imagine there's much to assemble, though." She examined the box sitting on the kitchen counter. The picture showed a black and chrome contraption with levers, spouts, tanks and knobs. She opened the flap and peered inside. "Huh, maybe more than I thought." She'd won the machine in a grand-opening drawing at a new coffee shop a week ago, but hadn't had time to take it out of the box yet. "Where is Grandpa?"

"He had a rough night. He was still asleep when I came out, but I think I'll go check on him." Monti closed her Bible, dislodged the protesting cat, and headed back to the big master bedroom. "Breakfast when I get back," she said over her shoulder.

Kit stood in the shower, leaning against the wall stretching his muscles, letting the hot water blast away at the knots. Monti peeked in. "How are you doing, love?"

He opened his eyes and smiled at her. "I'll survive. I won't need another dose. Doesn't look like I'll get the yard raked today, though." He straightened up and shut off the water. Monti handed him his towel. "Girls up?"

She nodded. "Barely. They're at the coffee now."

"You look scrumptious, by the way."

"Why thank you, kind sir," Monti said, and gave him a kiss. "I'll go start breakfast while you get beautiful."

Breakfast was cheddar apple muffins, scrambled eggs and orange juice. Noelle made the muffins, Monti did the eggs, and Jenny set the table in the kitchen nook. Gulliver, underfoot, didn't manage to cause any actual injuries or breakage, though he did try. Kit came in when everything was almost ready and dodged his way to the coffee pot. When they were all seated, Kit thanked God for the food and asked his blessing on the day's activities.

The conversation wound around the coffee, the espresso machine, Kit's war injury, Gulliver, the girls' classes and their social life until it got to Jenny's situation.

"Jenny, Noelle said last night the boy is acting nasty toward you. Does that mean he's threatened you?" Kit asked.

"Well, yeah, I guess so," Jenny said. "He'd never do anything, though."

Kit frowned. "Why do you think that?"

"Because half of what he says to anybody is BS. He promises, he threatens, he lies." She shrugged. "That's what he does."

"Did you report these threats to the police?" Kit said.

"No," Jenny said. "He was half-drunk and not making a whole lot of sense. I just decided to get out of there."

"Okay Jenny, I understand. But will you do me a favor?" Kit waited until she made eye contact. "Will you please write down everything you remember him saying? Just so we have a record."

Jenny shrugged. "Sure, okay I guess." She swiveled her eyes to Noelle and raised one eyebrow. Noelle shrugged, too.

Monti fetched the coffee pot and filled everyone's cup again. "On another point, have you and Noelle talked about what your options are?"

"Yeah. She thinks I should go to this Crisis Pregnancy Center and get an ultrasound. I think that'll just make everything harder."

"Why harder?" Monti asked.

"Because then I'll still have to..." Jenny trailed off, and shook the tears out of her eyes. "I won't follow in my sister's footsteps and have a baby, go back home and live on welfare. I'm not doing that, okay?"

Kit cleared his throat. "There are a couple of other possible scenarios, Jenny. All right if I tell you the ones I can think of off the top of my head?" Jenny wiped her eyes and nodded at him. "No particular order here, just random, okay? One, you could marry the baby's father." Jenny snorted. "I know, not likely at this point."

"Or at any point," she said.

"Okay, just laying out all the possibilities. Two, you could abort the baby. Three, you could have the baby on your own and keep it. Four, you could have the baby and give it up for adoption. Did I forget any options?" Noelle and Monti shook their heads but didn't comment. "Also, going home to your folks isn't inevitable, nor is welfare. You've made a tough situation for yourself, but it doesn't have to unfold the same way your sister's did."

"But I can't have the baby on my own. I have school, and no job except for ten hours a week work-study at the cafeteria. And I can't stay in that house, so I have no place to live. And my parents," Jenny said, and choked out a bitter laugh. "I can just hear them. They never thought I could do this...college," she said. "Even after the test scores and the scholarship they couldn't say anything good about the whole idea. Now they'll say this proves they were right, and I guess it does." Her voice broke on the last word. Noelle hugged her while she cried.

Monti and Kit looked at each other, weary already.

Noelle dabbed at Jenny's cheeks with a bright yellow linen napkin. Jenny took a deep breath. "I'm okay now. Sorry."

"You needn't apologize for tears, for goodness sakes," Monti said. "Tears are for a reason, even when we don't know what it is. And you certainly have reason enough to cry, Jenny. But let me ask you this. If there was a way for you to have the baby and keep going to school, have enough money and a place to live, would you do it? You're not set on an abortion, are you?"

"I'm not set on it, I guess. But there isn't any way to do all that."

"There may be a way, Jenny," Kit said. "We know some people who regularly take in girls and help them through an unexpected pregnancy. I haven't called them yet, but it's entirely possible they might help you."

"Why would they do that?" Jenny asked.

Monti laughed. "God told them to," she said. "That's what they'll tell you if you ask them. But don't worry, they're not crazy people. Opening their home is their way of serving God, and sharing his love with other people. They're very sweet."

Kit shifted on his chair, looking for a comfortable arrangement of spine and limbs. "So if they're available, that would solve part of the problem. They live in town here, so you could still attend your classes. When's this little one due?"

Jenny's eyes got wide. "I have no idea! I never even thought of that."

She looked to Noelle for help.

"Well, I don't know!" Noelle said. "Don't you have to ask a doctor or look at a chart or something?"

"No problem, girls," Monti said. "We'll have a talk in a little while," she glanced at Kit, "while Kit's feeding the fish, and we'll figure it out." She collected plates and took them to the sink. "Then there's the matter of what to do with baby after he or she is born. Sandy's the lady to talk with about that." Monti came back and laid a hand on Jenny's shoulder. "She knows how the different kinds of adoption work, and what the process is like. That way you'll have all the information you need to make the best decision down the road."

Kit levered himself out of the chair, suppressing a wince. He slowly straightened, then smiled down at the concerned faces peering at him. "It's all right. I'm just a little sore. I think I'll go feed those fish now. But don't forget, Monti, she needs to think about her job, too. When does it end, can she get more hours, you know."

"Yes, we'll talk about that, too." She put her arms gently about him. "Can I get anything for you, sweetheart?" He put the back of his hand on her cheek and she pressed into it.

"No, Monti. I'll be fine, thanks." He kissed her forehead and she let him go. They all watched his careful walk and occasional hand to the wall for balance.

"Is he okay, Grandma?" Noelle asked, tears filming her eyes.

"No," she answered. "He fights it doggedly, but he can't win. Degenerative means it's going to get worse, not better." She smiled at the two vibrant, healthy young women. "He still has lots of good days, though, for which I'm profoundly grateful. Let's get this stuff cleaned up, then we can figure out when the baby's due and make a list of things to do."

Live Rock

K it opened the blinds in the study and turned on all the aquarium lights. He checked to make sure all tanks were bubbling properly and all his creatures were swimming or crawling as they should be and not floating belly up.

He got the fish foods and prepared to feed everybody. The big tank needed cleaning. He would definitely need Brian's help this time. Maybe he'd supervise and let Brian do it all. He sank into the therapeutic, ergonomic, medically designed, expensive, padded swivel chair in front of the big tank. It had settings for heat and massage and was a gift from Monti, desperate to make him more comfortable any way possible. He wasn't sure it was worth that much of her hard-earned money, but he would never tell her so.

A huge Stars and Stripes Puffer ruled the big tank. Its spinning pectoral fins were hard to believe, even after two years of watching him do his helicopter hover around the aquarium. A snowflake eel peeked from his hiding spot to see if dinner was on offer yet. Canary blennies darted in and out of the live rock. Coral Beauties, Firefish, and a Watchman Goby swam in mellow fellowship in his low-maintenance tank.

Kit doled out to each its designated food, then examined the three rabbitfish in his quarantine tank. They looked healthy so far. The Benggai Cardinalfish in his nursery tank were brooding, and he hoped for a good hatch. He had a fifth aquarium ready and waiting for green mandarins, which should arrive any day now. Requests for the colorful fish were popping up among his small customer base of fish fanciers. He made a note to check his email for orders later today. Right now, though, he would spend a few minutes laying Jenny's situation before his Creator, and then call Ray.

Best Practices

"Life Choices isn't open until Monday. What's your class schedule that day?" Monti said. She had fetched a legal pad and pen, and was ready to make a plan.

"I'm done with class at eleven on Mondays, then I work lunch at the cafeteria until two," Jenny said.

"I can take her, Grandma, if you're busy," Noelle offered. "Or did you want to come, too?"

"I don't have to come," Monti said, "but I have time if you want me to go with you."

Both women looked at Jenny, who shrugged. "This is your idea. I don't really know why we're going there."

"Well, for several reasons, love," Monti said. "First, you haven't been to a doctor, right?" Jenny shook her head. "Well, they have a nurse at the center who, for starters, will make sure your home pregnancy test told you the truth. If it did, she'll check you over and make sure you're healthy and that there aren't any complicating factors like STD's. She'll give you vitamins and advice on things to avoid while you're pregnant." Jenny was starting to look panicked. "Don't worry, sweetie, we'll take it slow. One thing at a time. Due date. That's what we want to know first. Can you narrow down the range of dates when you might have gotten pregnant?"

"Uh, yeah. I can tell you the exact day and hour."

"She and Blaine were only together once, Grandma, and he was rough with her and rude afterwards. She didn't let it happen again. That ticked him off, didn't it, girlfriend?" Noelle said.

"That's one way to put it. He started calling me a tease and...other things. We broke up. Then I told him I was pregnant. He's totally being a jerk now. I'm afraid to go back to the house to get my stuff. Not that I have anywhere to take it to."

"Bring your things here temporarily, Jenny," Monti said. "And I know for a fact Detective Price would be glad to meet us at the house and keep us company while we pack up. You don't need to worry. Want to do that on Monday before we go to the center?"

"I have a couple pieces of furniture..." Jenny said.

"Of course you do. Right." Monti made a note on her pad. "We'll see if Kit can recruit some muscle and tackle that job when they're available. We wouldn't even need Detective Price in that case. We'd have our own bodyguard." Monti grinned at the girls. Jenny's eyes narrowed. "What's the matter, Jenny?"

"Why do you know how to do this? Why would a cop help me move out?"

Noelle rolled her eyes. "You have no idea, Jenny. My grandmother may look like a mild-mannered, well-dressed," ("Thank you, love," Monti murmured) "tea party lady, but she doesn't just sit around playing Scrabble all the time. She and Grandpa are on the front lines."

"Now, now, let's not exaggerate," Monti said. "And a tea party sounds like lots of fun. We should plan one. But Noelle's right, Kit and I have experience with these kinds of troubles, and we're familiar with what needs to be done. Detective Price serves on the Domestic Violence Task Force and he's made it clear we should call him anytime if we think his presence might keep a situation from getting ugly. I haven't had to take him up on that yet, but I wouldn't hesitate if I thought it necessary."

"Wow," Jenny said.

The phone rang and Monti picked up. "Risings," she said. "Hello Nick. Yes, she's here, one sec." Monti passed the phone to Noelle, arching one eyebrow in an exaggerated inquiring manner. Noelle made a comic grimace back and nabbed the phone.

"Hey, Nick. Yeah? Well, I have a lot going on today, but...that will work tonight, if I can bring a friend. No, silly, Jenny from math class. Okay. See you at seven." She hung up. "Now don't even start. He's just a boy from school. Jenny, want to go to the movies tonight?"

"Start what?" Monti said in mock innocence. "I'm sure you know exactly what you're doing and that the young man's full dossier with background check, academic and criminal record if any which there better not be, and character references will be available for our files within twenty-four hours. And though fortunately we *can* fit it in this time, best practices dictate that you give your chaperons at least two days' notice before requiring their services."

Noelle rolled her eyes and Jenny's mouth hung open. Monti laughed.

Kit walked in on this tableau and said, "What are you up to, Monti?".

"Why do you assume it's me?" she asked.

"It's always you," he said. "At least, it has been for the last forty years." He leaned down for a kiss and took the chair next to his wife. "Have you girls got a plan going at all?" They filled him in on what they'd decided so far. "Good," he said. "I called Ray, and their guest suite will be available in a couple of weeks. They'd love to meet you Jenny, and tell you about their place. Then you could think about whether you might want to stay with them until your baby arrives."

They all looked at Jenny, whose chin quivered. "It's okay, Jenny," Noelle said. "There's no pressure. They're just trying to help. Are we going too fast?" Jenny nodded and swallowed hard.

Noelle stood up. "Come on, girlfriend. Let's go upstairs for a while." She looked at her grandparents with wide eyes while she tugged Jenny out of her chair.

Monti whispered, "I'll bring up a pot of tea in a little while. I'll knock and leave it on the hall table, okay?" Noelle agreed silently and led her distraught friend up the stairs.

"That went well," Kit said.

Monti dropped her head onto her folded hands. "The desire to be helpful and the desire to be efficient do not always work well together," she said. "I forget until the tears start, that even though I know all the things she needs to do, she hasn't done this a dozen times before. She's still trying to absorb the bald fact that she's going to have a baby."

"Yes, and I guess I contributed to the tears, too," Kit said. He stroked her back. "We might not be the sharpest tools in the box, honey, but God hasn't donated us to a rummage sale yet. We'll do a little better next time."

Monti leaned her head on his shoulder. "Am I a hammer or pliers?" she asked.

"I think you're a putty knife," he said, without missing a beat. "You scrape people off the floor and help them find their right shape again."

"Well, that's put quite a picture in my head," she said. "You do have a way with words, love. On and off the Scrabble board."

Nick

Nick sat on the settle with Gulliver on his lap, watching Kit watch him. Kit was messing with his mind, doing his Intimidating Grandfather bit, Monti noticed the instant she walked into the room.

"The girls will be right down, Nick. Relax. He hasn't threatened you, has he?"

"What? No!" Nick said, looking even more nervous than before.

"Of course not. I don't mean to imply he ever would do such a thing." That got her a cocked eyebrow from Kit. "Um, what time's the movie over?" she asked.

"Uuhh, movie," Nick stammered. "I think it's around ten o'clock. I'll bring them right back home afterward," he said, dragging his eyes away from Kit to look at Monti. Gulliver adjusted his head position for better ear scratching, and Nick obliged without noticing.

"You don't have to come right home, Nick. Noelle likes a late-night snack. Sometimes we stop at Jamba Juice after a movie. Have you ever been there?"

"Yes, ma'am," Nick said. He relaxed a little. "I like the banana mango smoothie."

Kit cleared his throat and Nick jumped—actually jumped, poor thing. Gulliver dug in and Nick winced.

"I prefer the strawberry shake," Kit said. "But I wish they'd figure out a way to sieve out all those tiny seeds." Kit smiled, shelving the IG routine. "Are you in any classes with Noelle?"

"Yes, sir, we're in the Chorale together. They don't make you audition for that one...otherwise I wouldn't have made it in. But Noelle has a great voice."

Footsteps sounded on the stairs and the girls made their entrance, decked out in their finest "any old thing" outfits, each detail of which had undoubtedly been agonized over and analyzed for maximum impact. Noelle wore a vintage hand-knit sweater Monti recognized from their most recent treasure hunt, and a ruffled skirt printed with huge cabbage roses. Jenny had on one of Noelle's signature velvet blazers over a black t-shirt and jeans.

Noelle glanced at Nick's tense posture. "Nick, are they being nice to you? Gulliver, get down."

"Sure, of course," he said, and blushed most charmingly. "I don't mind the cat."

"They're a little scary on the outside, but they're cream puffs, really. Aren't you, Grandpa?" Noelle leaned down and kissed Kit on the cheek. He grunted and put on an unconvincing scowl.

"Well, scary was not the look I was going for," Monti said. "I was hoping more for casual but sophisticated elegance, with a dash of eccentric. I'd better go find a mirror and see what can be done." She lifted the cat off Nick's lap and cradled him in her arms, belly up. She scratched his tummy and he curled all his toes and rewarded her with loud purring.

"Grandma's turn to win tonight isn't it, Grandpa?"

"If she can," Kit said. "Drive carefully, young man. You have our favorite granddaughter in your care."

"I will, sir. Ready, ladies?" Nick opened the front door for the girls and off they went, looking much too young to be let out on their own in the dark.

They listened to the car driving away for a moment, then Monti rolled Gulliver down to the floor and said, "Well. Here we are then. Shall I set up the board?"

They'd been playing for about forty-five minutes when Monti leaned back and scanned the words on the board so far. "This one looks promising. We have a bit of a medieval theme going here. What with QUAG and HEX and MEAD and VAIR, I feel a story shaping up. Fun, fun."

"Let me read it first, this time. I should have some privileges." Kit said. He took five tiles from the bag and frowned at the results as he lined them up on his rack.

"Yes, I'm sorry about that," Monti said. She wrote down Kit's score and moved tiles around on her rack experimentally. "It's just that my Basic Skills class was whining about how hard it was to write a story. They didn't like it when I gave them a plot or setting idea to use, and they didn't like it when I told them to write whatever they wanted. I had to read "Vampires in the

Pool" to them to demonstrate how any arbitrary set of words could be developed into a pretty good story."

"Two problems with that, lover. One, they probably don't know what arbitrary means and two, just because your fecund imagination lets you spill stories into your computer as easy as breathing, does not mean your students can do anything of the kind."

Monti went very still, gazed intently at the board, at her rack, at the board again, and hooked JOINS to his QUAG for forty-five points.

"You're serious about winning this one, aren't you?" he said.

"I couldn't care less who wins and you know it," she said. Kit grunted, almost like he didn't believe her.

He did win the game after all, but only by three points. Before they slid the tiles back into the bag, Monti took a picture of the game board so she'd have all the words for her story. Another 'dash of eccentric' she cultivated was writing short stories containing all the words played during a particular Scrabble game. Kit thought it a great way to keep her busy and out of trouble.

Theoretically.

The Scrabble Story:
Bo and Anisette

Bo *Willem, a solitary man and* **plier** *of fine golden* **mead** *in the town of Westhaven, chewed his quill as he pondered his next words. Bo talked but little, and rarely* **wrote** *anything beyond the facts and figures required to keep his business in order. But this were important, and must be done just so. The girl's father, a well-to-do silk merchant, must be approached with care if Bo was to win Anisette for his wife.*

Anisette was a delicate creature perhaps a year **or** *two past the prime marriageable age. Bo had seen her* **AT** *her family home. Her slim figure glided through the background unnoticed by one and almost all. She cast her eyes down at the broad tiles of the floor if someone spoke to her. If pressed into conversation she spoke well, but vanished from the room as soon as she could manage it. Most men of the town probably did not know there was such an* **entity** *as Anisette Marlow. Bo thought even her father was hardly aware of her existence.*

But Bo had heard her sing.

He remembered the first time he had heard her voice. He had been delivering mead to the Marlow house as he did each Friday morning. The sun beamed golden light aslant through the house yard. Mist curled off the river, and the herb garden warming in the sun suffused the air with exotic perfumes. Bo was waiting for the steward when a voice like liquid silver flowed from an upper window. The girl sang a hymn to Jesu, and her song must surely have floated all the way to her Savior's ears in Heaven. Bo's knees weakened, and he sat abruptly **on** *a bench to keep from staggering. He had never encountered such beauty in his life.*

Bo inquired discreetly. A bottle of his finest mead made a friend of the steward, and the man told him of Anisette's delicate health and her isolated life in her father's house.

Several years ago, the steward told him, her father had arranged for her to marry the son of a local merchant. The suitor and Anisette had met in the garden to get acquainted while her nurse stood watch in an overlooking window. But the meeting had ended badly, the steward didn't know why. The man had left abruptly. He'd sent word refusing the match and wouldn't be dissuaded. Anisette would not say what his objections had been, nor relate anything at all about their conversation. Her father had made no further attempts to marry her off and she seemed content.

"But what might it take," Bo asked, "to meet the lovely maiden?"

"Oh, I might arrange it, sir," the steward said. "Miss Marlow customarily takes a turn about the garden at three o'clock or thereabouts. If you will come to the gate at that hour I shall be prepared to admit you..."

The next week Bo could not manage the afternoon variance in his schedule. He did, however, hear her singing again at his early morning delivery to the Marlow household. His heart pounded and he determined to meet her the next week no matter his obligations to his trade.

Bo's heart thumped even now as he remembered their meeting. He'd brushed his coat and hat. He'd polished his boots, donned a clean white shirt, and tucked a sprig of lavender into his buttonhole. At the appointed hour, he arrived at the back gate of the Marlow house. The gate was high and constructed of solid planks and he could not know if she were on the other side walking in the garden. He gathered his courage to knock thrice on the gate as arranged. After a moment, the steward opened the gate and beckoned silently for Bo to come in, then closed the gate after him and stepped quickly away toward the house.

*Anisette sat on a stone bench, her **neat** hands folded in her lap. She sat erect, perfectly still, gazing at him unafraid. She wore a pale blue gown trimmed with **vair**. The fur fluttered in the **lazy**, rose-scented breeze. Her honey-brown hair lay smooth against her head, pulled back into a pearled and netted snood.*

"My lady," Bo said, sweeping his hat off and bowing deeply.

"Master Willem, is it not?" she said in her melodious voice. "May I help you, sir?

"My lady," Bo said again. He gripped the brim of his hat with both hands, marring its form irreversibly. "I wonder if we might speak together, talk of this and that, or..." He stopped. He took a deep breath and plunged on. "My lady, you

sing with the most beautiful voice I've heard ever in my life, and I deeply desire to know the woman to whom the voice belongs."

Anisette ducked her head and a lovely blush warmed her neck and cheeks. She slowly raised her head and favored Bo with a splendid smile. "I have seen you in the yard. You looked as if you might weep."

"Yes," he said with a short laugh. "I did indeed feel I might. I would weep my eyes dry if I could but hear your song every day and hold..." His face reddened then. He hadn't meant to bare his heart so. He sank to one knee before her. "My lady," he began yet again. "I am no poet. Let me be plainspoken with you." He searched her face for signs of rejection or impending flight but found nothing amiss. "Could you, in the proper course of time, and if upon coming to know me you found me not objectionable, and if your father would allow, possibly consider me...as a husband?"

A small sound escaped Anisette. She gazed at him, taking in the details of his weathered but well-formed face, his fine eyes, his generous mouth. She touched his cheek with the fingertips of one small hand.

"Gentle sir," she said. "I believe I could consider it. I had given up hope of treading that path, but perhaps I might still..." She took back her hand, and Bo covered the place where it had been with his own. "You must ask my father's permission to court me, of course."

"Have I any chance there? Will he **deem** me worthy of you?"

Anisette's laugh was edged with bitterness. "He has ceased to bother with me at all. He may be a **grump** when asked to take any pains to be rid of me, but I think when he considers the matter he will think it a boon to have me off his hands." She gazed at her eager suitor. "There has been not a beau to test him for a long time. But I think you will do well." She tilted her head. "Perhaps a letter, to begin? T'will let him bluster his objections to himself, think it over, and by and by be courteous to you in person."

"A letter? I can write a letter. I shall do it this day. Thank you, my lady, for brightening my hope so I can scarcely bear it. I should be to you the best of husbands, the most tender friend, true in all things," he said, and ran out of words to express the lightness lifting his heart.

"I thought you were not a poet," she said, teasing him. "Send your letter, dear sir, and we shall see what good and perfect gifts our Savior has reserved for **us**."

Bo leaped to his feet, bowed again, and dashed through the gate without another word. He did not see her face tense into a frown of anxiety as she watched him go.

Beloved Infant

Monti sat back in her chair and rubbed her eyes. Enchantment or vow? How was she going to use HEX if it wasn't an enchantment? But she never did very well with anything magicky.

A cup of tea was in order. And what time was it anyway? Noon. Time to go pick up the girls and set out on their afternoon adventure.

Jenny was starting to feel comfortable with the Risings. She had stayed at the house when they went to church yesterday, which was understandable. Who wants to be smiled at and questioned and most likely judged by a group of old geezers who didn't know you? Monti was reasonably sure some such reasoning lay behind Jenny's cool "No, thank you."

But Sunday afternoon they'd all taken a leisurely stroll together through the cemetery across the road. Jenny had asked about it a couple of times. Cemeteries fascinated her, apparently. The girls brought paper and charcoal and did rubbings of the older stones. Noelle took pictures of the witty ones. Jenny found a baby's grave marked with a lamb statue. Engraved on the stone base were dates bracketing a lifespan of two months, and "Beloved Infant" in place of a name. That had brought the cemetery walk to an abrupt end, but Jenny cheered up readily at The Locket, where they had some supper before walking back home.

Monti had started her Scrabble story today right after breakfast this morning and, predictably, the hours vanished into a time warp bubble or something. Time to get up, stretch her back and figure out what critical tasks she had been neglecting. Grading papers, done. No class until tomorrow. Kit was out eldering until dinner. Gulliver stopped washing his face and looked at her, but not in a needy way. She pushed control+S and slowly rose from her chair, muscles and vertebrae protesting at being broken out of their morning-long configuration.

Exasperated with herself, Monti picked up the little digital timer next to her laptop. She'd bought it to remind herself to get up every hour and walk around a bit when she was working on a long project at her computer. It was pretty ineffective if she didn't remember to set the silly thing.

Monti went down the hall to the kitchen and turned on the gas under the tea kettle. She stood looking out at the garden thinking about Jenny, and about her own rocky initiation into adult responsibilities. She was pregnant at eighteen, too. But she had been raped.

She was on the Freeman High School yearbook staff, and volunteered for the annual trip to the local university to interview staff and students. Many of Freeman's students picked the college for their further education, so each senior class published a write up about it in their annual. She and Vanessa, the valedictorian, would accompany Rick—the captain of the football team. He would drive them in his dad's big Cadillac.

On the day of the planned excursion Vanessa was ill and couldn't go. It being 1967, everyone was cool with Monti and Rick making the trip unaccompanied. He drove them to the college. They interviewed the vice president, the student body president and random students. The spring weather was sunny and he took lots of pictures while she jotted notes about the campus.

On the way home the Caddy started having engine trouble. Or so Rick said and Monti believed, due to the sudden onset of jerking and revving. Rick turned off into the woods on a dirt road, shut off the motor, turned to Monti and punched her in the stomach so hard she couldn't breathe. Then he raped her.

It happened fast—before she could gasp a breath he had her pinned to the seat, his big hand clamped down hard on the side of her head, and the harder she struggled the harder he pressed her face into the leather seat. To this day she still smelled the acrid stench of stale cigar smoke that saturated the upholstery whenever she thought about it. Rick told her straight out she wouldn't be believed if she told anyone, so she'd better just keep her mouth shut and enjoy it.

Afterward she vomited out the door. He gave her his handkerchief to wipe her mouth and her tears. Then he helped her straighten her dress and tidy her hair, and combed his own hair in the rear-view mirror. When she had herself marginally under control he drove them the rest of the way home, calmly reciting to her all the facts of their relative standing at school and in the town. How powerful his father was. How sad it would be if her little brother got hurt during gym class. How she was a stuck-up bitch and deserved it anyhow.

She didn't tell anyone. She knew his star athlete status and big shot father would win out over the allegations of a skinny daughter of obscure retired missionaries. She decided to pretend it had never happened.

A few weeks later she figured out she was pregnant.

The teakettle whistled, bringing her abruptly back to the present. Time for one cuppa, and then she would go pick up the girls.

The Letter

Master Marlow sat in his chambers frowning like a thunderstorm. "So, does she **hanker** after a husband now? That Willem seems not a sod. He bottles a fine mead, I will say. Best have Lennox look about a bit, anyway, make sure he's not **poxed** or bankrupt. Then we'll see if he can be made to stick." He lifted the bell stationed on his broad desk and rang for his steward.

Five days later Bo received a letter, heavy with a brown wax seal. His hands trembled as he broke the seal and unfolded the crisp parchment.

Master Fritz Marlow, to Bo Willem:

Re your desire to court Miss Anisette, maiden daughter of mine, with intent to wed her. Permission is hereby granted, bearing in mind the necessity to come to certain fiscal arrangements between us. To accomplish such, please attend me in my chambers upon your next weekly delivery. Arrange your own meetings with the maiden, as I know not the vagaries of her daybook.

Your Servant,

F. Marlow

*Bo set the letter down on his desk, hands still shaking. He gazed with new eyes at the small chamber from which he conducted his business. The heavy desk bore a large register listing his customers and delivery schedules. The wall behind the desk was pigeonholed from ceiling to wainscoting and nearly every hole held a roll of parchment. Here was recorded the history and science of his mead making: his recipes, the precise location and condition of each cask of fermenting mead and each bottle of the finished honey wine. The weather, variations in flower populations each year, and every foray to his hives in the honey meadow were all documented in these closely written rolls, the **gist** of his success.*

The diamond-paned window beside the desk looked out on tall grass, the river and the quag beyond. His boat waited moored at a small dock and his tidy sheds lined the path from dock to house.

He walked slowly into the main room and tried to see it as a woman might, coming to make this her home. The hall was neat, but not what he would call charming. He must arrange for the walls to be freshly whitewashed. And the beams and tiles scrubbed. And the windows. But the yard? He dropped into the settle in front of the spacious fireplace. No. He would clean and repaint, but he would let her guide him regarding all else needed to make the house and grounds a fit setting for her loveliness.

But first, to meet her again and learn her mind on all things likely to matter to them both. And, if at all possible, to win her heart and her hand. He returned to his desk and wrote another letter.

Life Choices

Monti and the girls sat in the reception area of the Life Choices Pregnancy Center waiting for their turn with the nurse. Jenny fidgeted. Noelle grabbed her hand and held it. It was a little drafty and Monti stuck her hands in the pockets of her sweater.

Young moms carrying babies or pushing strollers kept walking past them. Jenny stared at each girl, several of whom were younger than she was. Some seemed a bit harried, but all looked reasonably happy and healthy. One couple came in, he carrying the baby and she the diaper bag, like they were playing grown-up. But Monti caught the eye of the young man and knew the days of pretending were long gone for him. They must be gathering for a support group meeting.

"Sorry to keep you waiting, ladies. Busy today," said a middle-aged woman wearing bright rubber ducky scrubs and a brighter smile. "Come on back." She led the way down a narrow, brightly lit hall smelling faintly of disinfectant and lined with framed photos of beautiful babies. "Haven't seen you for a while, Monti," she said over her shoulder. "How's Kit?"

"Reasonably well, thanks, Minnie. Good days still outnumbering bad, thank God. He's out eldering today so he'll be trying to keep up with Eddie and John. That'll come back to haunt him."

"What's eldering?" Jenny said in a low voice to Noelle.

"Oh, it's lots of things. It's not really a word, but that's what we call it. Grandpa's an elder at our church, and they're responsible to take care of the body—all the members of our church—when they need advice or comfort or a whack on the side of the head. Of course, they don't do the whacking thing even when people do need it, but they might strongly encourage someone to knock off the idiot behavior."

"Weird. I never heard of that before. It sounds, I don't know, like the Pilgrims or something."

Noelle laughed. "Maybe we can get them to wear those hats with the big buckles on them."

"Here we are," Minnie said. "Jenny, do you want company or shall we have them wait here?" Jenny waved Monti and Noelle to the chairs lining the hall and followed the nurse into the exam room.

After a while the door opened and Jenny and Minnie reappeared.

"Here's a shocker," Jenny said, "I'm pregnant."

"Well, it's good to know these things for sure," Monti said. "What happens next, Minnie?"

"Next, I check if Sandy is available. If not, one of her volunteers will help. They'll chat with you about options and what services we have available here. Hang on, I'll see who's around. You all head back to the reception area, it's a little more comfy." She disappeared down an intersecting hall.

The three of them went back down the hall slowly, cooing over the baby pictures. They were professional portraits and Monti noticed a local studio's sticker in the corner of most of them. Probably they donated a photo session to new moms.

They had just sat down in the worn leather chairs in the reception foyer when a slim woman with a stylish silver and blonde bob and a deep smile came to greet them. She held Jenny's file.

"Hey, Monti, good to see you," she said. A gust of wind rattled the glass door. "Brr. I keep forgetting to ask Sam about some weather stripping for that door." She paused, looking expectantly at the girls.

"Sandy, you've met Noelle I think, and this is Jenny Conklin. Minnie confirmed Jenny's pregnant, so we're here to talk about her options and maybe figure out a plan."

"That's what I'm here for," Sandy said. "Let's go in my office. Oh, Lynn," she said as they passed the receptionist's desk, "call Sam, will you, and ask him if he'll winterize that front door for us."

"Will do, Sandy," Lynn said. Sandy ushered them into her office and they all sank into faded, overstuffed sofas in a cozy corner. Sandy opened the manila folder in her lap.

"So, we have a baby due June 16." She looked up and smiled. "What do you think about that, Jenny?"

Jenny shrugged her shoulders. "It's gonna screw up my life, I guess. Monti and Noelle keep telling me I have lots of choices, but none of it makes sense yet. I don't know what to do." She looked at Sandy, apparently waiting for her to make it make sense.

"That's honest, Jenny, and a good place to start. There's one decision you have to make, on which everything else depends." Sandy radiated compassion at the girl. She waited a moment, giving Jenny a chance to respond. Jenny shrugged again and her chin quivered. "You're not sure about that, yet, honey?" Jenny shook her head no. "Okay, I understand. For now, let me explain some of what we have to offer here..."

THE THREE WOMEN RETRACED their steps without talking. They were wrung out. Noelle held the front door of the clinic open for them. Monti's phone warbled as they climbed into her Subaru. The ringtone, a clip of "Radar Love," meant it was Kit.

"Hi there, love," she said. "How's the eldering going?" She listened, a frown deepening as Kit talked. "Oh, no. Well, I guess we knew that would happen sooner or later. Everybody okay now? Yep, we're going to find a little lunch, then we'll head home. Yes, a plan is starting to form around the edges. Okay, love, see you at five-ish."

"What's up with the Gang of Elders?" Noelle asked. Everyone was belted in and Monti concentrated on exiting the parking lot. It was awkwardly situated at a busy intersection. Made her nervous every time.

"Grandpa's had an interesting day thus far," she said. "Mrs. Cahill's neighbors finally called the police about all those cats. She could hardly tell the guys about it between sobs. It was bound to happen. We've been trying for months to help her get them all spayed and neutered and given away, but last time I heard she still had at least a dozen animals. It's impossible to keep up. An eighty-year-old lady and twelve cats in a one-bedroom house." She shook her head. "Poor old lonely Agnes."

"So what are some elders gonna do about that?" Jenny wanted to know. "They can't do anything, can they?"

Monti looked at her in the rearview mirror. The girl understood so little about love. It was enough to break your heart. "They listened to her, Jenny. They cared about her, helped her clean up a bit, called her son in California, talked with the deputy. Just to have someone on your side in an awful situation can be a great comfort, even if the situation can't be magically fixed.".

Jenny's face reddened. "Right. I get that," she said, scarcely loud enough to hear.

"Um, I'm driving, but I don't know where I'm going," said Monti. "Where's our lunch?"

Stroll

Bo Willem and Anisette Marlow strolled through her father's gardens. A high wall around the property muted the noise of the town and stopped the dust rolling in. The gentle sun touched the blossoms the lovers passed, evoking from each its heady perfume. Dappled shade provided a breath of cool refreshment every little while as they passed beneath a rustling maple or a fragrant locust.

The couple did not notice these niceties. They were exploring the landscape of possibility, asking questions, sharing preferences and dislikes, tentatively offering fond dreams and tender hopes. Their heads bent closer and closer together as they walked on. At length, Anisette laid a feather light hand on Bo's arm.

"Come, sir, and sit beneath this willow. I want to catch my breath, and to broach a matter with you."

"Certainly, my lady," Bo said, and held aside the curtain of willow branches to let her into its shelter. They sat on the stone bench there and she folded her hands in the neat fashion that so charmed him.

"You know my father arranged a match for me long ago," she said. He nodded, a tiny frown creasing the broad space between his brows. "The gentleman broke it off," she said, bowing her head. "Do you know why?"

"No, how could I?" he asked. "But it matters not to me. The man must have been a losel to refuse you."

She reached for his hand and gripped it in both of hers. "You must listen to me, Master Willem. I cannot encourage you further without complete honesty and nothing hid between us."

"I hide nothing, my lady."

"Oh, and I meant not to imply that, sir. It is I," she paused and gathered her courage. "I must now be plain with you. The other gentleman broke off the engagement when he learned of an enchantment under which I have suffered these long years."

Pain

Monti, rummaging around in the kitchen, decided on late and light for their supper. She and the girls had thrown caution to the wind at lunch. The dessert cart had proved irresistible, and even though they had shared the towering Brownie Double-Dare it was still too much.

Kit had lunched with the guys, and they were no doubt plied with cookies and pie while making their rounds. No one would be hungry for a long while. She would make some stracciatella and have the girls put together a big salad. That should be plenty. If it were only she and Kit they'd probably just munch on a bowl of popcorn with their Scrabble.

A car pulled into the driveway and she peeked out the window. Kit opened the passenger door of Eddie's car but Eddie got out, too. He came around, opened Kit's door farther and leaned inside. Eddie practically lifted Kit from the car. Monti's heart hammered.

"Oh God—help," she breathed as she ran to the kitchen door and down the steps to help support him. His face was white and waxy as a candle. The three of them maneuvered up the four steps and through the door and lowered Kit into a chair. His face and neck were rigid with pain barely under control. "Kit?" She cupped his face with her hands.

"I wanted to take him right to the ER, Monti, but he insisted on coming home," Eddie said. She nodded and crouched down beside Kit's chair, her hand on his knee.

"Kit, what can I do? What do you want to do?" she asked, trying not to choke on the tears clogging her throat. He gripped her hand hard, his eyes locked on hers. He wasn't going to be able to help her decide.

Without taking her eyes from Kit's she said, "Eddie, go down the hall to our room and bring back every prescription bottle on the nearest nightstand." Eddie hurried to do it. "I'm calling Dr. Eastman," she said. Kit nodded slightly. She pulled her hand away and stood up.

Kit's doctor's numbers were written in bold lettering on a 3x5 card taped to the wall by the phone. She tried the office first. "Kristen, is Dr. Eastman still there? Yes. No, I've got his cell, bye." She dialed his cell number. "Charlie? Montana Rising. Kit..." she struggled to continue, "Kit is in a lot of pain. I'm not sure what to do for him...yes, he just got home, he's been out with the elders. ...I don't know, wait." She covered the phone. "Eddie, when did this start?"

Eddie jogged back down the hall toward her, clutching a half-dozen brown plastic bottles with white snap-on lids. "He seemed uncomfortable at lunch, around one o'clock or so. John had to head home then and I asked Kit if he wanted to call it a day, but he said no. We were clear out at Millers' when he got real bad. That was about four."

She held up her hand to stop his further explanation. "Started around one, very bad by four," she said. She listened, then turned to examine the medications Eddie had set on the table. She picked them up one by one. "Yes, I have it. Okay...Yes, Eddie will help me. Okay, see you in a bit." She hung up.

She filled a tumbler with water, took two pills from the chosen bottle and pulled a chair right up to Kit. "Love, Charlie says to take these right now and he's on his way. Can you swallow these?" Kit reached for the pills with a shaking hand. He tried to take them from her hand, but knocked them on the floor. Eddie got down to look for them while she shook two more out of the bottle. "Let me put them in your mouth, love." He managed a swallow of water and that was done, at least.

"Eddie, can you help me get him to bed? The girls are at the library."

"You bet. Like we did from the car?" he asked, and Monti nodded.

Ten minutes later Kit was stretched out on the bed, shoes and jacket off, with an afghan over him. She'd thanked Eddie and sent him home. Monti sat on a chair next to the bed and held his hand. The medication was starting to kick in and she felt a heady rush of relief as Kit's neck muscles began to relax. It was unbearable to see this powerful, gentle, brave man suffer such pain. He'd been her tower of strength for so many years. She was desperately afraid she would fail to be the same for him when he needed her.

He had come to her rescue, a real-life knight in an Army uniform, when she was eighteen. He was four years older and about to leave for his first duty assignment as a second lieutenant. His parents and her parents had been fast friends since their own college days, and Kit and Monti and all their siblings played together at rare intervals when both families were stateside. Monti's folks had confided in them about the rape and Monti's situation. The Risings shared their grief and offered their heartfelt sympathy. A month later Kit knocked on the Housels' door.

They fed him dinner. They asked him a thousand questions about his family and his plans and caught him up on all their news, too. Almost. They didn't mention Monti's pregnancy. But his parents had told him, and when the catching up was winding down Kit cleared his throat and asked permission to "speak freely, sir." Monti's dad was taken aback, but told him to go ahead.

"My parents told me about Monti's situation," he said. "I would like to offer her a solution that I hope will be a blessing all around. What I mean to say is, Monti, would you consider marrying me? I'm heading off to Texas soon and you could go with me, and have a fresh start, and we'll have the baby and raise it and, uh...live happily ever after, I guess."

Monti and her parents stared at him, eyes wide, stunned by this unexpected offer to rock their world. Kit blushed. "I know Monti and I haven't been around each other very much, but we've known each other practically our whole lives. I feel like we could fall in love real easy, and if we're already married when that happens then that works fine. Monti's baby needs a dad, and I'd love to have Monti as my wife.... What, uh, what do you think?"

Mr. Housel recovered first. He sat up straight and said, "Well, young man, that's quite an offer. It's completely up to Monti, of course." He looked at his daughter. "And...she might want to think it over and ask God about it. Monti?" All Monti managed was a wide-eyed nod.

"When do you leave, Kit?" her mother asked. She always cut right to the practical core of a matter. "How much time do we have for Monti to get reacquainted with you enough to make a wise decision?"

"I have to report to Fort Hood in five weeks. I don't have much in the way of household goods so I was going to box it all up, send it ahead and fly down. But," he said, and ran a hand over his blond crew cut, "if Monti will marry me I thought we might drive down and have a bit of honeymoon on the way there." His blush deepened, poor thing. Even his ears glowed a bright pink.

The next three weeks had been a whirlwind. Kit and Monti spent every spare hour together talking, planning, laughing, and praying. They found that sure enough they could fall in love real easy. Monti graduated on June sixth and they married on the fourteenth. Then they drove off into the sunset in a brand-new Mercury Cougar, a wedding gift from Kit's parents, and lived happily ever after just like Kit said they would. Not without their share of sorrow and heartache, to be sure, but oh so happy.

Monti bent down and pressed her lips to Kit's relaxed hand. The doorbell rang and she tucked his arm under the afghan and went to let the doctor in. Headlights swung around and backlit Charlie standing on the steps. Noelle and Jenny were home, too.

"Charlie, Kit's in our room. I'm going to let Noelle know what's up, then I'll be there." Charlie, never one to say one word when none would do, merely nodded and headed down the hall.

"Grandma? Was that Dr. Eastman? What happened? Is Grandpa okay?" Fear flitted across Noelle's face as she lugged her book bag into the kitchen.

"Your grandpa had a bad day. He was in a lot of pain, but it's easing off some now. Dr. Eastman is checking him over. I was going to make soup and salad for a late supper, but don't count on that now," Monti said.

"No problem. Don't even think about us, Grandma, we're fine and we'll stay out of the way." Noelle kissed Monti on the cheek and gave her a hug. "Give me an update when there is one?"

"Sure, sweetie." Monti left them and went to Kit.

Charlie was taking Kit's pulse. Kit was awake but groggy. "Eddie told me you started getting uncomfortable at about one o'clock, and it got bad by the time you were out at Millers'. Is that right, love?" Monti asked.

Kit nodded. "I took one a' those whatchacallits at lunch, Charlie, but it din' do any good," Kit said, struggling to not slur the words.

"And I gave him two of these," she showed him the bottle, "when you told me too. That did help."

The doctor put his stethoscope away and planted his hands on his knees. "Kit, when you keep pushing yourself when you're in pain it stresses your heart. You mustn't do it. Not only that, if you'd been alone when it got bad how would you have gotten home, or to help? You should have come home when the pain began. You must make yourself stop and rest, at home, when it flares up. You must."

Kit squeezed his eyes shut and nodded. Monti knew how hard that would be for him to do. Someone who didn't know him might assume it was pride that made him keep going and not acknowledge his limits. But she knew it wasn't pride. He was the first to admit his weaknesses. But her husband had the truest servant's heart of anyone she had ever met. He couldn't bear not to be of use. There was work needed done and he wanted to do it. She was glad Charlie was being firm about it.

"If the prescription you carry with you isn't working anymore then it's even more important you cease and desist at that point. Because I can't give you anything stronger that's okay for walking, let alone driving. You'll have to come home and take these." He took the bottle from Monti. "If you don't, the stress will eventually damage your heart. And I don't want that to happen, because I have other things to do with my evenings than tend to banged-up old hardheads."

Kit managed a weak smile. "Thanss for the pep talk, Charlie. I'll be sure and wry your boss abou' yer ezemplary bedside manner." His eyes would not stay open without effort, and he stopped trying. He was asleep in seconds.

The doctor and Monti stepped into the hall. He gave Monti instructions about when to give Kit another dose and handed her yet another bottle from his leather bag. Kit's nightstand pharmacy was growing to alarming proportions. "If it's really bad like this, have him take one of these. Only one, and hopefully not too often. We don't want to wreck his kidneys, too. And you'd better call Kristen and make an appointment for him sometime in the next couple of weeks. I need to keep a closer eye on his condition, okay?"

Monti sagged against the wall. "Is there anything I can do to make him more comfortable?"

"You do all the right stuff already, Monti. But heating pads and massage chairs are going to be of less and less use. The best help you can give him is to help him stay active, eat well, and rest when he needs to."

The doctor buckled his bag and Monti walked him to the door. "Thanks for coming by, Charlie. We appreciate it."

"Yeah, well. I'm billing you for it so don't get all mushy."

Monti laughed. "Well, I'll call Kristen tomorrow and make sure it does get billed. I know you, Charlie Eastman." They shook hands and he headed out.

She heaved a deep sigh. She'd better give Noelle the promised update.

The girls lay on Noelle's bed, listening to *Classic Yo-yo Ma*.

"Hey, G," Noelle said. "How's G?"

"He's asleep. Dr. Eastman gave us a stronger medication to use if he has an episode this bad again. Which I expect he will." Monti sat in the Stickley chair by Noelle's desk. "Are you girls hungry?"

"We were just thinking about going down to make that salad," Noelle said. "But we don't need any soup, do we Jenny?"

"I don't," she said. "What's the matter with Mr. Rising? Noelle said it's an old injury from the Gulf War. But how is that causing this much trouble twenty years later?"

"He got smashed up pretty badly in a HUM-V rollover in Kuwait," Monti said. "They gave him excellent medical care there and put him back together, but that was only the beginning." She turned her head this way and that, trying to loosen her neck muscles. "He needed extensive surgery and rehabilitation therapies once he got back home. The damage to his spinal column was horrific. He's never been pain-free, really, since then. And they warned us it would get worse as he got older, and it surely has. The last couple of years, especially."

"Man, I wouldn't have guessed," Jenny said. "He doesn't say anything about it."

"Oh, no. He's extremely disciplined. It amazes me every day what he endures. I've learned to recognize the signs when he's really hurting. I do my best to get him to lie down, take some medication." Monti rubbed the back of her neck. "It's more difficult than I expected to care for him without treating him like a child or a doddering old man. It takes tact. He's very gracious, mostly, when I get a little overbearing."

Noelle rolled off the bed and jumped up. "G, you need some tender loving care too, I think. How about if you go check on G and then take a nice hot bath, and Jenny and I will make a fancy salad. We'll serve and clean up, and then figure out some more ways to pamper you for the whole evening."

She took Monti's hands and pulled her up from the chair. Then she wrapped her arms around her and kissed her on the cheek. "Love you lots, G."

"I love you lots, too, Nellie. You make good plans. I think I'll keep you around."

"Ha. As if you had any choice about that!" she said, and shooed Monti out of the room.

Hex

Anisette looked into Bo's eyes, afraid to see his response and afraid not to see. But after a slow blink, he opened his mouth, closed it again, and sat silent. Anisette picked at the vair trim on her sleeve, then clasped her hands in her lap to stop it.

At length, Bo shifted on the stone bench and said, "What sort of enchantment, poor lady?"

Anisette let out the breath she had been holding. She stared at her clenched hands, then ventured a glance at his face. "When I was quite small," she said, "my father dealt sharply with an old mother of the town. She, it grieves me to say, dabbled in witchery. She put a **hex** on my father's offspring, present and future."

When she didn't **go** on, Bo said, "And what is the hex, my lady?"

She squeezed her eyes shut, "Whenever it rains I am compelled to cast off my shoes and stockings and run out to a patch of garden soil, whereupon I am changed." She swallowed hard, and went on before her courage failed her. "Whereupon I am changed... into the likeness of a tree." She took a deep breath and sighed it out. "I return not back to my natural form until the sun has dried the last of my branches." She wrung her hands and searched his face again.

A deep frown corrugating his forehead eased as she finished her tale. "A tree?" Bo laughed with relief, but sobered instantly. "'Tis...difficult to believe," he said.

"Aye, and I know it. I hardly believe it myself when I say it aloud. But 'tis true, and it drove my poor mother to her grave." Anisette stood and paced. "My father did not tell her of the hex, not believing in it himself. When next it rained, and I ran into the garden and was changed, she went wild. I was dimly aware of her torment and would have wept if I could." She sank back onto the bench. "When she learned of the hex she was terrified she might have another child. She locked herself away from my father and died within the year."

Bo grasped both Anisette's small hands. "My poor lady. What heartbreak to have endured. And each time, to be reminded so cruelly of your mother's anguish. How do you bear it?"

"Master Willem," Anisette said, tears filling her eyes and coursing down her pale cheeks. "You have not leaped up and run from me."

*"Why no, my lady. It is **none** of your doing. May naught be done to relieve your suffering?"*

"In truth, I do not know, sir." Her shoulders slumped in despair. "My father does not care to investigate the matter and I am never allowed to leave the grounds. I know not how to discover a remedy, if one there be."

Bo jumped to his feet at this. He strode back and forth in the willow bower. Then he returned to the bench and grasped her small hands once again. "Please do marry me, Anisette. I live on the bank of the river, in a lonely cove. You shall have there far more freedom than within these walls. And we shall seek for a remedy, far and wide. And yet, if there be no cure I shall care for you tenderly, and protect you and love you all the days of my life."

A great sob rose from Anisette's heart and broke out in a cry of pent-up grief and disbelief and joy and relief. "Can you? Will you, good sir?" she asked through her tears.

"I will, indeed." Bo took her in his arms and held her until she had calmed. Then he pulled away from her and lifted her chin.

"Your father," he said. "I do not wholly trust the man. He wrote of financial arrangements. I am to attend him in his chambers on the morrow to discuss the matter. What do you think? Will he try some trickery?"

"I would not put it beyond him," she said. "But if I am in the room I think it will be well. He is not so shameless as to try to profit from my misery whilst I am looking at him."

"Well thought of. Until then, do us both lay the matter before God, and we'll meet in the morning to settle things with your father." He kissed her hands, jumped up and thrust aside the willow curtain. "Until tomorrow, my Anisette." He departed as had the cowardly suitor of years ago, but with love and courage ensuring his soon return.

Muscle(s)

Monti stared into her closet. Surely she was standing here for a reason. Closet. Clothes. Get dressed. Yes, get dressed for work. She had classes to teach today. She closed her eyes and mentally blew at the cobwebs clogging her brain.

She had not slept enough. She'd tried not to move during the night for fear it might jostle Kit. She lay, tense from neck to toes, wide awake until midnight at least. She'd finally decided to sleep on the chaise longue, but just as she got out of bed Kit semi-woke in renewed anguish. She fumbled around finding the new medication Charlie had given her, and worked to get Kit coherent enough to take it. She collapsed onto the chaise, but it seemed like hours before she sank into exhausted sleep.

At least Kit was feeling better this morning. He was up and showering and apparently functioning okay, which was good because the project for this morning was to move Jenny's furniture to the Risings' garage. She hoped he would supervise instead of lift things.

But right now she had to get herself together for her nine o'clock class. She pulled out a classic no-brainer outfit: black slacks, cream turtleneck and dusty purple suede blazer. She'd wear those art glass earrings from the summer craft fair and call it good.

In the kitchen, she pulled a bag of huckleberry muffins from the freezer for the moving crew. The zipper split open and frozen muffins bounced across the floor. She rounded them up, invoked the 30-second rule and popped them into the oven to toast a bit. Then she spilled coffee beans all over the counter. She collected them into the grinder. Then she spilled freshly ground coffee all around the filter and into the empty pot. She rinsed everything and started over. When she had that going she took two mugs from the cupboard and a third fell out and shattered on the tile floor.

She put both hands on the edge of the counter and dropped her head between her shoulders. She was a grown woman. She would not have a hissy fit. She needed a cup of coffee and a few minutes in the Psalms to put things in perspective.

Kit appeared in the doorway. "Troubles, love?" he said. He grabbed the broom and swept ceramic fragments into a pile.

"Oh, you know. Have to exercise those klutz muscles once in a while. Use 'em or lose 'em."

He kissed the back of her neck. "Rough night, huh."

"I'm so glad you're better this morning," she said, and turned to embrace him. "Let's not do one like that again, okay?"

He laughed without humor. "Wish I could promise you, Monti." He kissed her softly. "Thanks for taking such good care of me."

She held him close. "Taking care of you is taking care of me. Completely selfish motives. I don't know what I'd do..."

"Hey, now. Knock it off, sob sister. I'm fine. I'm here for exactly as long as He decides I need to finish my basic training. Same as you. Isn't that the deal?"

She sighed. "I guess if I want melodrama I'd better finish my story. None allowed in the kitchen, apparently."

"Not before breakfast, anyway," he said, and kissed her again. "Got time for an omelet? I'll cook."

"Sure, thanks," she said. "I need to go early and meet with Alicia about next semester's schedule, but I have time." She ducked out of his arms to see if the coffee was ready. "There are muffins toasting in the oven. Is the plan all set for today?"

Kit nodded. "Eddie and his nephew will be here at eight to help lug Jenny's furniture over here. I won't be much use in the lugging, I don't think."

Monti stopped with her hand on the fridge door. "No lugging at all, okay? Supervise. Those guys, they're made of muscle—maybe even where they should have grey matter—so they need supervision..."

"Now, Monti."

"Okay, okay but no lugging, right?"

"We'll see. I won't push it, don't worry. I don't want two nights like that in a row."

Monti relaxed a little. "Okay then." She scanned for the next thing. "I'll feed Gulliver and get my laptop packed up." Gulliver appeared at the sound of his name and did his best to help her exercise her klutz muscles some more.

Done

The long hours until the morning meeting crept by with excruciating slowness, but at long last it was time to walk again through the Marlows' gate and change his life forever. He closed the gate behind him and carried the bottles of mead to the kitchen as always. The old steward met him there, curiosity peeking from the man's crinkled eyes.

"This way to the Master's chambers, Master Willem," he said. He led Bo up the back stairs to a wide, carpeted upper hall and a closed door, dark and polished. The steward knocked, and at a grunt from the other side opened the door and bowed, indicating Bo should enter.

"Close the door behind him, you dolt," said Marlow. The door was quickly but silently shut. Bo glanced around, marked Anisette perched in a window seat and relaxed a fraction. But he would not let down his guard until Anisette was safely his.

"Take a seat, Bo Willem." Bo sat in the chair facing Marlow's massive desk. "Let us settle this matter straight away. I have pressing business today."

"I can imagine no more pressing business than the future security and happiness of your only child, Master Marlow."

"Yes, well. As Anisette is my heir, you stand to inherit valuable property and business interests upon my death. Therefore, I will require for her bridal gift one hundred guilders. And a case of mead each month as long as I live."

"Father! That's ridiculous!"

"Done," Bo said. "Let us set a date for the wedding.".

Master Marlow's eyebrows rose into his hairline. He obviously had anticipated some haggling over the bride price. But he accepted the easy victory with the slightest smile, and slapped the desk. "Certainly, man. Let us set a date." He pulled a large ledger to him, and flipped several pages. "It will take some time to arrange the..."

"I suggest a week from Sunday," Bo said.

Marlow harrumphed and said, "It can't be done. What of the trousseau, the feast, the musicians and the clergymen? I must invite the proper people..." he trailed off. Bo imagined him picturing a late summer shower during the reception. The man harrumphed again.

Bo stood and paced the room. "I propose a small gathering of our closest family members only. We'll hold the ceremony here, in the gardens. My pastor will gladly marry us. I will speak with him this afternoon. Whatever food and music you may arrange within the week will be sufficient, will it not, Anisette?"

"Yes, my lord. And no trousseau is needed, Father. I have gowns aplenty no one ever sees."

"And to protect Anisette, Master Marlow, please do this: erect a small enclosed pavilion in the garden, encompassing a flower bed into which my lady may quickly run should the weather betray us." He turned to face Anisette. "Will you have time, my lady, to reach such a refuge?"

"Yes, my lord, I believe so." Her eyes lit with surprised joy at this brilliant plan. "Yes, that will be well."

"If rain forces Anisette to seek that shelter, I shall take it upon myself to explain it away to our guests. I will trust God to give me the words should I need them, to ease any upset without revealing my lady's suffering." Bo returned to his chair and sat. "Well, and how does this proposal set with you, Master Marlow?" Bo had listened with awe to his own voice, boldly dominating the room. Desire for the lovely creature sitting in the window had given him unimagined courage.

Marlow harrumphed yet again. Bo smiled to himself. This morning's encounter was not going how the man had anticipated, and he appeared unable to adjust to the current state of affairs. Anisette rose from her perch and went to her father.

"Father? Say you agree, will you not? 'Twill be very little fuss, and quickly done, and then I shall be gone from your house and no longer a burden to you."

He looked up at his daughter and caught hold of her sleeve. A frown creased his forehead. "A burden, daughter?" He pulled in his chin. "Indeed, I have treated you as such and it shames me. Forgive this selfish old man, little one?"

She put her arms round his neck and kissed the top of his head. "Freely, my father," she said, laying her cheek upon his head.

He did love his daughter, then. That is well, Bo thought. It might be a tense week, but he would not have to regard Marlow as an antagonist. The old man would do right by his daughter and see that she had a happy wedding day.

"It shall be as you say, young man," Marlow said. He rang the bell for his steward. "No time to lose now. Off with you both, I have many things to arrange."

Bo took Anisette's arm and they left the chamber scarcely touching the floor.

Rage

Moments after Monti left, Eddie banged on the kitchen door and let himself in. "Hey, is breakfast ready?" His nephew Brian followed him in, ducking to fit through the door frame.

Kit walked into the kitchen, empty coffee mug in hand. "Hi Eddie, Brian. Coffee?"

"Absolutely," Eddie said. Brian lifted his Redbull.

"Coffee?" Noelle said from the stairs. "I want coffee." She skipped down to the kitchen and kissed Kit on the cheek.

"Of course you do, young lady. You've wanted coffee every morning for the last five years or so. I don't see why there should be an exception today." He took down her favorite golden butterfly mug and filled it for her.

Jenny moved down the stairs more slowly, but smiling and inhaling the coffee aroma. Kit poured a cup for her, too. "Good morning, Jenny. Doing all right?"

"Yes, sir, thank you," she said. She lifted the edge of the plaid cloth covering the muffin basket and plucked out a hot muffin. The others followed suit.

"Okay, crew," Kit said. "Remember. As far as we know, Blaine will be in class this morning. But please be alert. We don't want any trouble, we just want to get Jenny's things and be on our way."

They all nodded, chewing their muffins, though Eddie and Brian gave each other a look, like they thought a little trouble would be cool. In short order they were fueled up and ready to go.

"Jenny, you and Noelle take the lead in her car, we'll follow in the truck," Kit said, and led the way out to the vehicles. Ten minutes later Noelle pulled up to the curb in front of a poor old Victorian painted lady. Her peeling paint matched the broken gingerbread trim and beach towel 'curtains'. A ratty lawn stretched from the sagging wraparound porch to the street.

Kit and the crew pulled in and climbed out of their rigs. Kit read grim determination in Jenny's set jaw. Everyone followed her as she stomped up the splintered front steps to the door. She stopped to pull out her keys, but Kit reached past her to try the knob and it turned. He motioned for them to wait, and stepped inside.

Kit's nostrils flared as a stale beer/locker room combo stench assaulted him. No one in the living room. A Schlitz sign buzzed and flickered in the front window. He checked the hall, turned to the dining room and kitchen on the right. No one.

"Jenny," he said out the door to where she waited on the porch. "Nobody's home, at least downstairs. Where's your room?"

She pointed down the hall. "First door on the left."

Kit nodded, grateful the narrow stairs to the second floor would not be involved in this project. "Okay, crew, here we go. Where's the hand truck?"

"I'll get it," Brian said, and did a 180 back to the truck.

"And the boxes," Kit hollered after him. "Lead on, Jenny."

She opened the door to her room and gasped. Kit stepped to her side and peered through the doorway.

Jenny's room was destroyed.

Wedding Day

The day dawned crisp and bright. A heavy, fragrant mist burned off as the sun rose, and nary a smudge of cloud marred the blue sky. The household staff, glad for the poor daughter to finally get a husband, festooned the gardens and banquet tables with bunting and ribbons. The cook produced a huge cake, rich with raisins and spices and layered with creamy filling.

Anisette and Bo worshiped together in the tiny chapel on the grounds. The guests gathered in the garden after attending their various churches in the morning, and as they arrived, added their contributions to a table set to one side. It was already laden with silver and carved wood, linens and tableware. Neighbors had got word of the upcoming nuptials and sent gifts. They weren't surprised not to be invited to the ceremony. Most were vaguely aware of some long-running tragic circumstance in the family, centering on Anisette. That she was marrying was an oblique indication the tragedy might be ending. They hoped so, and sent their good wishes in the form of crystal and fine fabrics.

At two of the clock, the hired musicians played a sacred march and Master Marlow escorted his lovely daughter to where the eager bridegroom waited. Pastor Wheaton read out the vows, the couple repeated them after him, and no one doubted they meant every word. The pastor blessed their marriage, bade them kneel, served them communion, and pronounced them man and wife. The band immediately struck a merry tune whereupon the ceremony became a celebration. The small company danced and feasted, happy for the young people and happy for an excuse to relax and indulge themselves. At some point during the festivities Bo and Anisette disappeared. Their absence was not marked for some time.

Bo handed Anisette down from the carriage hired to bring them to Bo's house by the river. No mead wagon for the new bride on her wedding day. He paid the driver and sent him off. Then he swept up his wife and carried her over the threshold of her new home.

"It is not as it shall be," he said as he set her gently down on her feet. "It is sore in need of your womanly touch. But it is clean." He lit a lamp, and then two more as the evening light faded. "Tonight, I shall show you every corner of the house proper, and on the morrow, we shall explore the grounds entire." Bo took Anisette's hand and led her through the rooms; great room, kitchen, store room, office and bedchambers. There were four bedchambers, for Bo had grown up in this house with his parents, a brother and two sisters, and their family retainer.

"Plenty of room for children," he said, looking into Anisette's eyes. She nodded, wide eyed but smiling all the same. "Tomorrow morning probably, Old Tom will arrive and commence banging about the kitchen. Don't be alarmed. He is my jack of all trades about the place. I inherited him from my parents and he does what he pleases, which is mostly to grumble and grouch and take care of me and the house."

"Why was he not at the wedding?"

"He's been away this month and more. His spinster sister passed on, and he were putting her estate in order. He'll not be pleased to find he's missed my wedding, but I would not put it off!"

Anisette smiled and blushed. "He will not mind a new mistress in the house?"

"Nay, fret you not. Tom has been nagging me for years to get a lady back in the house after my mother passed on. We will have a conference, the three of us, and divide the labor to everyone's satisfaction. You shall reign supreme in whatever realms you desire for your own." Bo caught both her hands in his. "Any further matters tonight, my lady? Or shall we to bed?"

Anisette blushed again and ducked her head. But then she raised her eyes to his, looked deep into them and said, "To bed if you please, my lord."

Blaine

"Don't touch anything," Kit said. "Jenny, I assume this isn't how you left it?"

"No, of course not!" she shot back. "Blaine—," she groaned and sank to her knees before her disemboweled dresser. Glitter and curved shards of glass sparkled across a heap of her clothing. Jenny picked up a miniature Eiffel Tower and choked back a sob.

"Lay it back down for a minute, Jenny," Kit said gently. "Noelle, got your phone?"

"Sure, Grandpa, want pics?"

He felt a swell of pride. Sharp girl. "Yep. Just the general idea. The police will take their own. Got enough light?"

Noelle adjusted the settings on her phone's camera. Then she stepped gingerly around the heaps of clothes and books into the center of the room, her phone flashing light and making that peculiarly satisfying fake shutter noise as she documented the wreckage of Jenny's small world. "What is that smell?" she asked, wrinkling her nose.

Kit sniffed. He knew that smell, and he figured they'd find wet spots shortly.

Eddie, arms laden with boxes, peered through the open door. "Criminy Pete!" he said, ogling the disaster. Blaine—or whoever—had been disturbingly thorough. The twin bed, desk, dresser and papasan chair would have crowded the room when in their proper configuration, but every drawer had been pulled, emptied and flung. The papasan chair was smashed apart, the cushion shredded. A dozen pencils stood, startled, where they'd been stabbed into the bed pillows. Jenny's cosmetics had been dumped, crushed, and smeared over the dresser top. Glitter winked from the mattress, and a B-52's tune started banging in Kit's head.

Empty hangers hung askew in the closet, every item of clothing having been ripped down and slung into the room. A tennis shoe was crammed into the glass dish of the light fixture, neon pink laces dangling, one long end tied tight around the neck of a tiny teddy bear. He touched Noelle's shoulder and pointed. She looked up, grimaced and snapped a photo.

Jenny burst into tears and they turned to her. She held a delicate figurine of two stylized girls embracing. The destroyer had knocked their heads off with dreadful precision. Noelle knelt beside her friend and put an arm around her.

"My sis gave me this for my birthday. She doesn't have extra for fancy presents and she must have saved for this..." Jenny gave in and bawled, clutching Noelle's sleeve.

A vein pulsed in Kit's temple as his hands curled into fists. Time to get these girls out of here. He stepped past Eddie into the hallway and barely avoided colliding with Brian pushing the hand cart.

"Sorry," Brian said, stopping short. "What?" he added, noticing the look on Kit's face.

Kit motioned for Brian to turn around and detour into the living room. He pulled out his phone and called Detective Price.

"CJ? Kit Rising here. Are you anywhere near the college?" He waited. "112 Elm. We have a situation I think you need to see. Okay. We'll be here." He put away his phone and stepped back into the bedroom.

"Girls? How about you go wait outside." He ushered them to the porch, where Noelle pulled Jenny down into the rickety swing.

He returned to the house. Brian had stepped into Jenny's room, where Eddie was pointing out the highlights. Brian gaped.

"Okay, gentlemen," Kit said. "We can't pack up anything, assuming there's anything left worth packing, until the police have had their look. Let's just relax until they get here." He ran a hand through his hair, wishing he was done with this. No reason he couldn't sit down for a few minutes, anyway, if he could find a spot.

"Is Jenny okay?" Brian asked, blushing a deep hot pink on each cheek.

Kit gave him a gentle smile. "She'll be okay. She's shocked of course. It's a damn shame what that boy did, but we'll take care of her." He examined the living room for seating possibilities and decided against both the inflated pool lounge and the bean bag chair. The sofa was so low he knew he'd never get out of it. He returned to the porch and lowered himself carefully onto the top step. Brian and Eddie followed and perched gingerly on the wobbly railing.

They sat silently in the cold November sunshine listening to the porch swing creak, until Detective Price and his officer arrived. Kit pulled himself up off the step with Eddie providing leverage and balance, and went to meet them.

"CJ, thanks for coming," he said, shaking the burly young man's freckled hand. He nodded to the other officer, a petite woman in her thirties. "Ma'am."

"You bet, Mr. Rising. This is Detective Ortiz. What's up?"

Kit motioned them into the house and led the way to Jenny's room, Brian on their heels.

"Well, sugar honey ice tea," Detective Price said when he saw the state of the room. "Anyone hurt?"

"No, it was like this when we got here, about twenty minutes ago." Kit rubbed his hands over his eyes. "We came to pack up and move the young lady's belongings. She and a boy who lives here had...a disagreement." He thought better of that. "Actually, he threatened her." Kit paused. "She's pregnant," he added in a lower voice.

CJ nodded, the simple motion heavy with world-weariness. "What's the boy's name?" Kit sent Brian to fetch Jenny, who supplied all the details the officer wanted about Blaine and the other occupants of the house. Sergeant Ortiz documented the destruction with her camera while they talked.

"Okay," CJ said, clicking his pen several times and consulting his notepad. "Miss Conklin, what would you estimate the worth of your belongings here?"

Jenny scoffed. "About 25 cents, I'd say." She caught the officer's frown and added, "Sorry. Let me think." She studied the room for a minute and said, "A couple hundred bucks?"

"More than that, Jenny!" Noelle said. She and Jenny tallied up this and that, and finally agreed $1000 was more like it.

Price jotted that down, clicked his pen off and slipped his notepad into a pocket. "I think that's everything," he said. He handed a card to Jenny. "If you think of anything else I should know, or if the young man harasses you or contacts you in any way, please call me right away."

"Thanks. I will." Jenny took the card and smiled a watery smile at him.

The officers took their leave and the crew got to work. Noelle found some black trash bags under the kitchen sink and they set about sorting the destroyed from the damaged-but-usable. Occasionally someone held up a completely unbroken object and everyone cheered.

When they were done, three bulging trash bags sat in the living room next to a pitifully small stack of boxes. The papasan chair was a total loss, but they loaded the desk, dresser and the bed into Eddie's pickup and piled the boxes and bags around them. They took one last look around and declared themselves finished.

Noelle opened the door of her car and leaned on the frame, her forehead furrowed with worry for her friend as she stared back at the house.

Kit didn't like to see Noelle worried. It made his gut wrench. "All set?" he asked Jenny.

"I guess," she said. She checked her watch. "I've got to hurry and get to the cafeteria for my lunch shift."

"Don't worry, you're seconds away," Kit said. As he opened the Geo passenger door for her, a bright orange GTO roared around the corner and slammed on its brakes upon finding the driveway occupied.

The driver rolled the window down and gestured at Kit. "Hey man. You looking for somebody?"

"No," Kit said. "Are we in your way? We're just leaving."

"Oh hey, Jenny!" the boy said. "You must be moving out, huh? Prolly a good idea. Blaine is like, really pissed."

"Yeah, Billy, we figured that out when we saw my room," she said.

"Yeeeah..." he said. "That was fucked up, man."

"You knew he did that?"

Billy snorted. "Kinda hard not to. They were bangin' and screamin' and knockin' shit around."

"And you just let him destroy everything I own?" Jenny said, her voice strained, her hands balled into fists on her hips.

"Hey man, I didn't wanna get involved, you know?"

"Yeah, thanks for nothing, Billy, you a-" she shot a glance at Kit. "You big coward."

Billy had the grace to redden but said nothing. Kit motioned for Jenny to get in the car. He leaned down and said, "When we get home, call Detective Price and tell him Billy witnessed this. He'll probably want him to make a statement." Jenny nodded and clicked her seatbelt.

Kit turned to Billy. "Do you know where Blaine is now?"

Billy shook his head. "I ain't seen him for a couple days."

"Is that unusual?" Kit asked.

"Not really."

"You said 'they'," Kit said. "Someone was in Jenny's room with Blaine?"

"Are you a cop?" Billy said, squinting up at Kit.

"What difference does that make?" he said. "Would you have different answers if I was or wasn't?"

"Hey man," Billy said, raising both hands, "like I said, I don't want to get involved, that's all."

"I hope that philosophy serves you well in your adult life, Billy. If you ever have one." Kit thought he'd better put a cork in it. He climbed carefully into the back seat of the crew cab and met Eddie's eyes in the rear-view mirror. "I think we're done here."

The Honey Meadow

B o dreamed of nightingales singing, flitting about his room and lighting on the windowsill. He opened his eyes reluctantly and the music continued.

She was singing.

He smiled, closed his eyes again and listened. She must be in the kitchen. Yes, there were dishes clattering, and water splashing. She had fetched water? Bo opened his eyes and sat up. He hurried into his clothes, smoothed down his hair and went to find his new wife.

He stopped at the kitchen doorway and watched as Old Tom stoked the fire. He must have fetched the water. Anisette stood at the table in an embroidered frock, a snowy apron about her waist, slicing bread. Tom filled the kettle, Anisette opened the larder to find...butter. The two moved around each other in an elaborate dance, as if they'd been working together for years. And to Bo's amazement, Tom was grinning.

Anisette caught sight of him and stopped her singing and her work. She smiled at him like a summer day.

"My lord," she said, and gave him a dainty curtsy. "Your breakfast will be ready anon." She set the crockery dish of butter on the table and came to him. "How is it with you this morning?"

He encircled her with his arms and said, "Well, and most excellent well. And with you, my lady?"

"Very well indeed. I have met old Tom, you see. He was already here when I wandered into the kitchen and he gave me a most gracious welcome. I thought you said he was grouchy."

Bo laughed. "He always has been until today. Perhaps you have inadvertently enchanted him?"

"No," she smiled, then grew serious. "But, if you would, do not make light of enchantments, Bo."

"I never shall again. Forgive me." He drew her closer. "I would not hurt you for anything under heaven." She lifted her face to him and he kissed her. Then his stomach growled. Anisette let out a peal of silvery laughter and pulled away from him.

"Sit here, husband, and we shall feed your stomach."

The three of them sat down to a breakfast of bread and butter, berries in cream, eggs and bacon and coffee. Anisette tried to rise to fetch the coffee pot once or twice, but Tom would not allow it, so she relaxed and let the man serve them as he wished.

"A fine breaking of the fast indeed," said Bo. "And now to the work of the day. Tom, you must give your new mistress free reign to determine what she will do, and what you may keep as your own work."

"Aye, sir. The mistress may have what she likes, only I do not like to see such a delicate creature doing any heavy work at all. If you please, mistress, take only what tickles your fancy, and let me be of use to you while still I'm able." The grizzled old man, who had got out his cob pipe and tobacco pouch in anticipation of a smoke while he did his outdoor chores, twisted the pipe in his hands, awaiting her answer.

Anisette placed her small hand on his to still the fretting, which made him jump. "Tom, I will need all the help you can provide. I know little of housekeeping. I can cook some few trifling dishes as our cook taught me when she had a mind to. I can mend, and do fine stitchery. But other than that, I am fit for nothing but the garden."

"But you will let Tom lift and spade for you, will you not?" Bo said.

"Yes, indeed. At my father's house the men helped with the heavy work, and I was grateful. Tom, you will not mind me tending the garden?" She smiled at him and Tom, flustered, pulled his pipe to pieces. Bo believed the old man would not have minded had she requested to pull his teeth one by one, and use them for gravel on the garden paths. Not that he had many teeth left.

"Nay, mistress. You shall direct me however you wish. I'll show you how things be now and you shall have charge over how it goes from here."

"Grand," Bo said. "If you work together in the garden as you did in the kitchen, all shall flourish. That takes care of that, it seems to me." He pushed away from the table and held a hand to his bride. "Lady Anisette, shall I show you the length and breadth of your new kingdom?"

Anisette stood and clasped his hand in both hers. "Yes, please. And may we take your punt onto the river?"

"Assuredly. We can pole out through the quag and introduce you to the bees. What about a packet of lunch, Tom, and I shall take my lady for a picnic in the honey meadow." Tom grinned and nodded and set to the task right away, setting aside his disintegrated pipe in his enthusiasm for the project. Bo gaped at him. Was this the same curmudgeon with whom he had lived from earliest childhood? Where had these grins and niceties been all those years?

He wondered if he had a silly grin on his own face. Anisette's presence had him a little off-balance, that was certain. Joy flooded through him in waves, making him press a steadying hand to a wall now and then.

He led her out the kitchen door and gave her the grand tour. They strolled through the garden, nothing so grand as her father's but bearing a bounty of fruits and vegetables, and mounds of flowers for the bees.

"I'm thinking of a walled refuge for you in the garden," Bo said. "Close to the house. Perhaps not a solid rock wall, but one with open arches all around. My love, how aware are you of your surroundings when the enchantment lies upon you?"

Anisette looked at him in astonishment. "No one ever thought to ask me that before—" she broke off, needing to swallow a lump in her throat. "How shall I ever love you enough?" She put both hands on his broad chest and gazed into his eyes.

He kissed her on the nose and wiped a tear away with his great thumb. "We will make it a game. I will try to love you more, and you try to love me more. We will play until we die, and see who wins."

She laughed at this. "We shall both win if we play the game well. It sounds a fine plan for a happy marriage." She sobered then, and said, "About the enchantment. I can sense the weather, and light and dark." She thought a moment. "I do not suffer from cold or heat. I sense if someone is near me, but I can't see them, of course."

"Are you afraid? When you can't see or move?"

"Curiously, I am not. I have often pondered that. When I describe it to you it sounds frightening, even to me. But I feel only peace, and a deep sadness, if you allow the two might exist together."

He nodded. They walked on in silence a bit. "So, a wall around your own bower, would it be well?"

She nodded slowly. "Do build it, Bo. It will be your way of protecting me when you can do naught else. And place within it a bench, will you not? Then if you will come and sit near me as my branches are drying, you will be the first thing I see when I am restored." She smiled up at him. "Could you ever conceive of a more bizarre conversation?"

He chuckled and shook his head. "No indeed. But Anisette, I intend to seek a remedy for you. I've not forgotten that promise. I have spoken already to Pastor Wheaton, and he is praying on it and consulting with trusted colleagues, true men of God. He will guide my search."

"It is well, my love. Thank you for that. I will leave it in your hands, and God's."

Content with the state of that problem for now, they walked on together. He showed her the neat row of big sheds set along the path, where he kept the mead making equipment and supplies; honey jars and vats with paddles, barrels of ingredients and flavorings, and a bottle washing contraption he had invented himself.

"Where are the bottles of mead?" she wondered, none being in evidence in the great sheds.

"In the cellar," he said, "under the kitchen. I'll show you anon. And here is my little punt." They walked down the gravel path and onto the dock and gazed down at the slender little boat. She bobbed in the water, spotless and in excellent repair. "The honey meadow is yonder," he said, pointing down river a ways and out across the **quags**. "It takes but a few minutes to float down the stream to the entrance of the swamp, and then an hour to pole through it to the higher ground of the meadow. None go there but me that I know of, as the way is circuitous and there be no reason to find it out but to tend the bees."

"That seems reason enough to me," Anisette said. "Everyone loves honey. Why do they not go and take it there?"

"Beehives abound. No need to wind through a swamp and risk losing your way, when in your own orchard or field you may keep a skep, or buy honey from your neighbor."

"Then why do you go to such trouble?"

"Ah. For mead, one wants only the best honey. My meadow grows thick with wildflowers and clover, and has even few fruit trees. I think it must have been an orchard many a long age ago, though I've never found remnant of a house or barn. The honey in my hives is transparent gold, like the streets of Heaven. I'm certain you will agree it is the finest honey ever to touch your tongue."

Crunching slowly down the gravel walk came Old Tom, his stiff frame leaning right, then left, over each bowlegged step like a ship and sailor combined. He gripped the handles of a covered basket with both hands and had a brown wool blanket folded across one arm. A grimace of concentrated effort made him look more like the familiar grouch of old to Bo. But when Anisette stepped lightly to him, the wide grin of this morning's vintage reasserted itself.

"Here be your luncheon, my lady. And a blanket for the grass, so you don't muss your fine gown." Bo gaped, nonplussed. Many a lump of cheese and a hard loaf knotted in a cloth had Tom sent with Bo to sustain him while working in the honey meadow. Judging by the effort Tom exerted to carry his basket, he must have loaded half the larder into it. Bo shook his head but admitted to himself he liked this new Tom. He was entertaining, if inexplicable. And it looked like the food would be better.

"Why thank you, Tom. Bo, perhaps you'd better put this in the boat? It seems to be quite heavy," Anisette said.

Bo jumped to take the basket from Tom and found himself grinning as widely as his old friend. A soft clink of glass against crockery meant wine and conserves. Fancy.

"A fine lunch indeed, it must be, or a basket full of rocks, to weigh so much. Perhaps you and your extended family are accompanying us to the meadow?"

"What extended family? I'm looking at my extended family right here. But the lady is so little...she needs feeding up some, I reckon." He gave Bo the old scowl for a moment. "Take care with her in the punt, now. Don't be tipping her into the quag." Bo favored him with an elaborate bow of acquiescence.

"'Twill be as you command, Tom. Thank you for the basket, and we shall be home before sunset. You'll manage..."

"Aye, aye with my eyes shut. Off with you." He shooed them into the boat and watched with a squinted eye as Bo pushed it away from the dock and let it float downstream, guiding it with the pole. At length the old man creaked back up the path to mind his master's business.

Bo steered the punt to the opening into the quag and followed the familiar route to the honey meadow. Anisette admired the bright blooms dotting the mounds of vegetation, while crinkling her nose at the tang of rot in the humid air. They spied a fallow deer and her fawn gazing at them while they chewed, unafraid. Anisette hummed, then sang softly, a hymn of praise for the beauty of the earth. Bo imagined she'd already seen more of it today than the last score of years. An impish breeze sprang up to disorder her honey-colored hair and she laughed, trying to smooth it. He could not imagine a more perfect day.

Like Crazy

M onti unlocked her classroom and set her things down. She'd had a good meeting with Alicia and next semester was all planned. Now to today's challenges. Her Reading and Writing Basic Skills students would arrive momentarily. Astonishing numbers of high school graduates arrived at the school without a mastery of the most basic skills needed to succeed at college. Her job was to help them fill the gaps in their education, in preparation for the more rigorous course work they'd face here.

Aside from Basic Skills three times a week, Monti spent two hours teaching Study Skills and two more on a College Transition course. She loved and hated these classes. It was satisfying whenever a student woke from his or her high school stupor and dug in. After a little while in her classroom, most realized what was at stake and what they needed to do to make up for lost time.

At the same time, it broke her heart to continually hear of parents' divorces, chaotic homes and violent relationships, and the rampant use of drugs and alcohol they all seemed to take for granted as a normal part of teenage life. The poor girls appeared world weary at eighteen. The boys often dragged about in a fog, whether drug induced or from too much time in front of the Nintendo, she didn't know. She took it one day at a time and offered each student as much love and wisdom as possible during their few weeks together.

After such a bad night, she would need to take today one *hour* at a time. Get from nine to ten, then from ten to eleven, and she might be able to snatch some rest before her one o'clock. Monti looked over her notes and caught up on some record keeping until a tap at the door made her look up at the spiky haired, liberally pierced face smiling in at her. She smiled back and got up, so tired already, to let Cody in.

"Hi, Mrs. Rising," the boy said. He thunked his back pack down on a front row desk. "I finished that story I said I couldn't write. You wanna read it?"

"Course I do," she said. This was another love/hate part of the job. She never knew what would turn up in their writing. Sometimes a childlike wonder emerged from under the Goth and the pseudo-sophistication and they wrote lucid, powerful stories that took her breath away, even as she struggled to decipher the badly spelled sentence fragments. But just as often a dark and angry bitterness flew off the pages at her, as the kids poured out their pain.

That Cody had written anything at all she considered a minor victory. That he seemed excited about it was truly encouraging. She took the slightly crumpled pages from him and dug in her pocket for her glasses.

"Not now, though. Later, when I'm not standing here, 'kay?" Cody's eyes pleaded with her to spare him that torture.

"Sure, Cody. I'll read it tonight," she said, and tucked it into her tote. "I'm glad you decided to do it after all. What made you change your mind?"

"Negative reinforcement, or I don't know if that's what you call it. I was b...complaining at home about having to write this stupid story, and my mom's boyfriend, a real loser, said to f...I mean, to just not even try it. He said I was probably too stupid to write my own name, let alone a complete sentence. So that p...ticked me off, and I sat down and wrote the whole thing." He grinned. "It wasn't that hard."

Monti winced inwardly. She did not look forward to reading the results of that source of inspiration. "Great," she said. "I'll read it with that in mind."

Her other students filed in, dragging or bouncing, silent or gabbing on cell phones. At nine she stood up. They knew her class rules by now. These were her fifty minutes to help them and they must put away the phones, sit down and pay attention.

When class was over Monti called Kit.

"Hey lover," he said.

"Hey yourself. You okay?"

"Sure," Kit assured her. "We're all done. The girls are headed to class and work, and we're loading up to head home."

"Good, I'm glad." She was relieved was more like it. Hopefully he would take some time to rest his back, but confidence was not high. Although, yesterday's pain episode was by far the worst yet. Maybe he would start to take it more seriously. "Was Blaine there?" she said.

"No. But uh, he definitely had been. I'll tell you about it when you get home, Monti."

"What? No way! Tell me now. What do you mean he definitely had been?" Monti said, sitting up straighter.

Kit hesitated, then exhaled. "He tore up Jenny's room and destroyed most of her things." Kit paused. "It was pretty bad. She's a bit shaken up."

"Oh no, the poor girl." Monti's jaw tightened. "That no-good...what did he have to do that for?"

"Yeah. Let's talk it over at home, okay? I called Detective Price. He came and documented everything, and they're on the lookout for Blaine now with a 'domestic violence' tag next to his name."

"Great." She took a deep breath and let it out. "What's next for you?"

"I'm on my way home, where I'm going sit in my wonderful chair and practice being an internet entrepreneur. But thanks for checking on me. I know you were worried."

"How do you know I wasn't just calling to complain about my lousy day and ask you to fix dinner?" she said.

He laughed. "It's Tuesday, and I always fix dinner on Tuesday. And you never complain about your lousy day. You just rant about how our culture is deteriorating and the education system is failing our kids."

"Oh. Right. Well, what's for dinner then? But really, you will rest?"

"Yes, Monti. I'll sit and write this newsletter I'm thinking up for my fish fans. By the time you get home I will have figured out how to send it to my whole list or given up trying."

"Wow. I can't see you doing the giving-up thing so you'll have to show me how it works tonight. Alicia wants me to teach Internet Skills, too, but I feel like I should take the class instead."

"We'll see how it goes and then you can pick my brain, even if all that's in it is six ways not to do it. You put your feet up for a bit, Monti, and have a rest before your next class."

"I'm thinking about going out to the car. I parked in the sunshine, and I might try for a wee nap. You probably need one too, after last night and all that non-lugging."

"I might. I want to do this project first. Okay, we're here. We have to get what's left of Jenny's belongings stashed in the garage. You have a good afternoon, love," he said, and hung up.

She did love that man like crazy. She wanted to get in her car and go home and pamper him to pieces. He'd hate that, though. Maybe she'd better try for that wee nap instead.

Tree

The punt bumped softly against the rising ground at the edge of the honey meadow. Anisette turned round to look. Bo stowed the pole, jumped out and pulled the boat up the slope a little. He tied it off to a sturdy stake he had dug in years ago.

"Stand carefully, Anisette, and take my hand." Anisette stood up, mindful to maintain her balance, and grasped Bo's hand. She stepped onto the till and leaped nimbly to the turf. Bo caught her about the waist and pulled her into an embrace.

"Welcome to my honey meadow, my lady," he said. He turned her around and let her take it in. A breeze pushed onto the island from behind them, billowing Anisette's skirts out before her and rippling the tall grasses into waves of gold and green. Domed bee skeps peeked from the grass here and there. A sweet scent of wildflowers teased her nose, stronger now, then dissipating, making her inhale deeply to catch more of the perfume. Bo noticed.

"You smell the nectar of the flowers. And so do the bees..." he crouched slightly and swept his arm across at the height of the grass. "See?" Anisette crouched also and followed his motion. Bees buzzed just above the flowers and grass, glowing in the golden sun, soaring and diving, landing and taking off again. The meadow hummed.

"They will not sting us?" she asked.

"Not likely," he said. They are about their business and we will not disturb them. 'Tis possible to frighten them and earn a sting. I carry always a salve of aloes in case that happens, but I rarely need use it." He leaned into the punt and lifted out the basket. He heaved it onto one shoulder and took Anisette's hand. "See the apple tree yonder? Let's spread Old Tom's feast there." They strolled hand in hand. A breeze whirled across the meadow, tossing the flower heads in a wild dance.

"*May I pick some?*" *she said, as a mischievous gust wrapped her skirts about her legs. She untangled herself with a laugh.*

"*Of course, my lady. God is extravagant with His blessings. If you picked armfuls every day the bees would not want for blossoms.*" *Anisette plucked a stem of velvety purple blooms. Fragrant white umbels caught her eye next, then bright yellow petals. She began to sing, a lively tune to match the bobbing flowers. Bo grinned and lowered the heavy basket to the ground under the apple tree.*

As he straightened again he heard a distant boom, which sent a faint thrill of alarm through him, though he knew not why. A second boom echoed across the sky. He stiffened and spun around. The sky above Westhaven had grown dense with dirty grey clouds racing toward the still-sunny meadow. Anisette stood stock still, the pink drained from her cheeks, her eyes wide. She looked at him, panic-stricken.

"*Bo!*" *she called to him. She dropped her bouquet and ran to him, into his strong arms.* "*It will rain!*" *she cried.*

"*It will! Forgive me, my love, for not thinking of it, for not watching the sky. We cannot get home in time.*"

"*I will be trapped here, alone!*"

"*No! Never alone again, little one. I will stay with you, no matter if it rains forty days and forty nights! I will not leave you.*"

The clouds burst and fat drops of rain splashed into the quag, knocked down stalks of flowers, splattered onto the leaves over their heads and soaked their hair. Anisette stiffened, trembled. A cry of anguish burst from her and she sank to the ground. She tore at her dainty shoes and her silk stockings until her feet were bare. She cast her gaze about frantically, desperate to find a patch of loose soil.

Bo realized what she was about. The grass grew sparsely near the apple tree. He took up a downed tree branch and roughened the ground between tree and meadow. He gouged at it, flinging clods until the stick broke. "*Will this do, Anisette?*" *he shouted. Thunder cracked nearby.*

Anisette jumped and stared at him, appearing not to understand what he said. He pointed to the loosened earth. She followed his gesture and her eyes lit up. She stepped into the soil and wriggled her feet into it, staring at him wild-eyed. It was nothing like the flower beds she was used to, but she was making do, the poor creature.

Anisette gasped. She threw her arms out and her head back and then...blurred. Bo blinked his eyes twice or thrice to clear his vision, and when he looked again she'd gone. He stood before a small tree, with delicate limbs and clusters of almonds on every leafy branch. He staggered back a step in the pouring rain. He tried to force his brain to believe what his eyes told him. Somehow, talking about this transformation with Anisette had not prepared him for the reality.

His wife was an almond tree.

Black and White

Ding. Monti startled awake, then rubbed her eyes. There was a small miracle. She'd fallen right to sleep, even while imagining Blaine destroying Jenny's room.

Monti put the little windup timer back in the glove-box and stretched as luxuriously as the front seat of the car would allow. Time to get back to work. She climbed out of her little Subaru, grabbed her purse and keys and walked to the building, trying to feel alert.

Monti's noon class was her favorite. This semester she had eight students in Study Skills. She was supposed to teach them how to manage their time and prepare for tests. She did that, but there were usually lots of other things going on in their lives interfering with their ability to do well in their courses. Sometimes helping a girl figure out how to shed an unfortunate boyfriend did wonders for her grade point average.

Today she would teach them some note-taking techniques. Then she'd go over their schedules with them individually, helping them plan the hours they needed to get papers written by their due dates, and learn to block out sufficient time to study for upcoming tests.

Seven out of eight showed up and everyone participated, another small miracle as far as Monti was concerned. As the class period wound down, she plugged in the coffee pot and pulled out a bag of corn chips and a tin of ranch dip. This was her last class of the day and a few students usually stayed after to chat for a while. Then she got to listen to their dreams and complaints, questions and troubles. She learned more after class than they learned during class, she was sure.

"Anybody know where Austin is? He wasn't in class Thursday, either." she said.

"Yeah, Mrs. Rising. I heard he's serving his time."

"He's what?" she asked, her shoulders slumping.

"Serving his 30 days. He got picked up for intent to sell a couple months ago and he finally got sentenced. Now he's got to do his time at the jail. That's f—, uh, I mean that's too bad, 'cuz I know he wants to be in school."

Monti appreciated it when her students chose alternatives to the colorful one syllable words that normally sprinkled their casual conversation. Of course, the fine jar might influence their word choice some but whatever motivated them, be it the honest desire to speak in a refined manner or the honest desire not to contribute to the next class snack, she was happy. She wasn't so happy to learn one of her pupils had been convicted on a drug charge. But she wasn't surprised.

"So, the county jail," she said. "I guess that puts a kink in his semester, all right. Tanya, how'd you do on your Algebra test?"

"86 percent," she said, smiling. "Thanks, Mrs. Rising. I never got that factoring stuff before. Hey, Marcie told me Jenny's living at your house now. Is that true?"

"Yes, she's staying with us for a while," Monti said.

"I heard she's pregnant," Bobby added. "Blaine was pissed off about that..."

"Quarter, quarter," several voices said in chorus.

"What! It's after class," he protested.

"Doesn't matter, you're still in the classroom," Monti said, and held out to him the jar with the slotted lid, shaking it to make the coins rattle.

"Yeah, yeah," Bobby said. He dug in his jeans pocket and found a quarter. "P...that word's not really a cuss word, you know." He dropped the quarter into the jar.

"Yeah, yeah," Monti said. "It's on the rude list and you know it. You have to learn to self-edit if you don't want to humiliate yourself in a critical situation. Like a job interview."

"But anyway, is she?" Kelsey wanted to know.

"That, my friends, is known as gossip. If you're concerned for Miss Conklin's health, you can ask her about it yourself. I'm sure she'd be pleased by your solicitous inquiry."

"Huh?" Bobby said.

"S-O-L-I-C-I-T-O-U-S," Monti said. "Look it up and bring me the definition, and you can have your quarter back." She put the empty dip container in the empty chip sack and stuffed them in the trash can. "I have to get going, kids. My hubby is home alone and liable to start raking the leaves if I leave him unsupervised for too long."

"He's not allowed to do yard work? My mom's always nagging at my old man to rake the leaves."

"Normally, yes, he may of course do as he pleases. But just now he's supposed to be resting and not exerting himself."

"Bad heart?" Bobby said.

"No. Old injury plus approaching old age...it's a scary combination at times."

"Bummer. Tell him to take it easy." The students collected their gear and she ushered them out the door. Lights off, door locked, and she was ready to go straight home to Kit. But she had to stop at the gas station, the bank, and the grocery store before she was allowed to shut the world out and concentrate solely on her husband's wellbeing.

An hour later she had conquered her 'have-to's' and she headed home. Traffic was light and lingering sunbeams slanted sideways through the cemetery across the street when she turned onto Engle Avenue. But the pleasure of this late autumn beauty evaporated when she caught sight of the black and white patrol car parked in their driveway.

Rain

B o walked slowly around Anisette. He wanted to put his arms around her and comfort her, but how did one embrace a tree? The rain poured down now, pelting her long narrow leaves and fuzzy drupes and soaking him to the skin.

She couldn't see him, but she knew he was near her. That's what she had said. The chill rain set him shivering, but she didn't suffer the cold, she'd said. He was glad to know it. Oh, why had he brought her here so far away from the garden, without consulting the almanac or even looking once at the sky to gage the weather? Fool! He must in future take more care to protect his vulnerable wife.

He peered up into the clouds. She would remain transformed until the rain ceased and she was completely dry. Those clouds were heavy yet with rain. It would be overnight, at least. What should he do? He would never leave her, no matter what.

Bo's stomach growled. He was suddenly grateful for Tom's infatuation with his master's new bride. The faithful old man had packed enough food to keep Bo for two or three days. He ducked over to the hamper and confirmed this with a peek under the lid. And here under the huge old apple tree the rain hardly penetrated. He had even a heavy wool blanket. God, knowing Bo's foolishness, had yet provided for his needs.

A fire would increase his comfort immensely, especially as it grew dark. He chewed a few bites of cheese and bread from the basket, and wondered where to build a fire. Under a tree was never the best idea, but in the rain would not work.

A fire wouldn't frighten Anisette, would it? He would keep it small and well away from her, and lie down between it and her. But would she sense it and be afraid?

No. He would do without a fire.

Thunder cracked again and the rain increased. He had better turn the punt over. "Anisette," he said, shouting over the rain. Could she hear him? He did not

75

remember what she'd said about that. "I go to turn the punt over. I shall be gone only a moment, never fear." He looked at her closely. Her branches trembled under the heavy rain. What on earth did he expect to see by way of a response? "I shall return!".

His shout was lost in a clap of thunder. He turned and ran through the meadow as a flash of lightning lit the way. Lightning must be terrifying to a tree! He turned to look back at her, his heart clenched with fear. Was she terrified? He quailed at the thought. He should have asked her all these things and been prepared.

Bo turned back to the boat. He pulled out the large piece of heavy oilcloth he usually set honeycombs on, a coil of rope, and the pole. Already a lake of water flooded the bottom of the boat. He heaved it over and pulled it a little further onto the grass. Then he hefted his supplies and ran back through the downpour to Anisette.

"I'm here, my love," he said, breathing hard. "I will not leave you again for a single moment." Bo set to work on rigging a shelter, experimenting with pole, rope and oilcloth until he had devised a meager refuge from the rain that didn't collapse when he touched it. He sat down under it. Surely Anisette could sense his presence here...only ten feet away. He shivered. Even a summer rain chilled you once you were soaked through.

He took off his wet clothes and hung them under the oilcloth where they might dry a little, and wrapped the dry blanket around him. Nothing remained for him to do except wait. How many hours until dark? How many hours of night? How long until the rain stopped? What a horrifying way to begin a marriage. He had had no idea what the reality of Anisette's enchantment, her curse, would be like. Had he made a terrible mistake? How were they to live like this?

Thunder rumbled across the whole of the grey heavens and a gust of wind slung a spray of icy water into Bo's face. He dropped his head onto his arms and wept. "God, help me. Help my beloved Anisette. I don't know what to do. I am so afraid."

Bo dreamed of woodsmen chopping down trees, their axes cracking loud as thunder with each swack into the wood. The trees writhed in agony, weeping and begging for mercy. Their tears wet his face. A final hacking blow of an axe started a towering tree creaking and slowly falling, right toward him. He woke howling and struggling to get away.

He stopped howling—stopped struggling with the blanket. Anisette! He leaped to his feet. It was still dark, but for the faintest yellow gleam on the eastern horizon. He turned to his little almond tree...there she stood, unharmed. He climbed into his damp trousers with a shiver and hurried to her, walking around her with his arms spread, aching to embrace her and keep her safe. He trailed his fingertips through her wet leaves.

"Good morning, my love. We have come safely through the night together." It was no longer raining. The rising sun had a fresh-washed sky in which to spread its golden light. "The rain has stopped, Anisette," he murmured. "Today, God willing, you will be restored to me and I will take you home.".

He dropped to his knees under the tree and wept again, remembering the terror of his dreams and thinking of the bewildering future of his marriage. He circled his arms about the trunk and rested his weary cheek on the smooth bark. "What shall we do, my lady?"

When Bo woke again, the air was pink and a dry breeze ruffled his hair, bringing to his nose the scent of myriads of wildflowers and a hint of almond, and to his ears the buzz of bees recommencing their labors. He smiled and closed his eyes again. It seemed only a moment later that the tree trunk about which he was wound began to wriggle to be free.

Bo came fully awake. When he realized his cheek pressed against creased muslin and that soft hands rested on his head, he sprang to his feet. Anisette was restored to him! They clasped each other tightly until they both believed everything was as it should be. Bo pulled back and looked down at his wife.

"Are you well, my lady?"

"Aye, my husband, I am well." She gave him a small curtsy and shivered. He let go of her long enough to fetch the wool blanket and wrap it about her.

"Please forgive me," he said. "I will take more care in future. I will not allow us to be caught away from home like this again."

"It is well, Bo," she said. "Do not fret. I can never blame you for any consequence of this hex. 'Tis none of your doing." She touched his cheek and kissed him.

"Home?" he said.

She nodded. She wiggled her toes. They were muddy. "Where might my shoes and stockings be?" she asked.

Bo had no idea. He searched the ground nearby and at length spotted them. He picked up the sodden mess of leather and silk. "I fear they are ruined, love," he said.

She giggled. "No matter. I will dip my feet into the river to wash them, and be a barefoot country girl this morning."

Truly, she looked none the worse for wear; not tired, nor frightened. She took the wet footwear from him and inspected the soggy pieces.

"Your transformation seems not to have done you any harm," he said.

"No. As I told you, I feel only peace when I am changed, and sadness. But, Bo," she said, looking up at him, "I was hardly sad at all during the night, as I knew you were with me, and even knew when you embraced me!" Her smile radiated happiness at him.

"But what of the thunder and the lightning? Did these not frighten you?"

She shook her head. "No. I knew you were here." She placed her hand on his chest. "And Bo, I trust Jesu to care for me, even while under the sway of this enchantment. He will protect me, or let me be killed and take me to His bosom. I am at peace with it."

"I pray He will choose to protect you yet many long years," Bo said, cupping her face with his hand. "And for my part, I will search to find what remedy may avail to release you from this curse." Bo froze as Old Tom popped into his head. "Anisette! Old Tom will be frantic with worry. We must pack these things and hasten to ease his fears."

"What can I do?" she said, looking around.

Bo realized he must disassemble the shelter he had rigged before they could go.

"Carry this oilcloth. I'll have it down in a trice. The basket is too heavy for you. Are you hungry?"

"Yes, indeed! But we may break our fast in the punt, may we not? We do not want Tom fretting over us any longer than we can help."

Bo agreed, handed her the folded bit of oilcloth and untied the rope from the tree. Anisette tucked her shoes and tattered stockings into her skirt pocket and took the coil of rope, too. Bo hefted the basket onto his shoulder, took up the pole, and they set off through the fragrant meadow grass, the sun warming their backs.

When they reached the water's edge Bo flipped the punt upright. He stowed all their gear and waited a moment while Anisette dipped one foot and then the other into the water to rinse away the clods of mud clinging between her toes. Then he helped his wife to her seat, stepped in after her and pushed off toward home.

Klutz

Monti's heart pounded in her ears as she tried to remember how to shift gears and where the brake pedal was. She pulled along the curb in front of the house and skinned her knuckles fumbling with her seat belt.

Groceries later.

She hurried up the driveway, tripped up the kitchen steps, banged her knee on the concrete like she was seven years old, and opened the door. Kit and CJ Price sat at the kitchen table drinking coffee.

"Hi Monti," Kit said.

"What happened?" she said.

"What? Nothing." Kit grimaced at the state of her knee. "Monti, what did you do?" He stood and guided her to the nook, pushed her down to sit where he had been. "Let me look." He squatted down with some effort.

She glanced down. Just your standard klutz scrape. She touched his head with her fingertips. *Sweet man.*

"Hello Mrs. Rising," Detective Price said. "I'm sorry if I worried you. I stopped by to get a little more information about the situation with Jenny and Blaine.

"Oh, of course," Monti said, waving away her concern. "No problem." It'd be great if her heart would settle down sometime soon.

"I'll get a band-aid," Kit said. He levered himself up and headed for the bathroom.

"Don't bother, love," Monti said, but he was gone. She took a deep breath and turned to the detective. "No, uh, no sign of Blaine?"

"No ma'am, not yet. But we've opened a case file and we're attempting to locate him. Domestic assault is a serious offense."

"It certainly is," she agreed. "But, Kit said Blaine wasn't there."

"Monti, you goof, you left the car door hanging open." Kit set the first aid kit on the table and looked at her. "Are you okay?"

"Yes, yes, I was just...I didn't know what was going on and I had to..."

"I know. You had to know right now," he said. He kissed the top of her head. "You really are a goof ball. I'll go shut the car door."

"There are groceries..." she said over her shoulder as he went out the door.

Monti leaned toward Detective Price. "I was afraid Kit had..." she gulped down the lump in her throat. "Had another episode, or something," she said.

"Episode?" CJ said, tilting his head.

"Pain," she explained. "Yesterday he had a bad pain episode, and today he was moving furniture. Probably. He was injured in Kuwait, and his condition is worsening with age."

"Oh," CJ said. "Wow, that's a tough one. Is he handling it okay?"

"He is, yes, as well as might be hoped. But I," she said, taking a deep breath. "I am sometimes a basket case. As you may have noticed."

CJ chuckled then jumped to his feet. Kit, loaded with grocery bags, was headed up the kitchen steps. CJ opened the door, took the bags from him and set them on the counter.

"I think I have everything I need, sir," CJ said. "We've put out a BOLO on Blaine and I'll let you know when I get any updates." He retrieved his notepad and pen from the table and tucked them into his pocket. "Is there anything else I should know?"

"Not that I can think of," Kit said, and stuck his hand out. "Thanks for taking this seriously, CJ, we appreciate it."

"Of course, sir," the young man said. He shook Kit's hand. "Remember the precautions we talked about," he said, plucking up his cap and settling it on his head.

"Yes indeed, I'll brief the ladies when everyone gets home."

CJ nodded and took his leave.

Monti waited a full three seconds after he closed the door.

"Precautions?"

Precautions

The girls arrived not long after Detective Price left. Kit sat them down and updated them on CJ's concerns. "They're on the lookout for Blaine, but no sign of him yet. So...shall we declare a private holiday from classes until Blaine's in custody? You could hole up here, sleep in, watch movies..."

Noelle was shaking her head before he finished. "I can't, really, Grandpa," Noelle said. "I have an exam on Thursday and I need to spend serious time at the library finishing the research for my lit paper. It's due Monday."

"I have a paper, too, and I have to go to work," Jenny said. "No work, no financial aid."

"All right, then we go to plan B." Kit lowered himself into his chair. "We'll plan for the worst-case scenario, in which the police are not able to take Blaine into custody tonight. If he's loose we don't *know* he'll try anything, but I'd rather have you safe than sorry. What's your schedule tomorrow?"

"You want them to write it down?" Monti asked. "Then we'll have it for reference."

Noelle fetched a pen and legal pad from the Stickley sideboard, and she and Jenny put their heads together and sketched out their combined day.

Kit took the pad, analyzed their schedule and noted in the margins when they should call home. "Now while you're on campus," he said, "stay among people. No walks along the lake, or wandering down deserted hallways, okay? How well does this boy know your schedule, Jenny?"

"I doubt if he knows it at all. We don't have any classes together."

"That's good." Kit straightened, stretching his uncooperative spine. "There's no reason to believe he'll go out of his way to find you. But we'll err on the side of caution until we get an idea of what's going on in his head." Kit looked over the schedule again. "Noelle, what'll we do about your chorale re-hearsal at five? I don't want you to drive home alone in the dark."

"I could call Nick. He's offered to give me a ride before. I mean, you might as well avail yourselves of his services since you've undoubtedly already gone to the trouble to do an extensive background check on him and everything." Noelle deadpanned, looking her grandfather straight in the eye.

Kit grinned. "You call him, sweetie. That would be an acceptable arrangement." Kit clipped the pen to the top of the yellow pad. "Sounds like a plan then. I hope Blaine will be on his way to jail in the next five minutes, but barring that I think we can get you safely through the school day."

"And don't forget we go to Ray and Dorothy's at seven tomorrow," Monti added.

"Right, but we'll all be together so that's no problem." He stood, rolled his shoulders and tipped his head to the right, then the left. "Time to eat."

"Oh, good!" Monti said. "The aroma in here is about to start me drooling."

Everyone did something toward getting the food ready for the table and the table ready for the food, and soon they were enjoying Kit's signature beef stroganoff, talking about anything and everything but Blaine. The girls washed up after the meal and Monti accompanied Kit to the study. He flipped on all the tank lights and sank into his ergonomic chair. Monti pulled her chair up beside him and sat down.

"Did you get that newsletter sent off?" she said.

"Yep. Turns out I'm a real web wiz. Look at that blenny backing into his garage. He likes to keep an eye on everything from that crevice in the live rock."

"Think you'll get much response?"

"Who knows? It doesn't really matter if I don't, seeing as how we're not relying on angelfish sales to keep food on the table." He leaned forward and straightened the cover on the small tank. "I just want to see if all the buzz about email marketing holds any water for the casual entrepreneur."

"No pun intended, right? You never get tired of trying new things, do you?" Monti said. She squeezed his hand.

"You try new things all the time. Where do you think I learned it?" He stroked the back of her hand with his thumb. "But I think I'd better put the brakes on that some. I don't want to start something I can't finish. I couldn't manage these tanks if Jason didn't help with the heavy work."

Monti hated to hear him talk that way, though she knew it was true. She bit her tongue to keep from spouting a 'you can do anything' platitude. "How do you make yourself look at life straight in the eye like that, Kit Rising?"

He snorted. "Believe me, woman, every shred of self-awareness I possess has been hard won. I like my delusions of grandeur as much as the next guy. But when you're flat on your back for long stretches of time it invites contemplation. I think that may have been his plan all along."

"You don't blame him for the rollover, do you?"

"Not at all. I'm pretty sure that was the fault of the truck driver who hit us at 50 miles an hour on a dirt road in the middle of nowhere. What I mean is, God's notoriously not much interested in our creature comforts. But he is concerned that we figure out the important things, and I seem to learn best in the school of hard knocks."

"And hard knocks indeed they are, love." Monti laid her head on his shoulder and watched a pair of dottybacks swim lazily through the rocks. The phone rang and she heard Noelle answer it. A few seconds later the girl peered in around the corner.

"They got him," she said.

Tom

T he water of the quag trilled along the hull of the punt. They were silent a long while. Bo pondered the night's events and imagined their future in light of this new experience. Anisette opened the basket and fed him bites of meat and chunks of cheese. She spread conserve on a bit of bread and giggled watching him try to eat it while working the pole with his other hand. The sun blazed by the time they had got through the quag and turned into the river. The last chill from their night outdoors dissipated. Bo put his shoulder into poling the little punt upstream, and nodded now and then at others plying the waters in their humble **crafts**, busy with the day's work.

Bo's eyelids were heavy and his muscles ached. He wanted to fall into his bed. He watched Anisette. Her eyes shone as she beamed a bright smile at him. He was glad her enchantment did not include the burden of weariness after a trans-formation.

At last the punt rippled the water around the last bend, and he spied his own dock in the distance. He squinted. What were afoot there? As they drew closer he saw that Old Tom stood on the dock, gesticulating frantically at a boatman on the pier. Bo increased his efforts to speed the punt along.

"Tom!" he shouted, hand aside his mouth. "Old Tom, ahoy!" The old man turned toward them. His eyes and mouth went round, he grabbed his wild hair with both hands and sank to his knees. Bo watched the fear drain out of him and leave the poor elder wobbly. Tom clasped his hands and peered up to Heaven in as eloquent picture of heartfelt thanksgiving as Bo had ever seen. He shook his head. He loved Tom and was sorry for his distress.

"Poor Tom," Anisette said. "We have worried the old darling, haven't we?"

"We have, but he will mend. We must take him into our confidence straight away so that any future...delays of this sort do not frighten him." Bo gazed at Anisette. "But I mean to do my utmost, my lady, to see you freed from this en-chantment."

"I pray you will succeed, my lord, an God wills it."

Here they were, home again. Bo maneuvered the punt to lie against the dock, jumped out and secured it to the pilings. Old Tom gripped the big man with both his gnarled old hands.

"I thought I'd lost you, lad, in the storm," he said, his voice quavering with remembered grief. "What mishap has befell you and the lady?" He turned to Anisette. "Is my lady whole and well?"

"Yes, dear Tom, I am well," Anisette said as Bo handed her from the boat. She went to Old Tom and kissed both his cheeks. "We are home, and you are not to worry anymore."

Each of them hefted items from the boat and they trudged up the slope to the house in company. Anisette put the kettle on and set about unpacking the basket. "We might eat another breakfast now, all from the wondrous basket," she said, lifting out bread, ham and cheese, the jar of conserve and the unopened bottle of wine. "Tom, you packed enough to feed the town." The men sat at the table, both exhausted from the frightful night, and watched her flit about the room taking down plates and knives, and fetching milk for the tea.

"Tom, there is something we need you to know," Bo said. "'Twill be a mite hard to take in, mayhap, but I tell you only the truth."

"Aye, and what is it, lad?" Tom said, following Anisette's every move, drinking in her presence like a tonic.

"Tom." Bo waited for Tom to wrench his eyes away from Anisette. At last he did.

"Aye, Master Bo, what is it?" he said, serious now and attentive.

"Our Anisette suffers under an enchantment," Bo said. Anisette stopped her preparations and stood still to listen. "And it prevented our return home yesterday. When it rains, she is transformed..." Tom groaned and trembled. Bo knew he imagined a hundred horrid beasts in that moment. "No, Old Tom, do not tremble so. She is transformed into a beautiful almond tree, that is all." Tom groaned again, with relief perhaps, and dropped his old head on his arms.

"We could not come home, you see, because she was rooted in the honey meadow. We were trapped there until the rain stopped, and she dried in the breeze."

Tom looked at Bo, a child's wonder on his face. Then his eyes **slid** sideways to Anisette. "She dried in the breeze?" he said, swallowing hard. "Rooted?"

"*Exactly so, friend. When she is dry, all her branches and leaves, she is restored to our lovely Anisette again.*" Bo patted the old man on the back. "*It does not hurt her nor frighten her. She only must wait for the sun's return, and she continues on as she ever was.*"

A long silence ensued, wherein Tom sat with fists clenched on the table while his face worked through a myriad of contortions until his eyes focused on Anisette again. "*What about bathing, if you'll excuse me. Or washing up. You get wet then...*"

Anisette laughed. "*No, Tom. Only the rain, truly. Oh, and snow, too.*"

"*But, can nothing be done for you, my lady?*" *Tom asked her.*

"*Bo has said he will search out a remedy,*" *Anisette said.* "*If God allows, he will find one, I doubt it not.*"

"*But meantime, Tom, we must form a strategy to protect her while the enchantment endures. We shall begin in the garden...*" *Bo said. Tom listened, nodding with increasing enthusiasm, until his newly accustomed grin once again lit his face.*

Flight Plan

The next morning Monti woke early and couldn't get back to sleep. She decided to get up and hit the Book, and then fix a fortifying breakfast for everybody. Banana chocolate chip muffins would be just the thing, along with a huge bowl of scrambled eggs and some apple slices and grapes. Fortifying, yes. Complicated, no.

Kit joined her as she was pulling the muffins out of the oven. By the time the girls tromped down the stairs wearing mix-and-match Hello Kitty collectible PJs, the basket of muffins sat steaming on the table, Kit was slicing apples and Monti was pouring the eggs into a skillet.

"Muffins and coffee on offer, scrambled eggs coming up," Kit said. Noelle's body got down a mug, scooped sugar and cream into it, and added coffee. Eventually her brain would switch on and catch up. Jenny poured her coffee straight into a big mug. She liked it black. While Monti stirred the eggs Kit dumped her cold half-cup, replenished the sugar and cream, and refilled it hot.

Five minutes later breakfast was on the table. The girls were perking up and Kit returned thanks, mentioning the BCC muffins particularly. They were his favorite.

"Well, I'm so glad we don't have to be on high alert all day," Monti said, scooping eggs onto her plate. "Nevertheless, remind me who's going where today and whether I'm supposed to be any particular place."

"Here's the schedule, Grandma, remember we wrote it all down?" Noelle produced the legal pad from last night's planning session.

"I thought you were staying home today," Kit said.

"I am. Unless I'm supposed to be somewhere else...oh never mind, it says right here I'm staying home today. Hey, we should make one of these every day."

Kit shook his head. "No amount of writing things down will uncross your crossed wires, Monti. If you're still a space cadet at your age, you're destined to be a space cadet forever."

"Well, even space cadets need a flight plan, right? And don't forget, we're going to Ray and Dorothy's tonight so Jenny can decide if they're too weird to live with," Monti said.

"*If* I end up needing a place to stay," Jenny said. That quieted them for a moment. Noelle bit her lip.

"Of course, young lady," Kit said. "That's your decision. And I guess you already know how we all feel about that, so we won't belabor the point."

"No pun intended," Noelle said. "Oh, good grief, it's nine o'clock already. I dibs first shower," she said, and sprang for the stairs. Jenny followed.

Kit refilled Monti's coffee again. "So what space cadet mission have you planned for today?"

"I'll be dragging out the laptop. I'm hoping to make some serious headway on my story," she said.

"Good. I'm staying home too. Fed-ex is supposed to deliver my new green mandarin dragonets today."

"You're raising baby dragons now?"

"Right. Chinese ones."

"Well they sound beautiful. I can't wait to see them," Monti said. "Gosh, I can't remember the last time we were home together all day!"

"Me either. I also can't remember the last time we had a good visit with Ray and Dorothy."

"I'm looking forward to it. I haven't talked with Dot more than five minutes at church for ages. And I'm sure Jenny will hit it off with them," Monti said. "No Scrabble tonight, then, huh?"

"Oh, you're ready for a rematch, are you?" Kit said, waggling his eyebrows up and down and grinning. "Any time, woman."

"Except tonight, of course."

Rogues' Gallery

Jenny peered through the car window, her heart thumping. Noelle nudged her. When Jenny turned to her she gave her a wink and a sweet smile.

Kit led them all through an arched garden gate, down a stone path, and up onto a deep wraparound porch. Dorothy must have been watching for them, because the front door opened before Kit had a chance to ring the bell. A plump, pretty woman pushed open the screen door and beckoned them in.

"Hello, hello. Come on in." She gave Monti a big hug. "Haven't seen you in a bazillion years, sister. Or maybe it was Sunday." She hollered over her shoulder, "Ray!" and ushered her guests inside. "He's down in the basement building...uh...I can't remember what he's building. Something that smells piney and generates voluminous quantities of sawdust, judging by the amount he tracks through the house." The lady stopped in front of Jenny and took both her hands. "You must be Jenny," she said. "I'm so delighted you're here." A shrill whistle sounded from the kitchen. "Oh, there's the kettle. Make yourselves comfy, I'll be back in a sec." She bustled off to the kitchen and stuck her head through the basement door. "Ray! They're here, honey. Dust yourself off and join us."

"Dorothy's your sister?" Jenny said. "You don't look anything alike." Monti and Noelle laughed. Dorothy was petite, with long shiny black hair beginning to grey around the edges of her olive-skinned face.

"She's my sister in Christ," Monti explained. "You acquire quite a few siblings that way. It's kind of a dysfunctional family, but lots of fun." Jenny was bewildered and it must have shown. "We're both Christians." Monti said. "All Christians consider themselves brothers and sisters in Christ, see?" She had no idea what Monti was talking about. "Don't worry about it, sweetie. Find a spot and settle in."

But Jenny couldn't settle. She wandered about the room, examining the knick knacks and photos. She paused to look at a wall covered with family pictures.

Dorothy returned carrying a huge tray crammed with stuff, which she set down on the broad coffee table. "Ah, you found my rogue's gallery!" she said to Jenny. "I'll tell you which ones have outstanding warrants later." Jenny's mouth fell open.

"She's kidding, Jenny," Monti said. Jenny felt her cheeks get hot. *Duh.*

"Help yourself, everybody. That's the Cominski House Rule. If you've been here for at least five minutes, you're to help yourself to whatever you need." Dorothy inspected the tray. "And tell me if I forgot anything."

Chocolate chip cookies, shortbread, and some kind of white, airy looking cookies were piled high on a big, bright red platter. A teapot, a coffee pot, a bright red sugar bowl and pitcher set, spoons and mugs crowded the tray. Noelle didn't hesitate. She poured tea for herself and Jenny and plucked a chocolate chip cookie from the platter.

"Oh yes, Jenny," Noelle said. "I should probably warn you. Dot's cooking is hazardous to your waistline. But then, you won't need to worry about that very much!"

Jenny took the mug of tea from Noelle, chose a chocolate chip cookie, and turned again to the wall of photos to examine a large, formal family portrait. She'd seen ones like this at the mall, advertising some studio, but she'd never seen one in somebody's house. It showed a way younger Dorothy, a man with thinning hair and a big smile, and a pretty teenage girl wearing jeans and a multi-colored vest over a big t-shirt, her dark hair studded with tiny butterfly clips. Must be their daughter. She looked at the other pictures on the wall. The same girl starred in lots of the photos at younger ages. Six or seven other girls, each holding a baby—one with twins—smiled at her from the wall, too. Not their daughters, she guessed.

A chubby man clomped up the basement stairs and came over to shake Kit's hand. "Hey, Kit, good to see you. Hello Monti, Noelle." He stepped into the living room far enough to grab one of the white cookies and popped the whole thing into his mouth. Then he stepped back onto the tile floor and said around the cookie, "How am I for sitting on your furniture, dearest?" He rotated slowly with arms raised to allow his wife a thorough inspection. She brushed sawdust off his sleeves and pant legs.

"She doesn't like man-glitter on the sofa," the man explained, which made Noelle snort tea.

"I'm sure you'll find a way to spread it around no matter how much I brush you, Mr. Sparkly." She finished swiping at him. "You'll do, husband," she said.

"Dorothy, Ray, this is Jenny Conklin," Kit said. "She may be needing a place to stay for a few months."

Jenny turned to meet the man from the family photo, now completely bald on top with a fringe of scruffy silver hair around the sides. Still smiling, though.

"Hello, young lady," he said, taking her hand in both of his. His skin was rough but his touch gentle. "We're happy to meet you."

Calm Down

M onti kicked off her shoes as she walked through the door. Her feet throbbed. Her molar throbbed, too. Did that mean she was throbbing from head to toe?

Noelle and Jenny had had their heads together all the way home from the Cominskis', and they were still talking quietly as they took off their coats.

"So Jenny, what did you think of Dot and Ray?" Monti said.

"They're sweet," she said. "Kinda weird, but in a nice way."

"I must have eaten half a dozen cookies," Noelle said. "At least. I'm so full."

"Yeah, I could get used to her cooking," Jenny said. "But I mean, your cooking is delish too, Mrs. R."

"Don't worry, Jenny. We all know Dot is the best cook in Kootenai County. I wouldn't dream of comparing myself with her in any culinary category whatsoever."

"Are banana chocolate chip muffins a culinary category?" Kit asked as he locked them in for the night. "Because you make the best I've ever eaten, no exceptions."

"Says the man who would eat them for breakfast every day if he had his way," Monti said, and kissed him on the cheek. "Every woman has to have a secret weapon or two in her kitchen arsenal." The phone rang and she picked it up. "Risings." She listened a moment, and frowned. "Just a minute, young man. You calm down." She glanced at Kit. He stood perfectly still, his jaw muscles tight, his body tense, listening.

"Wait. I'm willing to talk with you, but I won't tolerate that language or that attitude. No, I won't. You call back when you've calmed down." She hung up the phone. Then, hands shaking, she picked it back up and fiddled with buttons until she got it to display the number of the last call received.

"Who was that?" Kit said.

"He didn't get around to telling me that, he was too busy making threats. But I think it was Blaine."

The Bower

Next morning the sun warmed Bo and Old Tom as they paced off distances and pounded sharpened ash stakes in the garden. A few chrysanthemums bloomed on among the ripening hubbards and pumpkins, but the rest of the garden had been put to bed for the winter and this was a good time to redesign the landscape. Anisette sat in a window, singing as she mended one of Bo's shirts, distracting both men from their arithmetic.

"About fifteen feet across, I think, Tom. And quite a low wall. 'Twill allow the sun bright entrance to dry her, yet feel cozy and safe for her."

Tom grunted and paced off a distance for the next stake. "I heard tell of a similar enchantment o'er Bedford way, Master Bo. A little boy it were, turned into a frog whenever his mother cried. And o' course, the more he turned into a frog the more she cried, until he were more frog than boy and hopped away, ne'er more to be seen."

Bo stood and took in the circular area they had defined. "Yes, Tom, such tales abound. And no doubt many be true, but certain just as many are spun from thin air. Surely no mother could be so careless with her tiny hexed son." Then he remembered how carelessly he had poled off across the quag, never thinking of the danger. "But then, she doubtless loved him and grieved his loss."

He tossed his mallet onto a bench and took up the spade. "What sows dread in my heart is not being able to recall a credible tale ending with the enchantment lifted and the poor soul set free to live out his days in the ordinary fashion." He thrust the spade into the soil at the first stake and peered at his old friend. "Do you remember any such?"

Old Tom scrunched his face together and commenced to paw his clothing for pipe and tobacco. "Let me think on it. There be so many unlikely tales. But only a fragment comes any distance, and who can know how mangled be the truth of it after traveling so far." He found his pipe and stuffed fragrant tobacco into the bowl. "And people care less for a happy ending than a tragic one, God help us all."

"*True indeed,*" Bo said. *They fell silent. Bo dug fiercely, and after the pipe was smoked Tom took up another spade and joined him. Soon a shallow trench emerged. They pulled the stakes one by one as they worked along, until the trench was complete and the stakes lay in a heap in the center. A bit of rubble next, and then to fetch the stones. Bo was determined to have the enclosure built before the next rain.*

The two men worked steadily with the easy rhythm of long years together. By the time Anisette called them to the midday meal, they had the trench mostly filled with rubble from behind the shed. They leaned their spades against the house, washed at the pump at the edge of the garden and knocked their boots clean of clods before stepping into the house.

"*It smells delicious in here, wife. What fancy have you cooked up for us?*"

"*Oh, nothing fancy at all, my lord,*" *Anisette said.* "*We've a hot broth soup, a loaf of good brown bread, and meat and cheese from the larder. Sit down, Tom, and let me do it, if you will.*" *She gently guided the old man to a chair and set big bowls of steaming soup on the table, where the bread sat already sliced next to a dish of butter, and a platter of meat and cheese waited to be speared onto plates.*

"*Simple food is the best, I think,*" *Bo said.* "*It goes easy into the belly and renews the strength for working.*" *Tom grunted what could have been agreement. The meal was obviously to his liking, as he shoveled it into his mouth with only the barest attempt at manners. Bo and Anisette watched him, bemused.*

"*So, old Tom, the new mistress' cooking agrees with you, it seems.*" *Tom stopped and looked up. He grinned at Bo, gazed adoringly at Anisette, and got back to it. Anisette laughed her silvery laugh, sending shivers through her husband.*

"*Anisette,*" *he said.* "*Would you care to jolt along in the old wagon to town with me? I need to fetch a load of rock for the garden bower. We shall stop anywhere you like, for whatever you might be needing.*" *Her brow creased ever so slightly and he hastened to reassure her.* "*I have consulted the almanac, and old Tom, and the sky. There is not the tiniest cloud to be seen toward any horizon. Dry weather is expected for several days to come.*" *He took her hand and kissed it.* "*But if you do not wish to come or are uneasy, it matters not. Stay here where you are safe indeed, and old Tom will watch over you until I return. 'Twill be but a few hours.*"

Anisette smiled at him, relaxing. "I will go with you, husband. I cannot live my days in fear, and I have for so many years longed to be out in the world. With you beside me and God watching o'er me, I am not afraid."

Bail

Kit hung up the phone and turned to the three women waiting with wide eyes. "Blaine's father bailed him out this morning." He waited until the groans of disbelief subsided. "The number Monti got is Blaine's cell phone. Making threats, even over the phone, is assault, and that's been added to the charges." Kit sat on the bench at the table and wrapped his long fingers around a glass of water Monti had got for him. "Detective Price plans to visit Blaine's father tomorrow. How much good that will do I haven't a clue, but it couldn't hurt."

Monti put her hand on Kit's shoulder. He slid over and she sat beside him. She was suddenly exhausted. "Well. Daddy bailed him out. So either he thinks Blaine can do no wrong, in which case the police visit will do no good at all, or he's furious with him. I hope he's furious, and that he has some influence. Threaten to stop the cash flow or something."

"We can hope," Kit said. "But I've seen kids do unbelievable things to spite their parents even when the damage to their own lives is significant."

Noelle said, "Do you think Blaine will do anything worse?" Her voice wobbled a bit but she held her chin up.

"No way to know that, honey." Kit rubbed the back of his neck. "He'd never been arrested before, that's something. But it's hard to predict."

"I hope he doesn't come here!" Jenny said. "I'd hate it if you all got dragged into this."

Any more than we already are, Monti thought.

"I don't think he will," Kit said. "But if he does, the police are on it. They're looking for him to arrest him again, and CJ will have a patrol car cruise by here every little while tonight and tomorrow. Starting tomorrow you girls need to stick to the plan we made. Don't take any chances."

Monti leaned her head on Kit's shoulder. The girls stood hip to hip against the kitchen counter, gazing into their own thoughts. No one spoke for a minute or two. "Is anyone else as tired as I am?" Monti said. "I'm going to call it a night."

"Me too," Kit said. "I'm beat."

The girls stirred. "Yeah, I guess we'll head up, huh Jenny?" Jenny nodded.

Monti stood, kissed them both and shooed them up the stairs.

"CJ told me he talked to Billy," Kit said after a minute.

Monti sat across from him. "Billy..."

"One of the boys that lives in the house...he showed up as we were leaving after packing Jenny's stuff."

"You didn't mention that before."

"Didn't think of it. Billy thought someone was with Blaine when he tore up Jenny's room."

"Really. That's—unsettling."

He nodded, his lips pressed in a firm line.

Monti covered her mouth with both hands as her imagination took that idea and ran in hysterical circles with it. "You didn't tell the girls?"

He shook his head. "I probably should have, but there's nothing they can do about it anyway. That ray of sunshine will keep 'til morning."

"I agree. No sense *everyone* losing sleep over it." She stood again and took hold of Kit's hand to haul him out of the bench seat. "C'mon lover, let's hit the sack."

Intractable

A pale gold autumn sun shone through the kitchen windows on Thursday afternoon. Gulliver purred in the window seat and Monti sat with her feet tucked under his warm belly. She would have purred too, if she could. She soaked in the warmth, coffee cup clasped in both hands, eyes closed. Kit was working in the den, the girls weren't home yet, and she had a little while before she needed to start supper. She let her mind wander through the problems and quandaries that had popped up during the day. She thought through them, asked for mercy and guidance and made an effort to give each one into God's hands.

She hated the intractable nature of the problems she wrestled with. She most often couldn't fix them, and that vexed her. She was oh, so slowly learning to deliberately hand them over and not to fret, but it was slow going!

Blaine was the biggest wild card right now, of course, especially with a mystery sidekick thrown into the mix. Ruining her night's sleep was the least of it. He was a danger to Jenny and now to Noelle and all of them, and there was nothing she could do about it.

Monti sighed and forced herself to keep moving down her intractable problems list. Jenny would have to make her hard decisions about her baby, and live with the consequences. She shot up a prayer for protection for Jenny's little one.

Her student, Austin, was in jail. She didn't know if she had enough credibility with him to influence him one way or another, but she would go see him anyway.

Then there was Marla and her long chain of heartbreaking choices. And Kit. She couldn't solve that problem either...take his pain away, make him all better. Her helplessness jabbed at her heart. She gave that to God too. Again. The throbbing in her back-most molar made her realize there was at least one problem she could solve with a call to the dentist. Monti felt her favorite lips kiss the corner of her eye, and smiled.

"Hey, lover," she said.

"Hey," Kit said. He poured a mug of coffee, pulled a chair up to face her and sat down. He stroked Gulliver and the purring got louder.

"My cardinalfish has released his babies if you want to see them," Kit said.

"Sure, I'll come look after I get supper started! This is your first success with those, isn't it?"

"Yep. I think I made every mistake there is, but I finally got everything coordinated and ready in time. That guy in Portland helped a lot. Answered a hundred questions. I'll have to send him some pictures." He leaned forward and stretched his back. "You and Gulliver have a nice bask in the sun?"

"Yeah. I was just thinking through the day," she said. She swung her feet down and stretched her arms above her head. "Thinking about Blaine, of course, wondering how that's going to go. And Jenny and the baby. And I have to go visit one of my students in jail. I haven't done that for a long time, guess I'd better call and make sure the routine is still the same."

"Good idea. I hear they're switching to video visits pretty soon."

"Video visits?"

"Yep. Essentially visiting by closed-circuit television. No more face to face with only Plexiglas between."

"I don't think I like that idea. It's depersonalizing, or something. I wonder why they're doing that?"

"Don't know." He stood and pulled her up. "What's your student in for?"

She grimaced. "Selling drugs, they tell me."

Kit shook his head. "That'll put you in jail all right."

She opened the fridge and started taking things out. "The thing is, he doesn't seem like a bad kid. Granted, I don't know him very well but I like him. He's articulate, which is rare."

"Articulate does not equal moral. What are we cooking that needs ground beef, tomatoes, and strawberry jam?"

"What?" Monti looked at what she'd taken out of the fridge and put the jam back in. "Well, I'm going to go visit him anyway, and see what I find out."

"At least you'll have an intelligent conversation, if nothing else." Kit took a big onion from her hand and set about chopping it. "Monti, don't panic."

"What do you mean? Do I have more rogue ingredients threatening the menu?"

"No, sour cream and zucchini seem reasonable, and I already secured the maple syrup. I had in mind the fact that Thanksgiving is three weeks from to-day."

"What?" She froze, the meat half unwrapped. "Okay, I see how that's possible. I think it is November, isn't it?"

"Has been for days now," Kit said, getting out the big cast iron skillet. "I thought you might want to start thinking about it, is all."

"Well, yeah. I'd better make a list. When I have a minute."

Anisette Goes Shopping

A nisette turned to wave at old Tom, and grabbed at Bo when the wagon bounced through a deep pothole. Bo flicked the reins over the horses' **withers**. **Em** and **Jo**, the two old mares, responded briefly but soon settled back into their accustomed pace.

"Where might you like to shop a bit, my love?" Bo asked her. "Have you need of stitchery stuffs, or ribbons or..." No further possibilities came to mind.

Anisette giggled. "My mending basket wants replenishing, husband. But I know not where such things are to be had. At home, I was used to ask my nurse or the housekeeper for whatever I needed, and it was got for me. I've never been in a shop since I was a tiny child."

"Then we shall explore together until we find what is wanted. Old Tom does much of the marketing. Mayhap he would be a better guide, but we shall manage." He pointed out a gilded sign picturing a needle and thread. "I believe this place is central to ladies' necessaries. Shall we?"

As they stepped through the low doorway, Anisette's mouth made a sweet "O." Goods of bewildering variety lay stacked on tables and shelves, sat heaped in baskets, and hung from the ceiling on hooks and lines. Anisette's glance flitted here and there, trying to take it all in. Bo nodded to the mistress of the shop.

"Good Mistress Blackwell," he said.

"Why, Master Willem," the buxom woman said, arching her right eyebrow. "Surely you've never stepped foot in my shop before today." Her eyes moved to Anisette, and analyzed her head to foot. "Your new wife?"

"Yes, mistress. Anisette, this is Mistress Blackwell, wife to Bernard, a wool merchant. Mistress, meet my Anisette, daughter of Master Marlow."

"I am pleased to meet you, Mistress Blackwell. Your shop is wonderful." Anisette curtsied, and bent to examine a thousand buttons in a basket.

"She is not accustomed to find her way about a shop, so perhaps you might guide her somewhat?" Bo said.

Mistress Blackwell's eyes narrowed, then widened. "Anisette Marlow?" She dropped her voice to a whisper. "Isn't she cursed? Have you married into witchy doings, Master Willem?"

Bo scowled. His lips tightened into a firm line. "No, Mistress Blackwell. My wife is innocent of any such. She is a sweet child of God and..." He glanced toward Anisette, who had wandered away toward a table piled high with shimmery fabrics. "If you would help her find what she needs, I would be grateful."

Mistress Blackwell sniffed, then formed a sour smile. "Certainly, Master Willem," she said. She stalked off to where Anisette held a moss green velvet to the light. Bo watched her force herself to be courteous. "Mistress, how may I be of help to you?"

For the Win

Jenny and Noelle headed up the walk to the library, a chill afternoon wind making them tuck their chins down into their jackets and hunch their shoulders to their ears. They hadn't seen Blaine anywhere, but they were sticking to the plan. Noelle had called Kit to let him know they were studying for a couple hours and would be home late for dinner.

"I think I've decided," Jenny said.

"Decided what?" Noelle said.

"About the baby, of course."

"Oh! Of course. And...what have you decided?" Noelle stopped at the library door and held her breath waiting for the answer.

"I really liked Dorothy. And Ray, too. If I stay with them until the baby's born, that'll give me time to decide about keeping her or giving her up for adoption."

"Her?"

"Or him, of course. But I always think of the baby as her."

Noelle did an internal joy dance. If Jenny already thought of her tiny baby as a person, a little girl, that had to be good. "That's great, Jenny! That's super. Do you want to tell G & G tonight?"

"Yeah, I guess I'd better so they can get things arranged with Dorothy and Ray." Noelle swung the heavy glass door open and they stepped into the warmth of the library lobby. "I'm still kind of worried about school though. I want to finish my associates. If I keep the baby, how do I do that with a newborn?"

"Yeah. It'll be tough. But hey, she won't still be a newborn by fall semester. She'll be what, two or three months old? You'd have most things figured by then, you know, about feeding and diapering and stuff."

"I guess. We'll see. I can't think about that any more today. This math test tomorrow is gonna kill me." Jenny led the way to an empty table.

"No worries. I'll help you study. I have my paper mostly done. And if we need extra help, we'll call Nick. He was a math wiz in high school."

"Would you like me to pretend I don't understand your 'help' so you have an excuse to call Nick?" Jenny asked, her face all innocence.

Noelle stopped and grinned at her friend. "Why yes, Jenny, that would be most appreciated, thank you for your thoughtfulness."

THAT EVENING THE AIR in the dining room was redolent with the scents of buttered popcorn, Rusty Car organic coffee and polysyllabic words. Monti was a little giddy. She was enjoying a commanding lead, a rarity in their perpetual private Scrabble tournament. Kit sat tapping his fingers on the table, his mouth set. He had been eying the last vacant triple word score for the last five minutes, but he didn't appear to be making much headway with it. She decided to tidy the kitchen while he pondered the possibilities. She was rinsing the hand-crank popcorn popper when Noelle's car pulled into the driveway. The girls' giggles wafted in as they climbed the kitchen steps.

"Hey G & G," Noelle said. "Great news."

"Grrrr," said Kit. They all looked at him, astounded. "What? Two minutes, okay? I've almost got it."

"Okay, G. We'll go dump our books upstairs." Noelle looked a question at Monti.

"Take your time, dears. I've about got him beat," she said, earning another growl from her beloved.

By the time the girls flounced back down the stairs, Monti was holding the bag while Kit tipped the board to let the tiles slide in. She was grinning and he was not.

"Uh-oh. Final score?" Noelle said.

"384 to 326," Monti answered. Kit grunted.

"Well, Grandpa, it was definitely her turn to win, wasn't it? Haven't you beat her like three times in a row?"

"Oh, it doesn't matter who wins, right, Kit?" Monti said.

"Four times, actually," Kit said, apparently unable to let this inaccuracy stand.

Monti eyed him. "Like I said, we don't care who wins."

"That's a relief," Noelle said. "I wouldn't want you to stress about it or anything, Grandpa." She grinned and kissed his cheek, eliciting yet another grunt.

"Tell 'em, Jenny." She beckoned Jenny to a seat at the table. Kit and Monti set down the game pieces and listened.

"I want to have the baby, that's all," Jenny said, and was nearly drowned out by Monti's sophisticated and restrained whoop of joy. Kit just grinned.

"That's great news, young lady," he said. "Wonderful."

"We'd better call Ray and Dorothy and make your reservation right away," Monti said. "And Sandy will need to know, so she can round up maternity clothes for you, and the right vitamins, and arrange for prenatal care..."

"Monti."

"Yes, dear?"

"You're scaring the girl."

"Oh. Again?" She sighed. "Sorry, Jenny."

"It's okay, Mrs. R," Jenny said. "I'm kinda getting used to it."

Counsel

"Mistress Blackwell was such a help," Anisette said. "I fear I indulged my fancies a bit, and went quite beyond stocking the mending basket." She looked up at him, and he smiled as he shook the reins and bade the horses start the journey home.

"Aye, that is the manner of help Mistress Blackwell does best provide," he said. "'Tis good for business to have her customers indulge their fancies." He glanced at Anisette and was aghast at the stricken expression on her face. "My love, no rebuke to you, none at all. I would be glad to have you pack her entire stock into your basket if it pleased you. I only meant…oh never you mind. It was uncharitable of me. On, beasts!" He flicked the reins. The load of rock was more work than the mares wanted to bother with, but Bo insisted. Two or three minutes went by in awkward silence.

"Anisette?"

"Yes, husband," she said in a small voice, in which he thought he heard the choke of tears. He was a stupid oaf. He must take more care! He put his arm around her.

"Anisette, dear one, please do not cry. I want you to have every fancy there is. I'm sorry I spoke unkindly about Mistress Blackwell. I'm sorry…" What else had he bungled?

"Oh husband, do not apologize," she said, brushing tears from her eyes. "I see your meaning. 'Tis obvious now, how she drew me on to purchase more and more. But I had no idea…how foolish of me."

"And how were you to know of such wiles cloistered away as you were, as unworldly as any saint.".

Anisette laughed. "Hardly a saint, I assure you, husband," she said. "But ignorant of the world's ways, I grant you."

"Oh, and never mind it. You are stocked with ribbons and trims to transform my shirts and old Tom's trousers into works of wonder. Or, if you'd rather, *stitch them into some sumptuous garment for yourself. Yes, that might be better. We don't want old Tom expecting fancy finery as his due." He was rewarded for this effort at wit with the silvery laugh he cherished more each day.*

WHEN THEY ARRIVED HOME, *old Tom and Bo dumped the rock into the yard while Anisette went to make a pot of tea. Tom had a roast of beef and potatoes in the oven. Anisette peeked in and dared to baste the potatoes with the pan juices. Then she fetched her work-basket and stocked it with strong thread, sharp new needles, yarn for darning socks, and extra buttons.*

*She inspected the yards of ribbon and lace, the length of deep green velvet "just come from the **dyer**," and felt her face flush, her pleasure in them diminished by the memory of how easily she'd been persuaded to buy them. She straightened and set her jaw. She would not allow Mistress Blackwell to spoil her day. She would indeed fashion these beautiful goods into some sumptuous garment for herself. She felt sure that would make Bo smile, and she did so love his smile.*

*Next morning Bo and Tom set to work early. With no deliveries to make, they had the whole day available and were determined to finish the bower wall before sunset. Anisette bade them come in to eat a bite of breakfast, then brought coffee out to them midmorning. She exclaimed at their progress. They had finished a low wall to knee height all around, with bright white quartz pointing out each **quoin**. They now began to form the arched entry.*

At noon she brought them bread and cheese, a bottle of mead and one of water. The sun was high and warm, and they had that moment set the keystone at the top of the entry arch. It was complete. Anisette walked under it, back and forth. She stood in the center of the enclosure and looked toward the house.

"You shall be able to see me here, husband, from our bedchamber."

"Yes, I made sure of that. But remember I will set a bench here, so to be near you."

"Oh, but do not stay out in the rain, please," she said, and grasped his hand. "I do not wish you to take ill from sitting in the weather."

"Never you fear, mistress. I'll not let him do any such foolish thing," Tom said, as he filled his pipe. "I'll watch out for the both of you. Your husband is a ro-

mantic, and well I know it." He shook his head, lit his pipe, and squinted through
the smoke at whoever was crunching up the gravel drive.

"Good day, Josiah," Bo said. He wiped his hands on his shirt and shook his
friend's hand. The pastor, a stocky man about Bo's own age, took in the scene.

"Good day, Bo, old Tom," he said. "My lady, I see you are settling in well.
These two look to be flourishing in your care."

"Yes, Pastor Wheaton, they are a joy to me," Anisette said, and blushed.

The visitor studied the building project. "What pretty thing do you build
here, Bo?"

"'Tis to be a haven for my Anisette, for when it rains." It took Pastor
Wheaton a moment to process this.

"Ah. Of course. And it is touching that need I have come to see you both," he
said. "Have you a moment?"

"Of course, of course. Tom, take your time with your pipe, there. I'll be back
out afore too long."

"Go along with you," Tom said, shooing them in. Anisette hurried in ahead
and checked that all was orderly in the house, ready to receive a guest. She bid the
pastor sit, and offered tea.

"No need, thank you Mistress," Josiah said, and waved them to their seats.
She and Bo sat, eager to hear what he might have found for them.

"Now I see the hope on your faces, and don't wish to damp it overmuch, but
I've made little headway as yet. In fact, I want to caution you. It may not...it
might be that...oh, now don't be looking all forlorn at me." He scrubbed his face
with one hand, then laid both hands palm up on the table. "Let me begin again.
I have spent considerable time in prayer about poor Anisette's affliction. And I
thought it best to convey what is being taught me by our Counselor." He looked at
Bo, then at Anisette.

"Do not set your hearts on a cure to the extent that your joy depends upon it.
All marriages, all people, for that matter, have trials sore with which they must
contend. Some are passing and easily dealt with. But many are intractable. Barring a miracle of mercy from our Jesu, most of us must set our minds to endure
this or that ailment, some deep sorrow, perhaps an act of injustice or betrayal
done to us.".

He sought their eyes. "Do you understand, my children, what I am saying? I
will continue to seek among my brethren for a possible remedy. But it may be you

will have to gird your hearts to bear this trial until Jesu puts all such evil under his foot at last."

Anisette slid her eyes sideways to gage how Bo took this prospect. Tears started when she saw his ashen face. Josiah took in their reactions and said, "Now Bo, you must take care. You could so easily poison your home with bitterness. Your wife needs your unconditional love as she is," he said, punctuating his last words by poking the table with a finger. "And Anisette, do not be second guessing your mate's devotion to you, or fearing he may regret binding himself to you. Both of you, pay attention." He pounded his fist once on the table and they both jumped.

"I bid you heed my words and promise me you will abide by them. Are you listening?" They assured him they were. "The vital strategy you must ever employ between you is openness. You must not, either of you, harbor secret fears or resentments. If anything seems ever amiss between you, you must work together at the tangle until 'tis cleared away. Though this is the best way to make any marriage flourish, I cannot overstate how critical it is that you two vow to keep this always as your policy. You face a trial most couples could never dream of. You must be one in heart and mind to be sure of enduring it."

He sat back. "I am convinced each of you would give life and limb for the other but even so, if you harbor secret thoughts amiss 'twill undermine your devotion. Are my thoughts on this clear to you both?"

Anisette tried her best to choke it back, but a giggle escaped her. Both men gaped at her, which only made it worse. She gave in to it and laughed until she cried. The men watched, dumbfounded. When she'd caught her breath she said, "I'm sorry pastor. I mean no disrespect. I take your counsel quite seriously indeed. But such a vivid picture implanted itself in my mind. Bo, no doubt, would give his life, but I would give limb, do you not think?"

After a moment's silence, Bo said, "Implanted? A picture implanted itself?" They both laughed this time, and the preacher shook his head and waited for them to come back to earth.

"I do believe it will be well with you, my friends," he said. "I would say I believe your love will blossom and bear fruit, but I think it unwise to encourage you." They broke out again, Bo's booming laugh a counterpoint to Anisette's silvery peals. The visitor smiled his relief and stood to go. Mr. and Mrs. Willem stood also and grasped Josiah's hands.

"You are a dear friend to us, Josiah, and a wise counselor. I do vow to you, and to Anisette, to obey you in this."

"I, too, Pastor Wheaton. I will with all my heart."

"Ah well, and glad I am to hear it. And do not think I am abandoning my research on your behalf. That is by no means the case."

"We appreciate your efforts, old friend, truly. But I think you may rest easy about us. We will err, no doubt, and hurt each other all unintended." He looked at his beloved Anisette. *"But with the help of Jesu and friends such as Josiah Wheaton I think we will endure. What think you, Anisette?"*

"Amen to all that, husband. 'Tis the way of it indeed."

Austin

It was ridiculously hard to find government-type places in the phone book. Monti gave up, returned the seldom-used book to the top of the fridge, and went to consult Google. If she found it quickly there was just time to catch someone on the phone before she had to leave for class, she hoped.

As she opened her laptop, Monti wondered why she was going to all this trouble. Austin had been a marginal presence in her class, doing his assignments but never sticking around for snacks and conversation. She didn't really know him at all, and she had to be a non-entity to him. Nevertheless, she couldn't get him out of her mind and she knew better than to ignore that. Kootenai County Jail, there it was. She jotted down the phone number and checked the clock. She hoped a live person would answer the phone.

A live person did, and Monti shortly had all the information she needed from a surprisingly chatty deputy. The woman confirmed the jail would soon go to video visits, but for now she'd be able to see him in person between 8am and 9pm. Monti grabbed her tote bag and fished her keys from her purse. Time to go teach her one Friday class. Then she'd visit Austin.

MONTI PULLED INTO THE parking lot of the jail, still unsure of her motives. No, she did know. *Because God told me to*, while it sounded a little out there, was the truth. She leaned her head back on her seat and sent up a quick prayer for guidance, then climbed out and locked the Baja.

After depositing her keys, phone and purse in a plastic tub that stayed with the officer at the desk, she sat on a grimy yellow chair in the tiny waiting room, a faint funk of ammonia pinching her nostrils. She tried not to fidget. She tried to think of what kind of conversation she might have with Austin.

"Montana Rising?" A rotund officer holding her driver's license raised an eyebrow at her. "That your real name?"

She managed not to roll her eyes. "Yes, sir, it is." She stood and smiled benignly. She hoped the sarcasm pushing at the back of her clenched teeth did not show on her face. *No, I thought I'd use an alias today. No, that's my little joke. No, I'm on the run...*

"Follow me, ma'am," the officer said, and led her down the hall. She followed. The officer pointed to a tiny visiting booth similar to a study carrel at a library. Except for the reek of ammonia. And the institutional mint-green paint. And the thick sheet of Plexiglas separating her from where Austin waited in his matching mint-green carrel. Austin sprawled across a grey plastic chair in the de rigueur manner of his age mates, one long arm resting on the counter, fingers tapping the chipped wood-grain Formica. She sat in the chair the officer indicated and he walked off down the hall.

"Hello Austin," she said.

He picked up a phone handset at the end of a thick silver cable mounted on the side wall and pointed to it. She picked hers up and said again, "Hello Austin."

"Hey, Mrs. Rising," he answered. "Why are you here?"

She laughed, startled. "Well, that's a good question, Austin. I, uh..." She paused. "I was worried about you." She studied him. "Should I be worried about you?"

Austin pushed himself up a little straighter in his chair, ran one hand back through his unruly blond hair. "No...I don't think so. Why would you worry about me? You hardly know me. I was in your class what...three or four times?"

"That sounds about right," she said. "And, I guess I was curious. Do you mind if I pick your brain a little?"

Austin frowned. "About what?"

"Well, about why you're here. I mean, why did you choose this path?" She laughed at herself. "That sounded a little strange, maybe."

Austin stared at her. Stared through her. Mortified, Monti watched his eyes fill with tears. "Austin? I'm sorry...are you okay?" She glanced behind her down the hall. No one there.

He cleared his throat and leaned forward on his arms, gripping the handset. He glanced at Monti, and said so quietly she barely heard him, "It was inevitable, I guess."

"Inevitable?" She leaned in. "Why was it inevitable?"

"Because!" He smacked the table with a fist, making her jump. "Because my life is screwed up, okay? Always has been. Always will be."

Monti opened her mouth—then shut it on the pat reassurance she'd been about to blurt out. *Careful.* "Wow—always. You're what, eighteen?"

"Nineteen," he said.

"Nineteen. I get how your recent go-rounds with the law are screwing up your life now, but always?" She leaned toward him again. "How has it always been screwed up, Austin? Help me understand."

He looked at her then, his pale blue eyes searching hers, frowning, hesitating. She held his gaze, and her breath.

He nodded, having made a decision. "When I was five, on our way home from the playground my little brother Warren got mauled by a dog. I couldn't stop it."

Monti squeezed her eyes shut. *Just listen.* And she did. A flood of words poured out of Austin, about Warren's terrible scars, about his father abandoning them, his mother's drinking, her boyfriends, his step-dad. His overwhelming guilt at not being able to protect his brother...how his mother flung it in his face repeatedly over the years.

"I know it wasn't really my fault. I was only five, for crying out loud. But I heard it so many times I still kinda believe it, you know?"

Monti nodded. "Yeah, I know what you mean, Austin." She shifted in her chair. "Where's Warren now?"

"He's at home. I mean he's probably at school, but he lives at home with my dad and me."

"But, didn't you say your father left when you were little?" Monti seemed to have gotten her facts mixed.

"Yeah, yeah he did." Austin agreed. He sat straighter and jabbed the counter with his finger. "But I had to track him down, 'cuz my mother was wasted all the time." He grimaced. "She'd bring home these real losers, like, serious scumbags." He shrugged. "It wasn't safe for Warren, so I got ahold of my uncle Leroy and it took me a couple of months, but I found my dad."

Monti noted the careful pride in his voice. "How old were you— how long ago did you find him?" she asked.

"About four years ago," he said. "He came back right away when I called him. Like, he was here the next week. And at first it was great." Austin stared through the Plexiglas into the past. "He got this piddly little apartment, and we packed our junk and moved in with him." He snorted. "Mom didn't care. I don't even think she really noticed." He slid back down in his chair and scrubbed at his hair.

"Then, the funny thing is, mom got sober. One of the assholes she hooked up with beat her almost to death, and she spent a couple weeks in the hospital. She went from there to rehab, and she's been sober ever since."

"Wow, that's great!" Monti said. "Right?"

"Yeah, you'd think so, right? Except somehow things kept getting even more screwed up. She met this half-way decent guy—Brad—and they got married. Then they tried to get Warren and me to move back to live with them." He shook his head, a long slow swivel, over and over. "Brad's not a bad guy, you know? But Dad had kinda rescued us when things were real bad, and I would've felt guilty abandoning him after all he'd done for us. I mean he screwed up back in the day, but when he came back he was great. He worked hard. He kept us in groceries, bought us school clothes, made us do our homework, even went to parent teacher conferences. I couldn't just say thanks for everything and switch to Brad's team because Brad and Mom were renting a nice place and had a new car." He slammed his fist down on the counter again. "She didn't get that. And Warren wouldn't go without me."

Monti knew what had to happen next. "Who won custody?" she asked.

He blinked at her, surprised. He tilted his head and clenched his jaw. "Dad."

"Really! That's unusual. So, you got to stay with your dad...isn't that what you wanted?"

"Yeah, it was," he said, drawing out the words. "But I don't know what happened. It's like, Dad just stopped trying, which I don't understand because he'd been doing so well and we were really getting along and..." he swallowed hard, "we loved him. Warren and me, we love him."

A loud buzzer sounded and Monti jumped. "Five minutes, ma'am."

"Is that when you started screwing things up, finally?"

He stared at her, eyes weary. "Yeah, that's right. And about that time I destroyed my best friend's life, so that didn't help."

"What? What happened?" Monti asked.

Austin sighed deeply, exhausted at the very thought of telling that story, apparently. "Maybe another time, Mrs. R."

"Sure, okay. But that was the final straw, huh?"

"Pretty much. There wasn't gonna be a happy ending no matter what. And with the wisdom of maturity and perfect hindsight, I can now see I set out to piss off everybody I could, as bad as I could, in as many ways as I could." He flung his arm wide to encompass the visitation room and the entire jail. "And here I am. Again."

"And here you are. Success beyond your wildest dreams." The officer approached on Monti's right. "It looks like I have to go, Austin. But if I come back again will you tell me the rest?"

"Shit, I don't care," he said. "It's not a good story, I don't know why you want to hear it."

"I don't know either, but I do. So...will you tell me?"

"Sure. Whatever." He shrugged.

She stood and put a hand on the glass between them. "Okay, Austin," she said. "I'll be back next week. Anything I can bring for you?"

"Warren?"

She started to respond but he cut her off. "No, not really, I don't want him here." He hesitated. "Something new to read, though? That would be excellent."

Monti laughed, "Well, ask a teacher for something to read and you might be sorry! But okay, yes, I'll bring something for you to read." She didn't know what else to say. "Goodbye, Austin."

He unfolded himself from his chair and stood, suddenly shy. He stuck his hands in his pockets. "Thanks, Mrs. Rising."

Monti followed the deputy back down the hallway, collected her things from the plastic bin, and walked out into the clean, chill November air. She grabbed her phone to call Kit. One missed call. She pushed buttons until the name of the caller appeared— Unknown. That was helpful. But there was a message. She climbed into her Subaru and carefully touched the right icons to play back the message.

Her heart did a serious wham-thump in her chest when she heard the voice. She gritted back a howl of disbelief. Marla. Seven plus years with no contact except Noelle's birthday cards, and now she had missed a call from her daughter. She smacked the steering wheel. Not fair not fair not fair! What had Marla even said? Monti had no idea. She started the message playback again.

"Mom? It's me. I, uh...Mom can you call me?" A pause. "Please call me, Mom," in a whisper, and that was all.

Call her back now? Or wait until she was home with Kit? No, she couldn't possibly wait. Monti's hands shook so hard she hit a wrong button and growled with frustration as she cycled through several wrong screens before getting back to the right one. Return call. *Please, Abba.*

Refuge

As the afternoon sun slanted gold through the fragrant summer air, Bo looped his arm through Anisette's and led her to her garden haven. She admired the finished stonework. The arched openings in the walls all around echoed the entrance archway, and light would always flood into the refuge from one direction or another. Bo had ordered and installed a beautiful stone bench opposite the entrance. As the final step, this morning he had loosened a big patch of soil in the center of the enclosure, removed the rocks and grass, and ringed the area with the especially pretty stones he had set aside during the building of the wall. He'd also prepared a generous swath of dirt all around the inside of the wall.

"I've readied these beds for you, beloved," he said. "Plant what you will to brighten the place. Then we may all enjoy its beauty on sunny days as well."

Anisette sat on the bench. "It's lovely, husband," she said. "Thank you."

"If there were aught else I could do, I would do it," he said, scrubbing one hand through his hair. "But Simon at the market tells me we are in for three weeks of clear weather before a single drop of rain shall fall. Thereupon I was thinking, and only if the idea delights you, of attempting again our picnic in the honey meadow. Only should you desire it."

Anisette smiled up at him. "Truly, husband, you were more distressed by that than was I." She thought on it for a moment. "Though 'twould be a good thing, perhaps, to exchange that dreadful memory for a fair one."

"A sweet thought, Anisette," Bo said. He sat beside her. "Tomorrow and the next day I must tend to the casking. But after that I have only my morning deliveries, leaving the remainder of the day for an outing." It was decided. When they told Tom he began bustling immediately, determined, apparently, to outdo his previous portable feast by beginning preparations two days before the meal would be needed.

Marla

"Mom?" a voice said when the call connected.

"Marla? Is that you, sweetie?" Monti choked up instantly and swallowed hard.

"Yeah, hi Mom," Marla said.

"I can't believe it! Where are you, honey? Are you all right?"

"Yeah, I'm fine Mom. I uh...I'm in rehab."

"Rehab. Well, that's..." Monti squeezed her eyes shut and forced back a sob. "That's good, right? You're getting some help for..." She shook her head. She had no idea what Marla needed help for. "Tell me about that, sweetie."

"I don't want to tell you on the phone, Mom." Marla sighed—a heavy, exhausted sound. "They said I had to call a family member before they'd sign off on the next step."

Monti tried not to feel she'd been punched in the gut. "That's all right, love. It's so good to hear your voice—to know you're okay. Are you almost finished there if they're signing things off? Can you come home? For Thanksgiving maybe? We'd love to see you—Noelle would love to see you..." Monti couldn't quite stop the sob there. She had to get a grip. She clenched her fist and took a deep breath.

"No, I can't, Mom. I have a few more weeks," Marla said. "But maybe...maybe December? I can't promise."

"Sure, sure, December would be great. Oh Marla, you could come for Christmas! Please...please consider coming for Christmas. Or any time before that—any time, really." Monti pressed the heel of her hand into her forehead. *Calm down.*

"Do you really think Noelle will want to be around me? And Dad..." Marla's voice thickened and shut down.

"Yes, love, we all want to see you, and we all love you more than we can bear. Please—whatever is making you hesitate—if I'm being too pushy I'm sorry. Please come home, Marla."

"I will. I probably will. I have to go now, Mom."

"Wait!" Panic paralyzed her—she couldn't think. "Wait. Can I reach you at this number?" Idiot question, she just did reach her at this number.

"Yes. No—it's complicated." Marla sighed again. "I'll call you again, okay?"

"Yes, yes okay, honey. Marla? Where are you, love?"

"I'm in Florida. I have to go now, Mom, really."

"All right..." It was going to kill her to hang up. "All right honey, I'll talk to you soon, though, okay? I love you so much."

"I love you too, Mom." And she was gone. Monti put down the phone, leaned her head on the steering wheel. A moment later she began trembling and great sobs tore through her until she thought she might throw up. Only after the tears were spent and she wiped her face with tissue after tissue did she think to thank God for such a miracle. But she did thank him while she started the Subaru, and while she maneuvered out into traffic, and all the way home to Kit. Thanked him and pleaded with him for more miracles, because she didn't have her baby girl home yet.

Monti pulled into the driveway on automatic pilot, her mind racing ahead to her conversation with Kit. She hauled her purse and tote bag up the kitchen steps and dumped them inside the door.

"Kit! Where are you, love?"

"In the den," came his voice from down the hall. She took one step in that direction only to be stopped by Gulliver winding around her legs. Monti picked him up as the quickest method of getting him out of her way, scratched his head and tossed him down again outside the doorway to the den. Kit sat in his ergo-chair, working on his laptop.

"Marla called!" she announced, and went to kiss her shocked husband.

"What? When? Where is she, is she okay?"

Monti laughed, sat down knee to knee with him and described the call in minute detail.

He soaked it in, shaking his head, grinning, leaning in. "Where in Florida?" He asked.

"I don't know."

"What kind of rehab? For drugs?"

"I don't know, I don't know, I don't care! We'll figure it all out when she calls again!"

"But her number is in your phone. We could call her..." Kit said.

They talked it over. Would they be allowed to talk with her? Would she retreat if they were too pushy? It was nerve-wracking.

"Oh!" Monti sat bolt upright. "I wonder if she's anywhere near Dad and Mom?" she said.

"One more thing we don't know," Kit said. "Monti..."

"I'll Google rehab centers in Florida. That take women. How many could there be?".

"Monti," Kit said again.

"Dad and Mom would be there in a heartbeat if they knew where she was," Monti said. "I have to call them anyway. They'll be so excited!"

"Monti, listen!" Kit grabbed her knee and wobbled it back and forth until he had her attention. "We have to tell Noelle."

"Oh, yes of course! She'll be thrilled!" She looked at her husband and suddenly wasn't so sure. "Won't she?"

Kit sat back in his chair. "Take off your coat and let's think it through. Of course she'll be glad to know her mom's okay." Monti stood and shrugged off her wool jacket. "But how many years has it been?" he said. "Seven...almost eight. It might be a little unsettling for her."

Monti hung her jacket on the back of her chair. "And you know what?" she said. "She's bound to get her hopes up that Marla will come home, and then what if she doesn't?" She plopped back down in her seat. "Oh Kit, it's gonna be okay, isn't it? She will come home, won't she?"

Kit shut his eyes for a long moment, then looked at her. "I sure do hope so, Monti." He touched her cheek. "But she might throw us a curve." She started to protest but he cut her off, "No, we have to consider the possibility, the real possibility, because we don't want Noelle hurt if she does. Any more than is inevitable." He took her hands in his. "Better ask for help on how to handle this, don't you think? Before we talk to Noelle or decide whether to try to call Marla."

"Oh I have been, but yeah, we'd better." Monti's shoulders sagged. She was suddenly exhausted. Still, a little giddy exhilaration kept bubbling up from deep inside her, threatening to fizz over. She leaned forward and tightened her grip on his hands. "Kit, wouldn't it be the best Christmas ever?"

Anty-Hex

B o poled the boat lazily up the river, a contented smile playing across his face. Today in the honey meadow had been as sweet as the previous trip had been horrifying. He let the punt bump gently against the dock, tied her off and gave a hand to Anisette. He hauled the still heavy basket out—Tom had packed even more food than the last time. Just in case, he said. They hadn't been able to put much of a dent in the provisions.

They walked into the kitchen and plopped down at the table, warm and drowsy from their long day in the summer sun.

"Tea?" Anisette said.

"No, nothing. Thank you, wife." Bo frowned. "Where's Tom got to, I wonder?"

As if in answer, the back door opened and shut, and the old man hobbled into the kitchen. He carried a small, burlap wrapped bundle, which he set gently on the table. "Good evening to you both," he said. "Had a fine day, did you?"

"We did, thank you," Bo said. "What have you there, old Tom?"

"Sumfin'," he said. "Sumfin' as may help our lady." His grin displayed comprehensively the state of his dental health. "Old widow Tarmin gave it me today."

"Widow Tarmin!" Bo frowned and sat up straight. "She never gave you anything."

"Well, no, not exactly gave, of course..."

"But Tom, Widow Tarmin. I'm surprised at you."

"Now, now, don't be hasty. We be looking for a anty-hex for our Anisette, ain't we?" He began untying the twine around his bundle. He pulled it loose and quickly wound it into a ball, which he secreted in a pocket. The burlap fell away from an ancient, grimy glass bottle.

Bo's frown deepened. "And what might that be, exactly?"

"I told you, an anty-hex potion," Tom said. He looked from Bo to Anisette and back, and seemed taken aback by their marked lack of enthusiasm. "She said it were sure against any hex about trees."

"You told her about Anisette? Tom, what were you thinking? She'll have it noised all over town before sunset," Bo said. Tom's brow furrowed, and he bristled and spluttered a bit, but Bo's words must have percolated through his brain, because he gave up bristling and spluttering and wilted most pathetically.

"Tom," Bo said more gently, "Tom, old friend. I cannot give Anisette a potion from Widow Tarmin. She sells bait to poison dogs and rats. And people, I doubt not. I would never risk it." He laid a hand on the old man's shoulder. "Your heart is generous big, and I am true touched by your love for our Anisette. But surely you see...we cannot risk to give her such a potion."

Tom slumped further. He nodded but didn't speak. Anisette rose and went to him. "Thank you, dear Tom," she said, laying her soft hand upon his arm. "Do not fret on it. All will be well. I care not a farthing for Widow Tarmin's gossip." She patted him. "I shall fix you a hot cup of tea, shall I not? You sit down now and let me get it." She set about heating the kettle and getting the tea things. "'Twas a wondrous feast you sent with us this morning. Especially the conserve, it was most delicious. Will you teach me to make it, Tom?"

Bo watched his old friend slowly recover as she talked, firming up like a garden in the rain after a long dry spell. He smiled to himself. His dear Anisette worked a sweet anty-hex of her own, with an elixir of pure goodwill.

Noelle

Monti, cleaning veggies for a salad, heard Noelle's car pull into the driveway behind her Subaru and quickly dried her hands. She had no idea how this conversation was going to go, and she was feeling a little wobbly in the middle.

Noelle and Jenny giggled as they came through the kitchen door and dropped their backpacks on the floor. Gulliver, with his deep and undeniable need to be the center of everyone's universe, flopped onto his back in front of them and batted at their feet, causing the giggling to be about him. He risked getting fatally squashed as the girls tripped over him and themselves and their backpacks until Jenny picked him up. "Silly cat," she said, and scratched his ears while he licked her hair.

"Hi Grandma," Noelle said. She came and gave Monti a hug and kiss. "What's up?" she asked, her arms locked around Monti but leaning back to look into her face. Monti froze in place. Noelle said, "Grandma?"

"Hey sweetie. Uh, how was school?".

Noelle narrowed her eyes and peered at Monti with suspicion. At that moment Kit showed up to rescue her, as he always did.

"What your grandmother is trying to say, Nellie, is that your mom called today," he said. He joined the hug and kissed Noelle on the top of her head.

Noelle dropped her arms and took a step backward. "What?"

"Way to break it to her gently, Grandpa," Monti said.

"It's not bad news, Monti." He lowered himself onto a stool. "Your mom called Monti today. She's okay, and she's in Florida."

Noelle plopped down on the breakfast nook bench still in her coat, eyes wide and mouth open. "Florida?"

Jenny let Gulliver down and went to Noelle, held her hand and nudged her. Noelle automatically scooted over to let Jenny slide in beside her. Monti turned the soup off, sat on the other bench, and recounted her conversation with Marla.

When she finished, everyone was quiet for a minute. "But you didn't call her back yet? Can we do that now?"

"I think we have to wait for her to call back, sweetheart," Kit said.

Noelle frowned. "Okay. Did she say when she would call back?"

"No, love. It's complicated, I guess," Monti said. "Lots of rules in rehab."

"Oh," Noelle said. A thick silence hung for a moment. "But rehab...that's good, right?"

"Sure it is, sweetheart," Kit said. "She's getting help, and she's sticking with it."

"And when she's done, she'll come home. She can have my room, Jenny and I will share—"

"Now love, don't." Monti put her hand on Noelle's. "Don't count on her coming home. She might not, you know."

"Of course she will! Why would she call if she wasn't going to come home?" Noelle broke into tears now, as Monti had known she must at any moment.

Monti stood up and looked a plea at Jenny, who got out of the way and let Monti slide in and gather her granddaughter into her arms. "It'll work out, love." She stroked the long blonde hair, so like Marla's. "It'll all work out."

Jenny silently gathered the girls' bags and hauled them upstairs. Kit finished the salad and he and Jenny set the table. By then Noelle had recovered and agreed that dinner sounded pretty good. But she didn't eat and was largely oblivious to the conversation around the table.

After dinner the girls retreated upstairs to study, leaving Kit and Monti to bring each other up to date on their separate musings while they cleaned up the kitchen. They both had been thinking of Marla during dinner, and all the possibilities and complications her homecoming might bring.

They had plenty of room for her, but what would Marla do if she came home? They didn't know if she was ready to go out and find a job, or would need to hole up at home for a while. She was 43, nearly 44. Her birthday was two weeks after Noelle's. Did she have any plans or dreams, or were they all smashed? Would she let them help her? Would she come at all?

"I wish we could call her, Kit. The suspense is going to kill me. Even if she won't come, that's better than not knowing."

He nodded. "I agree," he said, rinsing the silverware. "Even when she calls back, if she calls back, I wonder how much we should trust what she says. In the past she hasn't been reliable."

"True. There are lots of places where this whole dream could break down. Do dreams break down? Where this whole...scenario...what would break down? A plan? A vision, a scheme? A car, obviously, but that doesn't fit."

"Monti," Kit said. "You're babbling." He took the dishtowel from her, dried his hands with it and pulled her in close. "It will all work out. She'll call, and she'll come home and we'll adjust to each other and learn how to be a family again. Or she won't come, and we'll be heartbroken again and then carry on praying for her to get her head straight."

Monti laid her forehead on his chest. "I know what you're going to say next," she said. "We have to keep it together and make sure Noelle doesn't get damaged."

"Yeah, something along those lines. And she has that scholarship essay competition tomorrow."

"Oh gosh, yes, I forgot all about that." Monti checked the calendar on the wall. "I wonder if she forgot?"

"I don't think so. Jenny mentioned it while we were setting the table. Noelle worked on some rough drafts of possible topics this afternoon." He kissed the top of her head, then tilted her chin up and smiled at her. "You want a game?"

Monti sighed. "I don't think so, lover. I'm wiped, to use my students' inelegant phrase. I doubt I could string more than three letters together, and don't you dare say 'so how would that be different than usual' or I'll smack you."

Kit chuckled and rubbed her shoulders. "Smacking, is it? I don't really think that would be appropriate behavior in an elder's wife, do you?"

"Mmmm." Monti leaned her head on Kit's chest again, loving the shoulder rub. "Don't tell me there's some Appropriate Behavior list I didn't know about. I'm doomed. I'm epic fail. Can I just go to bed and think about that tomorrow?" She looked up at him and offered her lips for a kiss.

"Bed sounds great," he agreed, and kissed her. They walked arm in arm down the hall to their room and closed the door behind them.

Almonds

The day dawned grey and Anisette mourned the departure of the long stretch of sunny weather. No more picnics in the honey meadow for a while. She wandered into the kitchen, poured a mug of coffee and went to find Bo. He and Tom sat in office finalizing the selection of mead Bo planned to enter in the upcoming faire competition, but Anisette could not attend to the conversation. She wandered out again, looking for something to put her hands to.

Clouds piled in thick heaps as the morning wore on and she grew more restless. She sensed the rain before she heard it and made her way to the back door, leaving her stockings and shoes just inside. Old Tom realized what was afoot and toddled out, his face creased and pale, but found Anisette already planted in her bower and heavy rain pelting her long, narrow leaves.

Tom stood in the rain examining the almond tree that was Anisette. He walked slowly around the ten-foot-tall plant growing where none had been an hour before. It very nearly filled the enclosure he and Bo had built. The branches hung low, loaded with ripening fruit. Some few of the drupes were split, and had Tom seen this anywhere else he would have plucked a handful to peel, crack open, and eat. But though his mind registered 'almonds,' the cruelest torture could not have forced him to break a single fruit from the smallest branch.

Bo jogged up the drive, hunched against the rain, and came to join Tom in the garden.

"Look at her," the old man said. "She's beautiful, ain't she? I mayen't hardly take it in."

Bo took the tour round the tree that Tom had just finished. He'd seen this before, but 'twas hardly easy to believe, even so. "Ripe almonds," he said. "In the honey meadow, her drupes were tight and green." He glanced at Tom. The old man shivered in the cold rain. "Tom! Please go in the house. You'll catch a deathly chill standing out here."

"*And you won't?*" Tom retorted. "*I clearly remember Mistress begging you not to stay out in the rain with her, do I not?*" Bo dismissed that with a wave. "*No, master Bo, I won't be ignored in this matter. I shall have mistress Anisette to answer to if you should take ill, shan't I? You come in, too!*" Bo looked at his old friend, chin stuck out and determined to have his way.

"*All right, Tom. I'll come too,*" he said. He ran his hands lightly over a bough or two. "*Fare well, my love,*" he said, and turned to follow Tom into the house.

Escalation

Monti dreamed she was making supper and dropped her mother's crystal salad bowl. It fell to the tile floor and exploded into a million pieces. She started sobbing. Kit shook her and she woke up. "What, was I crying? I had a bad..."

"Sshh. No. I heard a crash in the living room," he said, very low and breathing heavily. "I don't think I can get up without your help."

Monti's heart leaped about. "In the house?" she whispered. "What was it?" She got out of bed and threw on her robe and slippers, then came around to help Kit. A nearby car revved its engine and peeled out.

"I'm not sure. It sounded like glass breaking."

"Should I call the police?" she said. She put a shoulder under his arm and helped him sit up.

He drew in his breath sharply and gripped her arm. "Give me a second," he said, gritting his teeth. "You'd better dig around in the closet for that cane Charlie brought me."

Monti stared at Kit, shocked and afraid. The cane had heretofore been a forbidden subject. He must be in terrible pain. She hurried to find it. She rummaged wildly until the cane fell out and smacked her on her skinned knee. She grabbed it and limped back to the bed.

"Do you want a pain pill?" she asked him.

"Not yet. I want to get to the living room." Monti helped him with his robe and slippers, and then to stand. He wobbled, but got the cane in place and stabilized. Footsteps pattered above them. The girls were awake. Kit slid open his nightstand drawer and retrieved his service pistol. He checked it over and slipped it into his robe pocket.

The two made their way down the hall, one careful step at a time, until they reached the two steps down into the living room. The street lamp outside made a ghost of the front window curtains gently billowing in the chill breeze. Shards of glass shimmered in the light, a chaotic constellation cast across the living room floor.

"Grandma?" came a stage whisper from the top of the stairs.

Monti turned. "You girls stay up there. There's broken glass all over the floor down here."

"What happened?" Noelle said.

"We're not sure yet. We'll let you know."

Kit had maneuvered the steps and now examined the broken window. He turned from the gaping hole in the fractured pane, and looked into the shadows at the back of the room. "Turn the light on, Monti."

She did. "You've got to be kidding me," she said. At the far end of the living room lay a sizable rock with a paper attached to it, just like in the movies if you allowed for duct tape instead of string.

"Hang on, I'll get the broom and clear a path," she said. She swept up the glass, and Kit retrieved the rock. He lowered himself onto the settle.

"Monti, one of those pills now, I think."

When she returned with pill and water he had the tape off and was unfolding the paper. He read it and grunted. "I guess it's time to call the police."

Faire

A troupe of musicians whirled by, pipes trilling, tambourines jangling. Their bright costumes sparkled with shiny bits in the late afternoon sun. Anisette twirled and scanned the sky all round. Not a single cloud even yet marred the pale blue heavens. The heady aroma of roasted meat made her draw in deep breaths. She tried to take it all in and her head whirled like the troupe's dancers.

Bo smiled down at her. "What about a bite to eat, love?" he said. "I see they've lifted the boar from the roasting pit, and my mouth waters." Anisette nodded and looped her arm through his. They strolled toward the huge blue-and-white striped pavilion filled with rough benches and tables. They progressed slowly, as they stopped to admire the colorful wares in booths along the way, and had to dodge this way and that around thick knots of faire goers.

"How long until the prizes are announced?" Anisette asked. Bo glanced at the sun.

"Another hour, mayhap," he said. "Plenty of time to fill our bellies afore that." Bo lifted his wife lightly and stepped over a great lout stretched out on the turf before them, snoring loudly. "He's filled his belly with ale instead of pork, I think."

They joined the queue at the pavilion and watched the world go by as they inched forward. Ragged beggars, lords and ladies holding their finery above the muddying grass, gangs of filthy and deliriously happy children, staggering drunks, lovers arm in arm, the occasional juggler or roving seller of exotic novelties; a wondrous parade of people it was every moment.

In no time at all they arrived at the head of the line. Bo handed two coins to a frazzled, red-cheeked woman behind the table, and received two wooden trenchers. He passed one to Anisette. They presented them to the cook for great slices of juicy pork, and then piled them with bread and fruit and pickles and corn and sweets from the long buffet. A mustachioed giant of a man handed them mugs of ale and they threaded their way to an open spot at one of the tables.

"I've never been amongst so many folk," Anisette said in a low voice. "The noise is astonishing." Bo took two knives and spoons wrapped in a huge linen napkin from his pocket. Old Tom had tucked them there this morning before he shooed them out the door.

"Aye," her husband said. "And it only gets louder as the day goes on. And wilder. We won't stay long after the prizes are awarded. The risk grows large after sunset."

They ate for a few minutes in silence. The crowds provided ample entertainment as they worked through their dinner. After a while Anisette stared at the heap of food still on her plate. She would burst if she ate another bite. Bo lifted her plate and stacked it on top of his, and finished what she hadn't eaten. They wiped their hands and faces on the napkin and Bo cleaned the cutlery before wrapping and stowing it back in his pocket.

"Ready, love?" he said. "We might walk toward the stage and find a fair spot from which to watch the ceremony."

"Surely," she said. A thrill of anticipation somersaulted in her stomach. Bo was competing for a prize in Spirits and Ales. After several years of second or third prizes, he badly wanted to win first place. He'd told her the token monetary award mattered little, but if he won, the boost to his reputation as a mead maker would help business tremendously. He and Tom had had their heads together for days selecting what to enter. This morning Tom had packed the chosen bottles with tender care and charged Bo to drive gently. Every bottle had survived the journey unbroken, and upon their arrival at the faire Bo had handed them over to the panel of judges with solemn pride.

They would soon hear what the judges thought of Bo's best mead.

Busness

Grandma, can we come down now?" Noelle called from the top of the stairs. Monti peered up at the two young women perched on the top step, arms around each other's waists, looking like little girls in their jammies and fuzzy slippers.

"Sure, come on down. How about putting the kettle on, Noelle. I need some peppermint tea.".

"Okay. What happened, though?" Noelle said.

"Somebody threw a big old rock through the front window. How stupid is that?" Monti grabbed the cordless phone and joined Kit on the settle.

"What's it say?" Monti asked. Kit handed her the note and took the phone. She examined the penciled missive and read it aloud. "You should mind your own busness. No signature." She looked at her husband. "I don't feel like a bus, do you?"

"Get me Detective Price's card from the kitchen, will you Monti?" Kit said, ignoring her possibly inappropriate attempt at humor in the middle of—whatever this was. She fetched the card from the kitchen bulletin board. Noelle and Jenny followed her back into the living room.

Noelle saw the paper in Kit's hand. "There was a note? Who's it from?"

"No signature." Monti said. "But not too many people have adopted an angry and posturing threaten toward us lately, so the field of sendable probbers is small pretty, don't you think?"

"What?" Jenny said.

"She means Blaine probably sent it," Noelle said. "She has a hard time talking straight when she's stressed."

"I do?" Monti said. She sat down, folded her hands and pondered this idea for a moment. "You may be right, Granddaughter. I seem to remember my mother telling me to stop spouting nonsense more than a few times, usually when I was trying not to cry."

"Girls, how about going to the kitchen to discuss Monti's personality abnormalities," Kit said. "I need to hear, here."

"Hear, hear," Monti said, throwing up a fist and standing up again. The kettle whistled. She followed the girls back into the kitchen.

"Are you trying not to cry now?" Jenny said.

"Did he say 'abnormalities'?" Monti asked. She turned the kettle off. Her hands were shaking again. She fixed tea for herself and Kit, and left the girls discussing whether two a.m. was a suitable time to eat leftover huckleberry muffins.

"No, no signature." Kit said into the phone. "Yes, I'm being careful about that now, but I didn't think of it until after I'd already picked it up and unwrapped the note. All right, we'll be here."

"Careful about what?" Monti said, handing Kit his tea.

"Fingerprints," he said.

Monti thought of several possible responses to this, but decided she'd already been abnormal enough for one night. "They're on their way, huh?"

He nodded. They sipped in silence for a minute.

"It's escalating, isn't it," she said quietly.

He looked her in the eye and nodded again.

Noelle and Jenny returned bearing muffins on a plate. Everyone had a muffin to go with their tea, as if it were the middle of the afternoon instead of the middle of the night.

"Do we want to know what the note says?" Noelle asked. Monti looked at Kit, not trusting herself to answer sensibly.

"Mind your own busness," Kit said.

"Busness?" Jenny said. "Oh...what an idiot." A patrol car pulled into the driveway, and Monti went to let the police in.

Splendiferous

Bo and Anisette basked in the pale morning sun shining through the window, nursing one last mug of coffee. Bo glowed with contentment, the satisfaction of last evening's contest keeping a smile on his face since the moment he woke. And that made Anisette smile.

Tom burst into the kitchen, wild-eyed. "Master Bo!" he said. "There uh, there be visitors walking up the lane."

"Well, so be it. What ails you, man?"

"The visitors is, at least, they be a mite unusual hereabouts, sir."

Bo raised his eyebrows. "What, two heads?" He grinned at Tom. "No? Green skin?"

Tom jumped at that and narrowed his eyes. "Not precisely, no," he said, and clamped his mouth shut.

Bo and Anisette exchanged a glance as Bo stood to greet their mysterious visitors, who must by this time be at the door. A knock sounded that moment.

Bo, smiling, opened the door. Then he took an involuntary step back at the splendiferous sight before him. A man his own size stood at his door, arrayed in a glorious green and yellow robe, a dazzle of rich patterns sparked with gold threads. He gripped a tall walking staff topped with a carved lion head, and his skin was black as ebony. A beautiful, smiling woman stood at his shoulder, her robes dazzling in their own right.

The man bowed. "Mister Bo Willem?" he asked.

"Aye," Bo said. "May I be of help to you, sir? Madam?"

"That is my hope," the man said, and bowed again.

"Truly?" Bo said. "Then please come in, and I will do my best." Bo ushered them into the house. Anisette stood as they walked into the kitchen and curtsied, her eyes widening at the unexpected magnificence standing in her kitchen. Tom shifted from foot to foot and fiddled with his pipe. "My wife, Anisette, and our family retainer, Tom."

Bo pulled out the heavy oak chair with carved arms that sat at the head of the table, motioned for their visitor to sit, and held another chair for the lady. Anisette silently made another pot of coffee and handed Tom a seedcake from the pantry to unwrap and slice. He needed something to do to stop him shifting and staring.

Bo sat, too. "What manner of help may I be to you, mister...ah?"

"My name is Tumaini. This is my lady wife, Safia. We attended the festival this past day, and I was invited to taste your excellent mead. I wish to consult you on establishing a honey meadow in Morocco, and learn your methods, as you produce such a fine spirit."

"Why, I thank you, Mr. Tumaini. Where might Morocco be, exactly?"

"It is in the north of Africa, my friend. It is a place vastly different from this, but with its own beauty and bounty. I am stationed there as ambassador from Egypt."

"I would be honored to share what I have learned over the years, but I know not how well my methods will work in Africa. It is very dry, is it not?"

"Quite."

Bo frowned and thought of the usual weather that made his honey meadow bloom luxuriously. But surely not all flowers needed the same amount of rain. "Do flowers grow there, in Morocco?" he asked.

"Why, certainly," Tumaini said. "Many flowers, though not the ones I see in this country. Some few here I recognize, but ours are in large part much different."

"But they are pollinated by bees, yes? You have bees?"

A rich, soft laugh filled the kitchen. "Of course, yes, we have bees. I have traveled many lands, and cannot recall a place without bees."

"Is that so?" Bo reddened. His experience and knowledge were limited, he realized. He knew virtually nothing about the world beyond his own region. No matter, he was not too proud to learn, and the man had come to him for advice, after all. "Well, then, where there are bees and flowers I know nary a reason a fine honey meadow cannot be established."

Anisette served their guests, then sat beside Safia. The woman took Anisette's hand in hers and said, "Thank you, my lady friend, for your sweet welcome." Her smile brightened the sunny room.

The four sat long over coffee and seed cake, getting to know each other and exploring ideas for growing a honey meadow in the desert. Tom could not relax enough to sit with them, so Anisette kept him busy refilling cups and plates. At length Bo and Tumaini agreed a tour of Bo's mead-making setup was in order. The men stood.

"Would you come, Safia?" Tumaini asked, holding his hand to his wife.

"Oh yes, surely," she said, placing her hand in his. She turned to Anisette. "And thee? Anisette?" She pronounced the name carefully.

Anisette nodded, and the four strolled out the back door like old friends.

An hour later Bo and Anisette wiped their feet and came in the back door alone. They looked at each other, nonplussed. By the time they'd finished their tour, Bo had agreed to travel to Morocco to help Tumaini establish a honey meadow there. "I could not have predicted that result from a first prize in Spirits and Ales," he said. "It's a wonder."

"It is. Morocco! I'd hardly heard the name before today!"

"Neither I," he said.

"And I thought their robes the most magnificent things I've ever seen. They were dressed like royalty." She stopped, her cheeks suddenly pale. "Are they royalty?"

"I've no idea. He called himself an ambassador, but they could be, I suppose."

"We should go and find Tom," Anisette said. "He was so flummoxed I could scarce keep from laughing at the poor soul. We must tell him it's safe to come out from wherever he's hidden himself."

No Fretting

Monti took off her robe. The bedside clock glowed three a.m... The officers had recorded Kit and Monti's statements about what had happened, urged them yet again to be vigilant, eaten a muffin each and driven away with the rock and the note. Kit and Noelle had taped a big flattened cardboard box over the hole in the window while Jenny rinsed the tea mugs and Monti went over the living room floor with a damp mop to get up the tiny slivers of glass the broom missed.

The girls were safely back upstairs, and Monti climbed into bed. She lay exhausted and wide awake. Kit moved restlessly. "You okay?" she asked.

"Been better. Been worse."

"Need anything?"

"How about sleep? Any chance of that?" he said, a touch of sharpness in his tone. He lay flat on his back, knees bent over the cylindrical bolster he only resorted to when his back was badly aggravated. She touched his cheek.

"Well, not for me I don't think," Monti said. "I'll clear out and read in the living room for a bit."

"No, you don't need to do that," he said, his voice softer.

"But I'll toss and turn and bounce the bed and keep you awake," she said.

"Come here." He raised one arm and she rolled over and laid her head on his shoulder. "Just relax for a few minutes. You might sleep."

"I doubt it. Too many worst-case scenarios chasing each other through my head. Marla-Blaine-Thanksgiving-Marla-Blaine-Thanksgiving."

"But you're not fretting about them, right Monti?" He squeezed her shoulder. "And why is Thanksgiving a worst-case scenario?"

She sighed. "What will that boy try next? How do we keep the girls safe? When will Marla call again?" She whomped the comforter with her fist. "It's not fair."

"Right, no fretting," he said. "Listen, Monti. I have something I want to try."

"You're going to find out where he lives and throw a rock through his window?"

"No..."

"We're going to hire a PI to find Marla and go get her?"

"Tempting," he said. "But what I have in mind is an old-fashioned conversation."

"With who? Marla?"

"No, with Blaine. Or his father, or with both of them. As far as I know, there's no law against talking with the person who's committing crimes against you."

"But, hopefully he'll be back in jail soon," Monti said.

"Then I'll talk with him there. I want to understand what the kid is after, like you wanted to get inside Austin's head. Maybe I can clear up anything he's misunderstanding about Jenny. He seems a little young to be a hardened sociopath...something is making him feel threatened."

"Jenny thinks he was afraid she would try to get money, like child support, from him."

"Right. But then there's this mystery man involved too, for some reason, which makes me think it might be something else." Kit adjusted the bolster and grimaced. "I need to talk to his father first, I think. See what their relationship is like. If the people involved in these tangles would take the time to figure out why everyone is doing what they're doing, it might go a long way toward untangling them."

Monti raised herself up on one elbow. "You are the most incredible optimist I've ever met, Kit Rising," she said, and kissed him.

"Hmph. No fair kissing a helpless cripple like that. Maybe you had better clear out and go read."

"No way, José," she said, and snuggled back into his shoulder. "I'm awfully comfy right here. I'll just lie here and think of best-case scenarios for a while."

She was snoring softly within thirty seconds.

Topsy-turvy

J osiah Wheaton stopped regularly at the Willems' home. Each time he accepted a glass of mead or a mug of coffee, and gave an account of the new avenues
he'd explored toward a cure for Anisette. There were never any results to engender
hope. Occasionally Bo or old Tom or, more rarely, Anisette would lay before the
preacher some possibility of which they'd heard. Over time they all grew familiar
with the usual character of the touted cures.

Of tonics to take internally there seemed to be a universal recipe. Obtain one
or two obscure and preferably costly ingredients, steep them in a base of alcohol,
and add various herbs and one or more disgusting animal parts or excretions.
Spin a dark tale of its origins and charge an exorbitant price and you had a con-
coction irresistible to suffering folk.

Mysterious rituals intended to reverse hexes varied somewhat more, but a
surprising number featured moonlight, walking backwards, and disgusting substances like to those in the terrible tonics. They still mentioned the newest candi-
dates to the preacher, but even old Tom could no longer be duped into paying out
good coin for such quackery.

One Tuesday afternoon Josiah arrived at the house to find old Tom incoher-
ent in his greeting at the door. Inside, Bo and Anisette sat pale and shaken.

"Whatever is amiss, dear friends?" he asked.

Bo stared at his pastor, his eyes wild. "Josiah," he said, "what shall we do?"

"About what, my good man?" Josiah said, quite alarmed.

"Anisette is with child." Bo looked to his wife, as if he needed to have her confirm this yet again. She nodded, a little wild herself.

"Why, that's wonderful, man!" Josiah said. "Wha..." and then it sank in.
"Oh. Oh my." The four sat at the table in their separate silences for some moments. At length Josiah shook himself and remembered his duty to his distraught
friends. "How long have you known?"

"*Anisette consulted with goodwife Hannah this morning and they reasoned it out between them.*" *He took Anisette's hand in his.* "*We've not been able to think aright since then. We know not what harm may come to a babe should it rain, as it no doubt must sometime in a nine-month space.*" *He asked his pastor again,* "*Whatever shall we do?*"

"*Why, Bo Willem, what can you mean? There is naught for you to do but pray and hope, and take the tenderest care of your young wife.*"

"*But if it rains...*"

"*Bo.*" *Josiah brow grew thundery.* "*What manner of things might go awry during any lying in?*"

"*What? Diverse things. Many. And so?*"

"*And so, why should you expect to be exempt from the possibility? You have but a unique item to add to the list, is all. God will bring the babe to birth or He will not, as He sees fit. Is that not always the way of it?*"

"*Why, of course, but...*" *Bo crinkled his forehead. He gripped his hair. He held his breath and pondered. At last he let it out.* "*Why yes, of course, that is the way of it. Why did I not see that before?*" *He turned to Anisette.* "*Why did we not see that?*"

"*I...I cannot account for it!*" *she said.*

Josiah chuckled and they both turned to stare at him. He held up his hand. "*Forgive me, I do not mean to make light of your bewilderment. But you are such a picture of what I have seen a thousand times. We trust God, we say. Then our world goes topsy-turvy and we cannot even remember God exists in the face of whatever giant thing now looms o'er us.*" *He shook his head and smiled at his friends.* "*Take in a deep breath or two and the world will begin to right itself again.*"

"*Except I never knew a bairn to do aught but make everything topsy-turvy from morn' till night,*" *Tom said.*

"*Yea, and all through the night, too,*" *Josiah said.*

"*Right you be,*" *cackled the old man.* "*Why Bo, I remember one time when yourself was a tiny babe, you'd taken ill and was spewing your tiny guts out everywhere...and ye had the entire household up running about with candles in the wee dark hours o' the morning, making up tonics and comfits and washing baby and bed, and floors and walls!*"

After that, Bo and Anisette got a thorough and scarifying report on what they might expect as Tom and Josiah recalled tale after tale of havoc wreaked on peaceful lives by the smallest of infants.

We Love Her

Monti was still groggy from their shattered night. She'd risen early and seen Noelle off—Jenny was sleeping in—but was having trouble progressing to "awake." She pushed the start button on the coffee maker and wiped up the spilled grounds, wondering randomly how many pounds of never-brewed coffee she'd rinsed down the sink over the years.

Kit had the newspaper spread across the breakfast table, but gazed out the window.

"What?" she said. No response. "Kit?"

He gradually focused and finally looked at her. "Hmm?"

"Penny for your thoughts."

"Okay," he said. "You have the number Marla called from, right?"

"Yes, it's in my phone." She tilted her head at him. "Why?"

"What say we give it a ring?"

"Really?"

"Sure, what harm can it do?"

"Absolutely, let's do it!" Monti hurried down the hall and fetched her phone before he changed his mind. She sat down across from him and pushed her phone toward him as tiny squirrels did somersaults in her tummy.

"Ready?" Kit asked. She nodded. Kit found the recent calls and touched the line Monti had labeled 'Marla.' Monti sent up a silent 'help!' prayer and watched Kit listen to the phone ring. And ring and ring. Finally, some other-than-ringing noises leaked out of the phone and they both perked up. Kit cleared his throat.

But it was an answering machine. Kit's shoulders sagged and he said, "Hello, this is Kit Rising trying to reach Marla Garret. If possible, please tell Marla that her mother and I, and her daughter Noelle would like to speak with her, and that we love her. Here are several numbers at which we can be reached..." and Kit reeled off, in a clear and measured tone, all three of their cell numbers. He ended the call and set down the phone.

They sat looking at each other, the cold morning light pouring through the kitchen window revealing their clenched hands and tense jaws.

"Well, it was worth a try." Kit straightened, placed both palms flat on the table. Monti watched him gather himself, mustering what was needed to push himself up from the bench. "Time for the next thing, I guess."

They worked at next things together and separately. Jenny appeared for coffee and another muffin, then disappeared back upstairs. Kit and Monti were back at the table working out a Thanksgiving menu when the front door closed and Gulliver launched himself from Monti's lap toward the sound. By the time Monti decided she was, miraculously, not gashed from hip to knee, Noelle had appeared in the kitchen doorway clutching the cat, her mascara in a mess down her cheeks. Kit was on his feet instantly.

"What happened, Noelle?" he said. He moved to envelop her in his long arms.

"Nothing," she said. But she dropped the cat, hugged her grandpa and burst into tears.

Solicitude

Westhaven enjoyed a remarkably long and sunny autumn that year. The flowers in Anisette's bower garden continued to bloom as if it were July. Old Tom waited on his mistress hand and foot, loathe to allow her to bear the slightest burden or even to stoop to cut flowers for the vase on the kitchen table. She stifled her frustration and allowed him to pamper her.

When Bo returned from tending the bees or delivering mead he spoiled her just as much, and between them it seemed they had determined she shouldn't lift a finger for the next several months. Anisette tried to relax into this gentle care. Heaven knew she had never enjoyed so much solicitude for her wellbeing in her entire life. She endeavored to accept her new family's concern as a sweet gift from God.

She challenged herself to find handiwork that didn't send the men scurrying to help or prevent her. She read for hours. She wrote to her old nurse. And of course, there were many tiny items to stitch in preparation for the baby's arrival. To needlework they did not object.

She sought goodwife Hannah's advice on how many blankets, diapers, gowns and caps she should set by. Bo had Mistress Blackwell send a girl round with a selection of fabrics and notions, and Anisette chose what she liked. The girl did not urge her to excess as her mistress had, for which Anisette was grateful, though her cheeks yet burned at the memory.

She was selecting fabrics and flosses for the christening gown when a sudden splat of rain on the roof jolted her to her feet. Skeins of thread scattered and a bolt of white lawn rolled across the floor as she lurched to the back door. Shoes and stockings she pulled off at the threshold, and ran to her rock-walled haven.

TOM HURRIED OUT TO inspect her. Nothing appeared amiss. Bo examined her too, when he came from the sheds. She looked just the same, excepting her almonds were nearly all ripe now. The rain continued through the afternoon. Bo and Tom worked at indoor tasks; repairing casks and tallying sales. Bo tried to plan what still needed to be done before winter set in, but his head was muddled. Neither man voiced his worry, and the silence sat thick and dark between them.

At sunset Bo stepped out into the slackening rain to say goodnight, and when he went in again he set a lantern in the window facing Anisette. She might not be able to truly see it, but it gave him comfort. The men ate a silent meal, cleaned up and turned in early. Bo fell into anxious sleep, dreaming of lightning strikes and errant axes.

Next morning the early sun shot bright sideways beams through the windows. Bo woke fully in an instant, leaped into his trousers and dashed for the back door. The almond tree sparkled in the sun. He ducked back inside long enough to don a heavy shirt and his boots, and to grab a towel. Then he ran out to the enclosure.

"Good morning, beloved. I hope you are well." He dried off the bench and sat down to wait. The stone bench was cold but the sun peeked from the clouds and warmed his face. He was struck with an idea. He jumped up and stepped to the tree. Grasping a branch in each hand, he shook them gently, creating a shower of droplets. He grinned. He grasped two more branches and shook off the rain. This time several drupes fell off and dropped to the ground. Bo froze. That would not have hurt Anisette, would it? He bent and collected all the fallen fruit in his big hand, and set it on the bench. No more shaking of branches.

He sat and studied the split drupes. The seeds within were large and well formed. He could not bring himself to peel away the rind, let alone crack the shell to examine the almond within. That could wait. Unless—would the fruit disappear when Anisette returned to herself?

Tom came out then, bearing two mugs of steaming coffee, and sat beside Bo. "How does she seem this morning, master Bo?"

"As well as a tree may be," Bo answered, and took the offered mug.

"What have you there?" Tom said.

Bo reddened. "I thought to speed her return by shaking the rain off her branches and some fruit fell to the ground. It will not have hurt her, do you think?"

"Who can tell?" Tom looked at Bo's stricken face and hastened to add, *"But not much, surely. 'Tis only natural, after all, for ripe fruit to fall from a tree. Do not fret on it, Bo."* Bo did not seem reassured. *"Come in and help me get a breakfast cooked. We shall bring it out here to eat. Come, Bo."* He stood and tugged at the sleeve of his immovable master.

Bo rose slowly. *"All right, old Tom,"* he said. *"We shall do as you say."*

Tom and Bo clomped around in the kitchen, muttering and bumping into each other and the furniture. An egg splatted on the clean flagstone floor. Bo burned his fingers and Tom stubbed his toe. The oven smoked, the milk sloshed and escaping biscuits rolled across the table. A jam pot teetered on the edge of disaster and was rescued at the last moment by Anisette.

"M'lady!" Tom said. *"You are restored!"* Bo said nothing but enveloped his beloved wife in his capacious arms. Tom collapsed into a chair.

"Praise God and all his angels," he said. *"Are you all of a piece, m'lady?"*

Anisette peeked out at him and giggled. *"Why yes, Tom, whatever can you mean?".*

Bo made a low noise. *"He means I stupidly tried to speed the drying of your branches, and knocked loose some fruit. You are not hurt, are you my love?"*

"Not in the least." She pulled loose of him. *"Forgive me, husband. I should have told you. It does not hurt me to have the fruit plucked from my branches. My old nurse discovered that years ago. She plucked a handful unthinking, then suffered a terror of regret until I was restored, all unharmed."* She touched Bo's cheek. *"I am sorry for your unease over it."*

"No matter that. I am right relieved." He smoothed her hair and kissed her forehead. *"Are you hungry, love? We are cooking a good breakfast.".*

Anisette took in the state of the kitchen at a glance and bit her lip to hide a smile. *"Indeed, a bite of breakfast would be most welcome,"* she said.

Tom got up and pulled out a chair for her, poured her some coffee, put before her the cream and the honey pot and generally fussed like a mother hen. Bo got on with breakfast a bit easier with Tom distracted, and soon they all ate together, lighthearted as if no storm had wrested peace from their hearts just hours earlier.

When plans for the day's work had been discussed, Tom rose to clear away the dishes. Bo stood and offered a hand to Anisette. She took it and stood on tiptoe to kiss him. Next moment she gasped and doubled over in a paroxysm of pain, and fell to the floor uttering a piteous moan.

"Anisette!" Bo dropped to the floor beside her. He lifted her head and shoulders and cradled them on his knees. *"What is it, my love?"* There came no answer. *"Tom! Run for Doctor Fleming, and fetch Josiah!"* Bo gathered his wife into his harms and stood to carry her to their bed.

"Master Bo!" Bo turned to Tom, who pointed to the floor.

A pool of terrible red glared in the morning sun.

Truth

Monti's heart pounded as she filled the tea kettle, put it on to heat and listened to her sweet granddaughter cry. Kit's chest muffled Noelle's sobs but they were subsiding, thank God. Monti chose a box of tea at random and stuffed a bag in Noelle's favorite mug. If she had to wait much longer to hear what horrible 'nothing' had happened, she was going to explode. If it was anything other than the essay, she might explode anyway. But who knew *what* it might be in this season of room wrecking, death threats, and rocks through the window?

She grabbed the nearest box of tissues and stood ready to offer it when needed. Noelle had the hitches now, drawing in ragged breaths and striving to regain control. She pulled away from Kit a little and availed herself of the tissues. She blew her nose and wiped her eyes, then leaned her head back on Kit and heaved a piteous sigh. Kit took her elbow and guided her to the nook. He sat across from her. Monti hovered, too anxious to sit.

"Okay Noelle, let's hear it," Kit said, the command softened by his gentle tone.

She put her head in her hands and said, "I bombed the scholarship essay."

Monti needed confirmation that she'd heard correctly. "What?"

"My timed scholarship essay. I bombed it," Noelle said, her voice wavering.

Monti was ashamed to feel a great surge of relief. This was nothing. Truly nothing in the grand scheme of things. She sat down and hugged Noelle. "Oh baby girl, that's okay."

"No it's not, Grandma!" Noelle said. "It was critical for the Hamden journalism scholarship! I should have stomped it, no problem, but..."

"But you were up half the night," Kit offered.

Noelle nodded. "Yeah, that. And I just...couldn't concentrate." she said. "All I could think about was Mom calling, and Mom coming home, or not coming home, and how everything would change and be better, or worse." She stopped and looked at her grandparents. "Not that things aren't good, they're really good, but...wouldn't having Mom here be even better?" She scrunched her eyes shut. "Or it might be horrible and I feel horrible for thinking that."

Monti squeezed Noelle's shoulder. "Don't. Don't feel horrible for thinking that, because I go round the same circles."

"You do?" Noelle turned to Monti. "Really?"

"Yes, really," Monti said. "She's been gone for seven years doing all kinds of destructive things, and it scares me when I think about her living in this house." She checked Kit's face for his reaction to this shocking truth, but of course he knew her mind better than she did and was not a bit shocked.

"Me too," Noelle said quietly. Monti felt some of the tension melt from the girl's shoulders. "I want to be with her of course, I *do*. But it scares me too, remembering what she was like sometimes."

The kettle whistled and Monti went to pour the water. She motioned at Kit with the box of tea but he shook his head. Monti filled Noelle's mug and got down another. She was going to have a fortifying cup of peppermint, anyway.

"Sweetheart, I'm sorry this has been worrying you, especially today," Kit said. "But at least we have it out in the open. We all love your mom, but having her with us again would mean some huge adjustments on everybody's part."

Monti set the two mugs on the table and rejoined Noelle on the bench seat.

"But nothing is for sure, yet," Kit said. "Not by a long shot. Marla said she might come for Christmas. That's all she's considering for now."

Monti brushed Noelle's hair back from her red eyes. "I think she's as scared as we are. She knows she screwed up. She's afraid we won't truly be glad to welcome her home."

"Christmas," Noelle said, musing. "That's another month away. Maybe I can get my head around the idea by then." She grimaced. "Before then would be better. Final exams are mid-December. I don't want to bomb them like I did the essay!"

Kit straightened. "We should set a mid-December deadline for head clearing then. Your grandmother and I will do whatever we can to help you." He put his gnarled hand over hers. "Keep us in the loop, okay? We can't help if we don't know what's bothering you."

"I will, Grandpa," Noelle said, a tremor still in her voice.

"If we're in the loop, does that mean we're loopy?" Monti said. Kit and Noelle rolled their eyes in unison.

"Some of us, certainly," he said.

The Good Doctor

The doctor pulled the bedchamber door shut and came to join the three men who sat like stones at the kitchen table. He sank wearily into the chair offered him. Three faces stared at him, waiting for bad news.

"She's lost the wee baby," he said. Bo dropped his head onto clenched fists. Tom's chin wobbled, and Josiah looked as weary as the physician. "She's sleeping now, which is just what she needs. What, might I ask, what happened? Did some sudden fright or heavy work overburden the lady?"

To the doctor's surprise, Josiah and Tom cast sidelong glances at each other and had no ready answer for him. Josiah cleared his throat. "Nothing of that kind, Dr. Fleming. It is right hard to explain," he said. "Bo, should we not bring the doctor into our confidence?"

Bo lifted his head briefly and said, "I care not." Josiah pursed his lips at this.

"I understand, brother." He turned to the physician. "So, doctor, have you an open mind?"

"I believe so," said the man, "though not so wide open my brains are in danger of falling out." Tom snickered in spite of himself at that.

"Just so," the preacher said. "Just so. Well. In truth, doctor, Mistress Willem suffers under an enchantment." He stopped there to give this time to filter through, as he knew from his own experience it would take a minute for his words to make sense to the good doctor. Bo stood abruptly and disappeared into the room where Anisette lay. Josiah waited.

"An enchantment," Doctor Fleming said. "And...what might this enchantment be?"

"When it rains she turns into an almond tree," Tom blurted out, eliminating the hemming and hawing bound to tangle up this part of the tale. "It's God's own truth, as we three will swear to, will we not, Preacher Wheaton?"

Josiah heaved a sigh. "That is it in plain speech, doctor."

Josiah and Tom watched him closely. However the doctor may have received such a tale from plainer folk, he seemed reluctant to dismiss it outright coming from a man of the cloth.

"Truly? But of course," he said slowly, "such afflictions are not unknown. Though I have not encountered them personally..." He trailed off as he thought the matter through. "When it rains, you say?"

"Doctor, tell us. If the enchantment is the cause of the miscarrying, must it always be so? Shall they have any hope at all?" Josiah asked.

"Why, how am I to know?" the doctor said. "'Tis a singular circumstance!" Tom and Josiah nodded their resigned agreement. They sat brooding their heavy thoughts.

At length the preacher roused himself. "Well then, doctor, tell me this. I know they will eventually consult me as to the wisdom of future...attempts to have a family." He rubbed his tired eyes. "Would I be irresponsible, do you think, to encourage them to try again?"

The doctor blinked and raised his eyebrows, then frowned. "Hmm. My philosophy, Pastor Wheaton, is to align myself with nature as much as is possible in the care and treatment of my patients. Someone has wrenched nature cruelly out of her course in this case, 'tis true. But still, the most natural path is for a husband and wife to engender children. God in His mercy may deign to o'erpower the untoward effects of this enchantment and allow them a family. Anisette is young. I do not think they must give up the hope of children yet."

Josiah visibly relaxed at these words. "Encouraging words those are, Dr. Fleming. I thank you."

"Pardon," the doctor said. "Tom, what do you fondle there?" Tom had his hands in a wooden bowl on the table, peeling the rinds from the drupes they had collected from the ground around Anisette that morning.

Tom stopped suddenly, realizing what he had been doing without thinking. "These be the fruits my mistress dropped this morning, doctor."

"Truly? Fascinating. May I?" He reached for the bowl and Tom pushed it toward him. "They're quite large, are they not, and perfect in form. Lovely." He sniffed at one and finished peeling it. "Be there any objection to my cracking the shell and examining the seed?"

"No sir," Tom said. "Mistress Anisette said it don't hurt her none to have the fruit plucked or handled or even eaten, I'd wager, though I don't think I could."

"*That does seem awkward, doesn't it. Perhaps I'll ask the lady about that in more detail when she has quite recovered.*" He cracked a shell and a perfect, fat almond dropped onto the table. "*Beautiful,*" he said.

"*Nooo!*"

The doctor jarred the table in surprise, sending the almond skittering to the floor as all three men leaped to their feet. Bo's wail from the bedchamber set their hearts jumping madly. The door flew open, and they stared as a wild-eyed Bo half carried, half dragged his pale, struggling wife toward the back door. Out they went, and only then did the men realize the rain had started again.

Let's Do Church

Monti smoothed her skirt and did an all-over and round-the-back inspection in the mirror. She wasn't too sure about the over-sized black and white hound's-tooth checks. Noelle nudged her out of her fashion comfort zone now and then, and this nubbly wool pencil skirt was pushing it, that was for sure. A black turtleneck and black tights toned it down a little, but it was still kind of 'out there.'

Kit stepped from their bathroom scrubbing a towel across his crew cut. "Wow!" he said when he saw her.

"Wow good? Or wow I can't believe you were going to wear that to church?" Monti demanded.

"No, no. Wow good," he said. "You look scrumptious. Kind of...school marm with a spicy kick."

"I am a school marm," she said.

"And your kick is pretty spicy, too," Kit said, grinning at her. Leering, more like. She stole his towel and snapped him with it.

"Such talk!" she said. "And on Sunday morning!" She did her best to form an outraged frown but a grin kept getting in the way, so she stood on tiptoe and kissed him on the cheek. "What am I going to do with you?"

"Everything," he said. She tried to snap him again but he grabbed the towel and in an instant had her lassoed and pulled in close.

"G and G," came a voice from the kitchen. "Breakfast!"

Rats. They settled for a soft kiss, and Kit hurried to get dressed while Monti did another all-over appraisal. Looked like the skirt was going to fit into her wardrobe just fine.

THE PARKING LOT WAS half full when they pulled into the little church. Jenny had again declined to come with them, no surprise there. Maybe next week.

Kit held the door open for his wife and granddaughter. The mouthwatering aroma of excellent coffee greeted them. The beans had been sent to the church as a gift from their missionary in Rwanda. The hubbub of animated visiting was punctuated frequently by the unmistakable belly laugh of George, their lead deacon.

Dorothy Cominski touched Monti's elbow and opened her arms for a hug. Monti leaned into her friend's embrace and whispered in her ear. "I talked to Marla."

Dorothy's eyes popped wide. "Seriously?"

Monti nodded. "Remind me after."

"Oh don't worry, I will!" Dorothy said, nearly drowned out by exuberant bell ringing.

Five-year-old Joaquin careened through the fellowship hall, grinning from ear to ear and ringing a hand bell to call them all to Sunday School. He must have recited his memory verse perfectly last week to have won the coveted Beller job. George finally cornered him and gently confiscated the bell, tousling his hair and shooing him toward his mother.

"That was a bit much," came a familiar gravelly voice behind Monti. "I still say the bell should be off-limits to anyone under twenty- one."

Monti's shoulders tightened just a tad. "Good morning Faye," she said forcing her reluctant smile to behave and turning toward the elderly lady. "How are you feeling today?"

Faye said "Hmph," and trundled off to her class.

Well, all right then. Monti made a mental note to have Kit kick her if she ever resembled Faye in any way. Then she remembered the hard road Faye had traveled and her face went hot with shame. *Abba, forgive me. Please help Faye to feel your love and strength today.*

And me, too.

Kit headed off to teach his class and Monti went to help Dot in the nursery.

An hour later the bell rang again and she handed the last little one to the last mom. She was glad to be finished with toddler-wrangling for another few weeks. She loved them, but their energy level exhausted her. She tidied the room for a minute, closed the nursery door, made a quick stop at the ladies', then hurried to the sanctuary to slip into her pew.

At the piano Cathi filled the sanctuary with beautiful music, calming Monti's heart as she sat down and settled in, her back slowly unkinking. She closed her eyes to listen until a lateral attack jerked her to high alert. A tiny three-year-old girl wearing a tutu and pink framed eyeglasses had slammed into Monti's legs and stood grinning up at her, perfect little teeth shining, eyes scrunched shut from the wideness of her smile.

"Well hey there, Little Bit," Monti said. "I missed you in Sunday school." The tot traced the pattern on Monti's skirt and then poked each big white check, standing on tiptoe to reach and poke as far as she could. "You like my new skirt?" Monti asked. Little Bit nodded and twirled away to greet someone else. It seemed like Noelle was that size just a year or two ago, though Monti had only one blurry Polaroid photo of her as a toddler, and had never met her granddaughter until she was eleven. She could still picture Marla at that age too, and even that seemed not so long ago. Monti's heart convulsed in her chest. *Abba, help my baby girl. Bring her back to us. And to You.*

The piano music subsided and Lucy stood to read the announcements. The women's shelter needed blankets. A baby shower for Erica had to be postponed due to her being put on bed rest 'til the baby was born. A signup sheet for the Thanksgiving potluck dinner was passed around.

Thanksgiving! Monti sat up straight. *Oh bother, I haven't even begun to think about Thanksgiving.* She surreptitiously pulled her notepad and pen from her purse and started a list. Call Mom. Invite neighbors. Loner students? Order turkey from natural market?

Kit lowered himself into the seat next to her and she tucked the notepad away, feeling vaguely guilty. She glanced up to see what she'd missed. Ron was moving forward to lead singing. Kit looked a question at her and she put an innocent smile on her face. Ron announced the first hymn and the building filled with rustles and scrapes as they all stood. Time to have some church.

Distraught

T he doctor confined Anisette to bed. The weather had turned rainy at last, and Anisette stood in the garden sometimes two or three days at a time. When the sun periodically came out, Bo took her straight back to their room and she did not protest. They nursed her gently, and she slept a great deal. Bo slept in the room he had occupied as a child and at this she did protest, but he would not relent. A furrow deepened between his eyes, and old Tom grew despondent. Silence filled the house.

Throughout November, Anisette slowly recovered. On a fine day in December Bo entrusted her to Tom's care for a short outing into town for some necessary purchases. By Christmas she was nearly her old self, though still a mite pale, Bo thought. She did not fear the rain, and was delighted when a light snow took her out to root in her enclosure for an afternoon. But Bo still staggered under a heavy dread.

"Husband," Anisette said. "Shall we not cut fir boughs to hang in our parlor, and choose a Yule log?" She twined her arms about his waist and peered up at him.

He formed a smile in return, but could not keep it on his face. He put his hands on her shoulders and gently moved her away from him a bit. "We shall if it please you, Anisette," he said.

"Bo," she said softly. "I am well, my husband. Will you not return to my embrace, and my bed?" Bo's frown grew fierce and he turned and left the house without a word.

A few days later Josiah stopped in to see Bo while he took stock of the supplies in the bottling shed. He helped Bo move a few crates from one wall to another.

"And how fares your little family, Bo Willem?" the pastor asked, wiping his hands on a kerchief.

"We be well enough," Bo said. "Old Tom suffers some in his joints from the cold, a bit worse each winter."

"Aye, 'tis often the way of it in our elders. Mistress Springfield makes a wondrous tonic for such ailments. It soothes my own mother's aches. No bat ears or dung of any kind, I assure you!" he said, and frowned when Bo returned only a slight smile.

"Bo, my brother," he began again after an awkward silence. "Your lovely wife is distraught." Bo looked up sharply. The pastor raised his hand to forestall any comment. "I encountered her at the dry goods shop and asked after you all. She began to weep! I drew her to a side aisle, out of the traffic of the place, and endeavored to calm her. She regained her composure and apologized, I know not why, but would not say what was amiss. Therefore I ask you, Bo Willem, what is amiss?"

"Nothing!" he said. "Only everything. How can you ask!" Bo pounded a wall with his fist. "I near killed my wife."

"What?" The preacher's eyes widened, then he frowned in sudden realization. "Do you mean the miscarriage?"

"Of course, what else," Bo said. He dropped his head into his hands and pulled at his hair. "And now she begs me to return to her bed. I cannot do it." He looked into his friend's eyes. "I will not risk it, man," he said. "What if she conceived another babe? How should I bear to lose another little one and Anisette?" He choked out these last words and pounded the wall again and again.

Josiah's throat tightened in sympathy for Bo's grief and fear. What could he say? What would not sound trite and superficial? He asked Jesu for help, but no words of wisdom appeared in his mind. He put a strong hand on his friend's broad shoulder and gripped it. He prayed, pleading for a solution to this poor family's plight.

Jumpy

Monti closed the door and waved goodbye to Kit through the window. The girls, fortified with coffee and peanut butter toast and having assured Kit they would abide by the required safety precautions, had left for class early. She and Kit had enjoyed a leisurely breakfast together. Now he was headed off with the elders for the day, after patiently enduring Monti's firm reminders to Eddie and John to call it quits and get Kit home pronto if he started hurting.

The house was so quiet it distracted her. She wandered into the living room and examined again the damage to the window. Blaine's rock had done a job all right. Kit had called the glass shop on Saturday and a guy was supposed to come by this afternoon to measure for the replacement. That was going to be expensive. No standard Home Depot vinyl window was going to fit in their vintage bungalow. Where would they find the money for that bill? How much would the insurance cover? She made a mental note to find out. Not that she ever remembered her mental notes.

Glass crunched under her shoe. Amazed, she lifted her foot and plucked another shard from her sole. She'd better damp mop the floor yet again.

Okay, there were two things to remember now. She'd better write them down. Monti went back to the kitchen, grabbed her notebook and favorite pen, and climbed into the window seat. Gulliver immediately jumped up to join her, this being one of his favorite morning spots.

"Hey Guvluv," she said, and scratched his chin. He stepped onto her legs, purring and butting his head against her hand, requesting a shift in the scratching to his ears, please. She obliged. A car backfired down the block, Monti jumped and Gulliver dug his claws into her thigh. "Ack! Ouch, Gulliver!" Her heart pounded. She willed it to slow. She stroked the cat. "All right, lie down now, I have to figure out my day." She pushed him down to the end of the seat.

Gulliver made a snarfly protest sound but curled up on her feet. Monti opened the notebook and jotted down *mop glass* and *check homeowners' insurance*, then clicked the pen ten or fifteen times, floundering a bit on the subject of what else to do with the day. Not that she hadn't anything to do, but rather the list of have-to's, shoulds, and perhaps-I-coulds was so long it was overwhelming.

She leaned her head back. Surely a sixtyish woman should have a better handle on how to use a day. Oh, she had the basics down. She would first enjoy the luxury of some unhurried time in the Word and talk to her Redeemer about things, and listen for any small gifts of wisdom or guidance he might drop into her heart. She already had a load of laundry in the wash. The kitchen would take five minutes to clean, and supper was a known entity. The day was going swimmingly so far.

But now, since she had no classes on Mondays to structure her day, she must make a plan that would put the rest of her time to good use or else it would fritter away and be gone before she knew it. Was that her cell phone ringing? She waited...where was her phone, anyway? She wasn't sure, but it wasn't ringing. At least, not anymore.

She clicked the pen some more. Thinking of phones, she still needed to get Jenny a Hopeline phone and let Sandy know Jenny would need prenatal care. Did she need to help find maternity clothes? No, Sandy and Dot and probably Noelle would be all over that project. Jenny would be moving into Ray and Dorothy's in a couple of weeks.

She hoped Blaine wouldn't still be causing problems by then. She'd hate to see the Cominskis experience anything resembling their recent Blaine episodes. Dot hadn't seemed overly alarmed when Monti told her about the rock through the window yesterday, but Monti had determined to maintain a policy of full disclosure as they went along. Though it would take a lot to phase either Ray or Dorothy.

She wished she knew where Blaine was. She'd been fine over the weekend while Kit was home, but now she felt a little jumpy.

Thanksgiving, of course. She jotted that down and wondered what she'd written about it yesterday during church. She'd check in a minute. She had to invite her parents. She'd called them yesterday to let them know about Marla, but Thanksgiving had never entered her mind. She'd just call them again.

And she wanted to invite her neighbors to the south, a young couple who'd moved in recently.

And her Scrabble story. She should be able to fit some writing time in today and move Bo and Anisette along toward living happily ever after...though she wasn't at all sure where that story was going. She'd already used most of the words from the game board, she thought, but where was that list? She'd better check it.

The tale, as usual, had taken on a life of its own and she'd pretty much forgotten she was using a word list. She'd find it today and keep writing the story down, hoping for the best for poor Anisette. She was glad the girl had Bo to love her. She needed a strong, tenderhearted man to help her with such an improbable, challenging life. If only Jenny could find such a one. As much as she liked to see families stick together through tough times or reconcile after difficulties tore them apart, she didn't think Blaine would ever be Daddy to Jenny's baby.

Blaine again! Why did her thoughts keep circling back around to the unfortunate boy? He was so angry. Just like Marla. Monti sat up straight and smacked her forehead. Right! Blaine was angry, just like her daughter, which was why she couldn't stop thinking about him. Or her.

Friday's call had been the first communication of any kind since last December, and the first phone call in years. Monti had no idea how or when Marla had landed in Florida. Noelle had written to her mother after her birthday last year, but the letter had been returned, no forwarding address known. New Mexico had apparently lost its luster, like all the other places Marla had written from. She was sure Marla would remember Noelle's birthday next month. She had never missed sending her daughter a card on or before December 1. But now she had called, so maybe...maybe she would come home.

Monti pulled her legs up, wrapped her arms around her knees and rested her head on them. Nineteen years was such a long time to be angry. Marla was 23 when Stephen was killed in a training accident, before he'd had the chance to follow in more than one or two of Kit's footsteps. Marla had adored her baby brother from the moment he was born. They were best friends through thick and thin. His death ripped the center out of her world, and she took a nosedive every bit as steep as the one that smashed Stephen's plane onto the rock-hard desert. Monti only hoped it wouldn't be as fatal. She sighed, unfolded herself and got up to make some tea.

Nineteen years was a long time to feel guilty, too. Stephen's death, following hard on the heels of Kit's terrible injuries in Kuwait, had left Monti ill-equipped to help her daughter. She hadn't been available to grieve with the girl. She hadn't words of comfort on the tip of her tongue. For several months, it was all she could do to get out of bed each day, deal with her own grief and give everything she had left to Kit's recovery. By the time she had pulled out of her own threatening nosedive, Marla had turned to Derek for comfort. Kit and Monti foresaw a disaster in the making, but Marla wouldn't be dissuaded. Six months after Stephen's death, Derek and Marla took off for Las Vegas and got married. Less than a year later, Noelle was born.

Monti was grateful for Noelle, a silver lining if there ever was one. She brought joy to her and Kit every day. But Noelle couldn't erase their grief over Marla. And Monti didn't know how long Marla could survive, holding that old, poisonous anger so tight to her heart, unwilling to forgive or be forgiven. She'd lost her brother, her marriage, and her daughter. How close had she come to losing her life? Monti's heart clenched with familiar pain, yearning for her baby girl. *When, Abba, when?*

An hour later Monti had forced herself to get started and was deep into her project list when her cell phone rang.

"Hi, love. Guess what?" Kit said.

"What?" she said, stopping mid-motion as she reached for the dish towel.

"It's eleven-eleven."

"It is not!" She lowered her phone to glance at the time, 9:02am...and then the date. "Ooh! I bet you've been planning to say that ever since you left."

"Yep. Can't believe I beat you to it, actually. You're slipping a bit in your advancing years, Monti."

"You finally noticed. Don't know what that says about your keen-edged alertness." Monti dried her hands and headed back down the hall.

"Hey. I'm tarp as a shack, and don't you forget it," Kit said.

Heading Home

"Careful, Jenny," Noelle said. "It's still a little icy in the shade."

"Yeah, that's just what I need—to fall on my pregnant rump in front of half the student body." Jenny carefully picked a sunny path across the concrete in front of the library. "I'm so hungry! I wonder what's for dinner?"

Noelle fished for her keys in her hobo bag. "Thursday...never can tell. Grandma won't be home until after we are. Grandpa might be on it, but if he's not I know we have apples and peanut butter to snack on." She unlocked the Geo and they piled their packs and purses in.

As she pulled away from the curb and headed for the back road out of the campus, Jenny turned on the radio and surfed the stations until she found Train singing Hey Soul Sister.

"Put your seatbelt on, girlfriend," Noelle reminded her.

"Right, forgot." Jenny clicked her belt closed and leaned her head back. "I'm so tired."

"I thought you were so hungry," Noelle said, then scowled at the rear-view mirror. "Get off my tail, idiot," she said. She reached up and did her grandma's trick of pretending to adjust the mirror, which she swore made people back off nine times out of ten. But this particular idiot, driving a rusty black Camaro with a wide white racing stripe up the center of the hood, revved his engine instead and pulled around as if to pass them. In a no passing zone. She shook her head. "What a moron."

Jenny turned to see what the moron was doing. "Hey! That's Blaine's car!" she said, just as Blaine yanked his steering wheel hard to the right and barely missed hitting them. Both girls yelped. Noelle had instinctively swerved right and now she struggled to get the Geo back under control.

Noelle sped up, not sure if this was the right thing to do. "Jenny! Call my grandpa!" she shouted, gripping the steering wheel with both hands and watching Blaine from the corner of her eye. Jenny fumbled for Noelle's phone in her bag in the back seat.

A deep ditch rose into a steep embankment on their right. There was nowhere to go.

Noelle watched in disbelief as Blaine swung to the left and then cranked hard right again—she braced herself and gasped at the shriek of metal against metal as the Camaro slammed into them and slid along the side panel of her little car. Jenny screamed and kept screaming.

The Geo was forced onto the shoulder, one wheel kicking up clods of dirt and turf as Noelle fought to keep from getting pushed into the cavernous ditch. When Blaine swerved back left this time she floored the gas pedal. Jenny left off screaming with a gasp and dialed.

"Mr. Rising! It's Jenny," Jenny yelled into the phone. "Blaine is...he's ramming his car into us!" Jenny sobbed, fought it back. "Yes, no he's still...I don't know. Where are we, Nellie?"

"Almost onto Front Street," she said, gritting her teeth, hyper-alert, merging right onto the main road at a terrifying speed, praying for room in the traffic. A quick check of the mirror showed Blaine had followed them onto the highway.

"He's still following us!" Jenny wailed, twisted around to look out the back window. "Your grandpa says to drive straight home, he's calling the cops," Jenny said.

Noelle nodded, held her breath and swooped across two lanes of traffic and onto her exit in the blink of an eye.

"Shit! He's still there," Jenny said. At least the narrow streets lined with parked cars prevented him from pulling up beside them. Noelle drove as fast as she dared turning left, then right, then at last the final left onto their street.

A police car sat nose out in their driveway, its light bar stuttering its digital blue and red, its engine running. Noelle braked hard and stopped the little Geo at the curb in front of the house. The Camaro blew by and the patrol car blasted out after it, siren blaring.

Noelle turned the key with shaking fingers, put her head on the steering wheel and cried. Jenny undid her seatbelt, opened the passenger door and vomited on the lawn. Another patrol car entered the side road and pulled into their driveway as Kit hurried down the sidewalk to the Geo. He leaned into Jenny's open door.

"Are you okay?" he said, his voice hoarse with worry. He gave Jenny a hand out of the car, steadied her, cautiously let go and hurried around to Noelle's door. It was jammed, and it took him a couple of tries to wrench it open. "Noelle?"

Noelle fought with the seatbelt, got it open and climbed out into her grandpa's arms. He held her tight while she sobbed, clutching him, shaking uncontrollably.

Morocco

Anisette lay awake, alone in the big bed, staring at the shadowed ceiling. She had been turning the problem over and over in her mind for several weeks, feeling there must be a solution if only she could discover it.

Jesu had not yet allowed them a cure to rid her of her enchantment. Therefore, he must mean for her to live abundantly while in its thrall. She must not mope and moan over her misfortune. She must use her wits and think of how she might safely bear a child, because to have Bo keep to his own bed forever was not to be countenanced.

Bo's correspondence with the gentleman from Morocco danced around the edges of her mind, teasing her with elusive hints of some remedy for her dilemma. What was it?

She rolled onto her side. Before her miscarriage had put all plans on hold, Tumaini had meant to pay all expenses for Bo to travel to Morocco to help him establish a honey meadow and mead making business of his own. Bo was to have a share of the profits for his help. He'd fretted about it, because the desert climate in Morocco might not support a honey meadow anything like what Bo had here. Tumaini had assured him there were flowers and bees, but Bo struggled to envision a honey meadow in such a dry place.

Anisette sat bolt upright. That was it! Morocco was such a dry place, which must mean it seldom rained there. She leaped from the bed and ran to Bo's room. She threw open the door.

Bo rolled over and opened a sleepy eye. When he saw Anisette his eyes flew open. "What is it?" he said. "Are you well?"

"Yes husband, quite well, only..."

"Only what?" He sat up and scratched his chest, looking at her with suspicion.

"Only I have had the most marvelous idea," she said. She came in and perched on the edge of the low bed. "How long were you to be in Morocco to establish Mr. Tumaini's honey meadow?"

He relaxed a little. "Oh I don't know, beloved. That is all set aside for now."

"Yes, I know, but if you were to go how long would you be away?"

"I would strive to keep the time as short as may be, of course. But old Tom and young Ian would take capital care of you whilst I was away, never fear."

"Nay, nay, I do not worry on that account, dear man. But might the trip be made to last for a year?"

"What? Would you want me away for such a long while?" His forehead furrowed with confusion and hurt and she hastened to reassure him.

"I never would! But you must go, and I must go with you!" She clasped her hands together, excitement bubbling up and threatening to keep her from thinking straight.

"I do not think that would be wise, Anisette. The journey is arduous, and you are such a delicate creature..." He reached out to stroke a silken curl, hesitated, and drew his hand back. She kissed him on the nose and he jerked away.

"Oh, my dearest Bo. Think of this. If we go where it does not rain, and stay there for a year...?"

Bo went still. He stared at her with wide eyes and his face reflected the thoughts and calculations whirling in his head. He raised one finger as if to ask for a moment. It took several moments, and then he cupped his hand round her cheek and kissed her.

"You are a marvel," he said.

High Alert

Monti struggled to be patient in the traffic. She couldn't wait to get home. Kit had had a bad night and she'd hated to leave him this morning. The day had dragged on interminably, but now she was finally home. She turned the final corner onto Engle. The Geo was parked on the street and a black and white sat in their driveway, sending an electric shock of adrenaline through her. *You have got to be kidding me!*

She parked the Subaru behind Noelle's car and rushed into the house, a dozen horrible scenarios flashing through her mind between the street and the front door.

Kit stood in the living room talking with a uniformed police officer. Noelle and Jenny were right there on the settle, Noelle's arm around Jenny's shoulders, their faces white as milk. Monti sagged against the wall in relief.

Kit turned as she came in. "Everything's okay, Monti."

"What happened?" she said.

"Blaine followed Noelle's car out of the library parking lot. Tried to force them off the road over by the tracks. Actually sideswiped the car and scared them half to death." Monti went to Noelle and laid a trembling hand on her blonde head.

"You should've seen Nellie drive, Mrs. R," Jenny said in a wobbly voice. "I called Mr. Rising on her phone, and she drove crazy like Angelina Jolie."

"I called the police," Kit said. "A patrol unit happened to be in the neighborhood and pulled into our driveway about thirty seconds before the girls showed up."

"Blaine was still following us, but he took off when he saw the cops here," Noelle said.

"Those officers are in pursuit at this very moment," Kit said, his mouth twisted into an unnerving smile. Monti thought it was a mercy for Blaine that Kit was not in pursuit at this very moment.

"Officer Wells arrived right after the other unit took off after Blaine. Officer, this is my wife, Monti. She teaches at the college."

"Hello ma'am," the young man said and shook her hand. "I've taken the young ladies' statements. He scanned the battered notepad in his hand. "Vehicular assault and stalking are serious matters." He looked at Monti and at the girls huddled on the settle. "These young men are dangerous if they're willing to go to these lengths to frighten you. You need to be careful, extra aware of your surroundings and alert to the people around you. Hopefully we'll be able to take them into custody today, and we'll let you know if we do. Meanwhile, please be cautious."

"Them? Who's them besides Blaine?" Monti asked.

"Jenny thinks there was someone in the passenger seat," Kit said. He walked to the door with Wells. "We're already on high alert, Officer. Detective Price has us up to speed on what precautions we need to take, and the girls have kept to that plan."

Monti joined them at the door. "Should they stay home tomorrow? If you don't catch Blaine? The current plan doesn't seem to be keeping them safe."

"That might be a good idea, ma'am," Officer Wells said.

Kit squeezed her to him. "It'll be okay, Monti. Officer Wells has a daughter at school, too. He's on top of it." He reached for the policeman's hand and shook it. "I'll see you out." He opened the front door and the two of them talked on the step for a minute. Monti turned to the girls.

"Are you both all right?"

They nodded, eyes wide, lips tight. They were shaken and so was she. She dropped into the chair across from them. "Why is he doing this?"

"I don't know," Jenny said. "I can't believe I ever thought he was so wonderful. I must be an idiot." She gave in to tears again and Noelle hugged and rocked her.

Monti rubbed an unsteady hand across her eyes and tried to shrug the mounting tension out of her shoulders. She sighed and caught the fragrance of pot roast wafting from the kitchen. So Kit had dinner in the oven before things went crazy. That was a blessing. And no one was hurt, which was all that mattered in the end. Kit came back in and leaned down to kiss her.

"You okay, Monti?"

She got up and walked with him to the kitchen. "I can't seem to stop shaking. I've been anxious about you all day," she said. "Feels weird to have worried about the wrong thing for several hours. It's unsettling."

"You're not supposed to worry at all, lover. Do not fret. Right there in Scripture, plain as day."

She sighed again. "I know it. Someday when I grow up I'll learn to trust my husband and my Creator. Are you doing potatoes or noodles? Do you want some help?" She grabbed the dishrag and wiped at a smear on the counter.

"It's all together in the roaster. Just a salad to go with it, and that's already in the fridge. Listen, Monti..." She looked up at him. "You *can* trust me, you know. I understand I'm not twenty-five anymore, and I understand, even though I don't like it, that I have significant limits now." He held her shoulders and looked into her eyes.

"I won't push the envelope, because I can't stand even the thought of you having to take care of a broken down, helpless old man." She started to protest and he shushed her with a finger to her lips. "I know you would do it with all your heart. But I think I'll wait to try you out on that for another twenty years or so, okay?" She nodded as tears threatened to spill onto her cheeks. He tapped his finger against her mouth. "No worrying."

She shook her head and hid it against his chest. "I don't trust Blaine, though," she said into his shirt.

"No. That's a different matter. There we need vigilance, but not worry."

She tipped her head back to look at him. "Kit. This is miles beyond any situation we've had to deal with before. It scares me. What if Noelle were to get hurt?" She gripped his arms. "I couldn't take it."

Kit smoothed a thumb over the creases in her brow. "You're right, Monti. This is bad. But we know we're doing what we should be doing, and we're gonna have to rest in that. And I will take every precaution to protect the ones I love. We'll get through it, one day at a time."

He disengaged one arm and cracked open the oven door. "Half an hour before the roast is ready. Let's go get the girls calmed down and figure out how to tighten up the plan." He kissed her nose. And her forehead, and the outer corner of her right eye. "Okay?"

"Okay," she said.

In the living room Jenny was blowing her nose. Noelle wiped the mascara off her own wet cheeks and sniffed as she tucked her hair behind her ears.

"How are we doing in here?" Kit said. "Over the worst of it?" The girls nodded at him, looking more like eight than eighteen. "Good. Let's eat, try to get thinking clearly and see where we are."

Lying Low

Monti woke abruptly, curled tight in a ball, her jaw clenched and her head pounding. Bad dream? She couldn't remember, but tension throbbed through her body. A vision of Noelle's car crashing and tumbling off the highway sent a shudder through her and clamped a cold hand around her heart. She rolled onto her back. She opened her mouth and wiggled her jaw, wincing as it popped. *Relax, they're safe.* She worked at tensing and relaxing one limb at a time, then turned her head carefully to look at the alarm clock. 5:45 a.m. She rolled her head cautiously the other way, toward Kit—still asleep.

She needed a hot shower. Right after she checked on the girls. Quietly.

The girls were staying home from school and thus were, of course, sleeping in. She peeped in at Jenny's door. The girl lay sprawled across the whole double bed in her room, covers kicked off. Across the hall Noelle was curled up in the center of her bed, breathing evenly. Monti closed the bedroom door softly and slogged back down the stairs toward hot water. Coffee. Tylenol.

Kit met her at the bottom of the stairs. "What's up, Monti?"

"Nothing, just checking on our babies," Monti said. She put her throbbing head on Kit's chest and wrapped her arms around him, soaking up the exquisite therapy of his very existence.

He put his arms around her. "Still going to the dentist?"

"Ugh...I forgot all about it," Monti said. She considered, but only briefly, then straightened. "Yes, I have to go. One, that molar is getting more sensitive by the day. Two, they'll charge me fifty bucks if I don't show."

He patted her back. "Okay. Nine o'clock, right? I'll get the coffee started."

"Thanks. I'm for the shower."

"Better take something for that headache on your way there," Kit said.

"I didn't say..."

"Yeah, yeah. I know when you have a headache, Monti." He kissed her forehead. "Go."

Amazing man. She shook her head. Ow—careful!

At eight the girls were still asleep. Kit and Monti forced down scrambled eggs and toast with a pot of coffee. The memory of yesterday's attack filled the room like a toxic fog, making it hard to think, let alone make conversation.

Since Monti was going out anyway, they made a grocery list. She would replenish their pantry, including ingredients to make some serious comfort food. Hot chocolate. Beef stroganoff. Chicken soup. Apple crisp and ice cream would make them all feel better. She hadn't left yet and she already couldn't wait to get home and start slicing apples.

"I guess I can't be done until I get started," she said, and gathered her things to go.

SHE SURVIVED THE DENTIST and the shopping. The left side of her face was still a bit numb when she pulled around the last corner onto their street and relaxed. There was no police car in their driveway. Amazing how she used to take that for granted.

Kit came to meet her at the car. "Hey lover, how's your mouth?" he said, his open arms inviting her in for a hug.

"I don't know, you tell me," she said, and tilted her face to him for a kiss.

"Not bad," he said. "Whatcha got to haul in?"

"Just these old bones," she said. "And supplies to soothe and succor us in our sequestration."

"Did you practice that or did it just randomly roll out of your fecund writer's brain?"

Monti chuckled. "Spontaneous alliteration that time. A bit tricky around the numb tongue." She absorbed the hug for another moment, letting a little of the stress of the situation melt away. Then she let go to grab her purse from the front seat and shut the car door. Kit loaded his arms with grocery bags from the back.

"Any trouble?" Kit asked.

"Not a bit. No bad guys anywhere that I noticed. What'd I miss here?" she asked, holding the kitchen door open for him.

"Not too much," Kit said. "Got a call from CJ."

"Oh yes?"

"They got one print from the duct tape. It's definitely Blaine's."

"Well, I don't guess we had much doubt about that," Monti said.

"No, but it's good to have physical evidence. Strengthens the case."

"Right."

"We also talked about yesterday. CJ briefed the whole department on the escalating situation this morning. They're keeping an eagle eye out."

Monti slipped off her shoes and kicked them down the hall in the general direction of her closet. "Finding him and putting him back in jail would be better," she said.

"They're working on it, Monti," Kit said. He found the ice cream and stashed it in the freezer. "Let's see, what else. The glass shop called with an estimate."

"Should I sit down?" Monti sat down and scrunched her shoulders, bracing for impact.

"Yeah," Kit said. "$2100, including installation."

"Wowza," she said. They had a thousand-dollar deductible on accident repairs. "How do you feel about cardboard as a decor motif?"

"It's tempting. But I gave the go-ahead. They should have it fixed before Thanksgiving."

Monti lay her head on the table, then turned it sideways to look at Kit. "I haven't thought about Thanksgiving for a whole day. Maybe two."

"No need to stress, Monti. We'll invite some people, we'll make some food, we'll see what happens." He calmly continued setting cans in the cupboards.

She sat up. "You think like a man," she said, "broad statements and not a single detail." Though she had to admit, his perspective was therapeutic.

"Want more coffee?" he asked, ignoring her vicious taunting.

"I think I'll switch to tea," she said, and got up to put the kettle on. "What are the girls up to?" She hadn't heard any girl noise since she got home.

"They are, believe it or not, studying. They've been awake for a whole hour, they've been down for coffee, and they seem to be functioning reasonably well."

"Well, good," Monti said.

"And, I have an appointment to meet with Blaine's dad on Thursday."

"Wow, you've been busy. That's great, though," Monti said. "I hope it goes well."

"I had to schedule it through his secretary, like I was hawking insurance or something."

"Good grief. No casual chat over coffee with this guy, huh?"

"Guess not."

The phone rang and Monti jumped, spilling peppermint tea bags all over the counter. She had absolutely no desire to answer. She looked a plea at Kit, who nodded and picked up the receiver.

"Risings," he said. Listening, he started pacing as he always did. He lifted his eyebrows. "Really. That's good news. Mmm-hmm. Yes, they'll be relieved to hear it, thanks CJ." Kit gave Monti a brief crinkly-eyed smile as he continued to listen, and she grinned back at him. But then a frown replaced his smile. "What?" He stopped pacing. "What on earth was he thinking?"

Monti's grin faded. The suspense would kill her. The tea kettle whistled softly, the beginning of a crescendo that would soon dominate the room. She hurried to move it off the heat, glad of the distraction of pouring the piping hot water, trapping the tag of her teabag against the side of the mug with a fingernail, inhaling the cloud of peppermint steam. She carried the cup to the table and sat down.

"Yes, thanks. We'll be here the rest of the day," here Kit checked with Monti for confirmation and she nodded. "So anytime is fine. Okay, see you then, CJ."

"What?" Monti asked, the instant Kit ended the call.

Kit eased himself back onto the breakfast nook bench across from Monti. "They found Blaine and arrested him."

"Yes, and?"

He shook his head. "The boy is a mess. They searched his car, of course." He looked at Monti. "They found a can of gasoline. Rags, box of matches. All neatly packed together in a plastic crate in his trunk."

Monti put her head in her hands, visualizing very bad things that, thank God, hadn't happened.

"And a couple bottles of prescription painkillers that weren't his," Kit continued. He leaned back. "And his fancy smart phone. I imagine they'll analyze its contents six ways from Sunday."

"That'll be scary, I bet," Monti said. "Well, at least they got him. He won't be able to get out on bail again after this, right?"

"He shouldn't, no. CJ is going to stop by and talk to us about that."

"Shouldn't is not as good as won't."

Kit looked her in the eye. "No, it's not. But it's reality. We live in a world full of lawyers."

"What about the other guy?"

"No word," Kit said, shaking his head.

The girls came down the stairs, chatting together. At least they had some good news for them.

"Hey G and G," Noelle said, kissing each of them on the top of the head. "Why so glum? Or is that a stupid question?"

"No, not stupid. And we're not glum, we're...I don't know, what are we, Kit?"

"We are looking at the world through jaded glasses and letting that overshadow the good news."

"Which is?" Jenny asked.

"Blaine's in jail. Finally." Monti found she could smile at this, anyway. The girls whooped and hugged and that deepened her smile. They caught the bad guy. Now it would all be okay. Wouldn't it?

Plans

Anisette peeked around the corner into Bo's office. Bo and Tom were deep in discussion. Tom sat with his elbows on his knees, cutting a new pen as he listened to Bo, a scowl of concentration scrunching his craggy features. Scrolls and sheets of parchment covered the entire surface of the Bo's broad desk.

"We can do it, Tom."

"Aye, my boy, I believe we can," Tom answered, grinning broadly. He straightened his back, examined the pen nib, and set it on the desk next to two or three other quills lying by the ink pot ready for use.

She slipped into the room and set a tray on the window seat. Hot coffee, cheese, pears and seedcake would fuel their planning a fair while longer.

"There be two great cruxes in the matter which must be secured else the whole plan will tumble down." Bo tipped his head back, rolled it about and rubbed the back of his neck. "First, Master Marlow must supply us with the kit we need for the journey, and put his purse behind the business here in my absence." He looked at Tom. "But I think the prospect of a grandchild will be a powerful argument, do you not agree, Tom?"

"*Eh*? Indeed, lad, 'twill set him to writing cheques as naught else could, I wager."

Bo drew her into their brainstorming. "Anisette, he is a true businessman, is he not? A share in any profit, without additional investment...do you think that will appeal?"

"I think, husband, you have discovered two irresistible reasons for him to loosen his purse-strings: a sure profit and the prospect of descendants."

Bo nodded, satisfied. He stood and began to pace the room. "Then second, there's the matter of Ian. My brother, Matthew, has hinted once or twice at an apprenticeship for the boy and **lo**, here is the perfect reason to take up that idea straight away. It will take some time to arrange, even for the offer to make its way

181

to Matthew and their agreement to come back to us. But there is much else to see to, and we'll move the venture ahead on many fronts at once."

He sniffed the air, turned and discovered the tray in the window seat. "Ah, you spoil us. Coffee will do me great good just now!"

They worked at depleting the tray's bounty for several minutes, having discovered they were quite hungry. Anisette cleared away the tray, but hurried to rejoin the men. The three of them talked long into the night, imagining every possible impediment and devising remedies for each, making lists, writing letters to Tumaini and Matthew. All the while they dreamt of Bo and Anisette returning to Westhaven with a babe in arms.

Kit vs. the Furniture

Kit tapped his fingers on the arm of the deep leather chair. He'd been waiting for more than half an hour. And while he was willing to mortify his pride by waiting patiently a while longer, he would not be able to tolerate the chair more than another two minutes. Worse, he wasn't sure he would be able to get out of it unassisted. He should have brought the blasted cane, but of course that idea had been too humiliating. He tapped harder.

He would be humiliated one way or another pretty quick now. If he didn't want pride to go before a literal fall, he'd better get the secretary to help him up and find him a different chair. That wouldn't be as bad as being unable to get to his feet when the grand Mr. Rutherford was finally ready to receive him.

He cleared his throat. "Miss...I'm sorry, I didn't catch your name," he said. The secretary looked up.

"It's Mrs. Campbell, sir. What can I do for you?" Kit motioned for her to come over to him. She blinked rapidly, but rose and came to see what he wanted.

Kit's face flushed. He cleared his throat again. "I'm afraid, young lady, that I may need some help to get out of this confounded chair."

"It may be a few more minutes, sir, before Mr. Rutherford is available."

"Be that as it may, I need to get out of this chair now before I'm permanently welded in this configuration. Are you willing to help me?"

"Why of course," she said. "Exactly...er...how can I help?"

Kit shifted his weight, closed his eyes and groaned inwardly. "I'm going to have to grab your arm, I'm sorry to say, and pull myself up. If you'll brace yourself and hold still, I think that should work." His face flushed again. He was mortified, all right. Mrs. Campbell took a stance that didn't look too stable to Kit, balanced as it was on stiletto heels. She offered her arm. Kit took a deep breath and latched onto it. As he started to lever himself up, the door to

Mr. Rutherford's office opened and he stepped out. Kit's mortification level shot through the ceiling.

"Rondy, do you need help?" Mr. Rutherford said. Kit sank back into the chair.

"Um, possibly, sir," she said, her own cheeks reddening. "This is Mr. Rising, sir, your ten o'clock." Mr. Rutherford glanced at the large wall clock above an electric fireplace across from Kit's chair and winced. It was nearly eleven.

Kit said, "Well, I seem to have succeeded in embarrassing everyone in the room. I might as well carry on until we're all redder than a barn." He cleared his throat yet again, which he always did when he was uncomfortable, try as he might to break the habit. "Your kind secretary was attempting to heave an old man out of your excellent furniture, Mr. Rutherford. But I'm not sure she has the necessary ballast. Perhaps you could..."

"Of course, of course," he said. He leaped to replace his petite secretary. He was sturdy and athletic, a good fifteen years younger than Kit. Kit gripped the man's well-muscled arm and pulled himself up.

"Thank you," he said. "Most obliged." He straightened his shoulders. The three of them stood awkwardly for a moment before Mr. Rutherford recovered his businessman's bonhomie.

"Well! Come on in, Mr. Rising, I'm sorry to have kept you waiting so long." Mr. Rutherford ushered Kit into his spacious office and gestured toward a leather chair similar to the one from which he'd recently extricated his visitor, then realized his error. "Uh, perhaps not that chair?" Kit shook his head.

His host glanced around the room, but no promising furniture waited to be chosen. "Hmm. One moment." He poked his head out of the office. "Rondy, would you please find a suitable chair for Mr. Rising, something firm..." He turned to consult Kit. Kit nodded. "Something firm, Rondy, thank you."

The two men looked at each other, waiting. Kit decided he'd endured enough awkwardness for one morning, and took the lead. He stuck out his hand.

"I'm Kit Rising, Mr. Rutherford. Thanks for agreeing to meet with me."

The younger man shook his hand. "Call me Mike," he said. "This is about Blaine, right?" Mrs. Campbell came through the door with a straight-backed oak chair. Her boss leaped to take it from her and set it down. He'd done a lot of leaping so far. "Have a seat, Mr. Rising." Kit did, and Rutherford sat also, in one of the deep leather chairs facing Kit.

"It is about Blaine, Mike," Kit began.

The other man wilted a bit, and tightened his jaw. "Right. I'm not sure I'll be of much help in that area, but why don't you tell me what's on your mind."

"What's on my mind, Mike, is three frightened women living in my house." He tried to read Blaine's father's reaction to this. The man couldn't look at him.

"I don't know what to tell you, Mr. Rising," he said. "I don't plan to bail Blaine out again, just so you know. But his mother might." He did look at Kit then. "We don't always see eye to eye on the subject of Blaine."

"That can be difficult," Kit said. "But actually, I don't believe your wife will be able to bail him out." He shifted in his chair and knew he would have to head home soon. "I understand he's being held without bail pending arraignment."

"Oh," Mike said, visibly deflating. "I see. I haven't had a minute to catch up on his situation," he said. "Crazy busy." He reddened, obviously ashamed that Kit knew more about Blaine's status than he did. Another awkward silence stretched on for a few moments. "She's not my wife, FYI."

"Excuse me?"

"Lisa. Blaine's mother—she's my ex."

"Sorry to hear that, Mike. But regardless, the reason I'm here is to discover why Blaine assaulted my family, so I can work to protect them when he is released, whenever that might be." He paused, but Mike didn't leap into the silence. Kit continued. "Jenny says Blaine thinks she'll try to get money from him, or from you, I guess. But she assures me she isn't going to do that, and that she's tried to make that clear to Blaine. I'm at a loss as to what else can be driving him to these violent attacks."

Mike shook his head, staring at the floor. "I wish I could tell you, Rising," he said. "I wish I knew. He's all over the map, emotionally. Very angry much of the time. A pleasant young man other times. Occasionally."

He jumped up and paced the room. "Ever since Valerie and I married, he's...changed. We eventually had a doctor check him for, I don't know, chemical imbalances or whatever, but he didn't find anything wrong. Blaine won't go to a counselor anymore. He's nineteen now, we can't force him." He sat down again. "Not that it did any good anyway."

He looked at Kit. "He's getting worse, I know that. A year ago, I don't think he would've threatened a girl, let alone vandalized a house." He dropped his head. "And ramming your daughter's car. I still can't believe he did that." He looked Kit, imploring. "How do you get help for someone who doesn't want help?"

"That is a hard question, Mike. I'm familiar with that particular dilemma myself." Kit sighed and stared out the office's broad window, then back at the distraught man before him. "Our grown daughter is estranged from us. She's mighty angry, too, and the source of a great deal of heartbreak for her mother and me. Without our faith, I believe our marriage might have crumbled under the strain years ago."

"Yeah? I've been telling Valerie we should get back to church." He grimaced. "She's not interested." The two men sat lost in their separate thoughts a minute.

"Listen," Mike said. "I'm going to visit Blaine at the jail tomorrow. You want to go, too? I could pick you up."

Kit nodded, surprised. "I was hoping to talk with Blaine. So yes, that might be a good plan. What time?"

"Two o'clock work?"

"Sure." Kit stood up, pulled a business card from his wallet and handed it to Mike. "There's our address. Know where that is?"

Mike glanced at the card. "I think so, but it doesn't matter. Butch knows this town inside out."

"Butch?"

"He's my chauffeur. I don't drive. Those DUI's stick around a while, you know."

"Oh," Kit said, taken aback. "Right."

Mike leaped to open the door for him and Kit headed out without another word.

What's Truth?

E mpty your pockets here," said the officer. Kit and Mike emptied their pockets into little plastic bins. Both men followed the corrections officer down a hall to the visitors' booths. Blaine waited there on the other side of the glass, pale and sullen in orange scrubs. The two older men sat down. Mike picked up the handset and gestured for Blaine to pick up his, which he did without any enthusiasm.

"Hey there, son," Mike said, striking an awkward note of lighthearted affection. Blaine appeared unmoved. He didn't answer.

"This is Mr. Rising, I don't think you've met." Kit wondered what direction the man might go from there that wouldn't crank the awkwardness to extreme levels.

"Jenny is staying with the Risings..." Mike stopped abruptly. Awkwardly. "But right...I guess you know that." He gave up and pulled his hand down over his mouth. He offered the handset to Kit.

Kit took it, cleared his throat and breathed a brief prayer for wisdom. "Good afternoon, young man," he said.

Blaine glanced at him, then back down at his hand, picking at the chipped Formica. "Why are you here?" the boy said. "Try and scare me straight, or something?"

"Why, do you think that would work? I'll try it," Kit retorted. He unclenched his fist and sent up another prayer for wisdom. "Actually, I'm here for only one reason. To make sure my wife, my granddaughter, and Jenny are not endangered any further." He shifted on the plastic chair. "I thought learning what's going on in your head might help me with that goal." That hung in the air for a minute.

Blaine shrugged, and slouched down further in his seat.

"What does that mean?" Kit said, keeping his tone under strict control. "Does a shrug mean you don't know what's in your head, or just that you don't care to tell me?" Blaine glared at him a moment, then dropped his eyes. Mike gave Kit an uneasy glance, too. Maybe this wasn't such a hot idea. His temper was kicking in despite his best intentions. Mike wanted the handset back and Kit gave it up.

"I think what Mr. Rising means, son, is we'd like to help you. We'd like to understand and help you."

"What I'd like is to make sure you never come near any of the aforementioned women again," Kit said, loud enough for Blaine to hear. Both Rutherfords stared at him. Kit put his hand out for the handset. "Uh, scratch that. And uh, I will attempt to remain civil." He sighed and leaned forward. "I do want to understand, Blaine, why you destroyed Jenny's room, why you threatened my wife, why you threw a rock through our window and why you rammed into my granddaughter's car. I can't make sense of it. I don't understand what you stood to gain by any of that. If you'd explain your actions to me, I would appreciate it." He leaned back. That was better.

Blaine continued to stare at him, and the boy's father held his breath. Blaine shrugged again, then quickly said, "Sorry. I mean, I don't really know. What's in my head, I mean." He reddened. He sat up. "What I mean is, I don't know what I thought I was going to gain by...doing those things. I just did them. I was mad."

"You did all that, over several days, because you were mad?" Kit asked.

Mike wanted a turn. "Why were you mad, son?" Mike asked, and got a glare from Blaine. "What? Why were you mad? Why are you looking at me like that?" he said, louder with every word.

"Why are you yelling at me?" Blaine said. "Why are you all of a sudden acting like you freaking care?" He gestured toward Kit. "I'm sure he can tell you don't give a crap. I'm not the one...I didn't...Oh, forget this shit!" he shouted and slammed the handset into its cradle. He stood, flinging his chair back into the cement block wall. The clang resounded up and down the hall, and an officer immediately stepped into view behind Blaine.

"What's up, folks?" he said. "Rutherford, sit down." The man set Blaine's chair back up.

"No, I'm think I'm done here," he said. "I'm ready to go." The officer shrugged and led Blaine out. Silence settled sourly in the cramped booth, like a swamp fog.

"That went well, don't you think?" Kit said.

Mike Rutherford's face twisted around a deep and unhealthy-looking scowl. "Sorry about that, Rising." He hung up the handset and rose slowly from his chair. "Can't seem to hold any kind of conversation with that boy without it devolving into a shouting match."

Kit stood too, and they headed down the hall toward the exit. "Yep. He can probably get that reaction from you whenever he wants. He knows where your goat's tied."

"Hmph," Mike said. "You really don't worry about offending people, do you?"

"Sure I do, most of the time. But my family has been attacked. I thought I'd cut the crap just this once. What's needed in this situation is a generous dose of unvarnished truth."

"Hmph," Mike said again. "What's truth?"

"That question's been asked before," Kit said. They walked in silence to the booking desk. The sergeant plunked the bins down in front of them and they scooped out their belongings. Mike held the entrance door open for Kit.

When Mike's driver had the car on the road again, Mike said, "I don't know what to do about that boy. I don't know why he's so angry. I don't know where we went wrong, Valerie and me. Or maybe further back, when his mother and I were married. I just don't know, and he never will say."

"If Blaine won't or can't explain himself so we can address his problems, or misunderstandings or whatever," Kit said, "then my next concern is how to prevent him from being a threat to my family. Personally, I think jail is an excellent place for him." He paused and the silence thickened. "Do you have any influence with his mother? Can you convince her not to try to get him released?"

Mike huffed and shook his head. "My influence with her is minimal. But like you said, it might be a moot point. Even if they did allow it, bail this time would be set pretty high since he screwed up three times in a few days. Lisa wouldn't be able to afford the bond. She sure can't afford a lawyer."

"Good," Kit said. "Might not be enough to set Monti's mind at ease. Nor mine either, really." He sighed. "But, we can only control what we can control. I'll focus on the safety precautions we can take and trust God and the Coeur d' Alene Police Force to protect my family." Mike glanced at him with a look that suggested Kit himself might be a danger to society. Kit laughed. "What?"

"Nothing, nothing. I just...that's not a common attitude. In fact, I've never heard anyone but a priest say something like that. Trust God and the police. Are you serious?"

Kit nodded wearily. "Only way to live, Mike." He glanced out the window. "Hey, what about a quick stop up here. I think my girls could do with a treat."

The driver pulled to the curb at Floral Traditions and Kit climbed out of the car. He leaned back in and said, "I've learned over the years that anything with petals and perfume is tremendously soothing to a woman's soul." He grinned at Mike and headed into the shop.

"MONTI? WHERE HAVE YOU got to?" Kit paused at the kitchen counter, leaned into it to stretch his back for a moment, and eased back up. He let go the counter, made sure of his balance, tweaked the bouquet and hid it behind his back as he went to look for his wife.

He found her in the back yard snipping dead bits off the shrubbery. The girls rocked in the big porch swing, bundled in an afghan with faces lifted to the late autumn sun.

"Don't worry, I'm not touching your roses," Monti said, whacking a sizable branch off a perfectly innocent and apparently healthy azalea.

Kit was glad to hear his roses were not in danger of similar care, and wanted to believe it was true. Monti smiled at him, her eyes twinkling, pleased, it seemed, with the sanctioned violence of pruning. "You don't prune roses in autumn in this zone, Monti."

"Ah, good to know. Not in this zone. How'd the meeting with Blaine go?" she asked.

Kit grunted. "Swell," he said. "We had a nice chat, except for the part where I yelled at Blaine, and the part where Rutherford yelled at Blaine. Oh, and the part where Blaine yelled at us." He reflected a moment. "And the chair flinging, of course."

"Oh dear," Monti said, suddenly somber, her pruning shears dangling harmlessly from one hand. The girls stared at him, wide eyed and pale.

"But hey, it's okay. He's staying in jail this time. Probably." They didn't move. "At least until the arraignment..." Still nothing. He brought the bouquet out for inspection, "I brought flowers..."

How if it Should Rain?

B o and Anisette strolled along the path at the edge of the river. Their breath billowed miniature clouds into the cold, bright morning air. Anisette broke into skipping again. Bo grinned at her. Despite her chagrin at his steadfast refusal to resume her bed, Anisette shone with happiness this morning. "You frolic like a young lamb, Anisette!"

She stopped short, smoothed down her skirts, placed a hand on Bo's big arm and walked calmly for a few paces. But soon she was skipping again. Bo smiled, shaking his head, and returned to his thoughts. Anisette's father had agreed to finance their journey, and Bo expected a reply from his brother Matthew any day now. There were many tasks that must wait until they knew whether his nephew would come, and when.

Anisette exclaimed at a long skein of yellow and brown fluff meandering on the water. "Bo, look at the ducklings! Aren't they darling. So brave to be on the river when they're so tiny!"

"Their mother takes good care of them," he said, smiling. "See how they follow wherever she leads? She'll have them traveling all up and down the river before too long."

"Not long ago, up and down the river would have seemed an impossible journey to me," she said. "And now we're to travel hundreds of miles to a different continent!" She stopped walking. "Bo, the furthest I have ever ventured from my birthplace is your honey meadow."

Bo chuckled. "And that first journey turned out so very well. I would not blame you if you had refused to step over your own threshold ever again."

"Oh, but the next time was lovely! Still, I am lost when I sit to write my packing list. How do I know what will be needed on such a long journey?"

He guided them to a bench beside the path. The sun warmed their faces even as he pulled her close against the chill. "I am no great traveler myself, Anisette. Josiah Wheaton, though—many miles have passed beneath the soles of his boots.

He may advise us, as will Tumaini. I expect a reply from Tumaini 'ere long, and we'll consult Josiah soon."

"And Bess! We must have them both, because she has traveled with husband and children and will know everything I must pack. Shall we not invite them to sup with us this Sunday?"

"A sound thought. I know not why we haven't done it already," Bo said. "We shall pick their brains clean of all travel wisdom."

Anisette scrunched her face in disgust. "That is not a pretty picture, husband. Now I feel like a vulture. But aye, we must learn all we can from them. My head whirls whenever I think about sorting and packing and sewing and storing." She stood and pulled at his hands, moving him not an inch. "Let us be off to home, dearest Bo. Though I have only imagination to guide me until I speak with Bess, ideas about the journey continually spin into my head. I must catch the newest and pin them to a list."

A few whirling days later the expected letter arrived from Matthew, carried by Ian, himself! His arrival gave the journey a new tangible quality, and set off a flurry of activity. If Ian was here to take on Bo's work, then Bo must be going away!

The household welcomed him warmly. Though he were but fourteen, Ian was well-muscled and stood nearly as tall as Bo. He tripped somewhat over his fast-growing feet, and his smooth cheeks blushed at the slightest awkwardness, but Bo soon determined the lad was bright, and he set to showing him the basics of the business. Within a week the boy was making himself genuinely useful.

One evening soon after, laughter rang round the kitchen and Josiah plunked his empty glass down on the oak table. Tom refilled it with ale and Josiah thanked him with a nod. Bess, having heard all these tales before, sat smiling and rolling her eyes at a ridiculous detail now and then. But Tom, Bo, nephew Ian, and Anisette grinned, waiting for Josiah to continue the tale of his journey across the Middle Sea. Somehow, their friend made sea-sickness, pirate attacks, meagre rations, a fire on board their tiny ship and an infestation of rats sound hilarious rather than disastrous.

Bo checked Anisette's reaction now and again during the telling, but she laughed as much as anyone.

"By the time we make Tunis, two of the crew want no more of the whole adventure," Josiah said. "They scram overboard and disappear into the city. The *captain is none too happy about this, but when **Ed**, a giant of a man, walks up the gangplank the next morning and **joins** the complement, the captain quiets down. And that fellow does the work of three for the rest of the journey, so the captain is ahead."*

Ian said, "I wish I could be a sailor! Pirates! To fight pirates would be grand!"

Josiah shook his head. "Many a sailor dies fighting pirates, lad. It's no laughing matter when it's happening. Just as the Book says of temptation, 'tis far better to flee the encounter than stand and fight. E'en so with pirates, if you can!"

"What was Tunis like?" Anisette asked, being now profoundly interested in all things African. "Was it dry?"

"We arrived as the rainy season was departing. Only a few showers cooled us whilst we visited the brethren," Josiah said.

Bess responded to Anisette's frown. "But that were in April, dear girl. It nearly never rains, they tell me, in summer."

Anisette's frown grew deeper and she stiffened. "What is it, daughter?" Josiah asked. "Anisette?"

"How if it should rain while we are aboard ship?" she said, looking round at the others. They fell silent, the joyous mood gone as each friend unwillingly imagined it. A long moment passed.

Ian's eyes grew wide as understanding dawned. They had reluctantly taken him into their confidence the day after his arrival, it being bound to rain soon. The boy had gaped at the tale then, unable to believe it. The men's solemn reaction to Anisette's question obviously astonished him now, and Bo watched his disbelief trickle away.

Tom stood abruptly. "We'll line a big chest with tin, fill it with earth, and you'll cart it aboard with ye." They gaped at him.

Bo recovered first. "Well of course we will, Old Tom! That's just the thing." He frowned. "Is it not, my love?" He looked for assurance from Anisette.

She bit her lip, considering. "It may be. But husband, we must test the plan. I have always felt the strongest urge to get outdoors when it rains. I know not whether a chest of earth would...would do." She looked at Bo. "The chest must need be in our stateroom, not in the open."

"Of course, of course. And I agree, we need to be sure. Tom, will you do as you proposed as soon as can be? Ian will help you. We are bound to have any number *of rainy days this spring, and we shall test the idea and work out the best plan while we are still safe at home." He looked again at his wife and she nodded, relaxing.*

Tom grinned. "Aye, and we'll have it knocked together on the morrow. I know just the box, hid under a pile of sacking in yonder shed. And seeing we're to town tomorrow for supplies, I'll nip over to the smith for the tin. Be there chinkers for that, Master Bo?"

"Aye, certainly," Bo said, smiling at the old man rubbing his hands together, eager to take on a task vital to his mistress's wellbeing. "We'll leave that entirely with you, Tom."

That night as Bo and Anisette sat together in the darkening kitchen, mugs of fragrant chamomile tea steaming in their hands, Anisette voiced a related worry. "Bo, when you write again to Tumaini, inquire closely about the weather, will you not?" She gripped her mug and stared at the tea. "If Morocco has a rainy season...what I mean is, I had not thought of that possibility, but only of it being in the desert. If a whole season might bring rain, then our plan will come to naught!" She gazed at him, tears threatening.

Bo covered her hand with his. "I will, love. But I'm certain our plan will work. 'Tis a mercy from God, to bless us in spite of the enchantment and bring Him glory in overcoming it." Bo wished he felt as sure as he sounded. His stomach roiled as if they were already aboard ship when he thought of taking Anisette on such a dangerous journey, far from the safety of their home and the protected soil of her garden retreat. He squeezed her hand to reassure them both. God would see them through it, surely.

Jail Tales

"What shall I take for Austin to read?" Monti scanned the bookcase beside the living room window. "Do you think C.S. Lewis is too demanding for reading in jail?"

"I think C.S. Lewis is too demanding for most of your students no matter where they are," Kit said.

"You're probably right. But Austin is a thinker. Maybe *Out of the Silent Planet*." She pulled down a worn paperback and blew a layer of dust off the top.

"Been a while since you read that one, huh?"

"Oh, hush." She opened it to make sure "Rising" was marked on the inside of the cover, though that didn't always ensure a book would be returned. She didn't mind too much if it wasn't, it being a loaner copy. She didn't lend the volumes from her boxed sets.

"Noelle invited Nick to go with us to the movie tonight," Kit said.

"Hmm. I hear that boy's name a lot these days," Monti said.

"I'm thinking Thai for dinner. Chopsticks, unintelligible menus, spicy food. It'll be fun."

"You're wicked, Kit Rising. The poor boy." But she couldn't help a complicit smile. "What movie? I forget."

"Red. All our favorite old people in an action adventure."

"Perfect!" She slipped the book into her bag and checked her watch. "I think I'll go. I've got a lot to do today before we go on our group date."

"Yep, you better scram." He gave her a kiss and escorted her to the door.

MONTI PULLED THE C.S. Lewis book from her purse, and dutifully deposited her stuff in the plastic bin. The officer waiting to escort her shook his head.

"Ma'am, you can't take that with you."

"It's for Austin," she said.

"I'm sorry, ma'am, you can't give books to the inmates."

"Oh, really?" Her shoulders sagged. *No books!* "All right. But do they have access to books some other way?"

"Oh sure, the Chaplain's Corps keeps a book cart stocked. They make the rounds every week."

"Well, that's good," Monti said, pleased to know Austin could get a book if he wanted one. "What kind of books are on the cart?" she asked. "Where do they come from?"

"I don't know, ma'am. I never thought about it," he said. "But here," he pointed at a list of phone numbers on a bulletin board. "Jot down the number there and call them. They should be able to answer any questions about the book cart."

Monti turned to the officer who'd taken her things and said, "Um, could I have my purse back for a moment? Notepad..."

He scowled, but obliged. She wrote down the number, put her purse back in the bin with the forbidden book, and thanked him. She turned to her escort and said, "Ready!"

The officer led her down the hall and pointed to a booth before retracing his steps. Monti sat down in front of Austin, already sprawled in his chair waiting for her. They both picked up their handsets and she said, "Hey Austin. They wouldn't let me give you the book I brought."

"I know, I'm sorry about that. I talked to the book cart lady the day after you visited, and she told me it wasn't allowed."

"Oh well, we tried. Did you find anything promising on the cart?"

"I guess. I took a Jack Reacher novel and an old sci-fi. Ray Bradbury, I think." He sat up and leaned forward on his forearms. "What did you bring?"

"I brought sci-fi, too. C.S. Lewis. You like science fiction?"

"Sure, I like just about everything. But not romances. And I can live without the vampire crap, but other than that...Who's C.S. Lewis though?"

They talked about C.S. Lewis and books for a few minutes until Austin said, "Hey, I saw another guy from school in the cafeteria yesterday."

"Really? Who?"

"His name is Blaine."

"Blaine Rutherford?" He nodded. "You know Blaine?" Monti asked.

"Yeah, a little. We have—had—a class together." He looked at her. "And we both, you know, did some of the same stupid shit. You know Blaine, too?"

"Oh, yes. Unfortunately. Though actually I've never met him."

"What? How can you know him if you never met him? You're not making a lot of sense, Mrs. Rising."

"Really? My family is always telling me that." She sighed. "Blaine is in jail because of several attacks against my family."

Austin straightened in his chair, his eyes narrowed. "Wow. Did he hurt anybody?"

"No, thank God. But he ran my granddaughter off the road. And threw a rock through our window. And destroyed Jenny's room." Monti's fist clenched in her lap.

"Jenny's your granddaughter?"

"No, Jenny is...well, she's staying with us for a while." Suddenly Monti felt like she was gossiping. Her cheeks went pink.

"I heard him talking about her," Austin said. "To this other guy. Scary guy I seen around."

"Talking about Jenny? What did he say?" The gossip feeling intensified, but she had to know.

"They were at the same table I was. They were talking quiet you know, but seeing as how I was familiar with their...subjects of interest...I was kinda listening," he said. "They were both convinced that this Jenny had ratted on them, told the cops what they were up to."

"Huh." Monti sat back. "That's interesting. What were they up to?"

"Oh, you know. Your basic illegal recreational substances, small business style."

Monti translated this in her head and an unbeautiful scowl carved itself into her features. "We've been trying to figure out why he was so angry."

"You think she did rat them out?" Austin asked.

Monti shook her head. "No, I think she's clueless. About anything Blaine was doing, I mean. But now it's starting to make sense." She turned the various puzzle pieces over in her mind, then happened to glance at Austin, who was tapping his fingers on the counter. "I'm sorry, Austin. I'll think about that later." She leaned forward again. "Last time we met you said you'd tell me what happened between you and your best friend."

Austin went still and his face reddened. "Aw Mrs. Rising, that's not a good story. I ruined Rafael's life."

"That's what you said. But your story's not done yet, right Austin? You're writing the next chapter right now, and you get to decide how the next part goes," she said. "Even the story with Rafael's not necessarily over. You never know what might be possible." She watched him, hoping he would talk to her about it, though she dreaded to hear it. "You don't have to tell me, of course..."

AN HOUR LATER MONTI arrived home and went looking for Kit. She found him in their office, swishing a net around in a fish tank. She plopped into her chair.

"They didn't let me give that book to Austin," she said.

"I don't think you can give inmates much of anything these days," he said, bending to kiss her hello.

"Well, how come you didn't mention that this morning?" she said.

"This morning? I don't remember talking about it," Kit said.

"You teased me about the dust on the book..." she paused, but he looked blank. "Wow. That can't have been more than six or seven hours ago." She paused. "Actually, that makes me feel better. It's not just *my* brain turning to mush."

Kit ignored this, turned again to the tank and asked, "How about Austin. How's his jail experience been?"

"He's doing okay," Monti said. "He's had a tough life for such a young man. Most of it hasn't been his fault, but he keeps getting angrier as the years go by, and makes worse and worse choices. Today he told me a sad story about losing his best friend, Rafael."

"How's that?" Kit said, as he netted a wriggling creature from one tank and slid aside the lid of another to dump it in.

"Oh, they were roughhousing on the shore of the lake. Rafael shoved Austin, Austin shoved him back and Rafael fell in. He shattered his kneecap, which canceled his college football scholarship. And destroyed their friendship."

Kit frowned. "That's bad all right."

"I hate it, because he's such a sweet boy! If only a couple of things had gone differently, he'd probably be wildly successful. Thriving. But instead he's headed for disaster."

"Is he playing the victim?"

Monti slipped off her shoes as she considered this. "No...no he isn't. But he is having a hard time seeing a way forward. Oh, gosh!" She sat up straight. "He saw Blaine the other day."

Kit stopped scooping. "At the jail?"

"Yes, in the cafeteria. Talking to a 'scary guy.'" Kit laid aside the net and sat down while she filled him in on the conversation.

"I think you're right," he said when she finished. "Jenny doesn't know anything about Blaine being involved in drug deals."

"I'm sure of it. She would have told Detective Price."

Kit nodded. "The next question is, what do we do with this information?"

"Well, shouldn't we tell CJ?"

"Probably."

"Probably? Why wouldn't we?"

"I'm just thinking it through, Monti, give me a minute."

Monti rolled her eyes. He thought through everything to a degree that drove Monti nuts occasionally. Paint the dining room or hang wallpaper? Do the taxes or hire someone? Out to eat or stay home and cook? Go for the double word score or block Monti from the triple? Okay, some things needed careful consideration, but this! Obviously they should tell CJ. What else made sense?

"I'll give him a call," Kit said.

Duh.

CJ showed up shortly after Kit's call and asked Monti in minute detail about her conversation with Austin. The girls edged into the room upon his arrival, sat on the edge of the settle and hung on every word.

At last, the detective turned to Jenny. "Miss Conklin, do you know anything about Blaine being involved with selling drugs?"

"No, sir! But it doesn't surprise me, you know? I mean, he turned out to be such a creep it doesn't surprise me at all to find out he was selling, too."

"So you never saw him with any illegal drugs?"

Here Jenny hesitated and reddened. "Oh, you know...just weed. It was always in the house. All the guys..."

CJ's jaw tightened, but he said, "Don't worry. We're not making this about anyone but Blaine. You're not going to get in trouble, nor the other boys unless they were selling, too. It's important for you to be completely honest with me, because I'll have to talk to the others, and I don't want to find out you're hiding something or lying."

"Yeah, okay," she said, swallowing hard.

"It sounds like Blaine thinks you overheard him talking about a drug deal. Did that happen?"

"No, sir. I never did." She hesitated again and frowned. "But, one time I fell asleep on the sofa facing the TV—I was cramming for a test—and when I woke up Blaine and Stevie were talking in the doorway. When I sat up, they kinda went all weird."

"Weird how?" CJ asked.

"I dunno. I just thought 'weird' at the time, but now it seems like maybe they thought I heard what they were talking about, and were trying to be...what's that word...like you don't care..."

"Nonchalant?" Monti offered.

"Yeah, nonchalant," Jenny said, trying the word. "But also, kind of threatening me, real vague. 'You better watch yourself' and like that."

"I can see why that seemed weird," CJ said. "But you hadn't heard their conversation?"

"No. I was asleep. Man, now I think he wasn't so much pissed about me being pregnant, as this..."

CJ nodded. "It could be. Was this Stevie Jakes?"

"Yeah, Stevie Jakes, he's a real creep. How'd you know it was him?"

"Billy," CJ said, and glanced at Kit. "I re-interviewed him yesterday and he reluctantly identified Stevie as Blaine's accomplice in destroying your room. Do the other guys in the house know him, too?" She nodded. "Any idea where he lives?" She shook her head.

CJ consulted his notebook, flipping back and forth through the pages for a minute. Then he closed it. "Okay, that helps. Thank you, Miss Conklin. I think I'll have a talk with Austin, and then Blaine. And try to locate Stevie Jakes." He tucked the notepad away, shook Kit's hand, nodded to the ladies. Kit opened the door for him.

As he drove off, Jenny hid her face in her hands.

"You okay, girlfriend?" Noelle asked.

"Yeah. But I'm seeing my life at that house with whole new eyes," she said. "It was sleazy, wasn't it? I didn't even notice. How could I not notice? Weed and booze, partying all the time, creeps hanging around and girls sleeping over, and broken down and dirty..." She looked up at Monti, standing in the archway. "This is the cleanest, nicest place I've ever lived. I never realized...never in my whole life..." She started crying and Noelle held her, looking like she might start, too.

Monti stood speechless. Kit put his arm around her and she leaned into him. He motioned toward the kitchen and they left the girls to cry it out.

Packing

Anisette tucked a wisp of hair behind her ear and surveyed the room. Two great trunks stood open, half-packed. She and Bo had penciled detailed lists of what to take on a year-long sojourn in Morocco. After striking through many things they thought they might do without after all, they added just as many newly-though-of items at the bottom. They continued this great guessing game even as they began to acquire and pack the necessary articles.

The men had taken the wagon to town early this morning with the list of supplies needed to help with Tumaini's mead venture. Bo had had a letter from Tumaini yesterday. The regal African was eager to launch the endeavor as soon as could be, so the packing must be accomplished in short order.

Anisette was bewildered. The journey was a mist in her mind, a **nebula** of imagined encounters and situations. But she had her lists and she worked away at them, hoping that would be enough.

She took up one of the linen pillow slips they'd received as a wedding gift and snapped it open with a flick of her wrists. All the baby things she'd sewn would snug into two cases nicely, along with the extra fabric and trims.

Her eyes filled with tears as she fingered the tiny garments and grief again coursed through her. But she would not dwell on the loss—this was to be a journey of hope. She pressed her lips together, wiped her eyes and tucked the gowns, caps, and swaddling clothes neatly into the linen case. Then her sewing box too, filled with every possible necessity, had to have a place. She nestled it into the trunk.

Now for the kitchen things. They had decided to think of their voyage as an extended outing, and had thought through what they might need to stay in their own honey meadow for some days. 'Twas curious how few implements they settled on as essential. One tea kettle, one iron pot, one wooden spoon, one knife and a board for chopping. Plates, bowls and mugs, a spoon each and that made a tidy *kit. Anisette wrapped the things in toweling and packed them all in the picnic hamper.*

There was room, still. She pondered. What could she add that was feather light, but would be dear to have with them? An extra packet of tea weighed nothing at all. In it went. What of medicinal teas? They hadn't thought of possible mishaps or illness!

So many details! Anisette added this to one of the lists. What else? Ah, a cloth for the table or the ground, for who knew where they would be taking their meals? She chose from her wedding chest a sturdy brown cloth, worked round the edge with a Greek key pattern. She tucked it in over the kitchen things. She made note of the remaining space in her mind—they would need to use every available inch.

TOM HUMMED LIKE A SWARM *of bees, pleased as punch with how his project was turning out. He had fetched the metal from the smith, and had not explained himself even in the face of the smith's avid interest in why he needed so much tin. He was quite proud of himself for that. There'd been a little trouble with the measurements at first. Ian arrived at one sum and Tom at another, but in the end they agreed with the help of a stub of pencil and a margin in the almanac. Tom and Ian slid the finished tin lining down into the chest, Ian tapping it here and there with a mallet to encourage it downwards. Tom squatted and crab-walked around the box, squinting at the fit.*

"Right, lad, she's snug as a bug. Let's have those tacks." Tom hauled himself up straight again, took the hammer and nails from Ian and fastened the lip of tin down around the edges. He tested the lid. It closed tightly. He must show it to his mistress at once. He danced a little jig on his way to the back door, which alarmed Ian.

"My lady," old Tom called from the doorstep. He wouldn't go into the house with his boots dirty. Anisette appeared, list in hand.

"Yes Tom?"

He gestured grandly toward the box.

"Oh, you did it!" She came out to inspect the project.

"Aye my lady, 'twill hold the soil and never spill a crumb." His brow furrowed. "Now, it ain't too high for ye to step into, is it?"

"Well, let's see," she said, and held his hand as she stepped into the box. "Not a bit," she said.

"And deep enough, I reckon?" he said as he smeared the sweaty grime around on his forehead with a kerchief.

"I trust so. Thank you Tom, for this."

"Now, now!" he said. "No need fer that." He shooed her back toward the house. "Young Ian will get the dirt spaded in and then it'll be finished."

"All right, dear Tom. But you must both expect a treat at supper for such fine work." She swirled away and Tom did not see her smile fade, nor the sweat prickle across her brow.

A FEW DAYS LATER ANISETTE wiped her forehead with the hem of her apron. Another very long day was wearing on her. She smoothed her hair and took a deep breath, squeezing her eyes shut and trying to recapture the thought that had just flitted through her mind. She shook her head—nothing. Mayhap it would flit back again.

The air grew heavy. It would rain within the hour, she knew. She looked around at the jumble she'd made of their great room. The deadline loomed and the almanac predicted a stretch of wet weather before their departure. She had to get as much done as possible during the times she wasn't planted in the garden. She snatched her list, scanned down the length of it. She was nearly ready to close this trunk.

Bo scraped his boots on the rush mat outside the kitchen door, and stepped tentatively into the room. He took in the state of the room and Anisette and grinned.

"How does it go, wife?"

Anisette plopped down on one of the hassocks. "Tolerably well, husband. I have it nearly all in, I do believe." She consulted a list. "I know we fitted out a kit of medicines and bandages, but I cannot now lay my hands on it. Do you know where it's got to?"

He shook his head, came and knelt before her. She rested her small hands on his broad shoulders and leaned in for a kiss. "Don't fret, Anisette. It will turn up. Most likely Tom nicked it and is doubling its size and weight with items we didn't realize were essential to our survival." He sat back on his heels and levered himself onto the other hassock. "It will rain soon," he said.

"I know," she said. "Tom's box sits ready, but I.... It distracts my nerves somewhat. Glad will I be to have the first test over."

"My love, I will not leave your side the rest of the day. When the rain begins, I will be right there—if the box does not suit, I will straight away carry you to your bower."

Anisette shivered and gripped his hand. "Bo, shift the box into the bower, will you not?" At his puzzled expression she said, "To be safest—only a step between box and garden soil should you need to move me...yes?" The disturbing vision she'd banished from her thoughts repeatedly had returned in vivid detail. "I do not know...what will happen if the box of soil is not sufficient. I'm not distracted, Bo," tears welled up and she gripped him tighter. "I'm terrified," she whispered.

Bo drew her onto his lap and enfolded her in his strong arms. "We are in God's hands, and He is sovereign over hexes and boxes of dirt. He will carry us through this, I know it." Another tremor shook her, and she tried to relax into his arms. She could not do it.

Sisters

L ight snow meandered indecisively toward the ground as they drove, making it impossible to clear the windshield without the wipers screeching. Kit maneuvered through the crowded parking lot and stopped in front of the church door to let them out under the covered entrance. He'd have to park around back, poor thing. Monti grabbed her Bible and smoothed her skirt as she walked up the steps with the girls. They were running a tad late. Jenny had decided to come with them today, reluctant to stay home alone after all the recent goings-on.

As they walked into the fellowship hall, Monti thought she might be more nervous than their guest. She was determined that Jenny would not cross paths with one or two vinegary old ladies for a few weeks. Learning to love them required time and patience. She felt guilty for even thinking this, but it was the truth.

The girls headed for the bathroom and Monti made for the coffee pot. Dorothy appeared at her side.

"Hey sister, how's things?" She hugged Monti.

"Good. Pretty good. Jenny's here today," Monti said. "Where are the Hauritz girls? I wanted to introduce her."

"Haven't seen them yet," her friend said. "Is this the weekend they head to Seattle for quizzing?"

"I don't know! I hardly know when I'm supposed to head for Seattle!" Monti paused. "I'm not, am I?"

"Not unless you take me with you," Dorothy said. "Hey, we should do that! Last time was such a blast."

Monti nodded. "Write it down, Dot, or we'll never remember." Monti scanned the crowd and spotted Noelle introducing Jenny to the Hauritz girls and some other college students. Jenny was smiling and chatting, and appeared to know a couple of them already. Monti relaxed. "Looks like Jenny's doing okay."

"How are they after the car incident?" Dot asked, looking for an honest answer in Monti's eyes.

"Oh, they're holding up all right. I'm a wreck, but they're pretty resilient, as far as I've been able to tell. They have lots else to think about—Jenny's baby, end of the semester approaching, Nick."

Dot raised an eyebrow. "Nick? As in Nick Lightner?"

"That would be the one."

"Ooh, he's a cutie," Dot said.

"Uh huh. Noelle agrees. Nice manners, too. Kit tried to fluster him with Thai food and chopsticks last night, but Nick ordered four-star-spicy and chopped his sticks shiny as anything, smiling and gracious. Pretty irresistible."

"I hope Kit doesn't scare him off! There aren't too many of his caliber wandering the streets these days."

"Scare who off?" Kit said, taking off his snow-specked glasses and drying them with his handkerchief.

"Hi love, did you have to park a mile off?"

"Half a mile. Fred waylaid me," Kit said. "Heading in to pray with the guys now." He leaned down to kiss Monti's cheek.

"Good morning Mrs. Morgan," Kit gave a slight bow. Faye was making her way across the wide fellowship hall, one cane-assisted step at a time, and they were directly in her path. They moved aside.

"Who's that you got with you today?" Faye paused, jutting her chin in Jenny's direction.

"Her name's Jenny, Faye," Monti said, "She goes to school with Noelle.".

"Hmph." Faye put her head down without another word and resumed toiling toward her seat on the fourth row.

"See you in church," Monti said to Kit.

The Box

A nisette pricked her finger yet again. She growled, sucked on her finger and examined the seam she had been sewing—tiny stitches and great long stitches wandered over the cambric—she threw it down in disgust. There must be some task she could do competently. She would go and stir the soup. She shoved the gown down into her sewing basket and started for the kitchen. The splat of a few hesitant raindrops on the roof stopped her mid-stride.

Her heart raced—the tingling throughout her body intensified by the moment. The urgency to get outside was irresistible, as always. She sat abruptly on the bench in the hall and tore off her shoes and stockings—the rain pulled her outdoors.

Where was Bo? He'd been in his office a short while hence. "Bo!" she cried. "Bo, I need you, husband!" The rain began in earnest as she rushed out the back door. She ran to her bower, picked up her skirts and forced herself to step into Tom's box of dirt, sinking further down into it than she'd expected. She glimpsed Bo hurrying toward her as the world went silent. Peace now.

Bo stood in the pouring rain, looking at the full-grown almond tree planted in Tom's box. Once again he was befuddled by the way he never could quite catch the transformation happening. A blur, a blink, and she was gone. He examined the base of the tree. She seemed well-rooted. He sat on the stone bench and took a deep breath. Old Tom splashed up the path, shoulders hunched, Ian following at his heels. The lad stopped and gaped at the tree in the box.

"How is she, my boy? Is all well?" Tom lowered himself to sit beside Bo on the wet bench, his hair plastered to his wet head, all their promises to go in from the rain forgotten.

"She looks well enough," Bo said. But as he said it the slender tree shivered violently and several leaves dropped.

The men leapt to their feet. Another tremor shook the tree and more leaves fell. Thunder boomed and they all jumped.

"*What is it? Why be she tremblin'?*" Tom hollered.

Bo grabbed his hair with both hands, distraught. "*I know not! The box has not enough room, mayhap. Her roots—perhaps they need to spread more. We must move her!*"

"*How, lad?*" Tom grabbed his hair too, and danced a panicky jig round his master.

Bo ducked beneath the lower branches and grasped the almond tree's trunk. "*We must lift her out,*" he shouted over the downpour, "*and plant her in the ground! Take the spade and move some of that dirt out of the way!*"

"*I'll do that!*" Ian shouted, and lunged for the spade standing nearby. He madly shoveled dirt this way and that from the center of the bower.

"*Enough!*" Bo said. The tree trembled continually now, and drupes as well as leaves fell to the ground. Shaking with terror, Bo grasped the trunk and lifted with all his might.

"*A moment, my love, we'll have you in the soft ground!*" He heaved again but the box came up, too. "*Hold the box!*"

Ian flung the spade aside. He and Tom threw themselves on the wet ground and wrapped their arms around the box. "*We have it! Hurry, boy!*" Tom's ropy muscles strained and Ian held on with all his might, his face purpling as Bo heaved again and freed the tree from the box.

Bo staggered back, steadied himself and turned to gentle the tree into the hole Ian had dug. He dropped to his knees and scooped loose soil in around the roots. Tom let go the box, scrambled over on hands and knees and joined in, scooping with both arms and softly tamping down the dirt.

The tree shivered violently and loosed a flurry of wet leaves. A volley of drupes thudded to the ground.

Ian got to his feet, gasping, wild eyes sliding from the wrecked tree to his distraught elders, and back to the tree, which was his *Aunt Anisette.*

The two older men sat back, chests heaving. Narrow almond leaves plastered their wet hair and clothing. Clods of mud besmeared all three from head to toe.

Tom sat shaking, mouth open, groaning piteously. The sound shocked Bo and he turned to his old friend, fearing for his safety as well as Anisette's.

"*Father,*" Bo gasped, "*Father have mercy on us. Please, my Jesu, please...*" He broke down and wept with his head in his hands, unable to look at the raw pain on Tom's face, and his weeping rose to a howl at the unbearable thought of life without Anisette.

Lightning blazed, thunder obliterated Bo's howls, and rain lashed at the still-trembling tree.

Names and Places

Monti opened her laptop. Nine o'clock already. Time to get to work. She would not check email, she would get right to it. She picked up her Scrabble word list. What words had she not yet used? WITHERS. That shouldn't be too hard, either as part of a horse—what part of a horse exactly would that be? She didn't recall...she'd have to Google it. Or 'as the rose withers' would work, too. NEBULA. Oh, she'd used that, she could cross it off. It hadn't been easy to fit in, but she'd found a spot. Then there were all those two letter words to use. EM. JO. LO. She stretched, did backward circles with her shoulders, checked her posture.

Finishing a story was hard work. But still, it was easier than dealing with real-life stories. She'd noticed Jenny chatting with the Cominskis yesterday at church, and was glad that relationship was growing well.

She would miss the girl, she realized. She and Noelle were loud and silly and exasperating and absolutely fun to be around. It would get real quiet all of a sudden when Jenny moved out on Saturday.

Monti had to admit the prospect of fewer police cars in their driveway was charming, but she didn't regret them. She was glad the girl had taken refuge with her family while she adjusted to her new future, and was relieved she'd be in Dorothy's tender care for the rest of her pregnancy. Ray and Dorothy were unfazed by Blaine's assaults. Monti shook her head. They were the most rock-solid people she knew. Out of the fiery furnace of their own losses they had emerged fearless and selfless, totally sold out to serving God in whatever way he put before them. Monti wanted to be just like them when she grew up.

Monti decided another cup of coffee was required and went to fetch it. She would work for an hour to get Bo and Anisette to Morocco, and then she had to nail down some Thanksgiving plans since it was only...she froze mid-stride in the middle of the hallway. Thanksgiving was next week! What was the matter with her?

She turned and headed back to her desk. Where was her purse? She needed the list she had started yesterday—no, a week ago—in church, and then promptly put out of her head again. She found her purse and rummaged in the soft leather bag until she came up with the little notepad. She'd need bigger paper now—what would she do without her trusty stash of legal pads? She plucked one from the shelves above her desk.

One. Call aging parents. Well, she'd better do that immediately so she'd know how to plan everything else. She put down her pen and grabbed the phone. *What time is it in Florida?* she wondered as she dialed.

"Mom? It's Monti," she said, trying to find the right volume level so her mother could hear her, but wouldn't ask her to stop shouting. Always a challenge. Immediately a racket started outside—a lawn mower— good grief. Who was mowing their lawn in November?

"Well hey, Montana, sweetheart!" her mother said. "I was just thinking of calling you. It's almost Thanksgiving, you know."

"Yes, I know," Monti said. "Are you two coming up this year? We'd love to have you. I can't believe I haven't asked you about it before now, but things are, uh, a tad hectic. Can you come?"

"Oh, I'm sorry dear, we can't this year. We're co-hosting a lost boys Thanksgiving dinner and camping weekend. We were hoping you might get away and come play with us."

Monti chuckled. Everything was an adventure with her mom. And her dad. They never had quite grown up. "What lost boys, Mom? Sudanese?"

"Yes! Oh, they're so much fun. You wouldn't think they'd want to camp, after having to live off the land in such horrible circumstances, but they're quite enthusiastic. Why don't you come down?"

"We'd love to, Mom, but there's no way. We have a house guest, and Kit is struggling. I don't think he could tolerate a long flight right now. Are Mary and Oregon making the trek?" The lawn mower sputtered to a stop and Monti relaxed the hunch she didn't know she was in.

"Maryland and crew arrive the day before Thanksgiving. All eleven of them! Oregon is in Afghanistan. Or is it Argentina? Hmm. I don't remember, but he won't be home until after the clinic is finished, probably not until February, I think he said."

Monti remained profoundly grateful not to have been born in Zimbabwe. Montana wasn't too bad, and Maryland had it easy. But poor Oregon—there wasn't any way to turn that into a normal name. With Keith for a middle name, he didn't want to go by his initials. But it didn't seem to have any negative effects on him. Of course, for much of their childhood they had been surrounded by children with names like Madhukar, Abioye, and Yauwii. No one blinked at Oregon until university. And there, a name like Oregon Housel kind of made you stand out among your pre-med peers.

"I think it's Argentina, Mom," Monti said. "Well, you and Dad have a grand time with the boys, and send us some pictures, okay? We'll be thinking about you, and praying for a good safe adventure for everybody."

"Safe is overrated, but I agree we don't want any mishaps with the campers. Thanks, daughter." Her mom paused. "Has Marla called back yet?"

"Not yet, Mom. But she's never forgotten Noelle's birthday, so we'll probably get a card pretty soon." The lawn mower vroomed to life again. "I'll let you know when we hear more, okay?"

"Okay, love, and don't fret. She'll come around."

Monti teared up, unable to be stoic about this one thing, ever. "I hope so, Mom." She swallowed hard. "Love you lots."

"Love you too, daughter. Big hug for Kit from us, okay?"

"You bet. Same for Dad from us. Bye Mom." Monti put her head in her hands. No parents. No Marla, no Stephen. But she had Kit, and Noelle, and they'd fill the table with whoever else they could drag in. She could do this. It was just Thanksgiving. *And Abba, please forgive the pity party.*

Kit poked his head in the door. "Everything okay, lover?"

She turned her head sideways on her hands and smiled at him. "Yes, more or less. Just having a little poor me session." She stood and went to him. "All done now though, and on to the next thing." She moved in for a kiss. "What's up with you?"

Kit wrapped his arms around her. "I talked with Eddie. He and Brian will be here 9am sharp on Saturday to get Jenny's things moved to Cominskis'. Will you make that coffee cake?"

"Of course! Teenage boys can't work without filling their bottomless stomachs every hour or so. Nor can Eddie, come to think of it." She ducked under his arm and sat back down at her desk. "I'd better write it down though, or I'll end up with no eggs in the house that day, and have to feed them, uh, toast?"

Kit said "Hmm. Quite a backup plan. Who was on the phone?"

"Mom. Did you know Thanksgiving is next week?"

"Of course. The deacons have coordinated the turkey and fixings boxes, and the delivery schedule is all set. Elders are taking the in-town route, and deacons the outlying areas. Why, what's up?"

Monti blinked at him. "Did we contribute something to these boxes, I hope?"

"Of course. Where are you, Monti?' He smoothed the worry line between her eyebrows. "Are your folks okay?" He came and sat in his chair and pulled up to her, knees to knees.

"Yes, they're fine. I just...Thanksgiving hasn't entered my mind for more than a millisecond at a time. I called to invite them, but of course they have a grand adventure all planned. Taking Sudanese refugees camping."

Kip raised his eyebrows. "Ambitious."

She nodded. "Jenny will be at the Cominskis, so it'll just be you and me and Noelle, and whoever we can rope in to fill the empty seats." She swallowed and smiled to prevent the tears starting again, but it didn't fool Kit.

He squeezed her knee. "Okay, then we'd better figure out who has nothing better to do that day. Maybe Nick will be available. Noelle would love that. And how about your students—any lonely souls?"

She snorted. "Plenty. But whether any of them will voluntarily spend additional time with their teacher is another matter. Maybe I'll make it extra credit..."

Now Kit snorted. "I don't think we need to resort to bribery quite yet, Monti."

"Well, maybe not yet," she said, grinning sheepishly at him. "It's not that big a deal, is it?"

"That's what I've been saying, honey," he said. He slapped his knees. "Got an idea. How about I help you with the list I see you have started there, sort of, and then we pretend we're retired and get out the Scrabble board in the middle of the day."

"We are retired, sort of, and it's not the middle of the day."

"It will be by the time we're finished if you argue each point," he said.

The kitchen phone rang, cutting off a witty reply she would have thought up in just a minute. She made a face at Kit and went to answer it.

Five minutes later Kit came out to the kitchen to find her busy scribbling on another legal pad. "What are you doing?"

"That was Lucy," Monti said. "I got out of costumes and kid wrangling, and only committed to bring 4 dozen cookies for the Christmas pageant!" She grinned, waiting for Kit's admiration and amazement.

"Christmas? You're planning Christmas?"

"Well, not on purpose! Lucy started it!" Monti looked at him and her shoulders sagged. "She probably planned Thanksgiving in June."

Kit pulled her in for a hug. "Doesn't matter. Let's get back to what we were doing, okay?"

She snuggled in. "I don't know, this is nice. Let's do this instead."

"Oh yeah? I got better stuff than this..." Kit said, waggling his eyebrows at her.

Waiting

It poured for three days. Bo glowered as black as the storm, tension radiating from him in waves that crashed against anyone unwise enough to cross his path. He would not eat. He could not sleep. He spent hours on end sitting on the rain-slicked stone bench in Anisette's bower, or curled around the trunk of the almond tree. Tom's entreaties for him to come in met with harsh refusals. A proffered blanket was thrown aside. He accepted a hot mug of coffee now and then with shaking hands. But after a sip or two it sat forgotten on the bench, filling with cold rain while Bo brooded.

Tom and Ian did the chores in silence and ate their meals at the kitchen table, companions in misery. Ian was nigh to bursting with questions about Anisette and the enchantment, but when the first he gave voice to was answered with a tormented moan from poor old Tom, he dared ask no more.

On the morning of the fourth day, the rain eased. Bo had spent the night wrapped around Anisette's trunk. He woke and knew where he was after a moment. The fear and grief of the past days flooded over him and he squeezed his eyes shut again, curled more tightly about the tree.

But after a minute or two he grew aware of the lessening of the rain. He opened his eyes and sat up to take stock. Yes, it barely sputtered now, and the sky was unmistakably clearing. He pushed himself to his feet, groaning, every muscle stiff and aching from sleeping on the wet ground. He stepped back and examined the almond tree. It had lost at least a third of its leaves and many drupes, but no longer trembled. Rain dripped from every branch. There was no way to know if she were injured. He glanced at the sky again. The rain had stopped, but today would be wretched, waiting for her to dry and be restored to him.

The back door opened and Tom limped out to join him, followed by Ian bearing a tray. "And how is my lady this morning?" his old friend said.

"I cannot tell, Tom. I may go mad today waiting for her restoration."

Ian set the tray on the bench, and the aroma of hot coffee made Bo's mouth water. "Thank you, nephew. That's exactly what I am needing."

"There's biscuits and bacon, too. You must shovel them down, hungry or no. We know not what...I mean to say..." Tom scowled and bit out, "Eat your breakfast, boy."

Ian peered at the sky. "So the rain has stopped." He looked at the men. "What happens now?"

"Now we wait, lad," Bo said. "Until she's dry. Then she'll be restored to us, just as she ever was." His heart cringed at that. He was not at all sure she would be just as she ever was. He saw the same fear in Tom's eyes. The old man, he noticed, was filthy. He looked down at himself. "Meanwhile," he said, "I believe some washing up is in order. We do not want our lady to see us in this state."

The three of them polished off the biscuits, bacon and coffee in silence, standing where they were, then trooped to the pump to make themselves marginally presentable. Bo took a long look back to the bower, fear quivering in his belly. A little while only, and he would know how things stood.

Monkey Drums

M onti woke as a gorilla pounded through a vicious drum solo inside her head. She groaned and rolled onto her back, gripping her head. She opened her mouth wide and wiggled her jaw back and forth. Yep, she had been clenching her jaw in her sleep, a sure sign she was just a teeny bit stressed. She pressed the heels of her hands into her eyes. Rotten way to start the day. Kit still snored quietly beside her—she was glad he'd had a good night, anyway.

She sat up and instantly regretted it. She needed a hot shower and a cup of coffee to knock the headache down a few notches. Sliding out of bed she maneuvered to the bathroom, feeling for the wall and working to get her eyes to focus.

With hot water pounding the back of her neck, Monti's synapses started to fire. Thinking became a real possibility. Let's see, something easy to start with...what day is it? Ah, Tuesday. That meant three classes to teach, then a couple of errands, and home to eat whatever Kit cooked for supper. No meetings on Tuesday evenings, so maybe a Scrabble game. A smile started at the corner of her mouth. She could do this day even with the gorilla, though he pounded more like a baby chimp now.

Maybe she'd ask if any of her students were at loose ends for Thanksgiving. And that, she realized, was the source of her stress. All the Thanksgiving details still floated around in her brain, unsettled and not looking anything like a firm plan yet. She and Kit never had got back to the list yesterday...She liked to have things nailed down and she was having trouble finding any nails, let alone a hammer. Well, today would help. She'd try to finalize the guest list, which would allow her to move on to the shopping list.

She turned off the water and took stock. The monkey drums were backing off, that was a relief. She grabbed her towel.

Kit poked his head in the bathroom door. "Hey there, lover."

"Good morning, sweetheart. How'd you sleep?"

"Great! Really good night. You?"

"Can't complain. Headache, but it's retreating now." She tucked her towel around her, stepped into his open arms and tipped her face up for a kiss. "Got big plans today?"

"Not really," he said, and provided a very nice kiss. "I'm going to call Mike Rutherford and see if he'll meet for coffee. I want to stay in the Blaine loop." He tugged at the top of her towel with one finger and peered down inside with exaggerated appreciation. "I like your outfit. Sexy."

"Hmm. Maybe I should take a photo and add it to my wardrobe collection," she said. "Not sure where I'd ever wear it, though. I'll be interested to know if there's any chance Blaine will be let out on bail, if Mike knows that."

"Don't worry, whatever intel I dig out I'll be briefing you on promptly." He patted her backside and got out of her way so she could get dressed. "What about you? Normal Tuesday?"

"Yep. I'll be trying to convince my students that studying during Thanksgiving break is a capital idea. But my hopes are not high on that front." Monti scanned her wardrobe pics and chose a drapey cornflower-blue sweater and slim black skirt. Her chunky black and silver necklace and earrings would pull the outfit together.

"We never did finish the Thanksgiving list," she said with a sideways glance.

"I don't regret that one iota," Kit said, grinning. "Let's look at that this evening, if you want."

She grinned back, then glanced out the bedroom window. Her black wool tights, maybe, with her flat ankle boots. The fresh snow on the lawn didn't look the kind to melt off quickly. She'd consult Noelle about the correctness of ankle boots with tights.

"Okay, let's do. But I want to leave plenty of time for Scrabble." She pulled the sweater on over her head. "I'm thinking of reading the dictionary between classes, so get ready for a good game." Kit chortled and she said, "Made you laugh.".

"You always do," he said. "You prepare as best you can, lover, and may the best man win. I'm gonna go start the coffee."

"Best man, my eye," Monti muttered as she found her tights. "May the best woman win." It would be fabulous to win two in a row.

MONTI PULLED INTO THE parking lot with profound relief and loosened her death grip on the steering wheel. The roads were slick with ice and snow, and cars were sliding every which way. She had her studded snow tires on but that didn't help much on ice and she'd taken it nice and slow. Even so, she slid to within inches of the car ahead of her at a stoplight, and she witnessed two or three fender benders between home and the school. Monti rolled her head to ease the tension in her neck. It seemed to take a slick day or two every year for people to get reacquainted with their winter-driving skills. Add to that new drivers and imports from southern climates experiencing their first north Idaho winter, and November offered some serious white-knuckle moments.

By the time Monti wobbled across the equally icy parking lot and unlocked her classroom, four or five students waited in a huddle in the hall outside the classroom.

"Hey everybody," she said, glancing at their hunched shoulders and hands jammed into tight jeans pockets. Where were their coats? "Did you notice it's cold today?" She opened the door and waved them in. "Is it still uncool to wear a coat to school?"

"Naw, Mrs. M, it ain't that cold." This from Bobby, who was visibly shivering. Monti rolled her eyes and took off her coat. "It snowed, I'd say that means it's pretty cold." The heat was on in the classroom, anyway. She headed for the coffeemaker. It was never uncool to drink coffee, and it would warm them up.

"Hey Mrs. M," Tanya said. "Austin told me you went to visit him."

Monti turned, coffee scoop in hand. "Yes I did."

Tanya slid her heavy pack from her shoulders and dropped it to the floor, wincing. "I went to see him, too. We were neighbors when we were kids. He kept the mean boys from pickin' on me and my sister." She sank into her seat looking as weary at 18 as Monti felt at, well, at her age whatever that was, which she could figure out in a minute if she really wanted to.

"Well, how about that."

"I tried to get Rafael to go with me, but he wouldn't."

"No, I suppose not."

"They used to be friends, clear up to junior year, but after Rafael hurt his knee, they ain't friends no more." She shook her dark curls to emphasize this point.

Bobby, hovering about the coffee pot with an empty cup, said, "Man, that sucked big time." He shook his head. "Rafael lost his scholarship. That messed Austin up. Bad story."

"It is sad when a friendship falls apart," Monti said. She didn't want to encourage the conversation. It was gossip, really, and she needed to change the subject.

"Speaking of stories, bad or otherwise, I hope you all have finished your writing assignments. I want you to turn them in today, and I'll read them during Thanksgiving break. And let's talk about how you can use that time off wisely, too." *And maybe I'll discover a lonesome soul or two to fill up our table.*

Battered

A nisette pulled her feet from the soft soil, wobbled, and fell to her hands and knees. She frowned. Something was amiss. She was exhausted, when she was used to feel rested when restored to her true self. Oh, the box! A vague disquiet disturbed her still, an impression of terror and helplessness. She glanced round at the almond leaves and drupes scattered thickly about her, the churned-up soil, the footprints, the cast-aside spade and abandoned box.

Tears slid down her face, for her broken dreams and her lost hope. She could never travel to Morocco. "Oh Jesu, whatever shall we do now?" Anisette heard the door open and tried to rise. She collapsed instantly.

Bo rushed to her side and pulled her to him. "Are you well, Anisette? You're weeping! Are you hurt?" She shook her head but could not answer. She reached for his arms, buried her face in his shirt. He gathered her up and carried her into the house.

"Tom! Fetch the doctor! And Josiah." Chairs scraped and clattered as Tom and Ian rushed to Bo from the kitchen.

Tom took in the situation with one despairing glance and grabbed his hat. "I'll have them here quick as a cat. Ian! Stop gawkin' and help me with the horses!" Tom hobbled out the door with Ian on his heels.

Bo laid Anisette on her bed and sat beside her. "My love, what ails thee? What can I do for thee?" He smoothed her hair away from her pallid face, straightened her gown, plumped her pillow. She did not respond, but lay still while tears slid from the corners of her eyes.

Bo stood, frantic to do something. Noticing her muddy hands and feet, he grabbed the pitcher from her washstand and filled the basin. He clunked the pitcher back down, chipping the edge of the basin. He wet a linen cloth and gently washed his wife's limp hands, and then her feet.

"The doctor and Josiah are on their way, love, 'twill not be long. They'll know what to do." He finished cleaning her feet, and found he had dirtied the coun-

terpane considerably. He took up a towel, lifted Anisette's feet, spread the towel over the mess and set her feet back down. He ran his hands through his hair and turned on his heel, taking stock of the room. What else? Water! Surely she needed a sip of water. He rushed from the room and returned with a mug, splashing water on the floor, heedless.

"Wilt take a sip, Anisette? A wee sip of water?" She opened her eyes and looked at him from under heavy eyelids. Encouraged, he slid an arm under her shoulders, lifted her a little, and held the mug to her lips. She took a sip and sagged against his arm as he laid her back down. He set the mug on the washstand from where it promptly fell and smashed on the floor.

"You're a hoddypeak, Bo Willem," he muttered. He fetched broom and dustpan and swept up the mess. He hurried to dump it in the rubbish bin, but knocked his elbow on the doorpost and spilled it all on the kitchen floor. Letting out a low growl that would have been a howl of frustration if not for his wife lying ill close by, he swept up the mess again and disposed of it.

He returned to Anisette's side. She had sunk into a deep sleep. At least, he hoped it were only sleep. He watched her closely for several minutes. Her breathing was shallow but even enough. She didn't stir at all. After turning on his heel clear round again and finding naught else to do, Bo dropped to his knees and laid his head on the bed. He lifted Anisette's nerveless hand and held it to his lips. "Please, Almighty God...please...do not take my sweet girl from me..."

When Tom and Ian returned with Josiah in tow Bo still knelt, kissing Anisette's hand and murmuring pleas for mercy. Tom gripped his shoulder and shook him gently. "Bo, my lad. Pastor is here. And the doctor will be on his way, just so soon as he finishes splinting young Manfred Baker's broken arm."

Bo sat back, not leaving go of his wife's hand, and turned to his old friend. "Josiah, what...what can we do? What will happen to my sweet Anisette?"

Josiah knelt beside Bo and put an arm around his friend's hunched shoulders. "You are doing the work now, man. Keep battering at the door of heaven, and we will join you, and God will do what He will do."

Soup Love

Monti smiled as she pulled into the police-free driveway. Classes accomplished, car gassed up, banking done. No surly students, no ice on the roads, no traffic jams, no long lines—nothing but green lights both literal and figurative all afternoon. She pushed down the querulous whisper at the edge of her mind, the one wondering when the other shoe would drop. She sighed. How stupid was that, not to be satisfied even when everything went perfectly? Godliness with contentment would be great gain, indeed. If she could ever get there from here.

Kit opened the kitchen door and stepped out to meet her. She eyed him carefully. He was moving easily, that was a mercy. *Thank you, Abba*. She came around to meet him.

"Hey lover, what'd you bring me?" He leaned down and kissed her.

"Oh, same old stuff," she said.

"Mmm. My favorite," he said.

She rested for a long moment in his arms, always her best place. Then they stepped apart and she grabbed her bags from the front seat. "Dinner smells good." The aroma made her mouth water. "Have you been watching cooking shows?"

"Sure Monti, me and Paula Deen," Kit said, smiling. "It's just soup, love."

"Soup love. Huh. Well, I'll try anything once."

He rolled his eyes and held up the tea kettle. She nodded and he filled the kettle at the sink.

"Did you get to talk with Mike Rutherford?"

"Yes. But he's a bit fuzzy on what's happening with Blaine."

"How can that be? I'd sure know what was going on if my kid was in jail."

Kit turned the heat on under the kettle and turned to give Monti his military colonel stare. "Monti, where is Marla, precisely? How long has she been there, when will she be released? Where was she the last year before that?"

225

"That's not the same!"

Kit, infuriating man, having made his infuriating point, just shrugged.

She bit back another retort, using up considerable will power in the effort, and waited for the wave of self-righteous indignation to pass. She started emptying the dish rack, being extra gentle to compensate for how much she wanted to slam things around. She cleared her throat. "So, we don't know if or when Blaine will be out loose. That's disappointing."

"CJ will call us if he's released."

"Okay." The teakettle whistled and Monti cut it short. She filled their mugs. "Do I have time to work on my story a bit before dinner?"

"Sure, Noelle said they'd be home around six, so let's wait for them."

"Sounds good," she said, and laid her hand on his cheek. "See you in a bit."

Monti fished the teabag from her mug and retreated to the office. Back to Bo and Anisette. She was determined to finish their story. She opened the document on her laptop, and found her word list under her mug. In a sudden flash of brilliance—okay maybe that was overstating it a bit—she saw how she could use WITHERS, EM, and JO. She'd have to go back and find the spot where Bo and Anisette were going to town in the wagon...

Conspiracy

The doctor closed the bedchamber door behind him and went to join the menfolk in the kitchen. Four doleful faces greeted him, four pairs of red and weary eyes followed him as he pulled out a chair and sat, dropping his leather bag on the floor beside him.

After a moment, when no one asked him anything, he cleared his throat. "She's not in mortal danger, I think." He watched the tension ease away from Josiah and Ian, and even Tom, but Bo was not so easily comforted. The doctor plowed on. "She's exhausted. As if she'd..." He'd been going to say 'just given birth', but stopped himself in time. "As if she'd worked for days with no rest nor nourishment. Or been ill for weeks." He looked at Bo. "How long was she...in the bower?"

"Three days and a half," Bo said.

"But, that has never set her back so before, has it?"

"No. 'Twas not the rain—it was the cursed box."

"Box?" He waited, glanced around. No explanation was offered. In fact, the red-faced men would not look at him. "What box? What mischief have you been about here?"

"No mischief, doctor," Josiah assured him. "They built a box...for the journey." Josiah explained the idea, the custom designed and built box, and the miscarriage of the test.

"I see. My apologies, Bo Willem, for my tone." Catching sight of the wretched despair on old Tom's face, the doctor added, "'Twas a promising scheme, and carefully carried out. It might well have been just the answer needed." He studied the still gloomy faces. "But...I need not tell you, surely, that the box must be given up." Bo scowled at him and opened his mouth but the doctor put up his hands and cut him off. "I know, I know, that is full plain. But you grasp the need for me to be sure of you on this point. Now we must turn to the plan for bringing the lady back to health."

Doctor Fleming laid out strict instructions for nursing Anisette. What to feed her, when and for how long she might be allowed out of bed and so forth. Bo and Tom drank it in like a tonic. Here were tasks to do which would help their beloved lady, and not do her harm. They thanked the doctor and showed him out.

But after he left, silence sank once more around the solemn men.

Josiah roused himself. "Bo," he ventured. His friend made no response. "Bo, do not lose hope. Jesu will make the path clear, if it be only one step at a time." He gripped Bo's shoulder. "Today's step, my friend, is to begin to restore Anisette to health, yes?" Bo nodded, with an effort as though his head were cast of solid lead. "And whilst you and Tom are about that, we shall all ask for light to be shone on the next step, shall we not?" One by one the men lifted their heads and nodded at him. "Good. I had best be off home, afore my Bess begins to worry. I shall stop by on the morrow, shall I?"

Bo grasped his friend's hand. "Please do, Josiah. And we thank you for your counsel. It was sorely needed." He ran his hands through his hair. Crackles and pops sounded as he rolled his head around to loosen his cramped muscles. He looked toward Anisette's door. "I'll say goodnight, friend. Tom, will you show Josiah out?" He shook the pastor's hand and headed for the bedchamber.

When the door had closed behind Bo, Tom turned toward the door, but Josiah motioned him back to his seat. "Now, men, what's to be done for our poor friends? 'Tis quite a corner they are backed into. To take ship to the desert puts Anisette in danger. To carry a child in this place puts Anisette in danger. To dwell together without living as man and wife will break both their hearts and put the marriage in danger, and I daresay could not be endured for long. What is to be done?" Josiah shook his head. The three thought their own thoughts a while.

"Pastor Wheaton," Ian said. "I wonder, would you know of any maps we might borrow? I remember a man back to home that were quite a traveler. He were always rolling out maps and planning caravans to here and there, all over the world." Ian paused and turned bright pink when he saw how closely the older men listened to him.

"Go on, lad, spill out the rest," Tom said.

"Ah well, I wonder if an overland route might be discovered, to get Master Bo and Lady Anisette to Morocco."

"Overland! Why, 'twould be hundreds—nay, thousands of miles. One would need to travel around the Great Sea," Josiah said. "And no kind of safe travel, either."

Ian laid his hand on the table, palm down. "Even so, know you of any maps? I want to search out if there be any possible way."

Tom slapped the boy on the back. "And why not! It canna hurt to look into the thing now can it, Josiah?"

"No, no, of course not. Surely, young Ian, I have in mind some maps I might borrow. But, let's not be getting their hopes up! Not a word of this to the Willems." Josiah rose and collected his hat. "In fact, I think it might be best if you did your cartographical musings at the manse. I'll see if I might get hold the maps, and send a message to you. Will you be able to spare him tomorrow or the next day, Tom?"

"Oh, aye. He's mostly underfoot anyway," Tom said, and tousled the young man's hair. "Have mercy on us and put some bellytimber into him while you have him, will you not? He shovels down more than Bo and me together."

Ian blushed furiously but said nothing. Josiah smiled. "And did I not raise three strapping sons and a fourth yet in the house, Old Tom? I'm not likely to be shocked, however much Master Ian may 'shovel down.'" Josiah settled his hat on his head and glanced toward the bedchamber. "And may God bless our efforts, as I know not how much more the poor creatures can bear," he said, and took his leave.

The next afternoon a knock sounded at the front door. Old Tom, opening the door to find Josiah's youngest lad clutching a somewhat smudged and wrinkled note, hunched his shoulders, peered back down the hall, and hushed him with a loud "sshhh!" The boy, startled, stepped back off the front step but Tom motioned him forward again.

"Come here, lad, give it now," Tom said. "Is an answer wanted?"

"I don't think so," he began.

"Ssshhh!" Tom hissed. He peered back down the hall again toward Anisette's bedchamber. "Quietly, James."

"Er, Father did not say an answer was wanted," said the boy, bewildered at Tom's manner. "Is aught amiss, Old Tom?"

"Nay, nay. Hold a mite whilst I see what we have." Tom stepped out to join James on the step. He closed the door softly and unfolded the note. He held it

away, moved it toward him, then away again until the letters sharpened for him. He read the note, grimacing with the effort. A wide grin displayed his remaining teeth in all their sparse glory, and he clapped the boy on the back. "Tell your father that Ian will be round tomorrow sunup, or right thereafter, whene'er the chores be done."

"Yes, sir, I'll tell him," James said. Tom shooed him off the step and stuffed the note in his own breeches pocket. He opened the door a crack, peered in, and seeing no one in the hall slipped in and closed it behind him without a sound.

"Who was that?" Ian asked from behind him, and Tom jumped and fell to shushing again.

"It were James, Josiah's boy," Tom said in a hoarse whisper. "You're to go tomorrow morning early to look at them maps."

"Why are we whispering?" Ian asked.

"Do you not remember, you muddlehead—we're not to let Master Bo hear of the thing."

"Master Bo is down to the dock, tending the punt," Ian whispered.

Tom straightened and scowled. "Well you might have said so, lad!"

Ian spread his hands and opened his mouth, but shut it again. He knew Tom well enough already to realize how little use it would be to protest.

Message

M onti unlocked her classroom door, turned the lights on and deposited her tote on her chair. She had four classes remaining before Thanksgiving break. Today and tomorrow, then she would be free to concentrate on next week's definite events and a whole universe of possible Marla-related events. And hopefully no Blaine-related events. If she could concentrate on anything.

Already this morning she'd put on two different earrings, as she discovered during a last-minute check in the mirror before she headed out the door. She'd gotten halfway to the market before remembering she was meant to be going to school. She had stopped at a green light and almost run a red one. She'd finally made it to the parking lot without accident, injury, or moving violation, for which she was grateful and a bit surprised.

Monti started for the coffeemaker and jumped when her phone rang. Mitch ambled through the door with a wave as she changed direction and rummaged through her bag for the phone.

"Hi, Mrs. Rising." Cody and Jessica had arrived.

She nodded at them, located the phone and saw 'Marla' glowing at her from the screen. She froze. To answer or not? It was 9:02. She shouldn't answer, but that was impossible. She touched the answer icon and said, "One sec, sweetheart." She looked sternly at her students and said, "I'll be right back." Then she dashed out the door and a few steps down the hall. "Marla?"

"Mom?"

"Yes! Hi honey," Monti said, leaning against the wall, her heart hammering. "We called earlier."

"Yeah, I got the message. I'm not allowed—I don't have the phone with me all the time," Marla said. "Mom, did you tell Noelle I called?"

"Yes, of course, honey! She's so hoping you'll come home."

"Yeah? Are you sure?" Marla heaved a deep sigh. "I've screwed everything up royally. I wouldn't be surprised if she never wanted to see me again."

"No, Marla, no one feels like that. We've missed you terribly, prayed for you every day. We want you home more than anything." Monti bit her lip. She mustn't start crying.

Marla was silent a few moments. "Well, I'm finished here on the 10th. I have to give the counselor an address where I'll be headed." She paused. "Where I'll be staying."

Yes! "Sure, of course. You have our address, right?" Dumb question.

"Yeah, I do. The only thing is," Marla paused again, "I don't have enough money to get there, Mom."

In a flash, a complete plan appeared in Monti's head. No—two complete plans. Should she talk to her parents first? "Don't worry about that, Marla. I'm thinking of ideas. We'll get you here one way or another." Monti stopped, then decided to charge ahead. "How would you feel about spending a little time with your grandparents?"

"You mean Housels? I haven't thought about it. They're getting pretty old, aren't they?"

Monti chuckled. "It depends who you ask. They're 83 and 81, but still going strong. Last time I talked to them they were going camping with Sudanese refugees. The reason I ask, they might think it would be a wonderful idea to drive out here with you for Christmas. Or fly, maybe. I'm brainstorming." A couple of students had come in from outside and stared at her curiously as they walked toward the classroom. She turned away from them.

"Drive? I don't know, Mom. That'd take, what? A week? We'd be at each other's throats."

"I can't imagine my folks ever at anyone's throat, but if it sounds too stressful then never mind. We could fly you home, and ask if they want to come, too. Regardless, I'm sure they'd love to take you home with them when you're done at rehab, and take you to the airport whenever." Monti paused. Marla said nothing. "Does that sound like a possibility?"

After a long pause, Marla said, "Yeah, I think so. But you haven't talked to them?"

"No, not about this, but I will when I get home today. They'll love the idea, I promise."

"Okay. Well, I'll call you tomorrow." Marla cleared her throat. "I was thinking about calling Noelle, but..." her voice faltered. "Maybe tomorrow I could talk to her. You think that's a good idea?"

Monti straightened and took a step away from the wall. "I do. She will very much want to talk with you, Marla, she loves you. We love you."

"'kay," she whispered. "I gotta go now."

"All right baby girl, I'll talk to you tomorrow. Oh! But what time? Do you know when you'll be able to call?" But Marla was already gone. Monti stamped her feet and growled—then noticed Anthony staring at her, his hand on the doorknob. She smiled at him and motioned for him to go on and open the door. She followed him into the classroom.

After her ten o'clock class, Monti went out to her car to text Noelle and call Kit. Marla was back in contact and that news wouldn't keep any longer. She'd wait until she got home to try her parents—she didn't want to sit in the parking lot shouting into her phone. But now her phone announced an incoming text. Noelle, no doubt, wanting more details. Monti smiled and opened the app.

But it wasn't Noelle. And there was no message, only a picture. A cat sitting in a window. Monti zoomed in and looked closer. It was Gulliver, she realized, sitting in the front window of their house. Monti lowered the phone.

What on earth? Who would send her that, and why? Maybe Dot? Driving by, saw him in the window and snapped a pic...she checked the sending number but didn't recognize it. So, not Dot. A text bubble appeared.

There was a message after all.

Cat Pic

Monti's stomach churned and her heart pounded. She was being silly, probably, but she called Kit again. It went to voice mail and she decided not to leave a panicky message. Did she have CJ's number? Yes! She pushed call and tried to think what to say when he answered, which he did immediately.

"CJ! Montana Rising here, I'm so glad you answered. I just got a picture of my cat in a text message."

"Hey, Mrs. Rising. You got what?"

Monti described the picture.

"No message?"

"Oh yes, there was message," she said. "Bye-bye kitty."

"Shazam," CJ said.

"I don't recognize the number it was sent from," she said. "Should I be concerned?"

"At this point, Mrs. Rising, I think we need to be concerned about anything unusual that happens. It sounds like a threat." He paused. "Can you forward it to me?"

"I don't know, can I?"

"Sure," CJ said. Then listed off the steps. "Want to give that a try?"

"I can...but I'm worried I might accidentally delete it."

"I understand, Mrs. Rising. Hey, where are you? Maybe I should drop by and do it for you—show you. Then you'll know how."

"Sure, thank you CJ, I'm at the school." She told him where to find her classroom. "I'd better go, I have one more class."

"All right, I'll see you in approximately 20 minutes."

She hung up and rested her head on the steering wheel. What was going on? Wasn't Blaine still in jail? *Abba, help me think! And please, I need to calm down and function for the next hour.* She took a deep breath and opened her car door.

Monti waited until Tyree finished pouring his coffee before calling her twelve o'clock class to order. It was her last day with them before they scattered to the winds for Thanksgiving break. Except for those who had nowhere to scatter to...

"Hello, class," Monti said. "Let's retrieve your writing assignments from wherever they are, and pass them to the front, please." Much rummaging in backpacks and notebooks commenced. She noticed Tanya and Alex didn't move. Tanya bit her lip and swallowed hard. Alex just scowled and slouched lower in his chair. Bobby offered the four papers he'd collected; Monti deposited them in the wire basket on the corner of her desk and picked up a stack of her own.

"Thank you," she said. "Now, you have a whole week off next week..." She waited as two or three enthusiastic whoops interrupted. "But after that you have only two weeks until finals, and I know some of you will have term papers due also."

She distributed the sheets to the students. "So, here are my suggestions for what you might reasonably accomplish during your Thanksgiving break, while..." she paused again to give the collective groan time to dissipate. "While still allowing ample time for rest and recreation, and travel to wherever you might be going for Thanksgiving."

Her students scanned the page she had given them. "We'll spend a little time unpacking this page, and I want you to make notes to customize it for your own situation."

She picked up another stack of papers from her desk. "But first, have any of you decided that Thanksgiving dinner at the Risings' sounds like your first choice for next Thursday?" No one raised a hand, which didn't surprise her. They'd be reluctant to volunteer that in front of everyone. "Well, if anyone does want to eat turkey and pie with a slightly eccentric family with plenty of room at the table, I have directions here for finding our house. You can snag them after class." She put the papers back on her desk and breathed a quick prayer for someone to accept her invitation, or no one, or whatever would be best.

They'd been working on her handout for about ten minutes when CJ knocked on the door. She waved him in and retrieved her phone from her purse. "Thanks, CJ," she said in a low voice, as she opened the texting app and handed over the phone. She glanced at her class and found all six of them staring at her and the detective. She motioned for them to return to their work, with zero effect. She rolled her eyes and returned her attention to CJ. He forwarded the text and picture to himself, showing her each step, and he jotted down the phone number.

"I'll let you know what I find out," he said.

"Thank you, Detective," Monti said, and showed him out.

"What up, Mrs. R?" Tyree wanted to know. They were all goggle- eyed.

"Someone sent me a cat picture," Monti said.

"Like, a LOL cat?" Kelsey asked.

"Not exactly," said Monti, reluctant to explain. "It isn't anything for you to worry about, and it's probably nothing anyway."

"Wow, my grandma loves getting cat pics," Bobby said. "She never called no cops on it. You're one different lady, Mrs. R."

Monti smiled. "I think I'll take that as a compliment," she said. "Shall we call it done, kids? I'm ready to go home."

Universal agreement was evidenced by an immediate rustle of papers being stuffed into backpacks. The students laughed and horsed around, the gift of a few extra minutes of freedom enough to make every one of them cheerful. Monti leaned back against her desk as they filed out, and noticed from the corner of her eye that two of them took a copy of the directions to her house.

Bright Green

N ext morning Tom determined to make no noise as he set about lighting the fire, boiling the coffee and getting the breakfast up, while Ian hurried through the outdoor chores, fetching water and caring for the horses.

Bo they did not see, but Tom knew him to be stationed at Anisette's bedside, where he had been all the night judging by the untouched bed in Bo's bedchamber. Tom shook his head, grieving for his master and his lady, whom both he loved more than his own life. He looked a scowl toward Heaven for their trouble, then blanched and muttered a repentant prayer. God would do as He wanted, and that was only to be expected. Still, it were hard.

A door scraped and Bo emerged, creaking and bleary, from Anisette's room. Bo spared Tom the briefest glance before turning to the back door and heading out to the jakes.

Tom set down his knife and stole into the bedchamber to see how his lady fared. She lay perfectly still, pale as milk excepting the dark circles under her eyes. She slept peacefully. Her golden curls spilled across the pillow, her brow was smooth and she had no feverish look about her. Tom made bold to take her hand and plant a whiskery kiss on it, then grasped it in both his and begged God's mercy for the thousandth time.

Sighing, he placed her hand gently back on the counterpane and collected the ewer and towel. He could keep her in fresh water and linen, at least. He gazed at Anisette's sweet face a moment before turning to carry on with his chores. Closing the door softly behind him, he met Ian hauling in a bucket of water.

"Tom. Have you a biscuit or somewhat to put in my belly afore I head to Pastor Wheaton's?"

Tom shushed him, and motioned for him to follow him to the kitchen. He plunked a mug down on the table, and Ian poured in generous dollops of honey and cream. Tom filled it with piping hot coffee and put a plate of biscuits in front of the lad.

"Now don't be hurrying back, lad," Tom said, very low. "You search the matter out most thorough like. If there be any hope in it, 'twill do the master's heart good just to think on it." He watched the young man dispatch three biscuits between huge gulps of coffee. "Stay for dinner at least, I beg ye."

Ian made a face at him, chewing all the while. He drained the mug and rose to go. He grabbed his cap from his back pocket and pulled it down over his mop of hair. With a wink at Tom he palmed another biscuit from the plate and secreted it in his jacket. "I'll do my level best, Old Tom," he said, keeping his voice down likewise. "I don't like to see them so sad. If there be a way to Morocco from here that don't cross over the Great Sea and don't take a year's traveling, I'll find it."

A door closed and Tom's chin went up sharply. He peered down the hall. Bo had disappeared back into Anisette's chamber. "Aye, lad, and may God grant a fix to this wretched jam."

Ian left and Tom finished his own cup of coffee. It were maddening quiet in the house without Anisette's silver-bell laugh. It weren't to be borne. He hauled himself up and wandered out the back door to the bower.

The blasted box lay tipped where they'd thrown it. The air was still rich with the smell of churned garden soil. He should rake it smooth to be ready for his lady's next need of it. He fetched the rake from the shed and began tidying Anisette's sanctuary. A bit of bright green caught his eye. He stooped to pull it, wincing as he grabbed his knee with a gnarled hand for balance. He reached for the weed but stopped, cocking his head—it were a seedling, full six inches tall, standing amid the clods of earth. And there was another—and yet another. Tom lowered himself to his knees.

The little trees had sprung from—there could be no doubt— almonds. A look about revealed a score or more sprouted drupes scattered across the soil, drupes knocked from the tree during the frantic shift from box to bower just the day before yesterday. He was dumbfounded. What was happening? He knelt there in the dirt and tried mightily to make sense of what he was seeing.

Tell Me Everything

When the last student left, Monti called home. Kit answered this time. "Hey love, is Gulliver okay?"

"What?" He laughed. "Since when does the cat get top billing?"

Monti explained about the picture and text message. "Keep an eye on him, will you?"

"Monti, he never goes outside. I don't know how he can come to any harm, unless he gets the zooms and bounces headfirst down the stairs."

"Yeah, I know. But it has me a little spooked. Anyway, I'm headed home. I want to call my folks before it gets too late."

"Good, Noelle might be a little stressed when she gets home and you handle that better than I do."

"Oh, you do fine. A hug and a cup of tea do wonders, so you have the basics down."

"And tissues, don't forget," he said. "I always offer tissues."

"You're a pro, Kit. See you soon." She ended the call, packed up and drove straight home.

Monti couldn't stop thinking about the picture of Gulliver. It was invasive on several levels. Someone she most likely didn't know knew where she lived, had stood in front of her house and taken a picture of her cat, and knew her phone number to send it to her. And of course, this someone wished her ill. Wished Gulliver ill? That was ridiculous. He never did anything worse than shed on you. And drool a tiny bit sometimes. And try to trip you by winding through your legs. And puke on the rug once in a great while. Minor stuff. And definitely never inflicted on anyone outside the house. Monti gripped the steering wheel. Had someone been in her house?

By the time she pulled into the driveway she was freaking just a bit. Noelle's car was home. Poor Kit, he'd have his fill of female drama tonight.

Kit came out, took her bag and pulled her in for a hug. She burrowed in until he pulled back. "Monti, you're shaking! Is this about the cat?"

"I guess. I can't get it out of my head. How's Noelle?"

"She's all right. A little goofy. I wonder where she gets that from?"

"Did you tell her about the picture?"

"Uh, no. I was taught never to throw gas on a fire. I'll let you tell her."

"Chicken." They went in and Kit locked the door behind them. She raised an eyebrow at him and he shrugged.

"Hi Grandma," Noelle said, and hugged her. "Tell me everything."

She turned to Kit. "I thought you said—"

"She means about Marla's call," Kit said.

"Oh, of course."

"What." Noelle said, "What else is there?"

"Nothing to worry about, Nellie." Monti headed for the office, pulling her phone from her purse. "I have to call my folks first, then we we'll talk."

When she emerged from her office twenty minutes later, reeling and rattled from shouting at her deaf mother, she needed peppermint tea. In the kitchen she found Kit on the phone and Noelle hugging Gulliver, listening with wide eyes. Apparently, the cat pic was out of the bag.

Monti set about making tea, letting the ritual soothe her frayed nerves. She automatically set up mugs for Kit and Noelle, then thought to wonder about their house guest.

"Where's Jenny?" she whispered.

Noelle pointed at the ceiling. "Nap. She's wiped."

Kit ended his call and looked at Noelle out of the corner of his eye.

"What's up?" Monti asked.

"That was CJ."

Monti waited. "And?"

Kit sighed. "And Stevie Jakes sent you the picture of Gulliver."

A New Thing

"What have you there, Old Tom?" The old man jumped half out of his skin and twisted to squint at Bo behind him.

"Master Bo!" Tom tugged at Bo's sleeve. "See here," he tugged harder, until Bo squatted down beside him. "What make ye of this?"

Bo examined the bower silently. He stood and walked the border around the patch of loosened earth, absently righting the box and nudging it out of his path. He arrived back at Tom's side and squatted down once more. "Almond seedlings?"

"Aye, what else can they be?" Tom scrubbed his hands through his wild hair. "But, what do it portend?"

Bo touched a bright little leaf. His heart constricted and a fragile hope struggled to be acknowledged. He shoved the feeling down with unaccountable panic. "I know not," he said, and a chaos of thoughts bewildered him. Almond seedlings grew to almond trees. Almond trees blossomed and honeybees buzzed the blossoms. But these seedlings were of Anisette...would they grow to real almond trees? Were they cursed? Blessed? Would they change into...his mind reeled away from ideas he could not countenance. He shook his head sharply and pushed himself to his feet. "I know not," he repeated.

Tom got one foot under him and Bo caught his elbow and hauled him up. "Well one thing, Master Bo, is this. It surely will rain again afore two or three days pass. If you think as I do, that we should protect these wee treelings, then we must move them from the bower. Transplant them..."

"Transplant them to the honey meadow," Bo said, his brow smoothing. "I think redemption may be at hand for your box, Tom. Get young Ian to help you with the spading. I'll take them in the punt...," his enthusiasm faltered as he thought of straying so far from Anisette's side, "sometime soon."

"Ian is to town for...supplies," Tom said. "I can spade dirt into a box, Master Bo. I ain't dead yet."

"As you wish, old friend." Then he turned and went back into the house without another word.

Bo opened the bedchamber door to find her awake at last. "Anisette!" He hurried to the bed. "How is it with you, beloved?"

She smiled at him, still sleepy and pale as the moon. "I'm well enough, husband." She tried to push herself up to sit but her arms wobbled and would not support her. She fell back with a moan.

"No, no, little one, lie back. Or if you will sit, suffer me to help you." He put an arm around her, lifted her slight frame and pulled pillows up behind her, punching them into the shape he deemed necessary for her comfort. He eased her back. "There, will that do?"

Anisette thrilled him with a soft echo of her silvery laugh. "Yes, my love, I thank you." She examined him closely and frowned. "You look dreadful tired, husband, are you ill?"

Now Bo laughed. "No. Only fretting, Anisette, but I am better now you are awake." He smoothed a curl away from her cheek and his throat tightened. "I was afraid..." He looked away.

"Why, have I been ill?" Anisette asked, her frown deepening. "Oh..." she said, tears filling her eyes as she remembered again. "The box."

"Yes, the cursed box!" Bo said, and smacked his fist down on his thigh. "We must ne'er risk such an experiment again!" He looked at her, pleading. "I cannot lose you, Anisette. Nothing is worth that, not even children."

Anisette opened her mouth to protest, but closed it again. She stared down at her hands a long moment, and wiped away the tears that fell on them. "Was I so very ill, then? I remember—I am exhausted." She raised her eyes to his. "I suppose Doctor Fleming has been?"

Bo nodded. Silence grew heavy between them before Bo found strength to say, "Anisette, the journey must be given up." He watched her face crumple, and pulled her into his arms. He had had the long night to reconcile himself to this defeat, but it were a fresh loss for her. He stroked her back and kissed her hair as she wept.

When she at last quieted he said, "There is a new thing..."

She pulled back from him a little and wiped her eyes. "What new thing?"

"I would show you, but dare not take you from the bed quite yet. So you must imagine Old Tom tidying the bower this morning after—after the muddle

of moving you from the box to your bower." Anisette frowned at the mention of the old man laboring at this but Bo would not allow it. "Stop that, now, no one asked him to go nicening and neatening." He smoothed her brow with one big thumb. "He's tsk-tsking at the dirt flung here and there, when he spies a bit of green." Anisette looked at him, curious. "A wee bit of green amongst the almond leaves and drupes scattered about." He frowned. "For many, many leaves dropped from thee, my love, and a score or more drupes."

"Well, and what were the green?" she asked, pushing for the story to continue.

"Ah now, he could not tell straight away, having got purblind o'er the years, you know." Anisette tapped at his hand impatiently. "So he got down on his knees, and who may know how long that took..."

"Bo Willem! Wilt drive me mad!"

Bo chuckled, pleased to see some spirit in her. "All right then, 'twere an almond seedling. Several seedlings. Certain they were sprung from the dropped almonds, and stood half a foot high already."

"Truly? How very odd!" Anisette considered. "I do not remember ever seeing seedlings before, though there's been a drupe or two now and then, fallen where I had stood." She sat silent a moment, frowning. "And how a seedling today, when the drupe fell, when was it, Bo?"

"Not e'en two days ago. 'Tis a marvel, and no doubt."

"I want to see them." She made as if to get out of the bed.

Bo cupped her face. "You shall, love, but you'll not be walking out there today. When Ian comes home we'll fetch you out to see the wee things." He pushed gently at her and she lay back.

"Tom and I agree the seedlings should be protected. I think to move them hence to the honey meadow."

"A goodly idea, husband!" Anisette paused, "but leave one here for me to watch over? I am curious to know how it will grow."

"Aye, we'll do that. We only thought the bower soil must be cleared for when you may need it next. But if we choose one at the edge, that will be well." She nodded. "I'll go tell Tom, or he'll have them all snug in the box afore I can say jack robin."

Boots stomped at the back door, announcing Ian's return. Bo stood. "Back in a trice, love. I will just catch them up on how things stand." He kissed her fore-

head and strode from the room, feeling as if a hundred-stone weight had rolled off his shoulders.

Bo stuck his head out the back door. "Tom! Anisette would have you leave one seedling for her to watch over. One near the edge, as will not be in her way."

Tom straightened from his spading and nodded. "Aye, and we might have thought of that! I'll do it."

Ian stopped at the door, clutching several rolled parchments.

"And where are the supplies, boy?" Bo asked. Ian reddened instantly, opened his mouth, and looked to Tom, brows raised.

"Oh, ah...never mind that now," Tom said, waving the proclaimed errand away with a gnarled hand. "Take those in, lad, and scoot back and help me with this. Master Bo needs all these seedlings in the box, so's he can plant them in the honey meadow. Go along now." Tom peered under his eyebrows at his master. "He were on an errand for me, Master Bo. I'll tell ye about it later on." Bo got out of the boy's way but scowled at the parchments.

"What mischief are you about, Old Tom?" Bo said.

"No mischief, now, no mischief at all!" Tom said, raising his palms and his eyebrows in a declaration of innocence. "We're wanting to help Miss Anisette and yourself, is all."

"Help us...how?"

"Now, now, there's no need to gab about it this instant. Do you not want me to get these seedlings boxed up? We'll talk it over at supper, why not?" Tom recommenced spading with uncharacteristic enthusiasm.

Bo considered how much energy he would have to exert to pry any information from the old man before he was ready, and decided against the effort. Whatever harebrained scheme Tom had cooked up, he would hear all about it soon enough.

"Pardon, Uncle Bo," Ian said as he brushed past him and went to take the spade from Tom. Tom and the boy were in league, plainly. Bo shook his head. It might be amusing, he allowed. As long as Anisette were not hurt by their shenanigans, they could go at it all they liked.

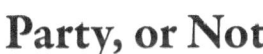

Party, or Not

M onti pulled into the driveway Friday afternoon and noted the absence of police cruisers, for which she was grateful. She was looking forward to a whole week off starting right now.

But first, unload the car. Was Kit home or would she be hauling everything in? She got out of the car and glanced at the kitchen door. Finding the key to the Subaru's tonneau cover, she worked at unlocking the persnickety thing. She loved her Baja, but this lock made her nuts. Kit could always get it open way faster. *Where is Kit? He always meets me at the car!* She gave up, jogged up the back steps, and opened the kitchen door.

"Kit?" she called. Nothing. She dropped her purse and keys on the table and walked down the hall, tripping and nearly falling over the cat, who was apparently perfectly safe but still dangerous.

She poked her head in the den. "Kit?" Not there. Her heart thumped. She pushed open their bedroom door. Kit lay on the bed, facing away from her. "Kit, honey," she said softly. No answer. She laid her hand gently on his shoulder, felt his deep, even breathing. She turned to tiptoe away, but Kit rolled over and squinted up at her.

"Hey Monti." He twisted to look at the clock on the nightstand. "I guess I fell asleep. Those damn pills."

"Was it bad today?" she asked. She sat on the edge of the bed, her heart slowing, and took his hand in hers. Gulliver jumped onto the bed and squirmed his way between them to rub his head on their hands.

"It got that way," Kit said. He maneuvered carefully, pushing the cat out of the way, and Monti stood to let him swing his legs down. "I went to meet Mike Rutherford for coffee at Calypsos, but he didn't show." He rolled his head, loosening his neck. "So I went by the church to chat with Josh. Satisfying conversation, we got some final Thanksgiving logistics figured out." Kit stretched his long frame toward the ceiling and rolled his shoulders. "But that leather sofa in his office about ate me alive. I didn't realize until too late."

He looked at her, his eyebrows drawing down into a fierce scowl. "Monti, I'm going to have to start taking that blasted cane with me," he said. "This was the second time this month someone's had to haul me out of a piece of furniture."

She squeezed his hand in sympathy, imagining his humiliation. "I think that's a good idea, love. Better to have it and not need it..." she paused, and decided she'd said enough about that. "Want to come help me? I have perishables locked in the car." She tugged on his hand. He tugged back and lifted her hand to his lips.

"Yeah, I can help with those. I'm all right now." He stood and wrapped her in his arms, kissed her and turned her around to head out the bedroom door. "That stuff just knocks me out, though. I hate that, sleeping in the middle of the day."

Monti turned back around to face him, hands on her hips. "That, Kit Rising, is what we common mortals call a nap. It's a time-honored, perfectly acceptable use of an hour now and then. You know, like between classes in my Subaru?" She arched an eyebrow at him. He was always encouraging her to rest and not push herself too hard.

"Touché," he said. He ducked his chin and she could swear he blushed, but all he said was, "We'd better get those perishables."

While they stashed the groceries, Kit filled her in on the church's Thanksgiving plans.

"Sounds like it's all figured out, and all I have to do is...what do I have to do?" Monti checked the note he'd stuck to the fridge. "Seven-layer salad and banana cream pie. Easy as cake." She put away the last sack and sat down in the window seat. Gulliver jumped onto her lap immediately and she stroked him.

Kit sat down too and scratched the cat's ears, causing loud purring. "Good. I'm glad you're not stressing over Thanksgiving anymore, at least."

"I have enough other stuff to stress over. Gulliver tried to kill me a while ago."

"Hmm. Maybe we should give Mr. Jakes a call."

"That's not funny. Any update from CJ?"

"Not yet," Kit said.

"Nor Marla?"

"No."

"Noelle at the library?"

Kit nodded. "Jenny, too. They'll be home before supper." The front door opened, letting a burst of giggling into the house. "Way before supper."

The girls brought their giggles into the kitchen. "Hey, G and G," Noelle said. "What's cookin'?" Gulliver jumped down and wound around the girls' legs.

"Nothing yet," Monti said. "Why, are you taking us out for dinner?"

"No, silly. Though actually, we were just saying how we should celebrate tonight." Noelle's face went pink. "Mom called me."

"She did? That's great!" Kit said.

"Isn't it?" Monti asked.

"Yeah, it was okay," Noelle said. "I didn't recognize her voice at first, it's so different. Kind of rough."

"She almost hung up," Jenny said.

"I'm glad I didn't, though. It was really good to talk to her. She sounds...I don't know...exhausted, or something. But also like she's done with all that, for real." Noelle bit her lip, then said, "She says she's coming home when she gets out of rehab, definitely." She smiled broadly, while tears filled her eyes. Monti saw joy and fear and hope flit across her granddaughter's face. It was heart wrenching to watch. "I miss my Mom," Noelle said.

Monti put her arms around her granddaughter. "Marla home for Christmas," Monti said. "Imagine that.".

Kit said, "That's enough reason to celebrate all on its own, but you girls also have a week off. And Jenny's moving to the Cominskis' tomorrow. I think we should have a family party."

"Excellent idea. Out on the town? Or bring the party here?" Monti asked.

"Let's stay home," Noelle said right away. They all looked at her with eyebrows raised. "I want to keep an eye on Gulliver," she said, sheepish.

"Sure, baby girl." Monti squeezed her tighter, then released her. "Now—menu and entertainment. What do you feel like?"

They brainstormed for a while, accompanied by much giggling and eye rolling. Bringing home Mexican food complete with a mariachi band was nixed as appropriate but impossible, and camping in the backyard with a campfire and S'mores, though admired as a concept, was postponed until summer. In the end they settled on ordering in Chinese and stirring up hot toddies (for the G's) and cocoa (for the girls) for dessert.

They'd drifted to the living room, and were debating a Scrabble tournament vs. a movie marathon, when tires squealed and a car peeled out on the street in front of the house. Everyone froze.

Kit motioned to them to stay put and went to check the street through the small window in the front door. After a moment he opened the door and went out. The women stared at each other, still not daring to move.

He came back in and went straight to the kitchen. Monti followed him. He was dialing the phone.

"What?" she asked.

"Take a look at the front lawn," he growled, his face a thundery scowl.

"Do I have to?" Monti said, and went to look.

A Storm

A pearly sunset glowed as Bo crunched back up the gravel walk after feeding the horses. He paused to examine the cheerful rows of seedlings in the big box. The one chosen for Anisette to tend stood alone at the edge of the patch of loose earth in her bower, the soil patted smooth around its baby roots, a circle of white pebbles marking its miniature territory. Bo shook his head. Old Tom would do anything for his mistress, and his fierce devotion revealed itself with surprising delicacy at times.

Bo went into to the house, hung his jacket on its peg, stopped at Anisette's door and peeked in. She instantly raised her hand to him. He was at her side in two steps, pressing her hand to his cheek.

A loud clang and a barrage of whispered rebuke met Bo as he stepped into the kitchen a few minutes later. "My lady is awake, no need to shush the boy."

He lifted a lid and flared his nostrils, drawing in the savory aroma of beef stew. His stomach growled. Tom and Ian clattered around him setting dinner on. Tom sent a shower of bread crumbs cascading across the floor as he moved the cutting board from counter to table. Bo winced as Ian, clumsy as a great puppy in the confined quarters of the kitchen, knocked a sizable chip from a mug as he stacked them. The boy froze and met his eyes, but Bo waved it away. Ian exhaled and resumed his tasks.

"I want to show Anisette the seedlings before the light fails." The two men stopped and looked at Bo. "I'll carry her. Ian, fetch out a chair to the garden and Tom, will you manage the door?" Without a word the two resumed moving, but on new trajectories, and with grins.

Moments later Anisette sat in the best chair in the house, precisely placed for her in the garden. She was wrapped in a warm shawl, and her feet rested on a cushion. Bo stood behind her, resting his hands on her slim shoulders.

"We got them all tucked in, y'see, Mistress," Tom said, after getting Ian to help him shove the box around so Anisette could see. She leaned forward to inspect the plantlets.

"And here's your little one," Ian said, having spied the lone bit of green still standing in the bower. *"Tom has it marked out, like,"* he said, swirling his finger around to indicate the ring of white pebbles pushed into the soil around the seedling. Anisette's luminous smile rewarded them both.

"Thank you both," she said. *"You are dears. It will be a wonder to watch it grow, will it not?"* Her voice faltered at the last few words, making Bo's heart twist. They wanted not to stay here and watch baby almond trees grow. He squeezed her shoulders gently. Then his belly rumbled again, loud enough that everyone heard it. Anisette's soft laugh got them all grinning again, and Bo gestured to set the whole process in motion again, in reverse. He lifted his wife from the chair and Tom scrambled to open the door for them.

Ian carried the best chair to Anisette's usual place at the table and Bo tucked her into it, shawl and all. Tom stirred the stew a final time, tasted it and declared it supper. As Tom ladled stew into bowls, Bo said, *"And now shall I hear of your mysterious errand, nephew?"*

"Uh...," Ian replied, looking to Tom for direction. Tom waggled his eyebrows and did an odd shrug-nod motion which Bo recognized, having seen it nearly every day of his life. It signified—Bo was not entirely sure what—avoidance, most like. *"Surely..."* Ian continued. But then Tom lowered a steaming bowl to the table front of the young man. His eyes followed the motion and his belly rumbled. Bo snorted a laugh.

"It will wait, Ian," he said, *"shall we return thanks?"* They all bowed their heads while Bo prayed, and then ate in appreciative silence for a few minutes. Whatever Tom's faults might be, he was an excellent cook. Eventually the rhythm of spoons clinking on crockery slowed, and the refrain of 'pass the bread, lad' and 'hand the butter,' petered out.

Bo glanced at Anisette. Her face was ashen and she struggled to keep her eyes open. He stood instantly. *"Wife, shall you to bed?"* She nodded and he scooped her up. He marveled again as he carried her, how such a feather-light girl could transform into a sturdy tree rooted in the ground, enduring **wind** and rain to no ill effect. He frowned. *Except when we interfere!*

He gazed at her drawn face as he lay her on the bed. She was asleep already. He tucked the covers around her, drew the door closed and returned to the table in no mood for foolish schemes. He lowered himself into his chair and placed both hands on the table, palms down.

"And now. What fadoodle have the two of you been stirring at all the day?"

Ian looked at Tom, who swallowed hard. "Now, Bo, there's no reason for thunder!" He drew himself up and motioned to Ian. "Go and fetch the maps, boy." Ian got to his feet and stepped lively to his room.

Bo's scowl deepened. "Maps? What maps?"

"Now, now, simmer down a mite, they're maps of the...the...of Africa and ways to get there."

Bo's face flushed. He went rigid. It took all the self-control he had not to shout the old man out of the room. Ian returned with his arms full of scrolls. He tripped on a chair leg and dumped them helter skelter on the table, where they rolled off in every direction. Tom and Ian snatched and gathered them all back into a pile in the center of the table. Bo grabbed one that came to rest at his fingertips and glared at the label. Europe. He found the edge and pulled the scroll open. In spite of himself, he was captivated. The map bore a wealth of detail, color, intricate shapes. Over it all lay a dense network of text labeling countries, cities, mountain ranges, rivers and seas. He stiffened again as he realized what Tom and Ian were about.

"Now Bo," Tom said, shushing him with his hands. "Keep your temper and listen to the boy for one minute."

Bo turned his glare on Ian, who stood holding two or three scrolls, petrified. "Well, then," Bo said, "and only because of Tom's pleading. Out with it, boy."

"Th-thank you, Uncle," Ian said. He lay the remaining scrolls on the table and Tom put a hand on them to keep them from rolling. Then Ian eased the map from under Bo's fist and opened it all the way. "I studied this out two ways." He plunked his finger down on the map. "First, I plotted a route from here," he slid his finger around in a wide curve, "to Morocco, entirely on land, barring a river crossing here and there."

Bo leaned forward and listened more closely.

"It goes through Hungary, the whole length of the Ottoman Empire, through Syria and down into Egypt." Ian straightened up. "Then across north Africa. 'Tis a very long journey."

"How long?" Bo asked.

Ian sputtered, shrugged, "I know not...months, it must be. Six months? Eight?" Bo slapped the table with a heavy palm. "What good is that, boy? Eight months travel? By horse? With a wagon? I know that cannot be done. I know Anisette could not do it."

"Pardon, uncle, another route..." Ian scrambled amongst the maps and pulled loose the one he sought. "'Tis much shorter. Two months or so, perhaps, with only the tiniest bit on board a ship. One day..."

Bo stood, shoving his chair into the wall behind him hard enough to gouge the plaster. "Nonsense. It's utter nonsense, and it pains me to know you've wasted I don't know how much time on this fool's errand, and how little you care for your aunt's safety." He swiveled his glare to Tom. "And you egging him on like an old fool. No more of maps now." With one swipe of his arm he swept the scrolls off the table and they clattered to the floor, rolling every which way.

"In fact, I see no reason for you to tarry with us, Ian. As we will not be making any long journeys, we've no need for an apprentice." He stomped down the hall, flung open the door, and went into the night.

Ian, his cheeks scarlet, stood stricken, staring at Tom.

"Ah, and don't worry on it now, son," Tom said. "It'll blow over. He wants you here, truly." Tom blinked and fumbled amongst his pockets for his pipe. "It'll blow over," he said again, working to convince them both.

Next

Monti peered through the window in the front door. She tilted her head and frowned. What *was* that? She opened the door and walked out to the sidewalk, then turned back toward the house.

You have got to be kidding me. Burned into the lawn in two-foot high letters was the word NEXT. What did that even mean? Next what? She still pondered this when Kit, followed by the girls, joined her.

"Next?" Jenny said. "Next what? Dang, Mrs. R, what's it mean?".

"I was just wondering the same thing."

"It can't be anything good," Noelle said with a tremor in her voice. Monti put an arm around her.

"Wait, isn't Blaine still in jail?" Jenny asked.

"He is," Kit said. All four of them stood in the pale afternoon sunlight, staring without a clue at the altered lawn for a moment.

"How did they do this?" Monti said, swirling her hand around at the letters. "It looks burned. How did they burn wet grass?"

"Who did this is more to the point," Kit said. "I want to know where Stevie Jakes was a few minutes ago. It's broad daylight. Someone had to have seen him. Or whoever." He rubbed his eyes and dragged his hand down his face. "CJ is on his way. I'm gonna go call Ray."

Jenny's eyes went wide. She shook her head, swallowed hard. "Oh man. This is all my fault—" her voice pinched off as she tried not to cry. "The Cominskis..."

"Hey now, Jenny," Monti said, and wrapped her other arm around the girl's shaking shoulders. "This is in no way your fault. You're trying to do the right thing—it's not you, it's them!" She squeezed both girls and said, "Come on, let's go in. It's chilly out here." There was no warmth in the November sun even at midday.

When they got inside, Kit was on the phone with Ray. "Right. I figured you'd say that, but I wanted to keep you updated." He listened. "Thanks, Ray, we appreciate that. When we find out anything I'll let you know. Yep, see you tomorrow."

"I knew it wouldn't faze them," Monti said.

"No, they're solid." He looked up at the sound of an engine. "CJ's here." He kissed her temple and headed out to meet the police, yet again. Monti went to find the girls.

"It's a threat, for sure," Jenny was saying to Noelle, huddled next to her on the settle in the living room.

"But, about Gulliver still? Or..." Noelle trailed off, reluctant to voice a worse possibility.

Monti sat across from them. "Grandpa called Ray, and he and Dot are not in the least worried," she said.

"They're still letting me come?" Jenny asked.

"Well, of course they are!" Monti said. "They've seen worse than this. There's no biker gang involved, I don't believe."

"Biker gang!" Jenny said. "They had a biker gang mad at them?"

"Oh yeah. And they came through that okay, so this will all be fine. Let's not panic. In fact, while Grandpa deals with the cops, let's finish our plans for this evening. Noelle, will you fetch the menu for Chinese Gardens? And Jenny, why don't you look through the DVDs and see if anything tickles your fancy." The girls moved to do as she asked. "I'll...do something useful, as soon as I figure out what that might be," she said, but was drawn to the window in the front door again. Then she stopped short and scanned the room.

"Where's the cat?"

Mistress Springfield

A heavy silence pervaded the house next morning. Contrary to Tom's assurances, Bo remained in a foul temper. He came to the kitchen to fetch a breakfast tray for Anisette and disappeared back into her room without a single word for Tom or Ian. Tom patted the boy on the shoulder, and sent him off to return the maps to Pastor Wheaton while he set about clearing up the kitchen with a heavy heart.

Ian had not been back from that errand long, and was cooling off with a long drink of milk, when a sharp rap on the front door made him jump and knock his mug crashing to the floor. Not the one he had chipped before, of course, and whilst it still was heavy with milk.

Old Tom opened the door.

"Tom?" said a bright little woman, standing on the step and clutching an enormous long bundle in her hands.

"Yes, m'lady?"

"Mary Springfield. I know not if you might remember me." She paused, watched Tom think about this, and rescued him. "I was used to deliver bread and pastries to the Willems when Bo were a boy."

Tom's face lit up. "Oh, yes, Mistress Springfield! I recall your apple dumplings mighty fondly, I do." He examined her fitments for signs of pastries, but saw only the green bundle and dimmed somewhat.

"How may I help you, Mistress Springfield? Will you come in for a cup of tea?"

"Yes, thank you, Tom." She followed him into the kitchen and sat in the chair he indicated, away from Ian on his knees wiping the white pond from the floor.

"This is Ian, Master Bo's nephew come to apprentice with him." Ian's eyes were glued to the bundle she carried. Mistress Springfield tilted her head to him. "Well met, Master Ian. I, um, is Mistress Anisette to home?"

Tom stopped filling the kettle and turned to face her. "My mistress is to home, m'lady, but lies in her chamber, gravely ill."

Mistress Springfield frowned at this and said, "Oh dear." She tilted her head and thought for a moment. "I cannot think why—" She stopped, then lifted her chin. "Tom, this may sound queer but I believe I am to give this parasol to Mistress Anisette." She laid it on the table before her.

"Ah, a parasol, is it?" Tom said. "I don't mind I ever saw one before." He paused. "What do it be, exactly?"

Mistress Springfield giggled. "Why, it's for, um, making shade to keep off the sun," she said.

Tom looked at her askance, as though he thought she made fun of him.

"Forsooth, 'tis its purpose." She gestured widely over her head. "It opens up, you see, and makes a, a sort of canopy, on a long pole. You've seen them in pictures." She could see he thought this highly unlikely and she giggled again.

"Aye, I saw such a thing last summer, Tom," Ian said. "A bishop or cardinal or some such grandee in his long robes, had a servant carrying one along behind him as he strolled in a parade down the avenue. All red and yellow it were, though, not green like this one here."

Tom blinked at this, it being so entirely outside of his experience.

"No matter, Old Tom, you will see anon." She looked him in the eye. "Now do not ask me why, as I will not be able to explain it, but the need is strong in me to give it your mistress." She smiled, "I inherited it from my Great Aunt Dorcas, who had it from her mother. It's been bumping around one corner or another of my house for ever so many years. I've no idea how our family originally came to have such an item. I've not seen another one, ever, except on some great porcelain vases at Mistress Canterbury's. Chinese antiquities, she said they were."

She shook her head. "I cannot think how we never put it in the parish rummage sale. I've never even opened it. One has not much use for a parasol in this climate, in any case." She stroked the mottled green silk and grinned up at him.

"Then yesterday it fell over and knocked me on the foot as I looked for...for...I cannot now remember what...in the wardrobe in our spare room." She paused, and her voice grew hushed. "Of a sudden, the thought came into my head, clear and golden-like, to give the thing to Mistress Anisette, whom I've never laid eyes on in my life, and only know of because she married your master." She peered at Tom, as if to gauge his reaction.

Tom blinked again. He reached out slowly and touched the perplexing parasol with one gnarled finger. He met his visitor's eyes. "What do it signify, Mistress?"

She stared back at him and shrugged.

Bo walked into the kitchen bearing Anisette's tray, and stopped short. He glanced at their visitor and frowned a question at Tom.

"Ah, Bo, you remember Mistress Springfield? The baker of apple dumplings fit for any king?"

Bo's brow cleared as he remembered his manners. "Surely, good morning to you, Mistress." He handed the tray to Ian and turned to her. "It's been...how many years since we enjoyed your pastries? You've been well, I hope?"

"Oh yes, quite well, thank you." Her eyes dropped to the parasol she had set on the table, and he followed her gaze. "I was, a moment ago, telling Old Tom here I felt compelled, I know not why, to give this old parasol to Mistress Anisette." Her cheeks reddened. "It seems foolish, mayhap," she said, then sat taller and squared her shoulders. "But I have learned, these many years walking with Jesu, not to ignore the urging of the Spirit, whether I can make fair sense of it or no."

The men stared in silence at the Spirit-urged sunshade on their kitchen table.

The little woman rose. "And gentlemen, forgive me this boldness, but I counsel ye also not to set the thing aside as an old woman's folly, but to consider what the meaning may be, and pray on it to determine what our Lord has in mind for ye." She smiled at them all. "I must be off," she said, and swirled to the door. Tom scrambled to open it for her, and she was gone.

Tom, Ian and Bo stood looking at each other in the kitchen, the green silk parasol lying across the table, its heavy gold fringe splayed on the smooth oak surface, its mystery tied tight with a gold brocade ribbon.

"Bo," came a silvery voice from the bedchamber.

Bo started, snatched up the parasol, and went to Anisette.

Moving Day

Saturday dawned grey and drizzly. Monti stared out the window in the front door. Sure enough, NEXT was still burned into the grass. Why couldn't it have rained yesterday and prevented the vandalism?

She moved to the kitchen window and gazed at the soggy back yard. Wasn't it just last weekend they were pruning bushes in the sunshine? The rain would put a damper on moving day. Literally. A damper? Why was that a thing? What was a damper? Something to do with a fireplace, wasn't it? She would have to look it up.

But before that she had, at last count, six people to feed in about an hour and a half. Monti shook off her melancholy. She didn't have time to indulge. First a minute or two in the Psalms, and then coffee cake, scrambled eggs, bacon, bananas, juice and coffee. She sat in the window seat, and Gulliver jumped up to sit with her.

"Bad kitty," Monti said. "Never do that again." They had spent 45 minutes looking for him yesterday afternoon, inside and out in the yard, only to find him sound asleep, curled up in the back of a shelf in the linen closet. Monti stroked him as she rebuked him, and he purred repentantly.

A little while later, with "Your faithful love is better than life..." echoing softly in her head, Monti put away her Bible and got out her laptop. She found her favorite coffee cake recipe safely stashed in Evernote, and started knocking about the kitchen turning ingredients into breakfast.

Eventually Kit poked his head into the kitchen, inhaling deeply.

"Coffee, check." He laid the newspaper on the counter and inhaled again. "Coffee cake, check. Bacon?"

Monti dried her hands. "Just ready to start that, lover." She stepped into his open arms and soaked in some enthusiasm for the day. Kit wrapped her up and kissed her. "How are you this morning?" she asked.

"Slept pretty well, had a hot shower, I'm doing okay." He smoothed her forehead. "What about you? Ready for today?"

"I'm getting there." Monti found a table cloth while Kit got out the bacon and breakfast prep became a dance they'd practiced together for many years and now performed flawlessly without a moment's thought to the steps.

By the time the bacon was just about perfect, Noelle and Jenny padded into the kitchen in search of caffeine. Noelle's Hello Kitty PJ top and "Keep Calm and Don't Blink" bottoms matched Jenny, who wore the Keep Calm top and Kitty pants. Little girls on a sleepover. Monti wished they *were* little girls, not young women already fighting the world, battle scarred and traumatized.

"Hey G and G," Noelle said. Gulliver twined through her legs and she picked him up. "Bad kitty," she said, and nuzzled him against her cheek. "Smells yummy in here. Is the coffee ready?"

"Certainly, young lady," Kit said. "What kind of a kitchen do you think we're running here? The coffee is always ready." He swept his arms toward the breakfast nook with a bow, inviting the girls to sit.

"Big day for you, Jenny," he said. He poured a mug full and set it in front of her. "Black, as you like it miss."

"Thanks, Mr. Rising." Jenny gave him a small smile and wrapped her hands around the hot mug.

"Sad day for me," Noelle said, dumping Gulliver to slide in next to Jenny. "The slumber party is over." She made a pouty face and leaned her head on Jenny's shoulder.

"Well, it must be done," Kit said. "The daily giggle quota has been ignored and exceeded in this house for too long." He set a steaming mug in front of Noelle. "At times, I've wondered how it's possible for you two to accomplish your daily tasks in the fragments of time available between giggle fests."

Both girls stared at him, uncomprehending. He stared back for a long moment. "Wait for the caffeine to hit your bloodstream. It'll all make more sense."

Monti frowned at the morning paper, just out of its plastic sleeve. "Isn't this Blaine's father?" she said. She sat across from the girls and smoothed the curled paper flat on the table. "Mike Rutherford, right?"

"That's the name. What's up?" Kit sat beside her, slid his glasses down his nose and looked where she pointed. "Coeur d'Alene man arrested in DUI collision," he read, taking the paper. "City police arrested a man on Friday who allegedly crashed into another vehicle while driving with a blood-alcohol level almost twice the legal limit." Here Monti made a rude noise. "Police say the incident happened about 8:45pm at the intersection of 4th and Appleway when Mike Rutherford, driving a black Cadillac Escalade, allegedly failed to yield the right of way and hit a Honda Accord crossing the intersection. Esther Millard, 76, the driver of the Honda, is listed in fair condition at Kootenai Medical Center." Monti growled. "Rutherford was arrested when officers at the accident scene found he had a blood alcohol level of .152. He was booked into the Kootenai County Jail."

Kit sat back and pushed his glasses back up. "He told me he lost his license. He has a chauffeur, for heaven's sake."

"Well, you can't visit him today, we need you to supervise the moving project," Monti said. She peered at him sideways to gauge his reaction to 'supervise,' as opposed to 'lift heavy objects'. He didn't seem to have heard her. He frowned down at the paper, evidently thinking dark thoughts.

The doorbell rang. Both girls froze. Here they were in their PJ's...Monti looked at the girls and at Kit. No one moved. The bell rang again. "Um, family? I'm blocked in here, will someone see who that is?"

The girls chose flight over fight and did a Keystone Cops routine scrambling out of the breakfast nook and up the stairs. "Kit?" Monti bumped him with her shoulder.

"Hmm?"

"Kit, the doorbell is ringing." It rang again.

"Hmm? Oh. Oh, right," he said, and unfolded himself from the bench. "I'll see who it is."

"Thank you," Monti said, rolling her eyes. They all said she was the wacky one. She got up too, and started another pot of coffee.

Brian ducked as Kit ushered him into the kitchen. "You'd better not get any taller, young man, or we'll have to feed you in the driveway."

Brian sniffed the air and grinned. "As long as you feed me," he said. "Hi, Mrs. R."

The bell rang again and Eddie hollered through the door, "Hey you're not eating without me, are you?"

Kit let him in. "Lock the fridge, Monti, Eddie's here." Eddie joined his nephew in the kitchen. By the time Eddie had his coffee—Brian nursed a Redbull as usual—the girls reappeared, looking like they'd spent the last hour getting glamorous, though Monti knew it hadn't been ten minutes.

Brian asked an enthusiastic blessing on breakfast and half an hour later Monti poured refills on coffee while Eddie and Brian helped themselves to second pieces of coffee cake and scraped the last bacon crumbs from the platter onto their plates.

"Monti, I'll be glad to move any amount of furniture from any place to any other place as long as I get to eat your cooking first," Eddie said. "I'm just saying, for future reference when you're rounding up muscle." He rubbed his expansive belly and brushed crumbs from his shirt.

"What's that round muscle you have on the front there, Eddie?" Kit said.

"Dinner muscle!" Eddie said without missing a beat. "You think it's easy, maintaining this figure? I work at it."

"Uh huh. I hope your lifting muscles are in working order, too. I'm supervising today."

Monti offered a silent *Thank You!* but said nothing.

"First, we need to fetch down a couple boxes and bags from upstairs. Those are ready to go, right, Jenny?" She nodded. "Good. You and Noelle bring those down and stage them here. Eddie and Brian, you come with me to the garage and load the furniture. Come on, crew, let's get this project rolling," Kit said. "You coming or staying, love?"

"I believe I'll hold down the fort here," she said.

"Okay," Kit said, and leaned down to kiss her. "Gonna work on your story?"

"That's the plan, man," she said. She waved them down the driveway, then cleared away the breakfast things while thinking hard about how to get Anisette to Africa.

The Parasol

Anisette sat up in the bed, pillows propped behind her back, and fingered the glossy gold fringe of the green silk parasol. It was no trifling object, being four feet long from the tip of its brass-capped point to the bottom of its curved and polished bamboo handle. Bo had just told her the story of Mistress Springfield's visit.

"I want to open it, Bo," Anisette said.

Bo furrowed his brow. "Oh, aye, certainly we'll open it," he said. "But, ah, do you know the trick of it?" He was embarrassed by his ignorance.

"I've no idea! I've never seen one before. But my nurse had a book of Chinese tales, and I remember one of my favorite pictures in it. A group of maidens in bright gowns of some sort, all had these parasols. Not monstrous great ones such as this, but delicate little things." She tugged at the ribbon, her eyes shining. "Shall we go out to the garden?" Anisette asked. "I feel stronger this morning. I would so like to sit on the bench...or in the chair if you like...and open the parasol and see how the sun may glow through the silk."

How could he refuse her anything at all? "Of course, love, we will do it. I shall have Tom and Ian to set the chair by the bench, and I'll sit with you a while, and see if this old relic may be in working order."

Anisette leaned her head back on her pillow and beamed at him. He kissed her forehead and went to direct his men to do her bidding. In a trice he had wrapped her in the shawl and carried her out to the chair. He set her down and tucked the shawl around her. The morning sun angled through one of the openings in the bower wall, setting Anisette's honey brown hair shimmering in the golden light. She seemed made of delicate porcelain, and was quite as fragile, Bo thought.

Ian handed him the sunshade and he sat on the bench to undo the tightly knotted ribbon imprisoning its ribs. Eventually the ribbon yielded to his determination, loosened and fell to the ground, wherefrom Old Tom immediately *snatched it up and smoothed it carefully before curling it round his fingers and secreting it in a pocket.*

Bo shook the parasol gently, and big crumples of tissue fell out. These Tom also plucked up and stashed away. Bo peered into the workings of the parasol to discover how to open it up.

A bamboo ring attached to slender ribs looked as if it might slide along the pole. He tried it gingerly, not wanting to damage the ancient thing. After a moment's resistance, it moved suddenly under his fingers and they all gasped as the ring slid up, the ribs spread, and the huge parasol unfurled like some otherworldly sail. It would not stay open though, but drooped down as if stalled in the doldrums.

Bo peered inside more closely, and spied a possible fastening gadget. He slid the ring up again until it caught on a cunning latch and stayed. The ribs arched stiffly, stretching the silk panels taut. It was splendid with the sun shining through, throwing spangles of light off the gold periphery. He presented it to Anisette. She took it eagerly and twirled it back and forth to shake the fringe. She rested it on her shoulder, closed her eyes and smiled a deep, happy smile.

The men watched her, speechless. Bo's heart tightened in his chest at her pleasure in this unexpected and inexplicable umbrella. Tom pondered the mystery of Spirit-urged gifts, and wished for apple dumplings. Ian's busy mind worried at the riddle of a gift that protected from rain and sun...and his thoughts leaped far ahead to the hot, sunny climate of Africa.

Kimberly

Jenny rubbed a clear spot in the fogged glass and peered out the window of the Geo as Noelle pulled to the curb. This was the first time she'd seen the Cominskis' house in daylight. The lawn in front was winter green/brown but neatly trimmed. Big rhododendrons, misty rain dripping from their deep evergreen leaves, made a tall hedge along the edges of the lot. Flowerbeds had been tidied for the winter, bushes wrapped with burlap and tied with string and...what was that word? Mulch. Everything was mulched with a deep layer of leaves.

And the house. The house was huge.

"Come on, Jenny," Noelle said, opening her door. She took Jenny's hand and squeezed it. "Ready?"

It was now or never, she guessed, and climbed out of the car. Noelle opened the hatch and handed her one of the duffel bags, gifts from Kit's military days to replace the black plastic trash bags. Noelle grabbed the other one and they toted them down the sidewalk and up the wide steps onto the wrap-around porch.

Light rain drifted across the yard, but the deep covered porch was protected and dry. She relaxed a tiny bit. As Noelle knocked, Jenny examined the big porch swing, four (four!) rocking chairs, and the flower boxes (more mulch) along the rail. You could totally live on the porch. There was enough room for a bed and a fridge out here.

"Here you are!" Dorothy said, throwing the door wide open and beckoning them inside. Jenny inhaled deeply. The house was fragrant with coffee and...she wasn't sure what but it made her mouth water, even though she was still full from breakfast.

"Drop those here, girls, we'll get the muscle to haul them upstairs later." Dorothy stepped over and rapped on the basement door, then looked out the front door, smiling as the truck pulled into the driveway. "And we're all here!"

Ray tromped up the basement stairs a moment later, brushing sawdust from his hands. He hugged Noelle gingerly, being still coated with tiny curls of wood, and shyly stuck his hand out to shake Jenny's. "Welcome, Miss Jenny," he said.

Kit and the crew stomped on the mat outside the door and trooped in. Eddie immediately said, "Maple bacon muffins! Dot, I love you forever."

Dorothy chuckled. "Well, I figured Monti would've fed you breakfast, but maybe you'll have room for a muffin dessert sometime this morning."

"I have room sometime this minute," Eddie said, and planted a kiss on Dorothy's cheek.

"Hmm, I think we have a motivational tool at our disposal," Kit said. "Dot, maybe you could keep those muffins under wraps until Elder Eddie here has taken some significant part in the haulage."

"What? Bacon gives a man strength to succeed!" Eddie protested, but pulled on his work gloves as he spoke. "Okay, okay, what's the plan, Miss Dorothy?"

Dorothy pressed her hands together in front of her. "Right. Jenny's room is upstairs, first door on the right. There's no carpet between here and there so don't worry about your boots, I'll sweep up later."

Ray said, "What do you have for furniture, Miss Jenny? Your room is furnished, but we can swap with your own things if you want. Or we can store yours in the shed."

Jenny blinked. "I have...uh, a twin bed and nightstand. A dresser, and a little desk. I used to have a papasan chair but it got trashed. And some crap in boxes." Her face went hot. "I mean stuff, stuff in boxes."

Ray smiled at her. "I have some crap in boxes, too. Yours will fit right in."

Dorothy led the girls upstairs and opened the door to Jenny's room. Jenny sighed with pleasure. It was pretty in a completely different way from her room at the Risings'. One wall glowed a soft yellow, another pale pink. The bed lay half hidden under a pile of pillows covered with bright, stylized daisies. Even the window shades had gigantic yellow flowers on a pink background, and were trimmed with bright blue. "Wow," she said.

"Do you like it?" Dorothy asked. "My friend Bonnie is a decorator, and she did this room as a gift to the girls who stay here."

"Yeah, I really do," Jenny said. It was more her style than the old- fashioned rooms at Noelle's house. She trailed her fingers through the beaded tassel on the window shade, and opened the hot-pink wardrobe.

"There should be plenty of room for your clothes in there. And there's a dresser here, and a desk, unless you want to use your own?"

"Oh no, everything here is so pretty." She turned to Noelle. "My stuff would look terrible in here," she said in a low voice.

Noelle came to her rescue. "Ray said you have a shed, right? For things Jenny needs to store?"

"Sure, of course," Dorothy said. "So...want to use this furniture and store yours?"

Jenny nodded. There was a lump in her throat for some reason. She'd never imagined having such a cool room.

The guys had carried up the boxes and duffel bags containing what remained of Jenny's belongings and piled them in the hallway. They poked their heads in at the door.

"Hey gentlemen, you won't need to haul any furniture up the stairs, I'm sure you'll be happy to learn," Dorothy said. "Ray will show you where the shed is."

Eddie let out a celebratory whoop and they retreated down the stairs to move the truck around to the shed.

Smiling, Dorothy turned back to the girls. "I'll leave you two to unpack. Let me know if you need anything, okay?"

"Thanks, Dot, we will," Noelle said, and hugged her tightly. "It's gonna be good."

As soon as Dorothy disappeared down the stairs, Jenny grabbed Noelle's hands, grinning from ear to ear, feeling giddy. "Can you believe it?" she asked in a stage whisper. "This room is fabulous!"

Noelle giggled at her. "I'm glad you like it. Dot's such a great lady. I'm sure you'll get along with her."

"Why do you call her Dot?" Jenny said.

"Dot is short for Dorothy. But it gets better. She writes web pages for a living. So her whole nickname is...wait for it...Dot Com."

Jenny blinked. Dorothy Cominski, Dot Com. "You guys have a weird sense of humor."

Noelle laughed. "Uh, yeah, I guess we do. Let's get your stuff unpacked. I'm looking forward to a muffin and another cup of coffee."

They hefted the duffel bags onto the bed and started unloading them into the dresser and wardrobe. "Hey, I forgot to ask you the other day," Jenny said. "Who's the girl in the family portrait downstairs? Is that their daughter?"

"Yeah. Very sad," Noelle said. "She died when she was about sixteen I think. Maybe seventeen."

"What? How?" Jenny stopped folding a t-shirt and waited for Noelle to answer.

Noelle fidgeted. "I don't want to say, Jenny. It's a horrible story." She shook her head. "Maybe Dot will tell you."

"Maybe Dot will tell you what?" Dot said, smiling in at them from the doorway. She held a stack of towels.

Noelle blushed until she matched the wardrobe. "Um, Jenny asked me about Kimberly's picture downstairs," she said.

"Oh, I see," Dot said. She set the towels on the dresser, picked up a stack of shirts from the bed and sat holding them on her lap, smoothing the wrinkles. "It's all right, Nellie. It was a long time ago, and God continues to work all things together for good for those who love him, and are called according to his purpose." She looked at Jenny. "I know that doesn't make any sense to you, honey. I hope it will someday.

"Kimberly died a week before her 17th birthday," Dot said after a moment. "I got a call from the hospital telling us to come right away, Kim was dying. I thought it must be a mistake because she was at school, they must have the wrong number or something." Dot cleared her throat. "But it wasn't a mistake. Or rather, it was a giant mistake, but they had the right number."

Jenny watched Noelle's eyes tear up and dreaded to hear what came next. Maybe she didn't want to know.

"Turns out, Kimberly had gotten pregnant. She was afraid to tell Ray and me, God forgive us, and instead confided in the counselor at her school." Dorothy's mouth closed into a tight line for a moment. The old pain still had vicious power. "The counselor and one of her teacher friends arranged for an abortion and drove Kimberly to the appointment."

Dorothy looked at Jenny. "It didn't go well. They didn't give her enough anesthesia, and she woke up...," her hands gripped each other tightly. "She woke during...and started choking, vomiting. Things went downhill from there, and by the time an ambulance arrived, quite a long while later, she was in a coma."

Noelle put her arms around Dorothy. Dorothy leaned her head into her young friend and continued. "She never woke up. A few days later she died. Since the abortionist hadn't even finished what he started, we buried our daughter and grandbaby together."

The room vibrated with grief and outrage. Jenny swallowed hard and didn't say anything. What could she say anyway? She looked to Noelle with wide eyes. Noelle gave her a wobbly smile.

"But that wasn't the end of the story." Dorothy patted Noelle's arm. "God is bringing good things from our family's pain. And you're one of them, Jenny. We're very glad to have you here, and we hope you'll settle in and feel at home."

"Thanks, Dot," Jenny whispered.

"Hey! Where'd those muffins go?" Eddie hollered up the stairs. "Furniture's stowed and I'm starved!"

Dorothy and Noelle rolled their eyes in unison, making Jenny laugh.

"Guess we'd better feed the help," Dorothy said. She stood and put Jenny's shirts back on the bed. Then she picked up the top one and fingered a long slice in the fabric, camouflaged by the zombie graphic. "How'd you do that?" she asked.

"Oh crap," Jenny said, grabbing the shirt from Dorothy. "Sorry. I...I thought I threw away all the cut ones."

"What? What do you mean, cut ones?" Dorothy stiffened, touched her hand to her throat.

"It was Blaine, Dot, the boy she was with?" Noelle said, resting her hand on Dorothy's shoulder. "He trashed her things, remember? We went through her clothes but it looks like we missed one."

Dorothy still looked concerned, but relaxed a bit. "Right, right, I remember." She waved it away. "Still. Are you safe? He's still in jail after the car chase thing, isn't he?"

"Yes," Jenny said, hunching her shoulders forward. "He's still in jail, waiting for arraignment or something."

"Do you know where the muffins are, the muffins are, the muffins are…" came warbling up the stairs.

Dorothy went to the door. "I believe I'd better go make sure the muffin man doesn't tear the kitchen apart looking for his goodies. See you girls downstairs."

"Oh my God, Nellie," Jenny said, and covered her face with her hands as she sank onto the bed. Noelle sat next to her, put one arm around her, silent. Jenny's mind was filled with the images downstairs, a whole wall full of young moms with their babies. What would make people do that to themselves, to be constantly reminded of their dead daughter? She didn't get it. It was insane. She lay down on the bed, curling up with her knees to her chest.

Noelle looked at her for a moment, then put away the rest of Jenny's clothes, blinking away tears as she did.

A while later Kit knocked on the open door. "Are you girls coming down for muffins and coffee?" He noticed Jenny on the bed. "Everything okay?"

Noelle shrugged at him. "Pretty okay," she said. "We'll be down in a minute, right Jenny?" Jenny sat up and nodded.

"Good. We'll visit a little, then I want to get home."

"Home without Jenny," Noelle said, pouting.

Dreams

Next morning Ian's eyes snapped open. He sat up, wide awake. Usually he slept heavily and struggled to get moving in the morning. But he had dreamt of maps and journeys and green parasols and the energy of it propelled him from his bed to retrieve a certain folded bit of tissue from the trunk in his room.

He spread the traced bit of map on his bed and pored over it, reviewing the possible routes, looking for a possibility he may have missed before. But finally he tapped the route he'd marked out two days ago requiring just one day at sea between the tip of Spain and the African coast. That was the best, the only way.

Bo would not hear of it, of course. Ian frowned, saddened by the grief he'd seen in his uncle and aunt's faces. Since he was kneeling by his bed anyway, he closed his eyes and threw heavenward a plea for God's help for his heartbroken family.

In the next room, God was at that moment working in the haze between sleep and awareness to move Bo's heart in the direction He wanted him to go. Bo dreamt of journeys and green parasols also, but in his dream the parasol, expanded to the size of a boat, floated upside down in the sea, the gold fringe transformed into a brass rail, blindingly bright in the sun. He and Anisette stood on board gripping the rail and waving, floating easily south toward a smiling Tumaini, inexplicably visible on the distant shore, beckoning them to come.

Bo opened his eyes. Then closed them, willing the dream to depart, but it remained vivid. He opened his eyes again. The meaning was plain of course, though Bo resisted it with all his might.

He rolled over and sat on the edge of his bed, his head in his hands. Then he straightened. He would not tell Anisette, nor anyone, of this dream. He would pretend it never happened. It was merely a dream after all, the nonsense a sleeping mind jumbles together, signifying nothing.

He stood and splashed water from the bowl onto his face and scrubbed it roughly with the towel. Time to get on with real life. He knocked lightly on Anisette's door, then opened it. She lay in the bed, her hair mussed, just waking.

"Husband," she said, smiling. He went to her and took her in his arms.

"How is it with thee this morning, wife?" He pulled back to look at her. The color was better in her cheeks.

"Oh, better and better, never fret," she said. "I had the oddest dream," she laughed and looked up at him. "You and Tom and Ian were—I don't know—waxing or lacquering or something—the green parasol," here Bo tensed involuntarily and she paused. "Are you well, Bo?"

"Yes, yes," he said, smiling, willing himself to relax. "Tell me your dream, little one."

"Aye, it was down to the dock, and you were slathering it with—whatever it was—and arguing with each other whether it was enough. Was it watertight, and how long before you could test it. Ian said it didn't need to dry and was ready now, and Tom kept poking his fingers into it, checking for stickiness." She laughed again and said, "You were all quite ridiculous!" She gave him a look as if he really had been ridiculous. "You were going to use it as a coracle, you see, and take it to the honey meadow."

The blood drained from Bo's face, but he forced the smile to remain. "Now that is ridiculous," he said.

"I know it," Anisette said. "But I won't soon forget your faces as you argued it so seriously." She snuggled into him with a contented sigh. "Did you dream, husband?" Bo hesitated. "No," he said. "I don't remember dreaming."

"Ah well." She paused. "Bo, I'm hungry."

"Oh! Then let's get you to the kitchen where..." he sniffed the air, "I believe there may shortly be some breakfast." Bo rose from the bed and helped Anisette up, wrapped her in her robe, and prepared to gather her up to carry her to the kitchen.

"Bo," she stopped him with a soft hand on his arm. "Lend me your arm, and I shall walk to the kitchen. I'm stronger today."

Bo ruffled his hair. "Are you sure?" She nodded. "So be it, then," he said, and stationed himself beside her, his massive hand covering her small one on his arm, and they set off down the hall.

When they walked into the kitchen, Tom was frying potatoes and regaling Ian with an elaborate description of his own dream. Tom relished telling his dreams in excruciating detail, which was sometimes quite entertaining. The old man had quite a convoluted sense of—everything—from beauty to morality to good cooking, and his dreams took those convolutions and twisted them into fantastical shapes.

This morning he described how he was building a new bower for Anisette. A storm had knocked down the bower's stone wall, so he was building a new one of oak beams.

"And then we started arguing about the roof," Tom said.

"What roof?" Ian asked. "There's no roof!"

"Aye, of course not, but it's a dream, lad, as will be e'en more plain when you hear what I was sweer should be used for the roof..." Tom paused dramatically.

"Well then, what?" Ian returned, when it was obvious Tom was waiting to be urged on.

"Yonder great green sunshade!" Tom crowed, and cackled at the ridiculousness of it.

Bo stood rooted in place. This could not be happening.

"Now that's a wonder," Ian said. "I dreamed of the parasol, too."

"And I also," Anisette exclaimed. "How odd!" Anisette told her dream of the parasol coracle while Bo bore down on his resolve.

"And uncle," Ian said, a wide grin on his face, "Did you dream of the parasol?"

"He did not, poor man," Anisette said, making a pout and patting Bo's arm. She turned her face to his, her eyes merry. "Perhaps you should lie down for a wee nap this afternoon, and a green parasol dream will come to you then."

"I need no naps, and I need no foolish dreams of parasols," Bo said. "Are we to break our fast this day or stand about spouting nonsense?"

The room fell silent. Anisette sank slowly into her chair. Ian gaped at Bo. Old Tom's face compressed into a fierce scowl and reddened.

Bo saw he had misstepped. Now a reason for his anger would be wanted. "I'll see to the horses," he muttered, and stomped out of the house.

The fresh morning, encouraged by a chorus of birdsong and bright with cool sunshine and scudding clouds, only mortified him. His face grew hot with shame. He slammed into the dim stable, making the old mares snort and stamp.

He had lied to Anisette! He gripped the top board of Jo's stall and hung his head, staring at his boots. What was he to do? They would all be convinced the dreams were a sign—that they should make the journey to Morocco. He was half convinced of it himself by this time. But he didn't want to be convinced, and he didn't know how to get himself out of trouble with his family. Blast the poisonous parasol!

Bo straightened and scrubbed his hands through his hair. He looked around, forced himself to do the next thing. He grabbed the hay fork and pitched hay to his horses, making soothing noises to calm them. He opened the grain bin and dug the big scoop into the oats. Murmuring to Jo, he dumped the oats into her manger, then fetched a scoop for Em. He leaned into her neck, breathing in the sweet scent of her, stroking the strong rippling muscles of her shoulder. She nickered and nuzzled him.

Abba, what shall I do? He no sooner thought this than the hard knot of resistance in him melted away. He was astonished! He searched for it—where was his determination to keep Anisette on this side of the Great Sea? His resolve to oppose any foolish adventures that would put her at risk?

Without thinking about it, Bo took up the curry-comb and set about grooming the big bay, the tension in his muscles ebbing with each stroke. So be it, Abba. If you want us to journey to Africa, we will journey to Africa, and I will roll the worry of it onto your shoulders. He made long strokes along Em's flank and back. The horse sighed, contented. Jo nickered, impatient for her turn.

But Abba, I have lied to my Anisette! He paused his brushing, resisting the tension creeping back. The mare nudged his shoulder, knocking him off balance. He snorted. He was off balance all right. He continued the grooming, finishing with Em and taking his time with Jo. By the time he was done, he was calm. Like a weaned child, came the verse to his mind.

He wiped his hands, glanced around to see that everything was set right, and squared his shoulders as he prepared to return to his family and set things right there. As he opened the stable door, a crack of thunder shocked him, startling him backwards, and he stumbled, twisting his ankle under him. Pain shot up his leg and he sat abruptly on the stable floor.

The rain let loose, pouring heavily down, thick as a river falling off a cliff. He stared at it through the open door and caught sight of Anisette struggling out the *back door of the house, hurrying to her bower. Old Tom peered after her, his face scrunched in concern, before disappearing back inside.*

Bo scrambled to his feet, calling to Anisette, wincing at the sharp throb in his ankle, and made haste to the garden enclosure. But she had already blurred and transformed and he could only stand in the rain, wishing with all his might he could tell her his heart.

Potluck

"Why is it starting to seem like everyone we know is in jail?" Monti said. She sat at her dresser, struggling to fasten the clasp on the art glass bracelet Noelle had given her last Christmas.

"Says something about our character, maybe?" Kit answered. He scowled, gripping his cane like it was the original serpent.

Monti, catching the scowl in her mirror, said, "Taking that with you today?"

Kit grumbled a response too low down on the growl scale for Monti to decipher, but he stood the cane next to the door of their bedroom. She doubted he'd take it into church, and would they let him take it in the jail? Seemed unlikely. But she sure wasn't going to say anything else about it. She got the bracelet fastened, finally.

Monti found her Sunday tote and slipped her Bible into it. She plucked an empty tissue packet from the bag and fetched a replacement from the bathroom cupboard. Wouldn't do to be caught tissue-less.

"Anything else need to go in the church bag?" She glanced at Kit.

He had retreated to the bed. She hurried to him. "Sweetheart?"

"I'll be okay. Just want to take the load off the spine for a minute."

Monti was alarmed. He'd only been up for an hour and he needed to unload his spine? She watched, helpless, as he rolled his head to loosen his neck while his jaw tightened. It was ramping up fast today.

"What can I do, Kit?" She said it softly, though her heart raced.

"Nothing. Just give me a minute, okay?"

She flinched at his tone and her cheeks went hot. "Sure, love," she said and returned to her dresser. She picked up earrings and put them away, closed a drawer, snuck a look at him in the mirror. Her throat closed and she swallowed hard. She forced herself to admit he'd rather get this under control alone. And besides, it would be stupid for her to cry when he was the one hurting.

"I'll be in the kitchen," she said and left, walking down the hall half-blinded by tears. She tugged a tissue from the box in the kitchen and wiped her eyes, careful of her mascara. She refilled her coffee cup automatically. She set the mug back down, took the dishrag and wiped the clean counter.

With a sigh, she retreated to the window seat and folded herself into it, hugging her knees to her chest and laying her head on her arms. *Abba, please? Relief for him, please?*

She was going to have to get better at this. This wasn't going to go away, and she couldn't start bawling every time his pain flared up. It was half self-pity anyway. *I offer help, he snaps at me. Whoopee. I want to stay and visit for the Thanksgiving potluck and he might not be able to adhere to my precious itinerary. Big deal. Ugly, ugly, Monti.* She groaned and curled her hands into frustrated fists.

Help me, Abba. Help me to know how to help him best. Forgive me. Monti heard Noelle springing down the stairs and sat up. She sniffed and dried her eyes.

"Ready, to go, Grandma? Jenny texted me and..." Noelle stopped, her brow furrowing. "Grandma? What's wrong?"

Monti waved it away. "Nothing, nothing." She stood up. "Well, not nothing, your grandpa's having a rough morning." She pulled Noelle in for a hug. "And your grandma isn't handling it very well."

"He seemed okay at breakfast," Noelle said.

"He was. He usually feels pretty good after a hot shower, for a while. But today that respite didn't last very long."

"My ears are burning, ladies," Kit said. He leaned his cane against the table and enveloped both of them in his arms. "Sorry for snapping at you, Monti," he said into her hair.

"Oh, hush. When you start to catch up I'll let you know." She examined his face. "Better?"

"No. But I decided medication made more sense than biting your head off, so I'll be better in a bit. We have places to go and people to see."

Noelle stood on tiptoes and kissed his cheek. "I'm glad you did, G. G's a basket case when you're not feeling well."

Monti made a face at her.

"I think they have medication for that, too," Kit said. "Maybe you should see someone."

Monti made a face at him, too. "I miss Jenny. She doesn't pick on me. Isn't it time to go to church, you smart-alecks?"

"Yep. Got the salad and the pie?" Kit said.

"Oh gosh, I would've left them in the fridge," Monti said, and pulled out of the hug to pack them up.

"Which is why I asked," Kit said. He gripped his cane and shepherded his girls out the door.

CHURCH WAS GOOD. THEIR missionaries to Ukraine were visiting, and they gave an encouraging report on the work they were doing there. The worship was heartfelt. Then the Selton twins sang a lovely duet, a treat for which Monti was always thankful.

At the conclusion of his sermon Pastor Winther recounted his blessings over the last year, in which he convincingly included his fight with cancer and their family car being totaled on a slick road last winter. Monti was glad she'd replenished the tissues in her church bag. By the time they stood for the final blessing, Monti was tired and happy and wrung out and soaring. And hungry.

Everyone had pulled out all the stops for the Thanksgiving potluck. She spied several dishes she knew were labored over only once or twice in a year. Turkey, potatoes, gravy, yams, salads and side dishes loaded down three cloth covered tables lined up end to end across one side of the fellowship hall. Tucked between casserole dishes stood diminutive hand- print turkeys glued to fringed yellow paper plates. Monti found Dot uncovering the desserts.

"Oh my, I may have to do dessert first," she said, surveying the spread. "That looks like Brenda's cherry pie." She turned to Dot. "Wait, can pie be an appetizer?"

"That pie is in a class by itself," Dot said, "I don't think the normal rules apply," thus encouraging Monti's iconoclastic potluck plan. She wandered over to look at the decorations on the dining tables.

Strewn across the tablecloths on all the tables, construction paper leaves in yellow, orange, brown, green and inexplicably, blue, were printed with "I'm thankful for..." and filled in with charmingly misspelled gratitudes. *I'm thankful for my litel poney* was illustrated with a recognizable Rainbow Dash. Monti was trying to decipher a leaf she thought said something about a puppy, or it might have been daddy, when the bell rang briefly to quiet everyone down, and Ray said a blessing over the food.

Kit appeared at her side. "Hungry?"

"Mmm-hmm," she said. "How you doing?"

"I'll make it," he said. "And don't worry, I won't be in a hurry to head home."

"Well good, because I have lots of visiting to do. But if it gets bad, just say the word." They got in line, and Monti kept a keen eye on the cherry pie supply as they inched toward the buffet tables.

Two hours later Kit found Monti in the kitchen with Faye and Lucy, wrapping leftovers in foil packets. "Time to take the apron off, Monti."

She turned quickly to look at him, trying to gauge his comfort level. A bit tight around the jaw, not as cheery as he had been. "Okay, sure. You all right to finish up, ladies?" She reached around to untie her apron strings, tied them in a knot instead, and growled under her breath until Lucy came to her rescue.

"Sure, we're about done anyway," Lucy said. She freed Monti from the apron and shooed her from the kitchen. "Scoot."

Monti thanked her, grabbed her purse and church bag from the pegs and smiled at Kit. Then she noticed he was using his cane. She couldn't quite prevent her eyes going wide.

"Yes, Monti, I'm using the cane. Let's go, now." They waved goodbye to the cleanup crew, and crunched across the gravel lot to the Subaru. Noelle waited in the back seat, texting.

Monti slid into the car and watched Kit fold himself into the driver seat. "You okay?"

"Sure, Monti, I'll be fine." He leaned over and kissed her cheek. "Let's go home. I might take a nap before I head for the jail."

"Oh, I forgot all about that! I'm sorry, we didn't have to stay so long," Monti said, putting her hand on Kit's arm.

"No problem, I was having a good time with George. He told me about his days on the Franklin D. Roosevelt. Rosie, he calls her."

"What kind of ship?"

"Aircraft carrier. First to take nuclear weapons to sea. He was stationed on her then, in 1950 I think he said."

"I love George's stories," Monti said. "He starts talking about chrome-plated chariots and going for pinks in his hottie, and I want to write it all down and translate it into English for posterity."

"I like it when he talks about how he met his wife," Noelle said. "It's so sweet."

"Yeah, he gets on a roll." Kit shifted in his seat and Monti knew he was gritting his teeth till he could lie down. They rode the rest of the way home in silence.

After some medication and a twenty-minute nap, Kit was back at it. Monti was glad she didn't have to go anywhere. She'd slept for a bit too, and she had just enough energy to sit at her laptop and see what Anisette would do with the parasol.

One Day

"**U**ncle Bo," *Ian called from the back door. "Is all well?"*

Bo turned slowly to the boy, and limped slowly over the sogging ground to the door. "Aye, well enough," he said.

"But your leg?" Ian said. "Have you hurt yourself?"

Bo sat on the bench by the door and pulled off his boots, wincing at the pain. "The thunderbolt startled me. I turned my ankle."

"The storm came up sudden like, whilst you were in the stable," Ian said.

"It did not escape my notice," Bo said. The rain had already eased. He scanned the sky. A spring storm, nothing more. It would soon pass. Sooner than the throbbing in his ankle, he thought, frowning. He glanced back at Anisette, shooed Ian back into the house and limped after him into the kitchen. Tom peered around at them, then continued to scrape the great iron skillet at the sink.

"Aunt Anisette dished a plate for you," Ian said, and set it, covered with a second plate, at Bo's place at the table.

Bo's first ridiculous impulse was to refuse the food. But he was hungry, and he was not keen to incur the displeasure of his Sovereign with further displays of ill temper. He swallowed back his pique and said, "Thank you, nephew." He removed the cover and set it aside. "Ian, Tom, please forgive my ill temper." He pushed his fork into a potato. "And please forgive me for lying to you."

The boy and the old man had started to brush away his apology but this silenced them.

"What lie?" Tom said slowly, a threat in his voice.

Bo's face flushed with heat. "Earlier. I mean to say, I did dream. Of the infernal parasol."

"You did?" Ian said. He sat down beside Bo, his eyes alight. "Tell us."

"You said you didn't dream," Tom said, pointing the scraper at his master and squinting fiercely.

"Yes, I know, Tom, and that were a lie, as I am now telling you." Bo, exasperated, took a breath and let it out. "I dreamt...that the parasol floated topside down on the sea, big as a ship, and the gold fringe was become a brass rail round the deck. We were sailing on it, Anisette and I, toward Tumaini, whom we saw in the distance, beckoning." He closed his eyes. There, it was out, and he could no longer fight the truth of it even if he wanted to. The room was quiet. He opened his eyes to find Tom and Ian staring at him open-mouthed. It evidently was taking some time for his story to penetrate.

Ian recovered first. "Why then, you must go after all," he said.

Bo nodded and ate his now-cold breakfast while Ian mentally regathered the fragments of the dashed-aside plan. The four or five days since Anisette's mishap with the box, and even Bo's outburst, had not pushed the project far from his thoughts.

"Uncle Bo," Ian said. Bo looked at him and waited. "Don't be angry."

Bo's face fell. "I think I have done with being angry, nephew, for a long while if God grants me mercy."

"That is well, uncle." The boy shifted his weight from foot to foot. "So...before I returned the maps to Pastor, I traced the route I had worked out, on a sheet of tissue from the parasol." He hesitated. "Shall I fetch it?"

"Surely, Ian. Let us make a study of it."

The boy rushed to his room, and appeared momentarily back at the table. He lay the crinkly tissue on the table and smoothed it carefully. It still bore the marks of having been crumpled for many years in the interior of the green parasol, but the lines of the traced map ran over and yon, clearly visible in heavy pencil. Three heads bowed over it.

Ian ran his finger along the route he had marked. "This route o'er the Gibraltar Strait would mean a crossing of only ten miles or so, easily done in a day. But, it be a long journey overland to the south of Spain to get there."

"One day at sea, you say?" Bo said, fighting the knot of fear in his stomach.

"Yes, uncle, I do not see how it could be more. And though it be a journey of mayhap two months to reach Gibraltar, once o'er the strait 'tis only another fortnight or so to Tendrara." Ian slid his finger lightly across the desert to the large oasis where Ambassador Tumaini lived.

"One day," Bo repeated. This was the crux of the matter, of course. Could he trust his Jesu to protect his lovely Anisette from rain for one day?

"Ian," he said. "Make hast to Pastor Wheaton's house and fetch back that map. I want to study it, and to show Anisette when she is restored to us."

Helluva Day

Kit eyed the terrible chair, a scooped out plastic monstrosity guaranteed to generate back problems if you didn't already have them. He leaned the cane against the counter, adjusting it until it stopped acting like it was going to fall over, unhooked the handset and sat. He looked up as Mike shuffled to the seat on the other side of the Plexiglas. His face was haggard, his hair wild. Heavy pouches under his eyes aged him ten years. No businessman's bonhomie today. He picked up the handset like it weighed fifty pounds.

"Hi, Mike," Kit said.

"Hey," Mike grunted, and sagged into his chair. He didn't look at Kit.

Where to go from there? The silence stretched out, tired as old elastic. "What happened, Mike?"

Mike looked at him then. His face crumpled and Kit thought he was going to cry. "I screwed up." He started shaking his head, small movements, like he didn't dare risk a bigger motion. "I screwed it all up but royal this time."

"I have to agree," Kit said, "but...why?"

Mike slapped the counter and leaned back. "Where do I start? It was a helluva day. First thing was a call from my broker at 7am, informing me my bulletproof portfolio had tanked to the tune of fifty grand overnight." He held up two fingers. "Second, before I leave for the office Valerie and me have a huge fight about the idiot sick cat."

Three fingers. "When I get to the office, there's a message from Rondy, rambling on about needing to focus on her family and not wanting to leave me in the lurch, but she's leaving me in the lurch anyway. Didn't even have the courtesy to show up and tell me in person." He kept adding fingers.

"My partner calls to tell me a huge deal fell through, one I worked on for six months. And Blaine's landlord calls to say he's sent me a bill for the damage to that girl's room." He stared at his five fingers splayed on the counter, but he wasn't done. "And I kid you not," he looked at Kit. "In the mail is a letter from my proctologist saying they need to take another look."

"So, I figure that's enough for one day, and have Butch take me home early. I walk in the door and step in a puddle of sick cat puke, in my $900 Mezlan oxfords." He paused, swallowed hard. "But fate, or karma or whatever, saved the best for last." He raked his hand through his hair, slowly, two or three times. "There's a note, in an envelope on the kitchen counter, from Valerie. She's gone and she won't be back."

Kit winced. No kidding, a helluva day. He shifted in the evil plastic chair.

"There was no liquor in the house." Mike stared at Kit. "And I wanted some. So I found the extra set of keys for the Escalade, and went and got some."

"The paper said your blood alcohol was .152," Kit said.

"Yeah, no doubt. I was working at it pretty hard. Started at some bar, I don't remember where, until they wouldn't serve me anymore. Then found a liquor store that would serve me—had to try a couple different ones—and then a quiet parking lot." He hung his head, his hand in a tight fist on the counter. "I should've slept it off right there." He raised his head and looked at Mike. "But I didn't." He hesitated, cleared his throat. "Have you heard how that lady is doing? I haven't had the courage to ask..."

MONTI KISSED KIT AT the door. "Mike?" she asked.

"Not good. I now understand why meeting me for coffee slipped his mind." She took his jacket, hung it on the coat rack, and followed him into their office.

"What happened?"

"He had a helluva day, as he put it, capped by his wife leaving him." He told her the details and Monti shook her head.

"I guess that could push a guy off the wagon all right. What happens to him now?"

"He'll be arraigned tomorrow," Kit said, lowering himself into his chair. "And charged with felony DUI, of course. Mrs. Millard is recovering, so it won't be manslaughter. But still, he's looking at mandatory jail time, anywhere up to 5 years. And a fine, and one of those ignition interlock things." He shook his head. "In other words, his life will never be the same."

"Nor will Mrs. Millard's no doubt." Monti had trouble feeling sorry for him.

"No doubt." He took Monti's hand. "I'll have to stick by him, you know. He doesn't have anybody else, as sad as that is."

Monti chewed her lip. He was right, of course. You couldn't abandon people because they did stupid, dangerous, hurtful, criminal things. You couldn't abandon people, period. "Yes, I agree. You'll be the fragrance of Christ in his stinky life."

Kit chuckled. "You and your turns of phrase, Monti."

"Did he say anything about him and Blaine being in jail at the same time?"

Kit sobered. "That's crushing him, Monti. He choked up when we started talking about Blaine. Then he broke down completely, crying, groaning, pulling his hair. It was hard to watch."

"Nowhere to go but up," she whispered, thinking of Marla.

"Exactly," he agreed.

Restored

B o checked the sky and cautioned the clouds to be on their way. He made several attempts to attend to his mead, but found himself ever at the back door, gazing into the bower. He silently cheered when a fresh breeze fluttered Anisette's leaves.

A rush of fresh air blew into the kitchen as Ian returned with the requested map tucked under his arm, out of breath and cheeks red from running the long way from the parsonage. He plunked the scroll on the kitchen table and dropped into a chair. Tom poured a huge mug of milk for him and he downed it in a single draught.

Bo came in from the back door when he heard the boy. He took the map and undid the ribbon tied round it. As he unrolled it, Tom set empty cups down on the corners of the map to keep it flat. Ian rescued the tissue copy which a stray breeze had lifted and deposited in a corner of the room.

"We can make notes on this one, Uncle Bo," he said. He smoothed it flat on the other end of the table.

"Good thought, lad, and where's my pencil?" Bo said, checking the most likely pockets but finding naught but a stem of hay and a hair ribbon of Anisette's. He gazed at the pale blue satin strand, puzzled.

"Here ye be," Tom said, and produced a reasonably sharp pencil from somewhere.

"Good. Now then," Bo said, as he stuffed the ribbon back into his pocket and took the pencil from Tom. He peered alternately at the map and Ian's notes. "The journey to Gibraltar is no less than 900 miles, you have here, Ian."

"Aye, uncle. As near as I can tell. A long way, ain't it!"

"It is, but if we made," Bo scribbled with the pencil, "thirty miles a day...and then another ten days or so to Tendrara, why that's forty days." He looked up. "Forty days and forty nights."

"Are we expecting a flood, Bo?" Anisette said.

All three men turned and grinned to see their lovely lady restored to them, pink-cheeked and well rested. Bo stood and fetched her to his chair. "No, my love, no flood. We're plotting our journey to Morocco."

"Morocco? What do you mean?" she said. "Are you to go without me?"

"No no, not a bit of it," Bo said. "Only, I have something to tell...to ask you." He sat in the chair next to her and held both her hands. "Do not be angry, Anisette." Here Old Tom gave Ian a sharp poke in the side as a non-too-subtle hint they should clear out. Ian followed him out, rubbing his poked ribs.

"I am not angry, husband. Everyone is out of sorts occasionally." She tilted her head and smiled at him.

"No, not that. At least, not only that." Bo swallowed hard, rubbed at the back of his neck, and confessed. "I lied to you, little one."

"You did?" A knife twisted in his belly when her voice faltered, and her eyes brimmed with tears.

"I did, please forgive me, Anisette." He kissed her hand and hurried on. "I told you I did not dream of the wretched parasol, but I did."

"You did?" she said again. "You dreamed of the parasol?"

"Yes, and I know we are being told to make the journey to Morocco. Together. I knew when I woke, but I didn't want to admit it. I was...afraid."

"For me. You were afraid for me." Anisette put a hand on his cheek and he pressed into it. They sat silent for a minute. Then she stood and pulled at him to stand, too. When he complied, she wrapped her slender arms about him and said, "I love you. I forgive you. Never do it again." And she made such a fierce face that Bo burst out laughing. She stepped away and tugged at his arm. "We must find Tom and cook something. I am so hungry!"

That evening Bo posted a letter to Tumaini to tell him of their new plan. The next day launched a month awhirl with planning, purchasing, and packing. The house grew crowded with crates and bundles, to which they added and subtracted continually in an effort to make small their baggage without finding themselves lacking vital supplies somewhere along the way.

Bo spent hours writing notes for Tom and Ian to consult in his absence. He had never realized how much of his mead making knowledge was in his head and nowhere else. Records and receipts he had, but every day he thought of several details that weren't written down anywhere. He hoped Tom and Ian would be able to keep the rhythm of the meadow and the mead humming along.

AT BO'S REQUEST, DOCTOR *Fleming came to the house and examined Anisette thoroughly. It had only been a week or so since the disaster with the box, though to Bo it seemed far longer.* "I want to be sure you are strong enough, Anisette," *he said.* "We will go, but mayhap the good doctor will have advice, or a tonic or somewhat to fortify you for such a strenuous journey."

Anisette screwed up her face at the thought of the tonics she had known, but submitted to the examination without protest. When he had done, Dr. Fleming put away his kit and said, "Mrs. Willem, I know not how it's possible for you be in the perfect pink of health so soon after falling so ill. It quite astounds me."

"No tonic, then?" *Anisette said, brightening.*

"No indeed. I would covet your advice at this juncture. What is your secret, mistress?"

Anisette laughed. "Well, and I have told you it is restful to stand in the bower, calm and sleepy."

"When you're not in a box," *he said.* "And when you're not with child."

"Yes," *Anisette said, dimming a little.* "Yes, quite so. But doctor, hope is a wondrous tonic, is it not? I can scarce contain the brilliant hope in me, that this journey will allow us to have a family."

"I hope God allows it to be so, Anisette." *He stood and walked with her out to the great room.* "I declare, Bo Willem, your delicate wife is healthy as a horse. You may take her wheresoever you will without fear, in my opinion."

A weight slid off Bo's shoulders and he smiled broadly. "Thank you, Doctor! That is sweet to hear." *He shook the doctor's hand, gave him the bottle of his favorite mead he'd fetched from the cellar and accompanied him to the door.*

A FEW DAYS BEFORE THEIR *planned departure, Tom led Bo to the box in the bower.* "Look at these wee seedlings," *he said.* "They be crowding each other now, and they need planted out."

"Aye, they do, Tom," *Bo said, examining them.* "And as they are to go to the honey meadow, and as I have meant to take the punt out there these many days,

*we shall make a day of it." He stretched with his hands at the small of his back,
and added, "We could all do with a bit of a lark, think you not?"*

*The next day they four set off in the punt and a rowboat borrowed from their
upstream neighbor, with one of Tom's prodigious hampers and the box of almond
seedlings. Anisette sat in the bow with her green silk parasol, like a young queen
in her men-folk's eyes. The brilliant morning sky allowed not a wisp of cloud from
horizon to horizon. The water rippled cool and fresh against Anisette's trailing
fingertips. Tom and Bo nodded to friends in other boats. The entire town seemed
to be on the river today. Anisette waved to one or two she recognized.*

*Bo guided them into the quag and poled them along the path to the honey
meadow, Ian and Tom following. Few others ventured into these parts, and they
had the musky, meandering maze to themselves, silent but for birdsong, bees,
and the plashing of the oars and pole in the water. When they reached the honey
meadow, Bo handed Anisette and the hamper out, and helped Ian haul the box
out of the rowboat while Tom secured both craft.*

"I say we eat first, then plant the trees," Bo said.

*"Hmm," Anisette said. "I know what generally follows after such a repast as
Tom has packed, and 'tis not physical labor."*

*Bo considered. "You may be right, love. Perhaps we'd better dig first, and
earn our after-dinner nap." He lifted his spade from the punt and gazed about
the meadow. "Seven seedlings. Let's start there," he said, and gripped one handle
of the box.*

*Anisette spread the picnic cloth and began to unpack the hamper. Ian loped
past, to dip a bucket in the quag for to water in the first seedling. "May I help?"
Anisette asked, but he just grinned and shook his head, as she knew he would.*

*She finished setting out the lunch things, and lay back on the blanket. She let
her mind wander as it was wont to do, to their approaching journey. She tried to
imagine riding a horse on narrow trails. Or sleeping on the ground. Or eating a
meal in an inn, or washing in a creek. She'd never done any of these things and
a thrill of anticipation, sharpened with fear, ran through her. She could hardly
wait.*

*Before she knew it, the men were finished. They wiped their necks with their
kerchiefs, and washed their dirty hands at the water's edge while she uncovered
the food and dished their plates. They all ate heartily and napped in the gentle
sunshine afterwards. As the shadows lengthened they roused themselves, packed*

up and climbed back into the boats smiling and lazy, to pole back home in no hurry at all. Anisette found she still wanted sleep as the day waned and the punt bumped against the dock.

She took Bo's arm as they crunched up the gravel path to the house. When they rounded the bend Bo stopped short, pulling her off balance. She looked up at him, startled, then followed his stare.

Standing at attention in front of their door were two gigantic soldiers.

Domestic Adventures

Monti was rinsing the shampoo from her hair when she remembered again she didn't have to teach classes today. She grinned and got shampoo in her mouth. A gift of extra time was always delicious (unlike shampoo). Yesterday had felt like a vacation even though she never had class on Mondays. She'd written several scenes in her story and gotten Bo into and out of a real mess, and both of them several steps closer to their Morocco adventure.

Monti's own Tuesday adventures would be of a more domestic nature, but still she'd better get a move on. She shut off the water and grabbed her towel. Now she knew what day it was, she looked forward to the window repair guy arriving at nine.

He'd probably need most of the day to replace the big front window, including the frames and even a bit of wall. Apparently, nothing whatsoever about their current windows was standard in any way, and the entire area was just a bit off square. Who knew? The shop had already warned them the repair would likely exceed the previous $2100 estimate.

She'd let Kit write that check and break the total to her gently later on. She was going to visit Austin one more time. He would be released next Tuesday, but a week was a long, long time in such places. She couldn't take him anything, but she could listen, a rare enough gift these days.

Monti threw on her robe and followed her nose to the coffee pot.

"Hey Monti," Kit said. He turned off the stove and kissed her. "You slept in."

"Somebody must have shut off my alarm," she said.

"I didn't see any reason you should get up early today," he said. "You were lying there snoring so cute..."

"Really. I guess I should be grateful you weren't in the mood for video documentation."

"How do you know that for sure?" He grinned at her, ducked her swipe at him, and handed her a cup of coffee. "Hungry?"

"You betcha. Snoring burns up all kinds of calories." She gussied up her coffee and asked, "You ready for the window guy?"

"Sure. I *will* document that. I want to see what the inside of the wall looks like. This house is over a hundred years old—you don't get to see old bones like that very often."

"You're interested in the oddest things. Though I suppose I'm glad 'old bones' is one of them."

"And I will resist saying how you fit into the 'oddest things' category, too."

"That didn't sound like resisting to me!"

"Well Monti, you craft these perfect openings..."

"And it's impossible not to walk through them, I know darling. Poor man, you're a slave to your wit."

"Get the jam out, will you?" Kit set two plates on the table, loaded with fat omelets and multi-grain toast. "I want strawberry."

"Of course you do." Monti opened the fridge and found a gigantic shrink-wrapped bird had taken up residence on the top shelf. "Why is there a turkey?"

"It's for the food boxes for church," Kit said. "Eddie will be by to pick it up. Aren't you supposed to collect ours today from Pilgrim's?"

"Yes! Though I never wrote that part down! Good grief, where's my purse?" She found it, dug out her notepad and wrote down 'pick up turkey'. "I wish I knew how many we were feeding," she said.

"Think about that after you eat. Your eggs are getting cold."

Monti didn't need convincing. They gave thanks, jammed their toast, and started in on the omelets.

"No girls yet? I mean, girl?"

"That girl is pretty good at sleeping in, even without disabled alarm clocks."

"She is that," Monti agreed.

Twenty minutes later Monti had a plan for her trip out, to include fetching a few final items for the Thanksgiving dinner. "Still no word from CJ on Stevie Jakes. I don't understand it."

"They're looking for him, Monti. But he doesn't want to be found, obviously. I think he has a little more experience, a better network than Blaine did, so it's easier for him to hide."

"That's even worse. The bad guy is in jail. The worse guy is out loose."

Kit shrugged. "We all do what we can. CJ's on the job. You be alert while you're out. I'll take care of Noelle at home."

"And the cat."

"And the cat," Kit agreed.

Anebni and Paru

Black as bog oak and heavily muscled, the two soldiers glittered with swords, spears, armbands and medallions. They wore dusty, heavy crimson cloaks, draped casually in deep folds around them, swept up and over the turbans on their heads.

Ian and Tom fell silent as they caught up with Bo and Anisette and saw the men. Bo gently pried Anisette's fingers loose from his arm, and indicated with a look at Tom that they were to keep her close. Breathing a quick, bewildered prayer, he went to greet their visitors.

One of the soldiers stepped forward and presented a letter sealed with red wax. As Bo took it, the man bowed slightly and stepped back into his place. Bo unsealed the letter and read it. He glanced back at the men, eyes wide, then turned to his family.

"Tumaini has sent them," he said, "as a bodyguard for our journey."

"Truly? Anisette said, and took a tentative step toward them. "A mercy to have them for us, and not against us."

"Have you any English, gentlemen?" Bo asked them.

"Yes," said the soldier who had given Bo the letter. "One little."

Bo smiled. "And I thank Jesu for that, as I have not a word of…what is your mother tongue?"

The soldier looked to his companion, who shrugged in the apparently universal sign for 'I know not what he says.'

"Never mind, we'll make do. My name is Bo Willem, and this is my wife, Anisette" he turned and beckoned for Anisette to join him.

Both soldiers bowed. The spokesman pointed to himself and said, "Anebni." His companion was Paru, who bowed his head when introduced. Ian and Tom joined them and they went over all the names again.

"Please, allow me," Bo said, and pointed at the door. They stepped aside to let him open it. Bo went in and motioned for them to follow him. They did, *each first shouldering his pack, then stooping to fit through the doorway. They filled the hall as it had never been filled. Anisette entered and threaded her way through to the greatroom.*

"The house is topsy-turvy," she said, snatching up a stack of blankets and looking about for somewhere to stash them. Open chests and piles of supplies cluttered the room. "It's all to be packed by tomorrow, you see."

"No fuss," Anebni said, smiling widely. "Long journey need...topsy in get ready."

"Yes, well, it surely does," Anisette said with a sigh, and dropped the blankets back where she'd picked them up from. "Are you hungry? Do you want food?"

Bo thought their eyes brightened at that. "Please, set down your things, and have a seat," he said. "We'll unpack Tom's hamper here and finish off the victuals." They were lost at first, but he pantomimed leaning a spear against the wall, and gestured to the kitchen chairs, and they got the idea. Tom and Ian set about unpacking the considerable stores left from their lunch, and Anisette put on the kettle.

An hour later, everyone could almost pronounce everyone else's name, and Tom had made an impression with his pipe and tobacco. Bo puzzled over where to put them for the night. He was sleeping in his childhood room and dared not do otherwise, so all the bedchambers were occupied. But Tom and Ian agreed to double up and give the Egyptians Ian's room.

"No need for sleep in house," Paru said. "Have cloak."

"Oh, please do," Anisette said. "We'll feel much more comfortable if we know you're comfortable."

Bo could see that didn't really sink in, but nevertheless Paru bowed. "As please you, mistress," he said.

Ian tapped Bo on the shoulder, and handed him the map. "Oh, good thought, nephew," he said, taking it from the boy and spreading it on the table as Tom cleared away the remaining crockery and Anisette wiped up the crumbs. Anebni and Paru leaned forward.

"We think mayhap forty days to travel from here," Bo placed his finger on their starting point, "to Tendrara. Would you agree?"

"Forty day..." Anebni frowned. "Thirty day we come here. We begin next day letter come to Bey Tumaini." Paru spoke to Anebni in rapid syllables. "Ah, yes, the lady," Anebni said. He nodded. "Not thirty, but forty day may be so."

"*Excellent news,*" said Bo.

Out then came the packing lists, and a tour of the great room and the chests. The Egyptians generally nodded in approval, but now and then made a sideways chop to indicate an item need not be included in their supplies.

"*Need go to horses,*" Anebni eventually said.

Bo hadn't thought about how they had got to his door. "*Where are they?*" he asked.

"*In stable,*" Paru said. "*We...ak...*" He turned to Anebni for the word.

"*We go in,*" Anebni said. "*No one home, horses tired, need unpack, water, feed.*"

"*Very sensible,*" Bo said. He stood up. "*I'll go with you and see if there be aught else you need for them.*"

When the horses, the family and the guests were all bedded down for the night, Bo and Anisette stood in the doorway of her room. She put a hand on his chest and peeked at him from beneath her long lashes. "*We shan't sleep apart for much longer, Bo.*"

A low growl rumbled in his chest. "*Best I do not dwell upon that just yet,*" he said. "*We've a long journey ahead of us. Are you ready?*"

"*I've no real idea what it would mean to be ready,*" she said. "*But I'm that eager to start I can scarcely breathe.*"

"*One day more,*" Bo said, circling her with his arms, "*to finish packing and on Thursday we set out, bright and early.*"

"*With our magnificent bodyguard!*"

"*Indeed. What an unexpected gift, that. It eases my mind tremendously, I confess.*"

"*And mine,*" Anisette agreed. "*But Bo,*" she whispered, "*What if it should rain? If 'twere just thee and me we would find a spot and wait it out as needs be. But I wonder how our companions would take in such a manifestation?*" She gripped his arms. "*Does it worry you?*"

"*Somehow, it does not,*" he said. "*I am so sure we are on the right path, I cannot feel uneasy about that detail or any other. He has decreed it. He will shower rain upon us or not, as He wills, and all will be well, one way or another. Might you rest in that?*"

She relaxed into him. "*Yes. Yes, I will, Bo. But you'll keep the spade handy, will you not?*"

He laughed. "I will, wife. I'll tie it to my saddle, as the parasol will be tied to yours." He leaned down and kissed her. "Sleep well, Anisette."

She kissed him back. "And you, husband." They released each other slowly, sliding their hands down each other's arms until they parted and retired to their separate bedchambers.

Thanksgiving

The alarm rang at 6 a.m. Monti rolled over and shut it off. She'd set it early because she wanted to move at a reasonable pace today, and not be rushing around like a madwoman in the hour before Thanksgiving dinner.

She flopped back over and stared at the ceiling. She still didn't know how many were coming today. One student had texted her yesterday with a tentative "Ill probly b ther." She looked over at Kit. He hadn't heard the alarm. She eased out of the bed, pulled on her robe and hurried to the shower. It was chilly this morning.

She managed to dress without waking Kit. Gulliver met her in the kitchen doorway and wound around her legs, purring. "Good morning, Gu-vluv," she said softly. "You hungry?" She fed him, refreshed his water, started the coffee and went to her window seat. She needed a firm foundation for this day.

By the time she'd thought through a few verses in Philippians and finished her first cup of coffee, the sun was shooting brilliant rays up through moving clouds. They might or might not get weather conducive to an after-dinner stroll through the cemetery.

But that was a long way off. She glanced at her menu, which would feed a dozen or more people and whose components were non-negotiable in the eyes of her husband and granddaughter. It was apparently impossible for it to be Thanksgiving without...fill in any item from the list. She started in on the sweet potato rolls, happy to be in her comfort zone, making good food for people she loved. And for hypothetical other people who might show up, or not.

Kit wandered in and kissed her. "You have flour on your nose," he said. He squinted at her, "and your right ear. And in your hair." He shook his head. "That's some talent, Monti."

"Wait 'till I get to the boiling cranberries," she said. "That'll be pretty."

"I bet. What can I chop?"

"How about breakfast? I'm kinda on a roll here."

"Sure, breakfast is the yeast I can do."

"I dough knead your help, thanks."

Noelle appeared, rubbing her eyes. "Sounds like a pun war," she said. "Is it over?"

"Well, we just got started but it's your grandpa's turn..." Monti cocked an eyebrow at him, a bold challenge.

"You're at least a cup of coffee ahead of me," he protested.

"I would say that's an unconditional surrender," Monti said, raising her floury fist in victory, and thus dusting her unfloury parts with snowy flakes.

"Whatever you say, love," Kit said, and poured coffee for himself and Noelle.

Dinner was set for one o'clock. By noon, everything had been chopped, assembled, simmered, or baked, and was staying warm or chilled. Except the gravy, of course. Can't do that ahead of time.

Monti was having a wee lie down with Gulliver curled against her. Kit was elbow deep in his aquariums. Noelle was...somewhere...on the phone, Monti thought. The plan was for Noelle to be ready to surreptitiously fit additional place settings onto the table every time the doorbell rang. If it rang at all.

The house was still. Gulliver purred quietly under her hand.

The doorbell rang and Monti jerked awake, scaring the cat who abandoned her to go trip up the new arrivals. She was probably all mashed and wrinkled. She rolled off the bed and hurried to the bathroom to take stock and repair any damage. Light steps moved down the stairs and Noelle greeted someone at the door. Bless her. Wait. Monti stopped combing her hair and listened. That sounded like Austin. How could it be Austin? She put her comb down and hurried to see.

"Austin! How can you be here?" she said, holding out her hands to him.

"Hey Mrs. R," he said, and took her hands. "They let me out yesterday. Best behavior, holiday week, you know. It's all good. Bobby gave me the map."

"And this must be Warren. Welcome, young man." Monti gave her hand to the skinny teen peering at her from under a shaggy head of curls. She noted the scars marring his mouth, nose and left eye, still shocking but mercifully faded with age. He and Austin were both pink cheeked from the cold, dressed in plaid shirts neatly tucked into worn but clean blue jeans.

"Nice to meet you, ma'am," Warren said.

"What about your family, Austin? Aren't they having a dinner today?"

"Yes, but not here. They didn't know I would get out early, so they're all in Wyoming at my aunt's. They'll head back tomorrow. Warren stayed home to take care of the animals."

"Happy chance for us, then. Come on in. You've met Noelle, our grand-daughter." Monti took their coats and handed them to Noelle, then led them into the living room where Kit met them, rolling his shirt sleeves down. "And here is my husband, Kit. Kit, this is Austin and his brother Warren."

Kit shook hands with them. "Welcome," he said. "Have a seat. I'm just going to light the fire." He squatted in front of the fireplace and opened a box of matches. "I meant to have it going by now, but I got lost in the fish tanks."

"Fish tanks?" Warren asked.

"Sure, I have some saltwater tanks set up. I'll show you after dinner." He struck a match, held it to the waiting tinder and the fire burst into life.

The doorbell rang again and Monti and Kit looked at each other, eyebrows raised. Monti opened the door. "Tanya! And Jeff, welcome!" She ushered them in, took their coats. Noelle poked her head out of the dining room to confirm the new count, then disappeared again. Monti did the introductions, adding Noelle when she reappeared.

"It sure smells good in here, Mrs. R," Jeff said.

"Thank you, I hope you're all hungry. I have to make the gravy, and then we'll be ready."

"Austin, dude, you're out!" Tanya said, and gave him a hug.

Monti left them to it. Kit followed her into the kitchen. "Seven's a good crowd," he said.

"Seven is perfect. And we have room for one more, easy. I'm kind of surprised!" She turned on the flame under the drippings.

"Somebody must have spread the word about your cooking," he said.

"Yeah, right. At school I feed them Rolos, chips and salsa from a can."

Kit shrugged. "They're here, that's all that matters. What's left to do?"

"Hmm. Open the sparkling cider? I think everything else is ready, it all just needs set on the table."

Kit left her to work her gravy magic and set about opening several bottles.

Ten minutes later they were all settled in their seats around the table, chatting like they ate together every week.

Kit said, "Let's say grace." Austin and Warren closed their eyes and bowed their heads. Tanya and Jeff looked blank, but followed suit. "Thank you, Father, for filling our house with young people. Thank you for a year full of blessings. Thank you for protecting our family, for allowing us to be useful, and for the gift of living in freedom and plenty. Thank You for this great food, and for the hands that have prepared it. In Jesus' name, Amen."

"Amen," echoed around the table. Then everybody got busy passing everything, then everybody got quiet eating everything.

"What are those green balls? They look like cooked marbles," Warren said, causing Noelle to snort cider up her nose.

"Those are Brussels sprouts, Warren," Monti said, arching an eyebrow at Noelle. "Though why they're named that I haven't a clue. You've never had them before?"

"Never even seen one."

"Our family is more into potatoes," Austin said. "Maybe carrots or green beans once in a while. They don't get too exotic with vegetables."

"Our kids used to call them bitter dwarf cabbages," Monti said. "But they ate them anyway."

"Where are your kids now?" Tanya asked.

Monti blinked, and her throat constricted, but Kit rescued her. "Our son, Stephen, was killed when he was 23, in a training accident. Our daughter, Marla, is finishing her time in drug rehab in Florida. We hope to have her home at Christmas."

That shut them up. Kit was never one for anything but the unvarnished truth.

Austin said, "Our mom was in rehab several times. For drinking. She finally did get sober, turned her life around."

"Glad to hear it," Kit said. "Pass the gravy, will you Tanya?"

She obliged. "My brother did rehab twice, but it didn't take. Then he ran off and got shot."

"Oh, honey, I'm so sorry," Monti said.

Tanya shrugged. "It was a long time ago. I was only five or six." She frowned fiercely. "Still, it p- it ticks me off when dealers come around our neighborhood. I wanna scream at 'em, but Mama says I have to be careful. They're dangerous."

"Your mother is right, Tanya," Kit said. "You should be careful. But you should also report it if you see any selling happening. The officers I know are serious about cleaning the dealers out of our town."

"You know cops?" Jeff asked.

"Sure, they're just regular guys, Jeff." Kit laid his fork on his plate and sighed. "And unfortunately, we've had them to the house pretty frequently in the last few weeks. Good dinner, Monti."

"That's 'cuz of Blaine, right?" Tanya said. "We heard he was, like, harassing you."

"He was, indeed," Monti said. "More than harassing! He attacked Jenny and Noelle in her car, threatened us all including the cat, and vandalized our house!" she said, feeling herself heat up.

"He didn't do all of it, Monti, he's been in jail for a couple of weeks now."

"Blaine has this drug dealer friend, Stevie Jakes," Noelle put in. "He took over when Blaine was arrested. He threatened Gulliver, and burned NEXT into our lawn. How stupid is that?"

"Man, I met that Jakes dude," Jeff said. "He's one bad—uh—bad dude."

Monti saw Kit's antenna go up. "You met him, where? At school?"

"No, at a place we hang sometimes. Kind of a club. Not really a good place, you know what I mean?" Jeff reddened and looked like he wished he'd never mentioned it.

"How long since you've seen him?" Kit didn't let it go. "The police are looking for him."

"I think I saw him there last weekend. But man, I don't want to get in trouble for bein' in that place, you know?" He looked about to bolt for the door.

"Don't worry, Jeff," Monti said. "Detective Price is very good at protecting people who are trying to help. Why don't you tell Kit the name of the place after dinner." She stood and collected the plates. "Right now, it's time for pie. We have pumpkin and banana cream. And coffee or tea to go with."

On the Road

Anisette woke with the sun. She snuggled in closer to Bo, for the morning air was chill and damp with dew. She gazed up through the leafy canopy above them and inhaled deeply.

She'd never slept outdoors before this journey, and though the first few nights had been frightening, filled with unfamiliar sounds and a feeling of exposure, she'd quickly grown accustomed to it. Likewise, she was not as sore now from the long hours on horseback. She and her horse had developed an understanding, and Anisette often dismounted and walked when the going was slow. She felt stronger than ever before in her life.

The first week or so, she had her sketch book on her lap continually, trying to capture the beauty of their surroundings. But after a few days she resolved to relax into the adventure and not try to catch every bit of it with her pencil and paper. She would let it soak into her heart and mind, and the memories would outlast any sketches.

Bo stirred. She wriggled up and kissed him on the nose, giggling at his startled face. "Good morning, love," she said.

"Good morning." He pulled her in for an embrace and she buried her face in his neck. He pulled back and inhaled. "Coffee? Have you been up and about already?"

"Not at all." She sat up. "But Paru grows quite fond of coffee. He has been most attentive as I prepare it." They climbed out of their bedrolls and rolled them up, found a large bush to serve as privy, then went to investigate the coffee aroma drifting toward them from the campfire.

Happy Birthday

Monti typed "The End" and sat back. Then she hit CTRL+Save and sat back again. She had agonized over the ending, but finally decided to make it turn out the way she wanted it to. It was her story, after all!

"That sounded final," Kit said, looking up from his computer.

"Now how did you know that?" she asked. "I just typed 'the end'."

"Heck if I know, maybe you were giving off completion vibes or something. Don't forget to save it."

"Already did, but thanks for checking. I still have some work to do on it, but the first draft is done, at least." Now, to back it up online...she decided to just email it to herself for today, she'd stash it in her documents cloud later. It was time to get dressed. She had no idea what she was going to wear.

"How's this?" Noelle asked, posing in Monti's bedroom doorway. She was decked out for her birthday dinner in a gauzy, bohemian-style smocked dress embroidered with silk ribbon, her newest score at a tiny hole-in-the-wall thrift shop. She wore over it a suede vest made mostly of fringe, had on her slouchy tall boots and dangled a tiny hand-tooled leather purse from one hand. Somehow, she made it all look pulled together and downright elegant. She would turn heads tonight. Gulliver eyed her fringe from the cedar chest and twitched his tail.

"You're gorgeous, Granddaughter. Did Jenny do your hair?"

"Yes, and I did hers. She has even more braids.".

"Did Jenny decide not to join us for dinner?" Monti asked.

"Yeah, she's tired, and not feeling too well. But we had a nice afternoon catching up. Ray and Dot are picking her up pretty soon."

"Wow," Kit said, emerging from the office across the hall.

"Why thank you, G," Noelle said, and granted him a kiss on the cheek.

He said, "I have an announcement."

"Okay," Monti said, and they looked at him expectantly.

"Should I make you guess?"

Monti and Noelle groaned in unison.

"All right, all right," he said, caving instantly. But he allowed himself a dramatic pause. "The dreaded kitty stalker has been arrested. Gulliver is safe."

"Woohoo!" Both women whooped, sending the safe but scaredy cat scrambling to hide under the bed.

"They found Stevie Jakes early this morning, hiding in his mother's basement."

"And that's why we have such enduring stereotypes about losers," Monti said, then raised her hand. "I shouldn't have said that, my apologies."

"Well it's true, Grandma. Only a loser threatens someone's cat. That was seriously lame."

"Monti means 'but for the grace of God,' I think," Kit said. "You never know what's happened in a person's life to set them on such a stupid path."

"Right, that's much better phraseology," Monti said. "It's good news, anyway. Two for two behind bars. That's a great 19th birthday present."

The doorbell rang. "That'll be Nick." Noelle and Gulliver both ran for the front door and Monti held her breath until she knew there would be survivors.

Good Travel

Bo let the reins slacken and watched the pale horizon, where distant clouds piled up and scudded along on a wind he could not yet feel. They'd seen scarcely a puff of cloud all the journey until now. Anisette seemed unaware of the change. She rode ahead of him beside Paru, chatting with him, trying to pronounce the words he provided in answer to her questions. She had quite an ear for their language, and already could make herself understood in simple sentences about flowers and horses and such.

Bo reached for the peace that usually undergirded his days. He would not fret about clouds, nor imagined reactions to Anisette's possible transformation. *Thou wilt keep him in perfect peace, whose mind is stayed on Thee. Help me, Jesu, to stay my mind on Thee.*

Anebni cantered up to ride beside him. "Sayyid Bo," he said, dipping his head in greeting. "We make good travel. Your lady more strong than I see before."

"Yes, she amazes me," Bo agreed. "You'd never know she spent the first twenty years of her life cloistered away in a private garden."

"Yes? What is closter?"

"Um, kept at home. She did not travel about, even locally." Bo wished he hadn't brought it up, and hoped Anebni would not press for details.

"Ah yes, protect from world. She have good father."

Bo stifled a snort and nodded. He scanned the horizon again. The wind pushed the clouds toward the north. "How many more days, do you think?" Bo asked the Egyptian.

"No many. Four?"

Bo nodded again. Their journey had been dreamlike, cloistered in its own way, the four of them moving in a bubble through town and country, unaccosted, apart. He had caught some wide-eyed glances as their unusual entourage clopped through the many villages on their path. But no one gave them any trouble. Anebni and Paru carried provisions, as did Bo and Anisette, but villagers also *sold them milk, cheese, fresh bread, and the fruits of the season. And now they were nearly to Gibraltar.*

His mind veered away from dwelling on the next part of the trek. The thought of Anisette on a ship in the rain still made his gut clench with horror. He shook his head to dispel the nightmare picture. It is one day, my Jesu. You love her more than I do. I trust thee.

"Does sickness harm you?" Anebni asked, concern furrowing his brow.

"No, no, all is well," Bo assured him. "I am thinking things over. It be nearly time to stop for the day, think you not?" His companion nodded and Bo clucked at his horse to catch up to Anisette.

THREE DAYS LATER THEY rode through Gibraltar, a city crowded and odiferous and bristling with battlements. The day after that they arrived in Tarifa. The four walked their horses down through the village to the shore, and peered across the rough sea to Africa as the wind whipped their cloaks about them. The horses snorted at the salt tang in the air and stamped on the damp sand.

Less than nine miles away, it was, though to Bo it seemed a thousand. Anisette reached for his hand. "All will be well, husband," she said loudly, competing with the wind. She smiled and drew her hair away from her eyes, whence the wind continually flung it.

He squeezed her small hand and drew strength from her confidence. "Yes, God willing," he said.

"You cannot doubt God wills it? He has brought us here sure as anything."

"Yes, I know it," Bo said, his cheeks burning with the revelation of his weak faith in the goodness of God. He leaned toward her. "I believe it. Help my unbelief," he said, pleading for her understanding.

"It is good journey," Anebni shouted. "I will get lodge, and ship for the morrow." He motioned to signify them all boarding a ship. He wheeled his horse about and trotted back to the village.

Bo inspected the sky in all directions. A high light haze blurred the sunlight, but the wind carried no clouds to mar the blue from horizon to horizon.

"Oh! Bo, look! See the great fishes?" She pointed into the waves at dozens of sleek grey beasts leaping through the white-caps.

"Dolphins?" Bo turned to Paru, who nodded.

"Darfeel."

They were magnificent. Anisette's silvery laugh rang out, sending a thrill up Bo's spine and making him grin.

"Dolphins. Darfeel. Are they not the very picture of joy?" She clapped her hands, startling her mare, who snorted at her and shook her mane. "Sorry, pet," Anisette said, and stroked the horse's neck.

They watched the dolphins until they disappeared. Anebni returned and led them to a tiny inn, where they gladly turned the horses over to a stable boy, enjoyed a hot meal of fried fish, and collapsed into their beds. At least, Bo and Anisette collapsed into bed. Anebni and Paru had fidgeted all through supper in the low-ceilinged dining room, and afterward declared they would check the horses. Bo thought they might decide to spend the night in the stable. They were not at ease in close spaces.

Next morning the screeching of gulls brought Bo awake at daybreak. Anisette woke when he moved and she sat up instantly, eyes sparkling. "Are we away, then?" she said, and threw back the counterpane.

"'Tis indeed the day we sail to Africa," he said, and hurried to catch up with her, as she was half dressed already.

"Do we have time to break our fast, think you?"

"Of course, Anisette. The ship is to sail at ten o'the clock. 'Tis barely dawn. We have plenty of time."

"That is good news, for I am famished."

"As are you every morning," he said with a grin. He pulled on his boots and joined her in throwing the last of their night things into the duffel.

"All packed then?" Anisette glanced round the room to be sure.

"Perhaps you want your comb?" He drew his fingers gently down through her tangled hair. "The wind is high in this place, and will be e'en more on the ship. You might bind it upon your head for the day."

"Yes, all right," she said, and rummaged in the bag for her comb and pins.

She was impatient with the tangles and Bo winced at how roughly she tugged through them. "Truly, Anisette, there is no rush," he said. "Be kind to your head, my love."

"Oh, I cannot help it," she said, but slowed her strokes, taking more care. "I so desire to be on board the ship, drawing nearer to Africa by the moment."

"You have been drawing nearer to Africa by the moment for a month now," Bo said. "Two or three more hours will not kill thee, surely."

Anisette laughed, and jumped up to embrace him. "Can you believe the day is here at last? I shall have you back in my bed 'ere long."

"I was in your bed scarce an hour hence."

"Ha!" She buried her head in his chest and squeezed him tight. "You tease me."

"How can I not? You are like a child at Christmas!" He kissed her and let her go. "Now finish your hair and let us see what our Egyptian companions are about this morning."

They conferred with Anebni and Paru, broke their fast and loaded the horses, Anisette hurrying them all the while. An eternity passed, but eventually the pre-departure tasks were done, and they walked down to the wharf.

Fire

M onti wondered how on earth she could have eaten so much. She so disliked feeling too full. She leaned her head back on the seat and closed her eyes while Kit maneuvered through the evening traffic. Christmas music played softly on the radio and the windshield wipers swiped lazily at the sleety drizzle. Noelle and Nick sat in the back seat chatting quietly. She could just about fall asleep.

"Grandpa? What are all those lights?" Noelle asked. Monti's eyes popped open as an unaccountable jolt of adrenaline coursed through her.

"It looks like fire trucks," Kit said.

"Oh no, where?" Monti said. "We're pretty close to...oh God, oh God, is that our house?" Her voice clamped off in a panicky squeak. She gripped the dash and tried to see through the slush on the windshield. Kit slowed the car, then had to stop. They had the street blocked. He turned off the motor.

Kit put his hand on hers, "Monti." She didn't want to hear it. "Monti, look at me, love." She dragged her eyes away from the flashing lights and eerie orange glow and made herself look at her husband. "I'm going to talk to the chief over there. Stay here for a minute?" he asked, touching her cheek with his hand.

"Okay," she whispered, gripping his hand, staring into his eyes. Her throat clamped tight, and tears poured down her face. Nick and Noelle opened the back doors and climbed out. Nick joined Noelle at the front of the car and put his arm around her.

Monti squeezed her eyes shut and clenched her fists. This was not okay. This could not be happening. She would wake up any second. *Abba, no. No, no, no on my house burning! Absolutely not!* She slammed her hands on the dash. She fought with the seatbelt, snarling, snapped off a nail, got the stupid thing off her. She opened her door and smacked her head on the frame getting out, which infuriated her. She slammed the door shut, saw she had dumped her purse onto the street, bent down to grab the spilled things in the lurid glare of the fire.

In the glare of the fire. She was picking up her lipstick and sunglasses in the glare of her house burning down. She left the things lying there, stood up and slowly turned to face her darling, sweet little bungalow—it was engulfed in flames.

Aah, no, no. A deep sob shuddered through her, tore at her throat.

Noelle turned at the sound and hurried to her, wrapped her arms around her. "Grandma?" Monti clung to the girl to keep from falling down. Her knees were wobbly. "Grandma, are you okay?" Noelle said, though her face streamed with tears, too.

"Oh baby, it's our beautiful house," Monti said. They stood holding each other, weeping. The wind changed and acrid smoke stung their noses as Nick moved to stand with them, his attention wavering between the disastrous fire and the heartbroken women. Kit approached, his face grim, his gait uncertain. Nick reached a hand to steady him.

"Sir?" Nick said. Kit shook his head and gathered his wife and his granddaughter into his arms. The chill sleet beaded up in their hair and on their coats, and joined the tears sliding down their cheeks as they watched the fire. But it did nothing at all to slow the hot, hungry flames devouring their home.

Africa

Their ship waited at the end of the wharf, rocking gently, creaking against the piles. *Saint Ive* was painted on the stern in elaborate script. *Other ships moored nearby dwarfed the one to which Anebni led them, but they were all immense compared to Bo's punt on the river at home.*

Sailors lugged cargo on board with their rolling gait, and scampered among the ropes high above, making Anisette's heart leap as she peered up at them. Gulls wheeled, screeching. Anebni left his horse with Paru and went to talk with the captain as he supervised the lading from the pier. Anebni presented the man with a parchment studded with wax seals from which red silk tassels dangled.

Anisette watched as the captain read the letter, nodded to Anebni, and summoned a sailor. Soon a young lad accompanied Anebni back to the group. He tugged his forelock as he bowed to Anisette and Bo.

"Ma'am," he said, "Kindly follow me 'ere."

Paru took their horses' reins. Anisette lay her hand on Bo's arm and followed the boy down the pier and up the ramp onto the ship. The Egyptians brought the horses clomping along behind them, their hooves making a hollow clatter on the boards. Anisette tried to take in everything but there was so much to see, and to smell! She wrinkled her nose at the odors the wind gusted at her.

Eventually their horses were secured, the four travelers found a corner of the deck out of the way, the ship pulled away from the wharf, and they were off!

Anebni and Paru minded the horses while Bo minded the sky. Anisette scanned the sea for dolphins while the land she knew grew tiny behind them, and a new shore loomed larger and larger ahead of them. At last an intensifying bustle on the ship signaled their imminent arrival. Her heart raced as the crew made ready to dock.

"Africa!" Anisette exclaimed as she gripped the rail and gazed at her new home. It looked much the same as the shore in Tarifa, but Anisette was not fooled. They were about to step into a different world.

Gulliver?

Noelle went rigid in Monti's arms. She pulled back to look at her grand-daughter, "What is it, love?"

"Where's Gulliver?" Noelle demanded, her red eyes narrowing with fresh outrage.

"Oh, no," Monti moaned. Her shoulders sagged. "Kit? Can we ask them if they've seen Gulliver?"

He gave a curt nod. "Let's go talk to the chief, Monti." He tipped his chin to Nick, who took Noelle's hand. Kit put his arm around Monti's shoulder and they walked up to a grey and grizzled man in his sixties talking on a radio and keeping a sharp eye on the labors of his firefighters. He clicked off the radio as they approached.

"Chief," Kit said.

The man turned to Kit, his eyes sad, his face all long lines. "Colonel Rising." He nodded at Monti. "Ma'am. I'm sorry about your home."

"Thank you," Kit said. "We wonder if you've seen a big grey tabby cat this evening?"

"His name is Gulliver," Monti added, "and he doesn't normally go outside..." she choked at the implications of that and squeezed her eyes tight shut against the tears.

"I don't recall seeing a cat, ma'am, but let me ask the crew." He walked over to a group of firefighters working with the fittings of a nozzle. They shook their heads, as Monti had known they would. She sagged into Kit, who tightened his arm around her shoulders.

"Excuse me, are you the Rising family?" A plump lady wearing a red parka with a white cross on it smiled at them, poised to consult her clipboard.

"Yes, I'm Kit Rising. This is my wife Montana."

"Hello dears, my name is Phyllis. I'm here to offer assistance from the Red Cross, if you would like it."

Kit and Monti looked at her, blank.

"Do we need assistance?" Monti finally said.

"Oh, probably. Of course, you haven't thought about any of that yet, that's perfectly normal. Is it all right if I ask you some questions?" Monti nodded. "Are there more members of your family?"

"Our granddaughter, Noelle..." Monti motioned back toward their car.

Phyllis asked them if any of them needed medical attention. She asked, calmly and gently, about medications, about other family in the area who might house them, about insurance, transportation, whether they would like the Red Cross to notify anyone about the fire, about pets...until Monti's knees threatened to give way under her and Kit said, "Excuse me Phyllis. I have to find Monti a place to sit down for a bit."

"Of course. Here you go," Phyllis said, and produced a folding chair from somewhere. Then another for Kit. "Robert, get these folks some water, would you?" she said to an assistant who'd appeared at her shoulder.

"You bet," Robert said, and trotted away.

"You're in shock," Phyllis said. "You take your time. Whenever you're ready, we'll figure how best to help you." She patted Monti's knee, then started making notes on her clipboard. Robert reappeared with two bottles of water. Monti and Kit accepted them mechanically.

"I guess we need a hotel," Monti whispered to Kit. "And your medication—"

"G and G, no sign of Gulliver?"

"No, sweetheart, I'm afraid not," Monti said. Robert instantly produced another chair for Noelle. She sat in it without noticing him.

"Where will we stay?"

Noelle looked a little panicky, Monti thought. "Don't worry, Nellie, Phyllis here is taking care of that for us for the next couple of nights. And then, well, we'll make a plan. It'll be okay." Monti said the words, but she could not feel them. Not at all.

Journey Complete

T he travelers fell back into the rhythm of their journey, though the way was
more difficult now. In single file they followed tortuous paths through the
desolate mountains of northern Morocco, pausing only to rest, eat, and care for
their mounts.

The Egyptians' weapons flashed in the sun as they rode, now displayed openly
instead of hidden beneath their cloaks as they had been on the trek through
Europe. One of them stood watch whenever they stopped. But they didn't seem
afraid, only alert. Bo watched them and found he could relax as far as they relaxed, trusting them to know the proper level of vigilance.

Anisette was oblivious to the heightened watchfulness, and she exulted in
the beauty of the new landscape. Bo couldn't see it, for the most part. Endless
pines grew straight from the rock of endless hillsides. Huge boulders choked tiny
streams, and the horses took care where they set their hooves in in fording them.
Their path was scratched into the sides of steep mountains, and now and then a
cascade of pebbles dislodged by the horses went shooting off the edge and set his
stomach churning.

But one day Anebni led them off onto a side trail. After an hour's ride down
a desperately narrow file, the path opened on the gravelly edge of a lake green
as emerald, surrounded by secret cliffs and freshened by a many-fingered water-
fall pouring into it. They dismounted and their horses splashed into the water to
drink.

"What a wondrous place!" Anisette said, laughing with delight. "We shall
picnic here, shall we not?" They did picnic there, and camped for the night after
washing everything and bathing in the chilly water. They fell asleep warmed by
a roaring fire, refreshed and soothed.

The next day, the mountains gave way to desert. For a week the sun glared
at them and the wind secreted sand in every orifice, every crease of skin, leather,
and cloth. Paru showed them how to wrap scarves around their heads and faces

to keep out both sun and sand, which helped greatly, but still Bo grinned with relief when a green smudge appeared on the horizon.

"Tendrara," Anebni said, pointing to the green. "Tonight our journey complete."

Baby

Anisette sat in the courtyard, basking in the morning sun. The heat would soon force her to retreat into the cool house, but for a few more minutes she turned her face to the sun and relished its warmth on her rounded belly. The baby kicked and she pressed her hand to the place. A harder kick thumped her hand and made her laugh.

Bo and Tumaini strolled into the courtyard, heads together in consultation over a document Tumaini held. They stopped at the sound of her laugh. "What is it, Anisette?" Bo asked, smiling.

"Oh," she said, shy in front of Tumaini. "The baby kicks."

"He will be a strong son," Tumaini declared.

"Please God, he will," Bo agreed. "Ready to go in, love?"

"I suppose," she said, and allowed him to help her to her feet. Tumaini bowed to her and said, "Until we dine, my lady."

She curtsied to him. When he had gone, she said, "It will be soon now, I think. Safia says perhaps a week more."

Bo pressed her hand on his arm and led her into the cool, spacious house. "Well, and it has been a long wait. I am glad it draws to a close."

"Could you ever imagine nine months with no rain?" she asked.

"'Tis a marvel. A blessed gift from God." He took her hand and kissed it.

"Have you thought more on when to return home?"

"Very little," he admitted. "There is so much more to be done here. Do you miss it terribly?"

Anisette considered. "A little," she said. "But I truly cherish our life here, too. Mayhap God will make clear the best path."

"As does he always. Until then, we have news today from home." He pulled a letter from his pocket with a flourish. "Old Tom is increasingly pleased with Ian's progress in learning the mead-making. He is a fount of practical ideas, it seems. And business continues to grow since our second Grand Prize in Spirits this last

July. Even our absence to journey to Morocco has lent a mystique to our mead it never had before."

"And happy I am to hear it, husband. Oh!" She hunched and gripped his arm.

"Anisette?" Bo said, his voice choked by the heart in his throat.

"Oh Bo, I do not think it will be a week more after all!"

After

Monti flared her nostrils and inhaled. *Coffee?* She opened her eyes and found herself staring at stiff curtains in a hideous pattern of huge green and tan diamonds. Was she dreaming? She sat up, realized she was in a motel room, and was caught off guard when a heavy sob escaped her. *My house is gone.*

Kit came and sat beside her on the bed. He put his arm around her and she leaned in. "Good morning, love," he said.

"Doesn't feel too good," she said, her throat tight.

"I know." They sat for a minute, thinking their own thoughts.

Monti straightened up. "Where's Noelle?"

"Right through there," he said, pointing to the door between their two rooms. "I just checked on her, she's still asleep."

She nodded, then fingered the fabric of her top. "I'm wearing flannel pajamas," she said. "I don't own any pajamas."

"You do now," he said. "But not much else."

"Is there coffee?" she asked, not willing to think about her losses just yet.

"That's debatable," Kit said. "I'm heading to Starbuck's in a few minutes. I don't think the stuff in the little pot there will brighten your day any."

"You're probably right. I seem to remember an inviolable rule. Motel coffee shall be execrable, to an extent precisely matching the hideousness of the drapes." She gestured hopelessly toward the green and tan monstrosities covering the window.

Kit laughed. "I think you'll survive," he said. He kissed her hair. "Any particular coffee requirements this morning? Or shall I surprise you?"

"I don't care, you pick. Bring some for Noelle, too."

"Of course. And donuts, too, maybe. I'll be back ASAP."

Monti stood to soak in his embrace for a minute, then let him go.

She headed for the bathroom and got a shock as she glanced in the mirror. When she came back out she studiously avoided the mirror as she bent over the sink. She scrubbed her haggard face with cool water and then a towel, keeping her eyes on the counter. She unwrapped a foam cup and rinsed her mouth with tap water. *Now what?*

She wandered back into the room, over to the window. She peeked out through the curtains at a parking lot indistinguishable from 10,000 other motel parking lots. The skies were grey, the asphalt slushy. She retreated.

On the room's little table lay a motel notepad covered with Kit's neat printing. She picked it up.

1. CLOTHES/SUNDRIES for next few days
    2. Insurance—process?
    3. Realtor/apartment
    4. College—Noelle, Monti's classes/sub
    5. New computer—data in cloud storage
    6. Call parents/elders/Ray and Dot
    7. Marla?
    8. Medication-call Charlie
    9. Fire Dept—salvage? Process?
    10. Call CJ—connection w/Blaine/S. Jakes etc?
    11.

Monti put the pad back down. She'd been doing pretty okay until she got to number 10. The gulf between someone breaking their window and burning down their house was so vast she couldn't process it. Couldn't believe someone would do it deliberately. She was deeply grateful Kit was on this, because she wasn't going to be much help, at least not today.

A small manila envelope lay on the table, too. Monti picked it up and tilted it. Several cards fell into her hand. Business cards from realtors and lawyers. A Visa gift card. One from a local supermarket. And one from Starbuck's. Maybe Kit wasn't exactly running on all cylinders, either.

The door to Noelle's room opened, and her tousle-haired, red-eyed, beautiful granddaughter, wearing plain old yellow pajamas, walked in and bright-

ened the day immeasurably. Monti held out her arms and Noelle came over
for a hug.

"You okay?" Monti asked.

"Sorta," Noelle said. But she started crying immediately and Monti held
her tight.

She was still holding Noelle when Kit returned with a tray of coffees and
a paper bag of pastries. Noelle perked up and gazed at him with an expression
that said there might be hope and a future. "You brought coffee?"

An hour or two later they had all finished their breakfast of foo-foo coffee, turnovers and muffins, and had showered and dressed in anonymous new
clothing from the bags Phyllis had given them last night. Monti felt like an
actor in a costume, but being clean and fed was heartening. Kit was ready to
launch into his plan, and she was ready to help him.

Phone calls first. They divided the list: Noelle took Ray and Dorothy and
her school adviser. The loss of her laptop was going to set her back on finishing her term paper. Kit dealt with the insurance, the fire department, their
doctor, and CJ, and Monti called her parents, left a message for Marla with
the rehab office, and arranged for a substitute to take her classes.

"Okay, what have we got?" he asked, when they had all finished.

Each reported on progress made, then Monti said, "I've got to get out of
this room before I go nuts."

"All right. The next round is out and about, anyway."

"Can we go back to the house?" Noelle asked. "Just to see if, you know,
maybe Gulliver is wondering where we are?"

Monti and Kit shared a look.

"Yes, we can, Noelle." Kit stood. "We'll do that first. We can't cross the
tapeline without an escort from the fire department," he said, "but we can drive over and park across the street."

"Well, let's go then," Monti said, and scooped up her purse. "We all still
have our ID's and credit cards, that's a mercy," she said.

"Find that sunny side, Monti," Kit said, and opened the door for them.
They filed out.

Monti's phone chimed after they'd been driving for a few minutes, and
she swiped it to look at a message from Dot. "Dot wants us to have lunch
with them today. That'll work, won't it?" Kit nodded. She noticed they were

approaching the corner of Government Way and Engle and her hands started shaking, preventing a reply to Dot. She put the phone down and made herself look as they approached the house. The former house. The sodden black heap that used to be their home and everything they owned. Monti's heart twisted with pain.

Kit slowed to a stop across the street and they all sat and stared. Finally, Kit opened his door. "I'm serious about not going past the tape. Our insurance agent and the fire chief both were firm about that requirement," he said. He consulted his watch. "I expect the chief will show before too long."

Everyone got out and huddled close, staring across the street.

"You can't see NEXT burned into the lawn anymore...," Monti said.

Kit's phone rang. "Kit Rising." He listened. "Yep. We're at the house. I know, I told them," he said. A motorcycle turned into their street, the heavy puhm-puhm-puhm of its engine making Kit cover his ear. "Okay, we'll be here." He pocketed his phone and turned to watch as the biker pulled into the curb behind their car and cut the motor.

The man dismounted, his leathers creaking. He smiled a brilliant smile and nodded at them. "Folks," he said. Then he turned to the back of his bike. HE>i was embroidered in huge letters on the back of his leather jacket, partially obscured by the wild curls escaping from under a bandanna on his head.

Monti caught a movement as the man worked at something on the rack behind his seat, and saw an animal jump down to the street. A cat.

He leaned down and said something to the cat in a low voice, then stood and pulled a shopping bag from the back of his bike and set it on the curb. He turned back toward them and nodded again, his smile bigger than ever. He got back on his bike, fired it up, wheeled it around and drove off.

"Gulliver?" Noelle said, her voice squeaky with disbelief. She crouched as the cat strolled over to her, purring loudly. He rubbed his head against her knees and tried to knock her over. "Gulliver!" She scooped him up and buried her face in the nape of his neck. "Where have you been?"

Kit stepped over and peered into the shopping bag. His eyebrows rose and he caught the handles in two fingers. He brought it to Monti.

"Scrabble?" she said, hardly believing her eyes.

Monti and Kit looked at each other, unable to make this scene compute. Noelle came to them. "It's Gulliver!"

"Sure enough," Monti said. She stroked her cat's head and glanced at the shiny new Scrabble game in the bag Kit held. Somehow the hurricane of questions and fears about Blaine and Stevie Jakes and the fire and Kit and Marla, plans and problems and unknowns...the storm had lost its power to overwhelm her. She wasn't sure what was going on, but she knew the Rock she stood on and she knew without a doubt, knew deeper than anything...they would be okay.

Rain

Anisette lounged on their bed, her chin in her hand, her other arm dangling into the cradle, fluttering her fingers to amuse the baby. He was so perfect she thought she might burst from pure joy. His little face scrunched up as he tried to focus on her fingers, and she giggled.

Bo burst into the room, smacking the door into the wall and scaring the baby, who started crying.

"Bo!" Anisette chided him, and moved to pick up their tiny son.

"Are you well, Anisette?" He put his arms out to take the baby from her.

"Yes, of course, what ails thee?"

"It's raining." He nestled the baby to his chest, went to the window and opened the shutter wide. Rain spattered the palms outside, falling heavier every moment.

"But...oh my!" Anisette stood stock still. They looked at each other across the room, not daring to hope. Anisette joined him at the window, and queried her body for the buzzing urgency to get outside that rain always stirred in her.

It was profoundly absent.

She stood calmly watching the rain for the first time she could remember in all her life. Bo pulled her close and the family watched the downpour together.

Don't miss out!

Click the button below and you can sign up to receive emails whenever LeeAnn Bonds publishes a new book. There's no charge and no obligation.

https://books2read.com/r/B-A-NDWE-EWDQ

BOOKS 2 READ

Connecting independent readers to independent writers.

About the Author

LeeAnn lives with her husband on the island of Saipan, in the Northern Marianas.

She has been writing since she discovered that telling stories is even more fun than reading them. She writes to encourage women to persevere through difficulties, and live a joyful life of faith, hope and love.

Montana Rising, Wordplay is her first novel (not counting the inevitable *first* first novel which will likely never escape from her hard drive).

Read more at leeannbonds.com.